GAME OVER

Compilation and Introduction copyright © 2004 by
Triple Crown Publications
2959 Stelzer Road Suite C
Columbus, Ohio 43219
www.TripleCrownPublications.com

Library of Congress Control Number: 2004115358
ISBN# 0-9762349-2-0
Cover Design/Graphics: www.apollopixel.com
Editor: Chloé A. Hilliard
Production: Kevin J. Calloway
Consulting: Vickie M. Stringer

First Trade Paperback Edition Printing February 2005
10 9 8 7 6 5 4 3 2 1

Printed in the United States of America

Dedication

To the Almighty Father for blessing me with dreams, courage, and the determination to follow through...

Acknowledgments

Thanks to my parents, Barbara and Melvin, for being my backbone. Mommy, you know you're my homegirl! Thanks for reading Game Over 50-11 times. My husband, Kevin, I thank you for being my support. My children, Taylor and Sydney, mommy thanks you for being her strength. And to my family, in both America and Trinidad, I thank you for being continued and renewed Blessings.

To my cousin, Taniesha, you are my favorite "girl" cousin in the whole wide world :)! I'm not sure if I ever told you, but I am so proud of you! Love ya girl!

To the my sistah-girlfriends: Lisa Gibson-Wilson, Danielle Santiago (my sister), Keisha Ervin (my little sister), Valerie Hall, Lisa Scofield-Ham, Lisa Polk, Sharonda Smith-Sims, and Nakea Murray (my publicist), I could thank you all a million and one times for being a part of my writing career, but that would only be a small portion of what I'm most thankful for. It's your friendship; the late night talks, the kids, boyfriend, ex-boyfriend, and husband swap stories that mean the most. I love you guys!

Vickie Stringer, the appreciation that I have for you there are no words to describe. Thank you for believing in me and for daring me to reach new heights. There are so many things that I could thank you for, but I'll only list one more; which is thank you for being my friend.

Danita Carter and Joylynn Jossell, thank you for being two very special people who opened themselves up and welcomed a new author like me, be forever blessed!

Triple Crown Publications' staff, all those seen and unseen, thanks for everything. Tami, thanks a million for being such a big fan it means the world!!!!

Philemon Missionary Baptist Church, your support means the world! Thanks for being a part of my Blessing.

Special thanks to: Creative Impressions (Ernest and Tracy) on 18th Ave in Newark, New Jersey. Kristy Burgess "Miss Thang" of 1075 in Bermuda (bermynet.com), Julian Wilson, Treasure E. Blue (be sure to check out 'Lil Love) Malik Whitaker (m-print-arts.com), Chloé Hilliard (thanks for all of your late nights), the book clubs, books stores, S.W.A.P., my co-workers, my mother's, father's, and my family's co-workers and friends. "Reydee" Jacqueline Ford, I want you to know that your strength lies within you and never ever forget that!

To every African-American author, those known and unknown, never forget that there was a time when it was illegal for us to read and write; let alone having our own books on the shelf. Therefore, whether we forever agree or disagree, let us do so peacefully and always hold one another's art in high standing; for we are all cut from the same clothe of excellency. Remember to respect my love for the written word, as I respect yours.

To the readers, the message board crew, and my fans (coupled with His grace) without you, none of this would be possible and for that I say thank you. I encourage you to visit my web site www.tushonda.com and to email me at info@tushonda.com! I would love to know your thoughts on Game Over!

Peace and Blessings,

Tu-Shonda

The Tip Off:

Once upon a time, I was a gold digger like a ma'fucker.
Robbing men left and right. Hustlin' their time, pimpin' their
money, and shittin' on their romance. I possessed the ability to
lace 'em with the power of the pussy and slam-dunk their asses
like a Shaq attack. I thought I had the game down packed. Then
with all the subtlety of a cool summer breeze or floating autumn
leaves, love came and turned my world upside down. Instantly,
I realized that my game had flipped and slipped through my fingertips.

I tried hard to retrace my footsteps in search of where my
game could be. But when I looked, all I had left in my hand was
my beating heart. Fully exposed to the elements, with valves
pumping blood into the air, like wild fire. All I could do was be
still and try not to move; at least until I got it together and could
stand without falling.

When that time came, I went in the bathroom and stood at
the sink, with the pinkish palms of my caramel hands resting on
the cool green marble. My hair was wildly hanging loose over
my shoulders and a little down my back. I pulled it away from
my face, twisted it into a bun on the side, and slipped on pear-
shaped diamond earrings. I could feel buried tears dancing in
my throat. My reflection seemed to be moving in an ocean
wave's rhythm as I stopped what I was doing and spoke quietly
into the mirror. *"Well, Miss Thing, seems to me, you're all fucked*

up in the game. Ya mama's still a junkie ass dope fiend, you're pregnant, and got the nerve to be in love. Vera, Lawd knows you got a thousand and one issues. Nevertheless, here you are: ready, willing, and able to let love into your life. But can you handle it? Without fucking up? Are you scared? Or are you straight? Whatever you are, we gon' agree not to run...at least try not to run. Amen? Amen."

I stared in the mirror, fully dressed in my black Be-Be halter top with matching jeans, 3-inch, black gator Ferretti boots, and draped across my shoulders a black chiffon shawl with beaded fringes.

After applying a full face of MAC, I took a deep breath and thought to myself, *All of this poetic happily-ever-after-bullshit has got to stop!* 'Cause on the real, my ass is in love and headed for trouble. I can't eat, can't sleep, and can't dream with out thinking about Taj Bennet. And yes, he's deliciously fine with a temple like a niggah pushin' weights in a prison yard, has a legitimate medical degree, but hell, nobody told me loving him would feel like this. So, here I am with no choice but to be done with the dumb shit. No more games, no more playing, no more lying about where I've been and who I've been with. Taj is it. No other dick, but his. Oh God, what in 'na hell am I gon' do? Not exactly having an answer to my own question, I grabbed my X5 keys and headed out the door, to meet Shannon, Angie, and Lee.

I know Shannon's gon' be running around Jimmy's Uptown, like a damn prostitute—her titties practically falling out of the tons of cleavage she's sure to be showing. Lately, she's been tryna kick it to the owner and side line him as an extra niggah. Poor Quincy, 'cause this bitch acts like being faithful is a crime.

Angie, Ms. O.P.P., has experimented and drank a bottle of *Desperate Ass Me*, cause this chick is fuckin' anything movin'. Now I'm not hatin', I'm just statin'; because some shit she backs it up for, is a bit much. Midgets and paraplegics?

Now Lee, since I'm only parked and haven't gone in the club yet let me pray right now. *Our Father who art in Heaven please*

give me the strength to not cuss Ms. Self Righteous out. I don't wanna molly-whopp dat ass. But Lord, You know she always tries to take me there. Amen.

When I stepped inside Jimmy's Uptown the music was live and the place was packed. The D.J. was blasting the club remix of Mary J's *"No More Drama."* As I walked closer to the bar, I noticed Shannon right away. She was leaning over the bar's counter, whispering something in the owner's ear. Girlfriend had more cleavage than a Lil' bit poppin' out! When she spotted me, she stood up. Immediately I noticed a tattoo of a tiger clawing and disappearing down her low cut, V-neck, lavender sweater, pointing toward her nipple. Where in the hell did she get that shit from? On her feet she had on lavender Moschino stilettos, with the heels slightly covered by her tightly fitted Ashley Stewart jeans. Every since Ashley Stewart's been advertising in her magazine, *Girlfriend's*, ole girl's been wearing the hell outta their clothes. Shannon winked her eye and pointed toward a small table over to the side, where Lee and Angie were sitting and sipping on their drinks.

"Look at you, hoe." I said, kissing Angie the cheek. "What the fuck you got on?"

"You wanna a bitch to model for you? 'Cause you know I'm sharp."

"Here we go." Lee said, as we greeted each other with a hug. "I ordered you some cranberry juice."

Angie got out of her seat so that I could admire her gear. This bitch knows she has a body to die for! She's got on tight ass, hip hugging, red Gucci leather pants, a red leather midriff top, and 3-inch Gucci boots, with the G's imprinted in the heel and running across the toe.

"Wait a minute, Angie." I said, noticing something hanging from her navel, "Bitch you got a belly ring? What the hell is wrong with you and Shannon?"

"Tell me about it," Lee sighed. "They need to cut it out and be conservative like me."

"Excuse you, Mary Agnes." Angie snapped. "but that long ass split you got running up your ass. In that glued tight, slip dress, you got on, doesn't hardly constitute as conservative. Hell, you look more like a lady of the night then I do. Shit, truth be told, every since Chanel came out with a big girl line, you done went crazy!"

"Don't hate me because I'm beautiful." Lee smiled.

"Kick rocks be'atch! Step with all that." Angie paused for a few minutes, "I need another drink, I'll be right back."

By the time Angie came back, Shannon was sitting at the table with us. "Vera, why you so quiet?!" Shannon shouted over the club mix of Snoop Dog's "Drop it Like Its Hot." *"When the Pimp's in the crib Ma, drop it like its hot...Drop its like hot...Got the Rolly on my arm...and I'm pourin' Chandon...And I roll the best weed cause Shannon got it goin' on...*This is my shit ya'll!" she laughed taking a sip of her Perfect Ten. "What the fuck? Talk, hoe. What's your issue?"

"We can start with me being about eight weeks pregnant and sitting in a night club, like a young ass video chick and shit."

"Well J-Lo," Angie said, stirring her Long Island Ice Tea, "shall I remind you that this wouldn't be the first time you've been pregnant and sitting in a night club?"

"Oh no you didn't!"

"Now, that ain't right Angie." Lee insisted, "She's gon' keep this one."

"Fuck all three of ya'll!" I yelled over the music.

"Nope," Angie smiled getting up from her chair and heading toward the dance floor, with Lee walking beside her. "Cause I'm trying to get ole boy at the bar to wet my dry ass coochie up!"

"That's why they make lipstick dildos and K-Y jelly."

"You ain't never lied!" Angie yelled over her shoulder.

"I'll be back Vera." Shannon said, "My jump off is at the bar."

"Shannon, what the hell is his name? Could you stop calling him a jump off?"

"That's Nile, girl."

"Damn Shannon, he's fine as hell, almost reminds me of Morris Chestnut." I said looking him up and down.

"Morris Chestnut? Girl please, Morris Chestnut looks more like Quincy. But Nile, Nile looks just like Tyler Perry! Oh hell yeah, that's wassup."

"You're right, he does look like Tyler Perry, but Shannon, you're back to messing around with Nile?"

"Sumthin' like that." She said walking toward him.

I can't believe this one. Nile's ass...again? This broad must wanna be a high-class hoochie for the rest of her life. Shannon gon fuck around and Quincy will have her on UPN 9 news with a spy cam bustin' up her cheatin' ass groove!

Damn, I need me some alcohol in this drink! I thought to myself as I clinked the ice around in my glass. I really can't believe I let them talk me into this shit. Look at em, every one of 'em horney as hell, with more issues than Monica Lewinsky! Shannon is the only one with some sense and she's running around chasin' Nile as if she's crazy. This is an after hours spot. It's Tuesday night, not Saturday night at the crunked up chicken shack. I swear you can't make three hoes into housewives!

They know I have a baby daddy and they know I'm tryin' real hard to be good. Nevertheless, they got me on the legalized hoe stroll in the middle of a night club, smack dab in the heart of Uptown; knowing damn well this was my gold diggin' stompin' ground.

I'ma just have to set their asses straight and let 'em know that I ain't feeling this. Well, not unless ole boy over there eying me, with the chocolate ball head, coco eyes, and a body that must've been chiseled by Adonis, comes this way. This niggah looks better than I imagine DMX with a stiff dick! But you know what? Fuck him! That's right; fuck him, because I got the original thugged out black god living in my house. I looked at ole boy, rolled my eyes, and shot his ass a look like, *Psst...niggah please.*

Goddamn, his ass is still looking. Why in 'na hell does he wanna do this to me? He gotta know that the flesh is weak. Shouldn't he have a woman? A man this fine standing alone? Shit, just staring at him has the heart in my coochie palpitating. See, I don't have no business doing this. I know damn well that I have a thousand and one issues—wait a minute—is ole boy coming over here? Oh, hell yeah, strike that, I mean, oh hell no.

He walked over and stood in front of the table, folded his arms across his chest and his whole body seemed to light up. He had on beige pleated dress pants, a cream raw silk button up shirt, slightly open and revealing black chest hairs that seemed to be singing a love ballet across his pecks. And when he smiled, boyfriend had the pretty-ass nerve to have dimples. Oh, damn, he is so wrong for that! Alright...alright, this is what we gon' do. I'ma remember that I'm pregnant with a crazy niggah at home, who would leave my ass high and dry, if he even suspected I was playing around. Therefore, I'm just gon' use ole boy over here to buy me some cranberry juice and hook my girls up with some Perfect Tens and Long Island Ice Teas.

He smiled, squinted his eyes real tight, and spit started flying out of his mouth, "Hoooooowa-wa-wa-wa, you dur'in?"

Oh...hell...no...What the fuck did he say? "Did you ask me *how am I doing*?" I smiled.

"Yup. Sho-Sho-Sho-Sho-Sho'nough."

Well, ain't this the answer to the million dollar question: Why ole boy was standing alone? He sounds like one of the Lil'

kids yelling out the back window of the short yellow school bus. But then again, maybe he had a bad moment. "To answer your question," I said, "I'm doing quite well and you?"

"Me-Me-Me-Me good. I-I-I-I's r-r-right nice!"

Oh, fuck no! I looked at him, square in his eyes and thought to myself, there's no way I can even play with the afflicted. I'll leave that to Angie and her crazy ass running around here with midgets and shit. But me, I don't wanna go to hell. So, I commenced to do the next best thing. I grabbed the napkin that was sitting under the juice I was drinking, and hog spit flem into it. Nasty, I know, but this is how you get rid of a niggah you don't want.

"Well, you take care," he said, stepping away from the table, and the niggah didn't stutter when he said it. Ma'fucker!

"Hey girl!" Angie and Lee said, sitting down and wiping sweat from their foreheads.

"I was hoping to catch ole boy over here," Angie said pointing, "That's the mofo I was eyeing at the bar."

"Chile please, you don't want him...but then again you might. But I'll tell you this, you won't be able to understand a word he's saying."

"For real? Mike Tyson type shit?" Angie sneared.

"Worse."

"Worse?"

"Much worse, more like that stuttering niggah in the Harlem Knights movie. It'll take you a year to know whether or not he's asking for some pussy."

"Well, knowing me, I probably would try. All I need to understand is that uhhnnn and ahhhhh Ludacris scream his ass gon' let out when he cumin'!"

"You never get enough do you Angie?" I chuckled.

"Girl, Vera, let me tell you. Remember that Lil' security guard from the Prudential building?"

"Yeah."

"Well the other day we were gettin' busy, this niggah suckin' my titties and shit. He's playing with the clit and I'm preparing myself to bust about three or four good nuts with this Chicken George ma'fucker. The next thing I know he humps twice and starts shaking. I looked around and said to myself, 'Angie, this mofo must be having a seizure, cause I know damn well he ain't cummin'."

"Was he?"

"Girlfriend, I got my shit spread eagle like a ma'fucker and the next thing I know he's practically got his femur in my pussy. Gruntin' like a damn animal about how he cumin! Slappin' me on the ass and screaming, 'What's my name? Tell me my name!"

"What you say?"

"I said '*Excuse me Minute-in'a-Half but I'll be needing my coochie back now. Thank you.*' I tell you it's a damn shame! How in the hell did the minute man get the magic stick?"

"What about the magic stick? " Shannon interrupted, slamming her drink down on the table, and flopping down in the chair next to Angie, "Vera, how'd you get ole boy over here? He was fine as hell, girl!"

"Bitch I don't know, but I don't want him. He can't talk worth shit."

"Yeah ai'ght, you know you wanted him. Hell, you don't need dick to talk all the time. Some of the best dick knows how to shut the fuck up! Humph, a many of dicks have talked their balls out of a good nut cause they say a buncha stupid shit. The real deal is Taj'll back slap dat ass if he catches you with another niggah. And yo ass is pregnant too."

"For real," Angie said giving her a high-five and singing like Akon, "Vera's ass is *locked up and Taj won't let her out.*" She and Shannon fell out laughing with spit flying out their half drunken ass mouths.

"You two need to be ashamed of yourselves!" Lee interjected, "Vera has a good man. And if I'm not mistaken you do too, Shannon. Quincy? So, both of ya'll need to stop. You're too old to be running around here like a buncha dick sick groupies!"

"Lee," Angie replied, "when's the last time you gave a niggah some head? Somebody need to bust up in your mouth so you can shut the fuck up!"

"You are so disgusting. I don't do those things!"

"Well, girlfriend," Angie smiled, "you don't know what you're missing!"

"Lee stop lying!" I said, "Remember Pastah James? Until the First Lady came along you had homeboy's entire shaft in your mouth. Straight flossing your teeth with his pubic hairs. See ya'll, look at her teeth and how they shine. That's called cumshine!"

"Oh no, you didn't?" Lee yelled out.

"Pretty much she did." Shannon added. "You better learn to give some head girl. That's why you can't keep a niggah."

Angie laughed so hard she started crying and making jerk off motions with her hand. "The poor mofo probably sittin' there beatin' his meat going, *'Never mind the balls, can I get my dick sucked please? Just a Lil' jawbreaker? Spit on it'* at least damn!"

"The men I chose to date," Lee said, rolling her eyes, "are far beyond asking, or needing me to perform oral sex on them."

"It's called, giving head." Angie snickered.

"No it's not." I added, trying not to crack the fuck up, "It's called, suckin' dick."

9

"Nasty bitch!" Lee growled, "And to think you're going to be someone's mother. How in the hell can you three talk about suckin' dick, like it's nothing? When you find a good man you should concentrate on keeping him, not sucking his dick."

"That's how you keep him." Angie looked at Lee like she was crazy.

"Lee," I said, "How the hell do you suppose a bitch should lock down a good piece of dick?"

"By being herself."

The three of us fell back in our chairs and rolled our eyes. This self-righteous shit with Lee is working my last nerve. Now, don't get me wrong, Lee is my girl and all, but this is one chick I just don't understand. She's lucky we're childhood friends, I'm telling you I would molly whop dat ass!

"Look *Lee*," Shannon stressed.

"Look Lee nothing," she interrupted. "The art to keeping a good man is to show him that you can take care of him and that's shown the first time you meet him."

"Lee," I said, "You can't be wife'n the dick from the first date, you gotta give good dick a chance to breathe. You can't lock it down right away. You gotta sit back and chill. Take a Lil' while and practice some sex moves. Rent some Vanessa DelRio and develop a Jennifer Lopez attitude, which screams, '*I'm the best hoe in Hollywood!*'

"Damn real," Shannon added. "Be a lady in public and a freak in the sheets. The big dick doesn't have to start off being yo' man, but if your plan is to snatch his ass up—" Shannon pointed to Angie.

"Then you better suck that dick like you slurpin' a jello pudding pop!" Angie snapped with her neck in full motion. "Afterwards, you swallow, catch your breath, hop on backwards, and buck that dick like Bin Laden lookin' for it!"

"Fah sho" I said slapping Angie a high-five. "Have that mofo call your name like you on loan from the bank! Take your time and showcase some skills. Don't just suck his *dick*, but hit his *balls*, his *toes*, play in his ass hole and kiss behind his knees. Put some ice in your mouth and let it drip while you bite his nipples. Then flip him over and run your cold tongue from the back of his neck to the bottom of his feet and watch him cum like a drought relieved by the rain!"

"Then you get up," Shannon said dusting her hands together, "Take a shower, slip on your clothes, and kiss the ma'fucker good bye."

"And I guarantee you," Angie said, pointing her index finger at Lee, "Not only will he be handing over his paycheck, but one day you will look down and have a red light beepin' from yo' ass. 'Cause the niggah done high jacked ya clit and slapped a low jack on it! Now the same ma'fucker that *you* use to sweat is sittin' on *your* jock nice and pretty!"

"Take it to church, Sista Angie!" Shannon shouted.

"Oh, ya'll don't hear me!" Angie patter her chin and forehead with a napkin.

"Fix it now! We hear you, we hear you." I said, clapping my hands.

"Well since you hear me, that sermon'll be coming from the book of Hush."

"Ya'll so stupid." Lee laughed, "Let's go!"

We gulped down the last of our drinks and grabbed our purses. On the way out the D.J. started bangin' the club remix to Lil' Jon and the East Side Boy's "*Get Low*."

"From the windooooow to the wall...to the wall...let sweat drop down my balls...and all these bitches crawl..."

Most of the people in the club rushed to the dance floor,

formed a circle, and started watching someone dance. Hell, the way the people were chanting *"Let me see you get low...you scared...you scared..."* Whoever they were watching must've been rippin' it! I started to go and check it out, but I was too tired to even look. As I went to throw my chiffon shawl over my shoulders I heard a female voice say, *"Show me whatcha workin' wit!"*

I know goddamn well that ain't who I think it is. The girls and I must've been thinking the same thing, because with out us saying a word we each headed toward the middle of the dance floor. As we maneuver through the thick of the crowd, I heard it again, *"Show me whatcha workin' wit!"* That's when I knew it could be nobody but Cookie Turner. I hope and pray that she is on the sidelines and this bitch is not workin' it out on the dance floor.

Oh goddamn, I can't believe this! Aunt Cookie and her two girlfriends, Carol and Janet are in the middle of the dance floor doing the Beyoncé Boodie Hop; while Lil' Jon grunts about 'sweat droppin' down his balls. Every time Lil Jon said, *"Stop and wiggle wit' it."* Aunt Cookie was shaking her ass like a Luke dancer. The next thing I know Aunt Cookie's sidekicks started break dancing. Ms. Carol's was doing the "pop and lock", while Ms. Janet occupied herself with the spin and freeze!

"Aunt Cookie!" I yelled, "What are ya'll doing?"

"We shakin' it like a salt shaker, Baby Girl!"

Before I could say anything the crowd, including Shannon, Lee, and Angie started chanting. "Go Aunt Cookie! Go Aunt Cookie!"

"Shake a shimmy girl!" Shannon yelled. I was pissed! And just when I thought things couldn't get worse, for the finishing touch Aunt Cookie and her two girlfriends, started doing the robot. Oh hell no! I gotta get the fuck outta here before I lose it! I turned to Shannon and said, "I'm out."

"Ai'ight, girl." She said giving me a kiss on the cheek, "I gotta watch this, this is some funny shit…Look, Vera they're doing the worm!"

***

"The pop and lock! Oh hell yeah…and remember lottos and shit? MCM suits with the dookey chains…oh baby that was the joint back in the day." Taj said lying in bed and propping his pillow behind his head.

"I can't imagine you actually rockin' that shit." I said lying against his chest.

"Hell no, I never wore that crazy shit. I was always the niggah with the army fatigue jacket, hoody, jeans, and Tims. Maybe some Nikes or Addidas but all that other lollipop, pimp-wearin' shit would never be caught on the kid."

"So, you were just thugged out since birth?"

"Don't sleep. Taj Bennet Jr. has always been the man…and once light skin brothas were played out, oh…it was on."

"Light skin played out? Taj please." I chuckled, playing with the hairs on his chest.

"Taj, please? Vera, you probably were one of the main ones, *'Oh he gotta look like Kid from Kid and Play, Heavy D, or Al-B Sure, otherwise Shannon, I ain't fuckin' wit' him.'"

"No you didn't just try and play me like that? You got my light skin confused, I would only fuck with Ice-T or Snoop."

Playfully he mushed me on the side of my head then pulled me on top of him. Stroking my back he kissed me lightly on the lips. "I want you to marry me, Vera."

"What did you just say?" I knew I heard wrong. "You want me to what?"

"I want you to marry me. I want to marry you."

"Taj, please. You don't have to feel obligated to me because I'm pregnant." I said rolling off of him and sitting up.

"Obligated? Taj said with a smirk, placing his head in my lap, "What would make you think that I feel obligated? Because you're pregnant? Since when has that ever kept a brotha? Vera, our baby, has nothing to do with the love I have for you. The baby simply adds to it. But I love you all by yourself."

"Tell me why?" I asked, somehow needing to be reassured.

"Girl, you're like my main man, my *dawg* and shit!" He laughed a little and then he quickly became serious. "Plus, I've never loved anyone the way that I love you. You make me feel complete. Everything that I need lies here with you. I laugh with you, cry with you, share my joy with you, and now…we're having a baby. That completes this picture. I want it to be a done deal. I wanna step to you with everything, every inch of my heart, every material possession that I own, everything that I am and say, 'Here baby. Here I am. Here's my world, and now it's yours."

"You would do *all* that for me?" I asked, stroking the side of his face.

"Ain't nuthin' but a word."

"Ain't nuthin' but a word? What kinda home boy hook up marriage proposal is that?"

"Oh, so you want a brother to beg?" he asked.

I shot his ass a look and pointed to the floor. "Down on ya knee, *dawg*. Oh…" I said stopping him before he could say anything, "Since I know you don't have a ring, being that you're proposing on the fly, just pretend."

"Pretend?" He chuckled, "Girl, somebody got to love you, because you're something else." Getting down on his right knee, Taj reached for my left hand. I sat on the edge of the bed; it felt like my heart was playing double dutch in its chamber. "Vera," he said, "Never have I loved like this. You are my everything and I want to be with you for life. Will you, Miss Vera Wright-Turner, do me, Dr. Taj Bennet, the honor of completing my circle by becoming my wife?"

I was speechless and my heart wanted to say yes, but nothing would fall out of my mouth. My eyes traced the creases in his face and I imagined still being in love with him, as we grew old.

"Close your eyes." He said.

I complied and closed my eyes.

"Now, open them."

When I opened my eyes Taj was holding my left hand and slipping on my ring finger a platinum, three karat, round, Tiffany solitaire. I started to scream and cry at the same time! I couldn't believe that he had me a ring. He really wanted to marry me. It wasn't something that he just decided on the fly; he wanted me to be his wife! I hugged him so tight that he started to cough. "Vera," he managed to say, "is that a yes?"

I started kissing him all over his forehead, on both sides of his face, and on his neck. I pulled gently for him to get off the floor. When he got up, I pulled him on to the bed, and rolled on top of him. I looked him in the eyes and said, "I would marry you every waking second. There is nothing more at this very moment that I want more than to be your wife."

I kissed him like an escaped slave arriving at the northern shore. He ran his hands up and down my thighs and I couldn't wait to make love to him. I stuck my hands in the slit of his boxers and pulled his dick out. I massaged it with my fingertips while he moaned quietly. I continued to stroke and kiss him straight down his thick neck, chiseled stomach, and then on his muscular thighs. Slowly, I slid to my knees, all the while massaging the gracefulness of his erotic manhood.

"Vera," he said, trying to lift my head as I kissed the tip of the dick, "If you keep doing that, I'ma cum."

"You gon' what?" I asked, while placing soft wet kisses around the head and sides. "Tell me again."

"Vera, come on baby and get on top." He hissed.

"No," I said licking him like a lollipop, "I thought this is what you liked."

"I do...but I want some pussy right now. Let's try something different." he begged.

"What?" I was sliding my tongue up and down the thumping vein on the side of his dick. "Try what?"

"Sit on my face."

Now, that threw me. What did he say? "Do what?"

"Sit on my face."

"Are you serious?"

"Yes." He said, playing with my hair and squeezing the base of his dick, making the head look as if it would explode. Damn, it looked delicious! I was enjoying this just a little too much. Is this what pregnancy does to you; make you horney ass hell? Still and all, sit on his face? Now that was a new one. For a moment I started to think, *'Where did he get that one from?'* Then I dismissed the thought and figured I was being a little too emotional.

Once I stop kissing his dick and lifted my head up, Taj moved to the middle of the bed and slid his boxers off, "Come here, Mrs. Bennet."

I started crawling next to him. "Wait, wait." He said, "I wanna watch you take off your clothes."

"Really?" I had a snide smile on my face.

"Yes, and do it nice and slow."

"You want me to dance for you, too?" I asked sarcastically.

"Yeah." he said, "Nice and slow. Turn on the CD player."

I can't even lie, I looked at him, thought about how much I loved him—not to mention the expensive ass bling-bling he'd just hit me off with, and I figured fuck this, this was my man. Taj was not only *that niggah*, he was *my niggah* and I'm sure you can understand that at this very moment, I felt a need to do whatever pleased him.

I got off the bed still wearing my black lace nightie. Closed the vertical blinds slightly, leaving them open just enough for the burning candles to reflect off the dampness of the windowpanes. The late September weather was misty; which brought in a seductive darkness from the outside, although it was mid-morning. The three feet tall candles glistened in front of the two floor-to-ceiling windows I have in my third floor master suite; complete with a walk-in closet, a sitting area with a butter cream leather sofa, chaise, 42'plasma TV, and a full bath with an octagon shaped Jacuzzi.

I turned on the CD player and slid in Maxwell's *Urban Hang Out Suite*, hit track number six, which was *"Til the Cops Come Knockin"* and placed it on repeat. I figured if Taj wanted a dance, then that's what he would get, a dance. As soon as Maxwell started hitting the first high note —where he seemed to jiggle it, hold it, and then set it free —was when I started to dance, twirl, and slowly get my grind on. Taj went to close his eyes. "Open them." I said, "You wanted a dance, now watch it."

He squeezed the base of his dick and his eyes told me he was speechless.

I worked my way around the room doing exotic moves, bending down and slowly coming back up, revealing the beauty of my vaginal goodness. By the time Maxwell finished singing I was undressed and climbing on top of Taj.

"Damn baby," he said, placing his hands on my ass and pushing me toward his face, "that was the shit!"

"Are you sure about this move?" I said, now covering his mouth.

"Shh," he said with the first lick to my clit, sending electric shudders up and down my spine, "I got this."

The Shot Clock is Running

After we finished making love, I laid in bed and kept staring at my engagement ring but Taj was walking around with his dick swinging. Teasing me and shit knowing full well that I'm weak when it comes to a gettin' a nut. "I wish you put some clothes on." I said, twisting my lips.

"I bet you do." He smiled, grabbing a pair of fresh boxers, "Ever dreamed of a big wedding?"

"I've never dreamed that I would fall in love, so who knows."

"Well, what do you know?"

"I know I want some mo' dick."

"Stop playing with me," he laughed "and be serious."

"Okay," I said sitting up, pulling the comforter above my breast, "The size of the wedding doesn't matter, what matters is that I simply want you."

"Well, hell, we must already be married because you already got me."

Why did he say that, now I can't stop blushing.

"Are you going to see your mother this morning?" Taj asked, standing in the bathroom's doorway, preparing to shower.

"Yes, baby, before I go to the shop."

"All right. When I leave I'll run by the hospital to check on her myself, and then I'm going to Jersey and hang out with my pop for a Lil' while."

"Don't forget about the Best of Both Worlds concert, tonight. We're meeting Shannon and Quincy there around eight."

"I didn't forget baby."

I watched Taj walk out the room, then I rolled over and called Shannon.

"Hello?"

"Hey girl." I said with a slight chuckle.

"Damn, some of us just crack the fuck up early in the morning. A He-he-he." She said, sarcastically.

"What's wrong with you?" I asked, trying desperately not to take Shannon's smart-ass comment to heart. "What? You ain't get none of Nile's dick last night?"

"Girl please, Nile is perfect. It's Quincy. Trust me, no matter how old men get they got ma'fuckin issues."

"Sounds like they ain't the only ones with issues."

"Vera, I'm sorry. I'm just stressed. I'm so tired of Quincy's ass, he's gotta go."

"Do what you gotta do." I sighed, tired of hearing the same complaint over and over again.

"Vera, please, you know it's not that easy. Plus, I don't wanna give Quincy up like that."

"I just love the way you talk out of both sides of your mouth." She huffed.

"I don't talk out of both sides of my mouth."

"Yes you do. I mean, really, make up your mind. What you wanna do? Do you wanna be a hoe or a housewife?"

"Oh wait a minute heifer, are you trying to read me? All of this because you got a good dick on lock? Slow ya roll homegirl! Anyway..." She said blowing me off, "I know you're not calling to cancel my hair appointment, you know we're going to the concert tonight."

"What did you say?" I said with my neck twisted, "I didn't forget the concert. I was calling to remind you and Quincy to meet us at eight tonight in the lobby. But just so you know, you really hurt my feelings."

"Why are you being so sensitive?...Oh hold up...Your pregnant ass got the nerve to be sensitive? How many more months of this do I have to go through?"

"You just did it again."

"What?"

"Hurt my feelings!"

"Bitch!" Shannon screamed. "As much shit as *you* talk to people and you have the nerve to be wearing your feelings on your fingertips? The next seven months with your ass gon' be a hot mess!"

"Whatever," I said with an attitude. "Anyway, just meet us in the lobby."

"Don't cry!" Shannon said extremely loud. "It's okay. Just be there for the photo shoot please...and don't forget about the concert tonight."

Did that just come out of left field? What is she talking about? "Shannon," I said confused as hell, "Are you feeling alright? What are you talking about? Photo shoot? We didn't agree to a photo shoot. I'm sick of you thinking that I should do your models' hair at the drop of a dime!"

"Shut the fuck up." She mumbled. She took her mouth away from the phone and tried to whisper, "Quincy, you know how Vera is. I'm just going to get her set up for the photo shoot, so she can do the model's hair for a story were running on Black hair. Then I'm going to run around with her for a little while before the concert. She's having a hard time dealing with her mom."

"Are you crazy!" I snapped, realizing she was using me to cover her lies. This heifer knows better than anybody, that Mr. 6 foot 3, 245 pounds Quincy Askew is nothin' to fuck wit'. I would have to climb a damn tree just to punch him in the face. "Shannon, didn't we agree that Quincy is violently retarded? You gon' fuck around here and make that niggah go off! And you know Dirty and Biggie ain't fuckin' wit' yo' ass!"

"Shut up," she said tightlipped. "Okay Quincy, I love you too, Sweetie." Then she paused, I could hear a door slam in her background. "I can't stand this niggah here. His ass is always trying to cock block a bitch. Can I get my grind on in peace? Damn!"

"I'm convinced you have lost your mind." I said in disbelief, "Suppose that retarded ma'fucker come by my shop and see me working there?"

"First of all, don't call him retarded. Second of all he won't do that, he trusts me."

"He trusts you, Shannon? Ha!" I said opening my walk-in closet, looking for something to wear tonight.

"Anywho…I'm going to meet Nile for a mid-day freak session and I'll catch ya'll about eight tonight."

"Keep fuckin' around. I've already told you that if you wanted to do Nile, then you needed to send Quincy home to his mama. That way, you can play as much as you want. You're not married to him and you're not pregnant."

"Ahhh, that would be the case, if that was what I wanted to do. But since that's not what I'm choosing at this moment, then I would ask you to mind ya business!"

"All right, you shall see."

"Uhmm hmm." She grumbled.

"Yo' ass love to be stubborn, Shannon. The grass might look greener on the other side but you got to mow that too." I said, taking out a cream Marc Jacobs' two piece, silk suit with matching stilettos.

"Shut up Vera," she snapped, "You sound like a fake ass playah. Damn near remind me of Lee."

"Lee? Oh hell no."

"Oh hell yes, ya do." Shannon sang, "You're on the borderline of fuckin' cornyyyyy!"

"Anyway," I said, "I got something to tell you."

"What? You're having twins?"

"Don't make me call you out your name Shannon." I chuckled, "Taj and I are engaged!"

"What? My girl!! Congratulations!!! You snagged that ma'-fucker. Now that's what's up! But let me ask you something Vera..."

"What?"

"Don't you ever want to cheat again?"

"No, hoe." I said listening for the grinding sounds of my gold diggin' shovel. "I'm satisfied. And you?"

"I could use an extra dick or two." She said sucking her teeth, "Quincy's ass is working my nerves, but other than that, I'm ecstatic for you! That's an honorable thing you're doing—

committing to one man. Marrying baby daddy and shit. Hell, anything is possible. So, I hope Lee and Angie understand that *I'm* the maid of honor. Maybe you can let them hold your train, carry the guest book around or somethin'."

"Shannon!" I screamed in laughter, "You know how they are. Don't start no shit."

"Please girl! But I can't believe you're getting married! The last time I thought about marriage, I was with Bilal."

"That's a name I haven't heard since college." I said, surprised that Shannon was talking about her ex-boyfriend.

"I know. I went by and left some flowers the other day."

"You miss him?"

"Girl, you just don't know how much. But anyway, Bilal was many moons ago. Back to you, I am so happy for you."

"Really?"

"Hell yeah! Girl, I just can't wait for the bachelorette party. We gon' get down and dirty."

"I'm pregnant Shannon. How in the hell am I going to be gettin' down and dirty at a bachelorette party?"

"Bitch yo' ass from the hood!" she snapped. "Don't be acting all high saddity. You know how we do. We get all on the tables, pulling on the niggah's jock strap. And then all of a sudden just like a jack-in-the-box, the stripper springs out a dick that looks like a tree trunk, and everybody in the place starts backin' that thing up!"

"Girl, you ain't never lied. Maybe we can have it in the shop. DeAndre's sweet ass is sure to enjoy that one."

"DeAndre will get his ass cut up in there. There will be no rainbow strippers. Straight up solid colors!"

I fell out laughing.

"Vera, how's your mom? When is she getting out the hospital?" Shannon asked.

"In another day or two. Taj and I are going to pay for her to go to a private rehab center in the Bronx. It's suppose to be one of the best."

"That's wonderful, Vera! When you see her, give her my love."

"All right, Boo. See ya later!"

By the time I got off the phone Taj was back in the bedroom getting dressed. He slipped on baggy jeans, a beige long sleeve shirt, his blue goose down Northface vest, and Tims. His dreads were hanging down and resting nicely on his shoulders.

"I know you wanna do me." he smiled.

"Boy, please. You ai'ight," I said, sitting on the bed, and waiving my hand from side to side. "Don't go getting your boxers all twisted up! This diva wasn't even thinking about you."

He walked over and pressed his forehead against mine, "*You* just better have my money."

"I'm tryin' Daddy." Playfully, I pushed him away, got off the bed and placed my hands on my hip. "Can't you see this niggah got me pregnant? But I'ma still feel that heat, beat that block, and get yo' money."

"Cut the shit." He laughed, "You better be thinking about me every chance you get. That ring you sportin' is somebody's yearly salary. Don't play."

"Bye Taj." I chuckled pushing him to the side. Before I could make it into the bathroom Taj ran behind me and picked me up. "What did you say?" he said playfully holding me in the air.

"Taj put me down!"

Instead of him placing me back on the floor, he held me tighter in his arms and started kissing me, on the neck. "Taj, you just got dressed. I thought you said you were going to Jersey?"

"I am, but let me get five minutes in the shower with you."

"Taj." I moaned while he started sucking my nipples, "We don't have time for this."

"Five minutes, baby."

"All right five minutes." I smiled.

After we finished our nice lil' shower episode, Taj jumped out before I did. What started out as only five minutes ended up being forty-five minutes. He ran in the bedroom and threw on new clothes. "Baby," he said, yelling at me in the bathroom, "I won't be able to make it to the hospital now. I'll call and check on Rowanda on my way to Jersey."

"Okay," I said stepping outta the shower, "I'm headed over there now."

I slipped on a pair of blue jeans with a DKNY tee shirt, a pair of blue and white throwback pumas, and my blue Norma Kamali midriff jacket. I felt the tears that I buried the other night wake up in my throat. As I thought about how my mother, Rowanda, had overdosed on dope and was now laying in her hospital bed, preparing for a second chance at life. I grabbed my keys and jumped in my truck.

On the drive to the hospital, I started daydreaming about Rowanda, something I've never done. Ever since social services took me away from her, I've been too scared to dream. I started dreaming about being married, having the baby, and Rowanda being drug free. Dreaming about all of us being a family.

I had to laugh, because I couldn't believe myself. This was totally out of character for me, but hell, everybody has a dream they want to come true. Mine just happens to be a mother who's not shootin' dope, or smokin' crack for once.

When I got to the hospital, the nurses looked at me strange. One of the nurses rolled her eyes when she saw me. I knew right away that the bitch had a thing for Taj. But it's all good, because when it comes to my man, I got a special alert radar. The kind that goes off when a hoe's libido jumps into overdrive and it screams, *"Bout to catch a case!"* So quite frankly I don't give a damn if she rolls her eyes, cause ole girl *really* don't know me, I'll punch her in the face first and talk later. Trust me when I tell you, it'll be the last time she tries to squat on my man!

I mean mugged the bitch, daring her to say something. She quickly turned away and I simply kept it movin'.

Just as I reached the doorway of Rowanda's hospital room, my cell phone rang. When I peeped at the caller I.D., it was Aunt Cookie. Oh damn, please don't let her be calling me about her boodie shaking episode in the club last night.

"Yes, Cookie Jolene Turner?" I said stepping into the room, and noticing how it was empty. My eyes wildly searched the room as Aunt Cookie started talking, "What you say, Aunt Cookie?"

"I said, that I want to talk to you about your mother."

"Uhmm hmm..." I said listening half-heartily, I noticed everything in Rowanda's room, from how the bed was freshly made to her missing clothes that use to hang on the back of the closet door. All of her things were gone. My heart jumped in my throat and it was climbing its way toward my tongue. I couldn't speak.

"Vera!" Aunt Cookie said, "Baby Girl. Where are you? Are you listening to me?"

I still couldn't speak.

"You in the hospital Baby Girl?"

"Uhmm hmm..." was all I could manage to say while biting my bottom lip.

"Vera, you know your mother loves you, but some times people need time to change. Please don't get upset."

"Aunt Cookie...I-I-I gotta go." I'm not sure if I hung the phone up or not, I just threw it in my purse. I couldn't believe that Rowanda wasn't here.

One of the nurses peeked in the room, "I remember you from the other night." she said, standing in the doorway with a chart in her hand.

"Yeah." I was trying not to cry, so instead I started rocking slightly from side to side, "Have you seen my mother?" I asked her.

The nurse looked at me and her eyes said it all. She walked toward me and said, "I'm sorry, but your mother demanded to be released this morning. There was nothing we could do to make her stay."

"You could've made her stay! Yes, you could've! You had my fuckin' phone number! You could've paged Taj!"

"Ms..."

"Don't fuckin' 'Ms.' me, fuck it! It's not your mother so don't you worry about it! Just go! Just leave!" I sat down on the bed and placed my hands over my face.

"I'm sorry." the nurse said softly before leaving out the room.

"Hey, Vee!" a voice said floating in behind the nurse who'd just left. When I looked up, I saw Queen, Rowanda's chicken head friend, standing there.

I couldn't even muster the strength to speak to her. Everything about her reminded me of the streets, from her twisted mouth, to her glassy eyes, to the way she just looked like the essence of a struggle. Everything about her screamed fucked up and I was sick of looking at her, mainly because she reminded me too much of my mother. All I could manage to say was, "Don't...say...shit...to me!"

Tears fell from my eyes like a lost stream. Queen stared at me like I was crazy. Then she looked around the room, under the bed, wildly opened the closet, and searched the bathroom. When she finished, she stood and walked back over to me, "She gon?"

"What the fuck you think?"

"Watcha mouth, Vera! I'm your godmother! I was the one who found you in the garbage. Found your mama shakin' on the corner when the police came. Me. So watch yo' nasty ass mouth, show some respect!"

"Godmother? You think you're my godmother because you found me in the garbage? Ya'll niggahs are a straight up joke!" I was laughing in disbelief and crying at the same time. "Goddamn chicken heads, one for a mother and another one for a godmother! If I don't ever see another ma'fuckin crack head or dope fiend for the rest of my life, it'll be too soon. I *am so sick* of having to deal with ya'll pigeon lookin' asses, that I don't know what to do! All I know is that every time I give this bitch my heart she breaks it. I don't have time for this! I'm pregnant. I have to take care of my baby. If I lose my baby worrying over her I'ma kill her and then I'ma blast yo stanken ass!"

"Stanken ass?" Queen took a step back as if she had to stop herself from acting on whatever she was thinking. "The only reason I'ma let that slide is because you're pregnant...Vera, you don't understand what its like to need a fix. You don't understand how it is to be a fiend."

"Fuck that! I don't give a damn how it is to be a fiend! I care about how it feels to have a mother. How it feels to be somebody's child. All my life I've been a dope fiend's kid, I'm sick of this shit! Fuck her! Fuck that dope! And fuck you and the glass dick you been suckin' on!"

Queen took two steps back. I could tell she wanted to slap the shit out of me, but my Aunt Cookie would'a killed her ass! So, I gave her a look like, *'you try it.'*

As much as I tried to calm myself, I couldn't stop the pain, no matter how much I wanted to. The hardest thing in the world is the feeling of wanting your mother to just, simply be your mother. I could feel the coldness of the white hospital sheets against my thighs. I ran my hand across dead dreams that laid on Rowanda's hospital pillow. I felt like a fool—a stupid fool—for letting her into my life, for the little time I did. I must be crazy to think that she could be anything but a dope fiend.

Suddenly, my stomach felt queasy. I rushed pass Queen and into the bathroom. Bending over the toilet, I started throwing up and gagging on my own vomit. Coughing and spitting out my daily routine of morning sickness.

I felt wiped out and placed my hands on the sides of the toilet. As I did that, I felt a hand rest on my shoulder. It scared the shit out of me! I jumped as I turned around and small bits of my vomit flew across the bathroom floor. Taj was standing there, seemingly unfazed by what had landed on his shoes.

"What are you doing here?" I asked him, grabbing some toilet tissue, wiping the corners of my mouth, and then handing him some for his feet.

"I found out that Rowanda left the hospital on my way to the Holland tunnel. I couldn't leave you here to deal with this by yourself. I know how you are and I don't want you internalizing it."

"You know how I am?" I said in disbelief, while flushing the toilet. "Please, I don't give a fuck! Is Queen still out there?"

"No, she left. She was crying on her way out."

"I just want her to stay the fuck away from me."

"Vera, Queen is not the issue. Rowanda is."

"Fuck Rowanda. So, she's gone, big fuckin' deal. You know what they say, once a dope fiend always a dope fiend."

"You know you don't mean that."

"I do mean that! I never thought that Rowanda would do something for me, or my baby. When you have a junkie for a mother then you ain't shit next to what the fuck she getting' high off of."

"Come here, baby." Taj said reaching for me.

"No!" I said, trying to boguard my way pass him. "Fuck that bitch! I can't take this. I just can't." I broke down and started crying. Taj pulled me closed and started rubbing my back, "its okay baby, its okay."

I cried so hard that my stomach started to feel queasy again. I knew I had to calm myself down, no matter how hard it was. "Well," I said, wiping my eyes, "I'll be all right. I knew she couldn't do it anyway."

Taj didn't say a word he just grabbed me by the hand and we left. He insisted on driving me to the shop. Then he called Shannon and asked her if she and Quincy could come and pick up my truck from the hospital's parking lot. I could tell that she asked what was wrong, because he looked at me. She must've guessed it, because he said, "You got it." She said something again, and he said, "Thanks."

I tried my best not to cry on our way to the shop; instead, I bit my bottom lip. When we got there, I looked out my window and flashbacks of being that little girl stuck behind locked doors of a pink Aries K flooded my mind. My heart was lost and I didn't know what to do with the part that loved and wanted my mother.

As we pulled up in front of the salon, Rowanda was pacing back and forth, still wearing her faded hospital gown, with the I.D. bracelet hanging loose on her wrist.

"What do you want?" I said getting out of Taj's Escalade.

"I need to explain something to you." she said.

"What? And make it quick."

"I left the hospital to get high."

"Tell me something I don't know."

"But I didn't." she insisted.

"You didn't what?"

"I didn't get high. But I spent my money and I bought a hit."

"Why are you telling me this?" I asked.

"You wanted me to be honest with you, so I'm trying to tell you the truth. Just listen. I couldn't take lying up there in that hospital bed needing a fix...needing something. I was so sick that I thought I would die. I needed to get high, the craving was so strong that I could damn near taste the left over dope in my system."

"Rowanda," I said cutting her off.

"Let me finish," she said, "I bought the dope. I carried it. I smelled it. And I squeezed it. I would've made love to it, if I could. But then, I looked at myself in the mirror and I didn't like what I saw. I was a used up junkie. I felt like less than rat shit. I scared myself so bad that I dropped my dope all over the place, some on my hand, some on my feet, and the rest on the floor. I panicked and threw myself down, scraping and brushing the dope that landed on the floor back into my hand. The rest of it I could lick off my skin. There was dust, dirt, and some trash from the floor in the dope, but I still wanted it. As I stepped into the kitchen, I dropped it again and it splattered on the floor. Once again, I fell to my knees, begging God to please help me...help me, to help me. So, He led me here, to your shop, where I'm beggin' for help. Vera, help me, to help me. Please, I need you."

It took everything that I had to keep my composure in the street. Taj stood there and I could tell that he had mixed emotions. I was so exhausted from the struggle of loving and hating my mother at the same time, that I felt like *I* needed help. I wanted to scream, I wanted to throw punches in the air, or slap the shit out of her for leaving a part me stuck in the trash dump!

As I watched Rowanda, tears were slowly building in my eyes and behind my throat. I rubbed my stomach to remind myself that I was now a mother, internally at least, and at this moment, my baby came first. I had every intention of hauling off and slapping the shit out of her. I had every reason in the world to throw her out of my life and never look back. But I couldn't and once I touched her hand and she squeezed mine and said, "Please." I couldn't do anything but hold her.

I knew that people on the street were watching, but at this moment, nobody else existed. I let go of Rowanda and softly backed away. Before I could say anything, Taj grabbed me by the hand and looked at Rowanda. "No disrespect, Rowanda, and please take this with love. But, I love Vera more than you could ever imagine and when she hurts, I hurt, and my baby hurts. And I ain't feeling that. Now medically, I understand why you left that hospital, I can describe what you were feeling better than you can. But, I'm not the doctor in this situation, I'm Vera's man, her child's father, and I will not stand by and watch them fall apart."

"Taj-" I said, interrupting him.

He shot me such a look that I knew to be quiet and let him finish. "Now anything that I have in this world I will give it to you to help you. But you see these two," he said resting his hand on my stomach, "I'm not giving them away to anybody that can't love them and take care of them."

"I love them too." Rowanda looked at him, "I just need some help."

"Then you got it…" he grabbed her hand, "Just remember that Vera and my baby are my life and I don't take kind to people playing with my life. I have too much to lose." He looked at me, "I really don't want you to go, but I can't make that decision for you. Do you want to go with me and sign her into the rehab center?"

"Yes."

"All right. Lets' go."

When we got to there I told Taj I felt too sick to get out of the truck. Actually, I didn't want to see Rowanda go inside and me come out with false hopes.

Once Taj finished with Rowanda, we were getting ready to pull out of the parking lot when he turned to me. "I love you." He placed his hand on my stomach. "It's all about us and what makes this work. No more drama and no more stress."

"We'll see Taj, because lately it's been the same shit, just a different day."

He tilted his head down, cradled my face in the palms of his hands, our lips touched lightly, "I got you," he assured me, "and that's all that matters."

Who's keeping Score?

"He got you!" Shannon shouted with her legs and bare feet hanging over the edge of my sofa, sipping on a glass of Moet. "You mean to tell me that since you sat on Taj's face, the ma'-fucker has taken control like that! And ever since then that's all he's been saying? *He got you*! Oh, shit! Does he have a twin? Fuck a twin, what's up with his daddy?"

The girls and I were all sitting around in my living room shooting the shit, sipping on Moet, with Ludracris' "P-Poppin," bumpin' in the background. I invited them over to peep out my big ass diamond, however only Shannon has spotted it.

"His *father*" Lee said, sitting on the floor, with her legs stretched out and giving Shannon the screw face, "is in a long-term and committed relationship."

"So was the last niggah *you* were with," Shannon said, in between sips, "but didn't nobody hate on you."

"Anywho," I said interrupting Shannon, "Taj's daddy got some undercover shit going on and you'll never guess with who. I peeped it the last time I went with Taj to Newark and Ms. Betty was on vacation."

"Where'd she go?" Shannon asked.

"To the Bahamas with her Bidwhist club."

"She left his ass home alone? She's too old to be that dumb." Shannon insisted, "She gon' fuck around and have a young girl like me, teach her why she should never leave her fine ass man alone too long. Now tell me, Vera, what sexy ass Mr. Bennet do, while the cat was away?"

"Yeah, I wanna hear this too." Angie said, as she gave a sly smile like she was the one creeping with him. Angie was laid back in my mint green, suede chair-and-a-half, with her feet propped up on the ottoman. "Who is he messing around with? He's too goddamn fine for Ms. Betty to be going to an out-of-town Bidwiss party, fuck that!"

Shannon reached over to Angie for some dap. "You ain't never lied. He's fine as hell and ya'll know me, I would hate to be Taj's step-mama, but I would do it. You know I would!" Shannon laughed, crossing her legs.

"Fa shizzle!" Angie said, "Ms. Betty's crazy, if them old ass biddies, couldn't play cards on my kitchen table, then guess who wouldn't be going? Humph, if she don't know she better ask somebody!"

"Well, she better not ask me," Shannon said, swinging her arms in the air and acting as if she had a whip in her hand, "cause I would be riding that dick and telling Ms. Betty, 'no he ain't cheatin'. Your man is more than faithful to both of us!"

We all started laughing. "Oh please." Lee said, "You have to be able to trust your man. Otherwise, what's the use? *And*, he should honor your trust and be faithful."

"See," I said pointing my finger, "That's why you're fucked up in the game now. A man has to *earn* your trust. You don't give it away like it's government cheese. If you start sleeping on his ass too early then the next thing you know, you're standing in church with your three best friends, callin' the pastor out for being the niggah you were creeping with."

"Don't bring that up!" Lee screamed. "That shit still bothers me!"

"Somebody needs to lay hands on you, you are way too sensitive." I swear Lee gets on my goddamn nerves.

"Oh, no your ass didn't!" Angie screamed, "Who was in White Castle the other day and cried because they gave you fries instead of onion rings?!"

"You talking about me, hoe?" I said. "I'm excused, because I'm pregnant."

"Oh please!" Angie sucked her teeth.

"Back to the subject at hand," Shannon interrupted, "Who was fine ass Mr. Taj Bennet Sr. creeping with, while Ms. Betty was out of town?"

"Guess." I said taking a swig of water.

"Who? Don't tell me the woman's sister or something." Shannon said.

"No, he ain't that dirty. I'll just say this. This isn't the first time that Ms. Betty has traveled with her lil' card group. The last time Ms. Betty went away, Mr. Bennet came over here and spent a week with us. Everyday that he was here, Aunt Cookie, would tip by here with her 1979 Dance Fever get up on, with her big ass rump shakin' and bringing Mr. Bennet lunch. A few days later, when it came time for him to go back to Newark, Aunt Cookie was dead on the job. It was her pleasure to carry Mr. Creep-Creep across the bridge. Needless to say, the next day when Taj and I went over there for his niece's birthday party, guess who was tippin' out the back door?"

"My girl!" Shannon screamed, "Aunt Cookie! That bitch knows she be puttin' her thang down!"

"Hell yeah." I said, "but her ass is too old to be a playah!"

"Don't hate," Shannon said. "Let Aunt Cookie do the damn thang!"

"Spare me," I laughed kicking my slippers off and laying back on the chaise. "Let me tell ya'll, when I saw that shit, I started to call her out, but I let it slide. When I saw her the next day, she told me to mind my goddamn business. I swear Aunt Cookie is a shiesty hoe." I laughed.

"Damn," Angie said, taking the last sip of her Moet, "Aunt Cookie gon' fuck around and make Uncle Boy lose his mind!"

"Don't say that shit, cause Lawd knows I can't take him quotin' club songs again."

"That was some funny shit!" Shannon said. "But look, let's get back to the sit on his face move. Show ya girl how to work that! Maybe I can grow up to be like Aunt Cookie one day. "

"For real, I gotta see this!" Angie said, reaching over to give me a high-five, which judging by the way she and Lee have been acting, a high-five seemed a bit much. These two have been acting real shady, not returning phone calls, only coming into the shop to get their hair done, two-waying each other right in my face, laughing at inside jokes and shit. Quite frankly, pissing me the fuck off! I only invited them over here for drinks because I wanted to show them my ring, but since they've been here, they haven't spotted me using my left hand for everything. That is unless they've seen it and have been ignoring me.

"Don't be giving me no high-five, hoe! With your funny acting ass!" I said to her.

"Funny acting?" Lee said adding her two cents. "Please, spare me the pregnant dramatics."

"Was I talking to you?" I said pointing to her, but looking at Angie and Shannon, "Did I miss something or is she in my business again?"

"Anyway," Shannon said, ignoring my sarcasm, "Getting back to your freaky ass, you actually sat on Taj's face? That's some good shit, so tell me," she said getting up from the sofa, bending down, and posing like Brandi on Vibe's cover; with her knees on the floor, ass in the air, and hands folded under her breast. "Was it like this?" she smiled, "Or were you like this?" she said bustin' into a split.

Juvenile's "Slow Motion" was now bangin' in the background and half empty flute glasses of Moet were sitting on the marble coffee table. I had a bottle of spring water sitting next to my bare feet. Since Shannon wanted me to show her my P-poppin' moves, I rose from the chaise, threw a pillow on the floor, and placed it between my feet. Then I squatted over it and started doing leg bends, "This is how you work it!"

"Oh shit!" Shannon yelled. "One more time!" She grabbed a pillow from the sofa and threw it on the floor. Now we were both squatting over pillows. Shannon started moving up and down; we both were handling our business! We raised our hands in the air and started singing along with Juvenile, *"Uhnnnn...I like it like that!...She's workin' that back..."*

Angie started laughing. "I got ya'll asses beat, check this." She changed the CD and put on the "Magic Stick," with Lil' Kim and 50 Cent. Then to all of our surprise, don't you know this skinny bitch sat down on the floor, wrapped one of her legs around the back of her neck, and started buckin' on the floor like she was riding the best dick in the world! Our eyes popped open, I couldn't believe that shit! This bitch had me beat! I ain't never seen a move like that! For a moment, I forgot about the shade she'd been throwing my way.

"Oh hell no!" I said throwing my hands up in defeat. "I ain't fuckin' wit you!" As soon as I said that Angie looked at my hand and unwrapped her leg.

"Let me see that ring bitch!" Angie jumped to her feet.

I held my hand out so they could admire my bling bling. "Boo'yah! Bling!" I was cheesin'. "Now see, had ya'll shut up and stop complaining when you walked in the door, you would have noticed it right away."

"Goddamn bitch!" Angie screeched, "I'm blind!"

"That is beautiful, Vera!" Lee said just as excited as Angie.

"Can you spell f-l-a-w-l-e-s-s?!" I said.

"That niggah got you sprung! Is the dick that good?" Angie asked.

"Got me sprung? I'm the one with the ring bitch! Anyway, since you're wondering," I said shaking my head and slapping my thigh, "My shit be going through cardiac arrest when he hittin' it!"

"Party over here!" Shannon screamed.

"Oh hell," Lee said, sitting back down and sipping on her Moet, "Have you three ever heard of HIV and AIDS? Ya'll wanna be jump-offs all your life? Sex education goes far beyond which block has the most heat? I swear you three are the most un-educated tramp ass hoes in the world."

"Much like yo' man!" I screamed, "Oops, I just remembered you don't have one!" Shannon and I fell out laughing. In the midst of laughing so hard, it took us a few minutes to notice that Angie and Lee weren't laughing at all.

"Girl don't even sweat that, they're just mad because they won't be on the cruise." Angie sat down on the floor, next to Lee.

"Cruise?" Shannon frowned.

"Oh," Angie said, holding her hand over her mouth, with her eyes popped open, like the kid from *Home Alone*, "You two didn't know? Do you want to go?"

"When and where are you going?" I asked, thinking that maybe I could rearrange my schedule.

"The cruise is a Hott 1075 cruise with Bermuda's very own Miss Thang." Angie said, as she and Lee gave each other a high-fives. "Its gon' be off the hook!"

"By the way the ship leaves in the morning." Lee smirked.

"In the morning!" Shannon screamed.

"What's the issue?' Lee asked, blinking her eyes real fast. "Didn't you two, oh excuse me, you four, including your men, just go to the Best of Both Worlds concert and didn't invite us? Do either of you recall that?"

"That was different." Shannon said.

"Different? And how is that?"

"R. Kelly showed his steppin' ass, that's what. Plus ya'll know Taj and Quincy are old friends from Newark. Hell, why wouldn't we all go out?"

"Ya'll some lyin' hoes" Angie said, "Them negroes didn't meet until ya'll started fuckin' 'em. But it's all good because the cruise is different too. It's for singles."

"That's right!" Lee coldly interjected, "No Stepford Wives allowed."

No, this bitch did not. No, she didn't! Oh hell no. "I can't believe ya'll two." I said, "I just can't!"

"All you and Shannon do is think about yourselves." Angie said rolling her eyes, "You have been around here treating me and Lee like shit. So you know what, we decided that we didn't have to take that anymore and guess what? We're going on a cruise and ya'll are staying home. Now what!"

"That's right!" Lee chimed in.

"Have you lost your goddamn minds?!" Shannon shouted, "Oh, these skeezers really don't know me!" Shannon said looking around, "Can't nobody help it if ya'll still alone. Or, Ms. Angela Adams, if your husband left your frail ass for the Keyfood welfare-to-work chick. Hell, you need to stop being so choosy. Don't no niggah care if you're a size eight with a bangin' body! You're fucked up, plain and simple!"

"You ain't never lied, Shannon!" I said rolling my eyes and twisting my neck.

"What is that suppose to mean!" Angie looked at us in shock.

"I got this, Vera." Shannon pushed me to the side. "What it *means* is that nothing's ever good enough for you. You got mo' fuckin' complaints than anybody I know! That's why men always leave you."

"Oh, no you didn't go there!" Angie jumped up from the floor and started pointing in Shannon's face.

"Shannon Simone, you're dead wrong!" Lee screamed, standing up next to Angie.

Fuck this, I couldn't let these two think that they could gang up on Shannon, and I was just going to stand there, "Yeah she went there!" I said. "And what? You better take a break and rec-ognize, you know how I do it," I said, sounding like Aunt Cookie. "Both ya'll bitches are sick! Ya'll some naggin' ass, mis-placed attachment havin' hoes. Ya lips always yappin' and com-plain' about a niggah. That's why ya'll sleepin' alone. You com-plain if the man is too tall, too short, if he's he too light, or if his dick is purple. Then you make up shit, if his breath stinks he must have a mouth full of cavities, if he has a baby then he must be broke from paying child support. Get a fuckin' life! You're so stuck on a whole buncha superficial nonsense that you gon' fuck around and have a coochie so dry that potpourri's falling outta the shit!"

"Don't ever speak to us again!" Lee said.

"Whatever!" I said, "Beat it!"

Angie and Lee started grabbing their things. Angie picked up her half empty glass of Moet, filled it up, and went to walk out the door. "Give me my ma'fuckin'glass!" I said walking behind her, I snatched my glass from her hand and some of the Moet spilled on the floor. I looked at them and said, "You ain't got to go home but you gotta get the fuck outta here!"

"Fuck ya'll!" Angie screamed.

"I wouldn't give you the satisfaction!" Shannon replied.

"I'm not talking to you, or you!" Lee said opening the front door and stepping onto the stoop.

"You already said that!" I snapped, "Now get ta steppin'!"

"I've been thrown out of better places." Lee smirked.

"Good, then your fat ass will leave easily. Be'atch!"

"Have fun!" Shannon yelled sarcastically, standing beside me at the front door. "Love ya'll."

Angie turned around, on the steps. "Love you too and by the way, we need a ride to the pier in the morning, can either of you take us?"

If looks could kill, I would've blasted this bitch! "Die slow ma'fuckah!" With that, Shannon and I slammed the door in their face. Then we went back into the living room and sat quietly on the sofa. I looked at Shannon and Shannon looked at me.

"I ain't messin' wit' them no more." she said.

"Me neither!" I had tears forming in my eyes. "Fuck them hoes!"

Blind Pass

"How many pregnancies have you had? Any live, still born, miscarried, or aborted?" I felt like I was being harassed. This is some ole bullshit. Is this mofo tryna be funny? He's suppose to be an OBGYN, one of the best in Manhattan, and this is the shit that he asks me...and in front of Taj? See, I should'a got me a sista and not this tight ass brotha, who looks like my Aunt Cookie wouldn't even fuck him. Damn, I'm startin' to feel dizzy. I got outta my chair and fixed me a glass of water. I sat back down, looked at the doctor, and said, "Is that important?"

Taj, who was holding my hand, suddenly replaced his I'm gon' be a daddy smile with a look that said, *No, this bitch did not.* "Answer the question, Vera." Taj said before the doctor could comment.

I was sitting there feeling like shit, thinking of all the abortions that I had and all of the times I swore to myself, "this will be the last one." Only to be laying on the table six months later, making the same fake ass promise to myself.

"Vera..." I said, five years ago, sitting by myself in the waiting room of the abortion clinic, *"this shit has gotta stop. What is this like, number four? You on some ole bullshit. You know what Vera? Let's just have the baby and go from here...I know the councilman is married. I know he has other children and will never own this child, but you're not a kid anymore, you're 26. You've used him enough, ain't nothing else to gold dig."*

As I went to grab my things to leave I thought, *"What are you doing? You don't want any children...at least right now...you know how hard it was for you not to have your father, so why would you do that to your child? Grow up! Get the fuckin' abortion and keep it movin'. Just do it."* After I had the abortion and the anesthesia wore off, I left the clinic. The councilman and his driver met me outside in a white Mercedes Limo. I got in the backseat and sat next to him. "We're done. I'm not fucking with you anymore. Go home to your wife and kids and leave me, the fuck alone." The last time I saw him he was running for the mayor of a major city.

But now, I'm 31, with my own shit, a new man, and he wants this baby, and I want this baby. But I never expected to be pulled on the carpet and made to think about how many babies had actually taken up residence in my uterus.

I knew Taj would have a slight attitude if he thought I was lying, but I lied anyway. "I've been pregnant twice. I had a miscarriage and I'm pregnant now."

The next question the doctor asked was, "Have you ever been tested for HIV or HPV?" I almost passed the fuck out! Why would he go there and ask me that? This is supposed to be a happy occasion, not a recap of Think *real quick about every-niggah-you-ever-fucked*. I can't believe this. Now, I'm sitting here trying not to squirm in my chair. Don't ask me why but, my pussy feels like it's burnin'. I can't even lie, I was droppin' it like was hot, if the right niggah had some dough. Although most of the brothas were strapped, there were those who got away and shot up in me like a L.A. drive by. *Oh my God...what the fuck was I thinking?*

As I started to revive myself from dick flashbacks, I looked at the doctor and said, "Yes, I've had one of those. When I was getting private health insurance for myself and my staff." The doctor seemed pleased, but Taj wasn't buying it.

"It'll still be a part of your testing," the doctor said, "But I always like to ask."

I could've died.

The doctor looked down at my file. "Family medical history?" he asked. Of course, all of Taj's shit was straight laced. No retardation, no STD's, some high blood pressure, and an uncle with diabetes. No drugs, no still borns, just a perfect fuckin' set of fraternal twins, a girl and a boy.

Now here came my shit, Taj took a deep breath and bit the corner of his lip. The doctor was trying to hide his thoughts, but I felt like they were waiting for the weapons of mass destruction to be uncovered. "I don't know my family's medical history that well." This was the first honest thing I've said since I've been sitting here. "My mother was a drug addict. I was born drug addicted and no my mother didn't have any prenatal care." I decided to leave out the part about her placing me in a Hefty Cinch sac. "My father's family has a history of diabetes."

I got that piece of information from Aunt Cookie. She doesn't know much about her family either, but she has always said, "All black folks got sugah." So, the diabetes part I threw in there.

The doctor wrote down what I said, then he looked at me, as if I had just said that the sky was blue, and all was well with the world. I felt like crawling under a rock. I was so ready to leave that I didn't know what to do.

The doctor looked at us. "I'll be right back, I need to get the room ready for your ultrasound."

"Why did you lie?" Taj asked me, as soon as the doctor closed the door.

"I didn't lie." I insisted, getting out of the chair, looking out of the office window, staring at how small the cars looked, 28 stories down.

Before Taj could come back with a smart-ass comment the doctor returned, "The room is ready."

I laid on the exam table and the doctor poured blue ultrasound gel on my belly. I shivered a little because it was cold. I was so pissed with Taj that I didn't even look his way. The doctor positioned the ultrasound screen so that we could both see. Then he started pushing the ultrasound wand softly into my abdomen. I could hear the baby's heart beat before anything appeared on the screen.

"It sounds like a stallion running through water." Taj whispered to me.

The ultra sound screen was in hues of red, black, and electric white. As the doctor pushed the wand, deeper into my abdomen a small bubble began to appear and inside the bubble was my tiny baby, moving from side to side.

"There's your baby!" The doctor said, excited. The first sign of emotion he's shown since I've been here. "And all of that moving he's doing" the doctor continued, "is why you're so nauseous."

I couldn't believe it. My baby. Floating around inside of me, living, breathing, and depending on me. Taj squeezed my hand tight and said, "From this point on, this is all that matters."

The doctor printed out ultrasound pictures of the baby and handed them to the proud daddy. He wiped the gel off my stomach and I fixed my clothes.

"The gestational period for the fetus is nine weeks plus three." He said more to Taj than to me. He knew Taj was a doctor, but hell, Taj wasn't carrying the baby, I was.

"Excuse me," I said to the doctor, so he would realize he was speaking to Taj only.

"Oh," he said seemingly taken aback, then the ma'fucker started speaking in layman's terms like I wouldn't know what a fetus and a gestational period was. "Vera, the baby's due date is April 2nd. That's means your two months and one week pregnant." I swear I wanted to slap him. He was talking to me like I was stupid and Taj was a rocket fuckin' scientist.

As we were leaving and Taj was fixing the rear view mirror, he said, "The next time don't lie to the doctor. Ask me to leave, if you don't want me to hear."

"Taj—"

"Vera, understand this," he turned to look at me, "and I'll only say this once. When I fell in-love with you, I fell in-love with you. So, stop it with the word games. If you don't want me to know something then ask me to leave. But quite frankly, I can handle it. I already told you, I got you, Ma."

***

"Whatcha workin' wit' Baby Girl!" Aunt Cookie said taking a hard pull on her cigarette and then mashing it into the ashtray as I came into the kitchen to sit down. "You want something to eat?"

"Yeah, Aunt Cookie, I'm starving," I said, taking a seat at the table. "We just left the doctor's office. I have some ultra sound pictures."

She fixed me a plate of fried chicken, corn, collard greens, and fried corn bread. "What the doctor sayin' about Nana's Lil' Flip?"

"Lil' Flip? What the hell? Aunt Cookie you will not be calling my baby a damn Lil' Flip."

"Well ain't this some shit, what the fuck wrong with Lil' Flip? But bigger than that, I've been telling you this since you were a little girl to watch the cussin and you continue to do it."

"You're right. I'm sorry." I said with a mouth fulla chicken.

"Humph, you better take a break and recognize, you know how I do it...Now let me see these ultrasound pictures."

I reached in my purse and handed them to her. "Vera," she said reaching for her reading glasses, "I ain't never seen nothing like this. Which part is the baby's head?" she was frowning her face and turning the picture upside down.

"Aunt Cookie...I'm scared."

She placed the ultrasound picture on the table. "Scared of what?"

"Of how fucked up my life has been. *Rowanda and Larry*?"

"And what the hell are me and your Uncle Boy, chopped liver? You need to stop being scared and start being a mother. That baby won't care what your mother and father were like; the baby will care what *you're* like. So you be the mother that you always wanted for yourself."

"That's true..." I said more to myself than to her. "Aunt Cookie, you think that Larry ever thinks about me and my mother?"

"Chile, please." Aunt Cookie said, looking away.

"Why are you looking away?" I said trying to look around her face.

"Because you done talked up the damn devil, honey. That niggah was by here the day before yesterday."

"Day before yesterday and you're just telling me?" I couldn't believe this shit.

"Vera, please. Since when have you wanted Larry around? What'd he ever do for you? Don't come up here with no lil' girl fantasy 'bout a daddy that doesn't exist. You know I ain't never played that shit and I ain't playing it now. Your daddy is the same one that you saw when you where ten. The same niggah I almost cut for fuckin' with you. He was so drunk up and high that Boy had to put him outta here. He still runnin' around with that same girl as before, the one with the painted on eye brows, and both of them look they kissed hell's ass."

"What did he want?" I asked her.

"He wanted to work my goddamn nerves is what he wanted. He came talking 'bout 'What it be like Sis?' I just looked at him and that strumpet he was with looks as if he beats her up everyday.

"Did Larry ask about me?"

Aunt Cookie cut her eyes at me. "He asked about you and your mother."

"Really?"

"Yes, Vera he did. Don't worry though because I told his ass off. And chile, you'll never believe it, but after he, left I cried. I swear that thing hurt me to my heart, to see my brother like that. I can remember a time when I was a lil' girl and he use to protect me from things in my life. I can remember that like it was yesterday."

"So, he was a good person?"

"Honey," Aunt Cookie said, taking my fork and eating some of my greens, "Your daddy had a heart like gold."

"What changed?"

"He went to the war and got put out the army."

"The war?" I said squinting my face up. "What war?"

"The Vietnam War. Larry went over there and lost his mind. Vera I'm telling you, he came back and was different. At first, we didn't notice it, but then he started staying in his room all the time. And when he came out, he would be standing in the middle of the floor and having flashbacks. He couldn't' stand to hear a baby cry and shit like that. My mother swore that he had a spell on him."

"What about your father?"

"I didn't know my father. All my mama told me was that his name was Cook Turner."

"You never wanted to find him? Do you wonder if he's still alive?"

"No. I'm good." She smirked.

"Why not?" I asked surprised.

"I just didn't, now do you wanna hear about your daddy or mine?"

"Mine." I said defensively.

"Well, then. Larry was discharged early from the war for trying to kill himself. In the midst of trying to commit suicide, he shot one of the other soldiers. The army sent him back to the states and he was supposed to be stationed in Fort Lee, New Jersey. The next thing we know, he's in Brooklyn with us and the Army reported him A.W.O.L., not to mention the charges he was facing for shooting the other solider.

My mother was so scared that she gave Larry the money to leave and go to Georgia with her people. Larry didn't listen and he took to the street.

Some of the people I played cards with would tell me how my brother was living in Lincoln Street projects with a woman and her two daughters. Turns out the woman was your grandmother, Wanda, and her twin daughters, Rowanda and Towanda. Larry was the biggest got damn pimp and drug dealer that anybody could stand to see. This niggah had block after block locked and money for days. They were happy and higher than a ma'fucker on Lincoln Street, until your mother got pregnant with you. It was Larry's baby, and all the while Larry was supposed to have been your grandmother's man. That's when all hell broke lose. Your grandmother called the police on Larry for sleeping with your mother, who was fifteen, after that he was arrested and sent back to the Army to face the charges.

Not too long after, I got a letter from Larry saying that, he pled guilty to assault with a deadly weapon and sex with a minor, in exchange for a lesser sentence. He ended up serving eight years.

The next thing I know, eight years have gone by and Rowanda's on my front stoop, looking like the same used up little girl that I knew from years ago, crying and screaming about her baby being taken by social services. And the rest, Baby Girl, is pretty much history."

"What about Larry's girlfriend?" I asked Aunt Cookie. I felt like I needed to know everything.

"Strangely enough she reminded me of Rowanda. She looked to have been a pretty woman in her time; but she had sad eyes. Hurt me to my heart to see a woman so lost. I ain't seen a woman look like that since my mother was getting her ass beat by my step-father."

I couldn't help but say something to her when they showed up here the other day, so I told her, 'Honey chile, please leave my brother alone, what good is he doing you?' Trust me, Vera, I've been in the streets long enough to know what the walking dead looks like."

"What did she say?"

She just looked at me and never opened her mouth. Larry was falling all over the place. Screaming 'bout Rowanda was his baby and where his child at. How he needs to see Rowanda. Here this woman sat looking at me with eyes that seemed to wanna break with tears at any moment, while, Larry, was screaming 'bout another woman right in her face. 'What you need to see Rowanda for?' I told him, 'Leave her alone!'"

"And what was his reason?" I asked.

"He didn't have no reason. Just claim he needs to see her before he dies. I looked at him and thought about all the pain that he caused Rowanda and I told him, *'Be sure you rent a*

speedboat when you bust through hell! Cause you will have to die before I tell you where she's at.' Vera, trust your Aunt Cookie, I know that he's your daddy, but Larry is poison for Rowanda and she don't need to see him, and you don't either. That's why I didn't call you over here. Trust me Vera. Larry was a sad sight."

"What about his girlfriend?"

"Vera, she looked crazy as hell in the eyes. The love she got for Larry is the kinda love that's gon' kill him. Trust and believe that. Aunt Cookie ran the streets long enough to know."

"What now?" I said, biting my bottom lip.

"What now? Baby Girl, we gon' live out life 'till the good Lawd tells us otherwise."

"But Aunt Cookie—"

"But Aunt Cookie nothing," she said cutting me off, "I can't talk about that no longer." She cleared her throat and I could tell she was holding back tears. "Respect that please."

I just took a deep breath.

Aunt Cookie mustered up a smile; "Boy!" she yelled looking toward the kitchen doorway, where Uncle Boy could be seen making a mixed tape, "Come on in here and look at these ultrasound pictures of our grandbaby."

Rebound

As bad, as I have to pee the phone would ring! I grabbed it and ran into the bathroom. It was Shannon. "Vera how long we gon' be mad with the girls? They've been back from the cruise almost two weeks and I wanna make up. Plus, Angie left me a message that she brought me back some Jamaican rum, and I wanna drink it."

"Fuckin' lush! So what she brought you back Jamaican rum? She still showed her ass. I don't wanna make up!"

"Vera, be reasonable."

"Reasonable? Fuck dem hoes! Do you Boo." I frowned, "I don't have time for the drama."

She sucked her teeth, "Bye Vera."

"Bye." I hung up. Then I thought, *Fuck 'em. I miss 'em too, but a bitch ain't gon' beg just to be their friend. Fuck that.*

Still sitting on the toilet I convinced myself not to go back to bed and instead get ready to go to the shop. I flushed the toilet and just as I started the shower, the phone rang again. I peeped the caller I.D. and it was the Bronx Rehabilitation Center, where Rowanda was. I started to let the answering machine pick it up, but then I changed my mind.

"Hello?"

"Hey Vee!" Rowanda said.

"Hey Rowanda."

"It's been a while," she said. "I've missed you."

I was determined not to cry. At some point, I had to accept the fact that my mother was a drug addict. Still I couldn't say anything so I listened, "This kickin' dope shit ain't no joke, Vee."

"Really?" I mumbled as escaping tears slid into my mouth.

"Heck yeah! After detox it took me the rest of the month to collect my thoughts and start to get myself together."

I knew if I spoke, she would hear the cracking of my voice and more tears would follow.

"Vee," she said, "Would you come and visit me?"

"Yes." I said, anxiously.

"Thank you Baby. I'ma tell you," she sighed, "not until the high leaves you, do you realize just how fucked up your life has been."

I didn't respond to that.

"I love you." She said, "See ya soon."

I hung up the phone, swallowed the hard lump in my throat, and wondered how I would face Rowanda without her being high and me being in pain.

I called DeAndre and he agreed to cover my clients for today. After jumping in the shower, I put on my Talbot cargo skirt and matching V-neck sweater. Slipped on my signature Louis V. loafers, and headed for the front door. For it to be early October, it felt like a spring day. Once I got in my X5 I started to think about how dope had been my mother's lover. A selfish lover, that required her to spend her time and money wallowing in the shit that dope deemed important, like getting high and staying there.

Driving to the rehab center. I kept wondering what my mother would think of me, especially since she was sober. Would she see that I love her and want my childhood soul to rest? Will it be safe to share with her that my deepest desire is to be a woman with a mother and not a little girl in desperate need of one.

Once I pulled in the parking lot, I sat in my truck for a minute, feeling as of I had to gather the scared pieces of my heart and say, "It's show time!" Walking into the rehab center felt like the longest walk that I have ever taken. Once inside, I noticed how the walls were concrete and brick, all painted in primary colors: red, yellow, and blue. There were pictures and crafts all over the place, some in glass cases. Posters about AIDS, STD's, and the effects of drugs and alcohol during pregnancy. The entire hallway looked like an anti-drug commercial. This place seemed to be in a world all of its own and instead of me feeling embraced, I felt like an outcast.

I signed my name in the visitor's book and sat in the lobby waiting for Rowanda to come from her dorm area. When she came, I stared at her and she stared at me, both of us seeming amazed that we were here, looking at each other, maybe even wondering some of the same things. As she came closer, I was reminded of how much we look-alike. Almond shaped eyes, naturally arched eyebrows, full face, and soft mocha skin. The only difference is, I didn't have a scar on my right cheek, shaped like a half moon. The last time I thought about my mother and me resembling one another was when I found her overdosed, stretched out on the kitchen floor of an abandoned building.

As she walked over, I could tell she had gained some weight. She had on a pair of blue jeans, a white tee, and a pair of white G-Units, which my cousin, Dirty, called me the other day bragging about. Instead of looking like a frail size four, now she looked like a healthy size eight. Her hair was in the same style ponytail as mine. Pulled to the side with the front swooped around.

Rowanda grabbed my hand, pulled me close, and we melted into each other's embrace.

"Hey Bryce, this my baby, Vera!" Rowanda yelled, holding me in her arms with my head against her bosom. "I told you she was all grown up and beautiful. Look at her!"

I raised my head to see who Rowanda was speaking to…and I had to do a double take. Bryce Miller? I couldn't believe it. It really was him. Ain't this some shit, who knew? Bryce was the first guy that I actually liked, almost loved. When I first started dating him I use to trick this niggah outta all of his part time hustlin' money. But not long after we started dating did I really start to like him. We had fucked up shit in common, like mothers who were junkies. Bryce and I spent time together, chilled together, and one lonely night, after his mother, Queen, embarrassed him, we made love for the first time. That's when I started getting scared of falling in love. I was only seventeen and on my way to college. He was eighteen and on his way to the Marines. He wanted to marry me, but I didn't want that kinda love in my life. I was gold diggin' and trickin' niggahs out of dough. I had no time for a full time love…so, I broke up with him. Shortly after that, he went into the service. I haven't seen him since. But I never thought that years later I would find him in a drug rehab. I know a bitch did him dirty, but goddamn.

"How are you Ms. Vera Wright-Turner?" he asked, grabbing my hand.

"Engaged and pregnant." Damn, I didn't mean to say that. "I'm well and you? Do you work here?" I said, nervously biting my lip.

"I see you still have that nervous habit, biting your lip." He smiled, "And yes I work here."

After all these years, he remembers that I have a nervous habit. Shit, why is my heart beating like this? Oh God, I think I have butterflies. What the hell is wrong with me? I haven't seen this man in 14 years and he got me goin'. Damn, he is fine as hell—6'1', at least 210lbs, cinnamon glazed complexion, with thick eyebrows, long eye lashes, and a body for days. This is unreal. I shook his hand, not with a firm grip, but one that would allow me to place my left hand on top of our handshake, so that my engagement ring would be visible. I noticed him checkin' me from head to foot, then he stared at my stomach a little. Since I'm early in my pregnancy with a small pouch, I knew he couldn't quite figure it out. In an effort to break the monotony of the stare, I said, "I'm about ten weeks."

He smiled and the clef in his chin lit up. "Congratulations. I hope the daddy knows how lucky he is."

"*He does*." Rowanda said, in a voice to let us know she was peeping the situation.

"Your mother tells me you own a full service salon." He was still holding my hand, massaging it with the softness of his thumb.

"Yes, I do." I bit down harder on my lip. Shit! I can't take this.

"Perhaps I'll come by and check you out, I'm looking for someone to braid my hair." His hair was beautifully styled, in zigzag cornrows.

"Who braids it now?" I asked, gently pulling my hand from his embrace.

"My ex-wife."

"Oh, you got married?" *Damn, why did I ask him that?*

"It's a long story." He continued. "Look, I'll let you go. We'll talk. I'll be sure to stop by the salon."

"Okay, see ya soon." Don't ask me why, but my coochie was live! I couldn't believe this shit. Here I am pregnant, with a man at home, that is more than the complete package, and I'm standing here having electric-like current run rampid through my coochie over an ex-boyfriend.

After Bryce walked away, Rowanda and I went into a small conference room, with a small plaid couch and color T.V. We sat down on the couch, facing each other. "Girl, Vee, you lookin' good!" Rowanda said, stroking my hair, "And it seems that Bryce thinks so, too. He is fine though." She said looking toward the doorway, "If Queen wasn't his mama, I would push up on that."

"Rowanda!" I said, surprised, "That's just a bit much. Don't you think you're a lil' too old for that?"

"Vera please. I'm only fifteen years older than you...and while we're on the subject of his mama, you owe her an apology."

"What?" I looked at Rowanda like she had lost her mind.

"You heard me. Queen told me about how nasty you were and how bad you treated her. You're lucky I didn't mention it to Cookie. You know Cookie don't play that shit and from this point on, me either. Granted you're grown, but just so you know, if you ever lose your mind and talk to Queen the way you did at the hospital I'm step to yo' ass."

"You're threatening me?"

"No. I'm providing you with information. Now call her. She hangs out at the Fox Trap on 133rd."

I sucked my teeth. I couldn't believe her. If I wasn't mistaken, she really didn't know me that well to be ordering me around. "Rowanda," I said looking at her like she was crazy, "You haven't *been* telling me what to do for all these years, so don't start now. Queen got on my damn nerves, so she got what she was beggin' for. *And* don't think that because I came up in here to see you that you can start ordering me around and shit. Please."

"Hold up now, let's get this straight, you will not disrespect me. Now, I love you and I know that I need to devote a lot of my time getting to know you, but I'll be damned if I will have you treating me any kind of way. Now, call her like I said 'cause you're pissin' me off !" This time she raised her voice a little.

I rolled my eyes because I knew she had lost her mind. "I'ma just do this for now, but the next time don't count on it. What's the number?"

"Call information."

"That shit cost $1.75!"

"Vera Wright-Turner, call her!"

Hesitantly, I agreed. Information connected me. "Fox Trap!" yelled the person answering the phone.

I sucked my teeth, "Queen there?"

"Dis Queen. Who dis?"

"Vera." I mumbled.

"Who?"

"Vera." I mumbled again.

"You gon' have to speak up and I hope this ain't Young Blood's wife callin' me and shit. I done told you bitch!"

Ill! Young Blood? I thought. *Even dope fiends have relation-ship drama?* "Please Queen this is Vera. Rowanda's daughter."

"If you call me a stanken ass chicken head, I'ma have to put my thang down on ya. I swear to God. I don't mean no harm, but I ain't toleratin' that no more."

I took a deep breath, "Whatever. I called cause Rowanda said to apologize."

Rowanda pinched my thigh, "Say it again."

"I'm sorry about what happened between us. The way I spoke to you and everything. I won't speak to you like that any more."

"You better be sorry withcha grown ass self. You been a

fuckin' grown ass for the longest and somebody need to calm your tongue down. You act just like that damn Cookie Turner."

Now the bitch was pushin' it, 'cause I don't play anybody talking about my Aunt Cookie. "Alright right Queen that's enough. We cool?"

"Long as you remember who's the child and who's the adult, we all good."

Making the point that I'm almost 32 years old wasn't even worth my time. "Bye Queen. Later." I hung up. "You satisfied?" I said to Rowanda.

"Quite satisfied. Now, let me look at you. Girl, Vera, you got some hips on you."

"Yeah hips from you and this ass from Aunt Cookie."

"Chile, Vera, you ain't never lied. That's that Turner trade-mark and Larry surely blessed you with it."

Larry? This was the first time that Rowanda ever mentioned Larry to me in any kind of way, other than telling me that he use to be her pimp. For a moment, I thought maybe she still cared about the man. "Larry, huh?" I asked.

"Well," she said folding her hands, "I got to get over that shit I got with Larry. For all I know that niggah might be laid up some place not thinking about you or me. Cookie don't even know where he is."

I shook my head, as I thought about how right Aunt Cookie was when she said that Rowanda was in no condition to hear about Larry looking for her. He was her real problem. I thought about telling her the truth but then I changed my mind. "Why are you wondering about Larry?" I asked, frowning up my face, "I hope you haven't been looking for him?"

"Chile, please. I saw the devil so much when I was in detox that God knows if I saw Larry I wouldn't know whether I was coming or going."

"Now, my father is the devil?"

"I didn't exactly say that."

"Yes, you did."

"No, I didn't."

"Yes, you did. I heard you, but it's all good." Shit, I feel the tears creeping in the back of my throat again. I can't stand all this damn crying!

Rowanda tilted her head and looked at me. "Let me explain something to you. Vera, I was in love with your father. No, we didn't have a fairytale story or a happy ending, but it was love. One of them sad dope fiend things that I can add to my list of the things that broke my heart, but there's no mistake it was love."

"That's what you call love?" I frowned.

"It made you didn't it? I would tell anybody that my chile was made out of the love I had in my heart for that man. Pillow talk is something else and although I was fifteen you don't know what my man confided in me. The only time I felt like something was when I laid next to Larry. It's only now that I'm realizing something was wrong with that."

"You're talking an awful lot of love shit for a woman who placed her baby in the trash. You really think that Larry loved you, he was your pimp. He made you turn tricks. He turned you out and he was the only man that loved you? Well, shit, hate me then." I said waving my hands in the air.

"Vera, even my placing you in the trash was outta love. I didn't want you going through what I was going through. I loved Larry, but I knew the love I had for him would be one of the very few things that grew from my personal hell. I didn't want that for you. Vera, Who do you think I was? A normal teenager reared in a two parent home with no problems. Hell no! I was a fiend with a shit load of problems. I took love from anywhere that I could and ran with it. I know what Larry was to me, better than you know. But, I have to deal with my life the best way that I know how, and sometimes the realities of life hurt a lot worse when you're sober then when you're high."

"So, you're still in love with him? That's ridiculous."

"Vera, allow me to get over my issues, my way."

"I'm sorry, but I just don't understand that. That's silly if you ask me." I was getting angrier by the second. Here this niggah treated her like shit and she wants to try to analyze her love for him.

"Well, I didn't ask you!" She snapped. "Vera I don't want us to argue, I called you here so that I could talk to you and prayerfully move on with our life."

"All right." I said swallowing the hard lump in my throat. "I'll listen."

"Vera, I'm sorry."

Don't ask me why, but at that very moment I could have hauled off and slapped the shit out of her. "What?"

"I'm sorry...sorry about everything...everything that I have done to you while I was getting high."

I swear to God, if I could have floored this bitch, she would be stretched out! I looked at her with raised eyebrows, "You're sorry? Really? Well guess what? Me too!" She went to continue her apology, as if what I just said didn't register. I raised my hand up, signaling her to stop. "*I'm sorry?* Do you really think that that's strong enough for the shit I've experienced because of you? At the feet of *your high! I'm sorry?* Fuck that! How about I'ma be your mother, Vera? I'ma love you Vera? What's your favorite color Vera, what do you dream about, what are you scared of, what happened the day that social services took you away from me?"

"Vera—"

"No, Rowanda." By now the tears that I was so destined to hold back were starting to take control over my words and my voice began to tremble. "I'm not finished." I was standing up and trying to sound stronger than I really was. "Since you're *so* sorry and you love me *so* much, how about asking me, how I feel about Larry Turner not being shit? How about when he told me how I looked like a whore and that there was nothing he could do for me. Or, wait, wait, wait…I got it…how about asking what did I think when I went to live with Aunt Cookie, who was a stranger to me. How about asking me, why did I spit in your face when I was nine? Well, I spit in your face because I hated you…I hated you because I felt like nothing. Rowanda, didn't you *wanna* see me? Did you even look for me?"

"I use to go to the playground and watch you!" Rowanda shouted. "Every Saturday, Boy would take you, Lee, and Shannon to play double dutch. You always wanted to jump, but you never wanted to turn. That was love Vera. I always loved you, that's why I stayed away and never let you see me sitting there watching you."

"No!" I said pointing in her face, "You stayed away because you were high! I was garbage remember?"

"Why do you keep talking about that?"

"Because nobody ever let me forget that shit. Nobody. Grandma use to tell me every chance she got how you threw me in the trash. Then here comes Queen, the goddamn super hero, *'I saved you from the trash. I found you, so I'm yo' godmother.'* Do ya'll even think about the shit that you say, let alone the shit you do? Then you look at me and tell me that you're sorry? You're killing me, that's what the fuck you're doing to me. I'ma die fuckin' around with you and this shit. Instead of killing me, get to know me."

"I wanna get to know you."

"Please." I sucked my teeth. "That's straight up shit you talkin'. Since you wanna get to know me, why don't you ask me if Aunt Cookie beat my ass for stealing food when I went to live with her? Or instead did she make me put it back and then wake me up every morning, to show me that the food wouldn't disappear? You know why she did that? 'Cause I didn't eat when I was with you, I starved. When I saw food in her house I thought that it would disappear, but she taught me differently."

"Vera, please stop." Rowanda said, holding her head was down.

I pretended like I didn't even hear that. "I got some more questions that every mother should ask. When did you get your period Vera? What was your first boyfriend's name? How about asking, are you scared now? How do you feel about becoming someone's mother? What about those things? Huh? I'm sorry? Fuck I'm sorry! As you can see, sorry ain't never done shit for me but cause me a buncha fuckin' problems!" I stood up, looked down at her, and said, "I don't want your sorry, I want you to be my mother!"

"That's all you want?" Rowanda stood up with tears pouring down her face.

"Yes." I said holding my head down, trying to stop my tears from escaping down my cheeks and sliding toward my neck. "What else can I use in the midst of all of this, except a mother?" I lifted my head to look at her. "I can't start from day one, that time is gone. Don't apologize to me about something that you can't change, just show me differently, please. Sorry reminds me of too many things. I wanna start from right here and now. I can't handle any more than that."

Rowanda wiped my tears and reached for my left hand. "I'll try not to revisit the past or catch up on bad memories. But it works both ways. Don't haunt me with shit that I've done and I won't apologize for it anymore."

"Rowanda—"

"No," she said calmly, "I'm talking and what I have to say is simple. I just wanna say that I love you and I want to start over from here. What you can do," she smiled "is tell me, what's your favorite color. Then tell your mother what's up with this ring?"

Illegal Contact

Shannon and I were parking in front of DayO's Caribbean and Soul Food restaurant, when I saw Angie parking her midnight blue Range up the street, across from the hospital. Then I noticed Lee's olive green Infiniti FX 45 was parked right behind Angie. At that moment, I could've slapped the shit outta Shannon Simone.

"Shut up." Shannon said, as she clicked the locks on her car door, "And don't open your mouth."

To say that I was pissed would be an understatement. Shannon had fucked up my whole plan. My original plan was to ignore Angie and Lee for at least a month, do fucked up shit to 'em, like spam their asses, send them chain letters and shit, call their houses and flush the toilet in their ear. Crazy shit, that I knew would piss 'em off.

As we walked in the restaurant and sat down, Angie was following close behind. "Don't say shit to me." I mumbled to Shannon.

"You talkin' about me?" Angie said, sitting down, across the table from us, next to Lee.

Lee was staring at us, with her marble Jackie-O, sunglasses resting on the tip of her nose, and her floral Tiffany scarf thrown loosely around her neck. If I knew I could get away with it, I would take that scarf and choke the shit out of her. Instead I rolled my eyes at Angie, "Don't nobody have time to be talking about you, so please."

"I'm tired of ya'll treatin' us like shit." Angie complained.

"Doesn't bother me," Lee said looking over the menu, "Fuck 'em. They just jealous."

"I'm sick of yo' fat ass." I said to Lee, massaging the side of my stomach. "Every time you get a good piece of dick, somebody owes you something, or somebody's jealous of you and shit."

"Oh don't hate." Lee said with a smirk. "And how did she know about my good piece of dick, *Shannon?*"

"Lee, paleeze," Shannon said. "You knew I was gon' tell it. That's why you told me."

I wanted to reach across the table and stab Lee's ass with my fork. "Up yours. That's why Shannon said all you've been doing is giving the niggah all your money cause the dick got you wide open. I bet yo' ass suckin' dick now, doin' jawbreakers and the whole nine. But check this, cuz I gotta announcement for you. When all of your money is gone the dick comes outta your mouth, and goes with him."

"You're the one living in sin." Lee rolled her eyes and twisted her neck, "Shackin' up and shit. Having a baby out of wedlock, mind you. You gon' fuck around and the raft of Satan gon' come down on you!"

I looked at Lee and barked like a big ass mad dog. Angie and Shannon looked at me like I had lost my mind. Before I could go on, the waitress came over and took our orders. After she left I shot Lee a nasty look. I took my hand pointed it like a gun and pulled the trigger. Then I said, "Don't nobody care about you and your man. You better make sure that ma'fucker got a green piece of paper in his wallet that says permanent resident, cause if you fuck with me, I'ma call immigration on his ass!"

"Oh, no you didn't!" Lee screamed, bangin' her fist against the table. "My man is legal. Not every foreigner that comes here is looking to use an American."

I curled my lips, made another imaginary gun with my hand, pointed it toward Lee and pulled the trigger three times. Then I held the trigger to my mouth and blew the smoke from it.

"Stop it." Shannon said slapping my hand down.

"Look," Angie said, attempting to make peace, "How long are you going to have an attitude?"

"Why? You wanna make up now?" I snapped.

"Look, I got some shit to tell ya'll." Angie said, "And yes I wanna make up."

Shannon bumped me on the arm and mumbled, "here it comes." That's when Lee got a dumb look on her face.

"You been running your mouth?" Angie asked Lee.

"No, I haven't. I didn't say anything about you and Daddy-O.com I mean Lil' Love. Absolutely nothing."

"Lil' Love?" I frowned.

"You're lying!" Angie screamed at Lee, "You stank ass tramp. You know we agreed that what happens on the ship stays on the ship."

"I know." Lee said, "That's why I didn't tell her nothing about what happened on the ship. I only told *Shannon* the part about you having to make him a doctor appointment."

"Doctor's appointment?" I said giving Angie the screw face, "What kinda nasty lil' ma'fucker you messin' wit', that need you to make him a doctor's appointment?"

"Nasty?" Angie smirked, "See that's why I didn't want to tell ya'll anything because you and Shannon always have something smart to say."

"All right. We're sorry." Shannon said to Angie, kicking my leg with her foot. I couldn't look at her because I would've fell the fuck out laughing and been stretched out on the floor.

"Look," Angie sighed. "I ran into Eugene on the cruise."

"Eugene?" I said, knowing damn well that Eugene was nobody but the midget better known as Daddy-O.com.

"The midget." Lee said nonchalantly. Angie couldn't comment right away because the waitress was sitting our food on the table.

"Shut up! Leola!" Angie screamed, as soon as the waitress left.

"Yeah, Lee," Shannon said taking up a fork full of potato salad. "Shut up and let Angie talk."

I picked up my fork to eat, rubbed my stomach, and reared back in my chair so that I could really listen to this shit.

"Ya'll know that things are tough with me and men." Angie sighed sipping on her tea mixed with lemonade. "And sometimes I feel like I just can't deal. I can't even lie, that ma'fuckin butterfly dildo gets cold after a while."

"Did you try the warm water and the shower head?" I asked, cutting Angie off.

"Fuck the warm water." Shannon interjected, breaking off a piece of her cornbread. "I told you don't sleep on the silver bullet. Nile blind folded me and slapped that shit on me, I felt like my pussy was goin' through convulsions. The whole ma'fuckin block knew I was cumin'."

"Goddam, the whole block knew you were cumin'? Now that's wassup!" I smiled.

"Yeah." Shannon said, "It'll have you cumin' like a kid bustin' bubbles on plastic wrap."

"Damn I'ma have to try that!"

"I'm tellin' you," Shannon said, stuffing chicken in her mouth, "it's the best thing next to a big dick with a crook in it."

"Yeah," Angie signed, "but in the end, ain't no strong back to hold onto. Its still just you all by yourself. Let me tell ya'll about the shit that happened on the cruise. It was the first night. Lee and I got dressed and went to dinner. Well, guess who was assigned to our dinner table, you won't believe this shit. Goddamn, Daddy-O.Com! I was so embarrassed." She said wiping her brow. "I thought I would never see this niggah again, and there he was dressed in the same tight ass We-Be-Kids Easter suit, smiling at me with the patch over his eye. At first, I tried to ignore this ma'fucker, but then I couldn't do it. He kept looking up at me snortin' and shit like a lil' pig, twistin' his lips, talkin' 'bout, 'How long you been looking for Lil' Love?' I almost threw up, I swear I did.

'Lil' Who?' I frowned at him. "The last I checked your name was Eugene and at most, Daddy-O.com."

'Lil' Love is my attribute.' He grinned.

I simply just got up from the table and left his ass sitting there. For three days, I swear he was following me around. Making shouts on the ship's radio with the D.J. Ms. Thang. Dedicating songs to me and shit."

"Don't forget the poem." Lee snickered.

"Poem?" Shannon frowned, with a mouth fulla food.

"Yes, hoe a poem." Angie said shaking her head.

"How did it go?" Shannon asked.

"It went like this, *A lil' bitta love is all it takes...A lil' bitta love goes a long-long way...Come on Angela Adams and get up on a Lil' Love...Ahhhhhh...Oh God,*" she said shivering, "Just plain nasty!"

"No that niggah did not break out a New Edition throw back!" I said falling out laughing.

"Yes he did." Angie said "and the whole goddamn ship heard it."

"Where was Lee?" Shannon asked.

"Don't worry about me?" Lee interjected, in between bites of potato salad.

"Lee was acting like she had never had any dick in her life." Angie said, "Don't let this silly trick fool you, she had ole boy up on the cruise, fuckin' him and shit. Left me in the cabin all alone."

"You weren't hardly alone, Ms. Thing."

As bad as I wanted to say something smart, I couldn't. A part of me felt proud, Lee winked her eye and gave me a thumbs up. I looked at her and mouthed *"You better work that shit girl!"*

"Anyway," Angie continued, with a slight chuckle, "Eugene started wearing me down, because he was bugging the shit outta me. So, one day we were on the top deck, poolside. I was stretched in the lounge chair, sipping on a Grey Goose Martini, reading a new book by Tu-Shonda Whitaker, and this lil' niggah walks up to me, with nothing but boxer shorts on. Looking like the midget from Universal Soul Circus!"

"He had on boxers at the pool side?" I asked with my face frowned up.

"Boxers, bitch!" Angie screamed, "But wait, this is what killed it, the lil' niggah had on boxers and the spilt was open!"

"The spilt open!" I screamed. I couldn't even eat my food with this visual running around in my head.

"And," Angie continued, "you know I was eye level with his waist so you know the dick was just pointing at me. Head all swollen and shit."

"That's a scandal!" Shannon said, "A midget with a dick. What is the world coming to?"

At first, I wasn't going to say anything but then I couldn't hold it in anymore, "How the fuck does a midget's dick look?"

"Vera!" Angie screamed. "This lil' niggah was packin'! No lie. You know your girl ain't gon lie to you about no dick and especially not about no big dick. After I saw that shit, for a moment, I envisioned his ass being six feet tall with a dick ready, willing, and able to bust my back wide open. Divas, I can't even lie, after seeing that dick my coochie was clapping!"

We all fell out laughing as Angie continued her story. "His ass must've known that I was staring at his dick, because he reared back on one leg, while I sat in the lounge chair, pulled down my round eyed Gucci shades, and looked at him. Then I growled at his ass and told him to shoo. I swear to God he looked just like one of the three lil' pigs! That's when I told him, '*Get away, before I huff and puff*!' With his nasty ass! It should've been a sin; his ass is too greasy to have a dick that big. Finally, I broke down when I saw that he wasn't moving, and asked him, 'What do you want from me?'

'Check it.' He said. 'Lil' Love got something to say.'

As he said that, I realized this ma'fucker didn't have the patch over his right eye. I almost fell the fuck out! Here he was standing three and a half feet tall, with his slit to his boxers popped open, and his eye rolling around. All I could see was my reflection going round and round in a circle. When he saw me staring, he squinted his eye closed but you could still see the imprint of the ma'fucker roaming around underneath the closed eyelid.

Anyway, this negro takes a step closer and says, 'Lil' Love sorry about the way he treated you when we went to Soul Café last year. I shouldn't have done you like that. That's all I wanted to say."

"I can't believe he apologized." I said.

"Believe it." Angie chuckled, "As he was walking away I felt a little sorry for him. He was little and shit. Big ass head, but hell judging from the way he acted the last time we were together he needed to apologize. Well, the next day at breakfast, while ole girl here," she said pointing to Lee, "was getting' her grind on, who was sitting at the table in his booster seat, reading *Girlfriend's* magazine? *Eugene.*

'Hi Eugene.' I said as I sat down with my plate of food. "The magazine you're reading is my girlfriend's Shannon publication. She's the publisher and the Editor-and-Chief.'

'Word? This ya girl shit? You think she could hook Lil' Love up with a photo shoot? Let me get up on that cover jammy?"

"Hell no!" Shannon interjected. "Tell his ass that he can keep right on makin' cookies in that fuckin' Keebler Elf tree house."

"Well," Angie said, taking a sip of her drink, "I wasn't exactly that rude. I simply told him 'No, I don't think so Eugene."

'Don't be so formal,' he said, ruffling the magazine, "Just call me Lil Love, or Bigger Love, if ya nasty."

I had to laugh because I couldn't believe that he thought he could was the mack from a booster seat. "I will call you Eugene.'

He laughed and said "Alright, no arguing for today. We only have two more days here and then that's it. Let's just enjoy each other's company."

I agreed, plus I was tired of arguing with him. We talked and soon we started laughing, and enjoying each other's company. After a while, he got serious and broke down telling me some of the things that were bothering him.

'What the hell could be bothering Lil' Love?' I asked him.

'Angela,' he said, taking a deep breath. 'To be honest, it's not what you may think.'

'Tell me.'

'You promise not to laugh at me?'

I just looked at him and smiled, 'I promise.' I slid my hand under the table and crossed two of my fingers.

'Well...the truth is, that my height doesn't bother me. I got people in my family like this...but truthfully it's the eye.' He said, sounding as if he was getting choked up. 'It jacks a lil' niggah's game up! Look at this shit." Then the nasty niggah opened his eye all wide and shit. Scared the hell outta me. I had to tell him to close it. "But look at,' he cried, 'It ain't focused. It won't stay still. Nothing! I mean it just fucks Lil' Love up."

"Girls," Angie said, "Can you believe his ass was crying?"

"What?" we all said. "Crying?"

"Crying ya'll! So, I asked him has he ever considered getting it looked at and he said, 'I'm too embarrassed. Can you help me?'

'Me?' How am I going to help you see about a crooked eye? Who do you even call for some shit like that?'

'Never mind!' he said hopping off his booster seat. 'Fuck it!' Immediately, I felt bad for hurting his feelings. I went to grab his arm as he jumped down, to stop him from leaving. Well, the next thing I know he ends up bumping his chin on the edge of the table and his neck snapped back."

"What did he do then?" Shannon asked, still cracking up.

"Girl, he got that Taco Bell chiwawa look in his eyes like he wanted to attack me! I looked at the ma'fuckah and said, 'I'll mace yo' ass!'

The next time I saw him he had a neck brace on. I felt so bad that when we docked in New York I begged his forgiveness and we exchanged phone numbers. That's when I told him I would help him with the doctor's appointment."

"Did you?" I asked.

"Uhmm hmm," Angie said, sounding embarrassed. "I called and the doctor kept clearing her throat and shit. Then she said, 'Well Ma'am what kinda eye is it? A lazy eye? Is it crossed, halfway closed? Is it a different color than the other?' Hell, I ain't know. I clicked over and called Eugene to ask him, 'What the fuck is wrong with your eye?' That's when it hit me and I said to myself, *what the fuck are you doing Angela Adams? Just hang up.* And I did. I hung up and now I can't get him to stop calling or emailing me. I keep spamming his ass, but he keeps instant messaging me from different names."

Shannon and I fell the fuck out. Shannon, she was laughing so hard that she was banging her fist on the table. The only reason Lee wasn't laughing is because she was on the phone talking to her man.

"Jerell says '*hello*', everyone." Lee smiled.

We all just looked at the dumb bitch and resumed our conversation. "Angie," I said, "Don't sweat that shit. You'll find someone; you just have to be patient. Just be happy with yourself for a while."

"Fuck that!" She spat, breaking off a piece of her cornbread, "I want someone who loves me and wants to be with me."

"I understand that Angela." Lee said clicking her cell phone off, "But you need to become a little more refined and try not to be so gangsta like. Be a lady."

"I'm not a gangsta, you just a square ass broad!"

"See, look at how you're talking. Square ass broad? That's what I mean. It's too rough neck. You didn't grow up in the projects…" she paused and looked at me. "No offense Vera. But Angie, you have to stop acting like bruh man's wife. So I tell you what, would like you to meet Jerrel's friend, Keith. He's a store manager and he's a nice guy. That's what matters."

"Uhmm hmm, his ass better not be the store manager for Quick Check and shit."

"Wait a minute." I said frowning at Angie, "You just gon' let this chick set you up on a date? I wouldn't let this broad hook me up with a niggah if she said Jesus was the chaperon."

"Oh see, you need to mind your business. Everybody doesn't have a hustlin' ass doctor in their back pocket."

"You tryna talk about my man? I'll take my fist," I said balling it up, "and stuff it down your ma'fuckin throat."

"Do it. I dare you."

"Lee," Shannon said, hitting my hand, "No offense but don't you think you need to slow down just a little with Jerrel."

"Oh, I know *you're* not giving out advice." Lee rolled her eyes.

"You know what Ms. Leola Jones," I said, as if a light bulb had just gone off, "By golly I think I got it. You suffer from B.D.S."

"B.D.S.?"

"Yes, Big Dick Syndrome! It makes you retarded. A niggah don't need to do no more to you than finger fuck yo ass."

"Whatever!"

"Yeah, whatever." I snapped.

"Anyway, what's the book for the next book club meeting?" I asked everyone.

"*Me and My Boyfriend* by Keisha Ervin." Lee smiled, "It's the bomb. I've read it three times and after that it's *Chyna Black*."

"I'm choosing the next book Lee." Angie snapped, "So take it down."

"Oh boy, I guess I better get ready for some shoot'em up boogie."

Back Court Violation

"Happy mother fuckin' birthday." I said to myself, standing in the mirror, ass naked and six months pregnant." It's December 31st and you're 32 years old. Ever think 32 years would look like this? Titties swollen, legs swollen, can't breathe, always wanna eat, and some how in the midst of all this you got the nerve to be engaged. Ole girl, you know fa sho' that you got some shit with you."

I hopped in the shower and when I came out, Taj was sitting on the edge of the bed holding a large garmet bag with a box ontop, anxiously waiting for me to open it. "Vera, I can't wait for you to see what I got you!"

"What?" I smiled with the towel still wrapped around me.

"Open it."

I zipped open the garmet bag and oh my God! "Taj, a full length chinchilla with the matching hat! How'd you know?" I said giving him a hug.

"I think the note you left me a month ago that read *'On December 31st I'll be 32 and I hear a full length chinchilla callin' me'*, was all the hint that I needed."

I kissed him and then I slipped on the fur and modeled around in it with my towel still wrapped underneath. "This is the shit baby! Wait until I show Shannon, Lee, and Angie. Oh! They gon' be sweatin' me!"

As I went to take a second look at myself in the mirror, the phone rang. "Happy Birthday, Vera!" Aunt Cookie yelled in the phone. "Whatcha workin' wit, Baby Girl? Thirty two years? Damn girl you gettin' old while I'm getting' better! Come on over before you go to the shop. Aunt Cookie need to talk to you."

"Aunt Cookie, I have a busy day today. Er'body and their mama will be in the shop getting their hair done for New Year's." I said, slipping off my new fur. As I did that Taj walked over, unwrapped the towel, and started caressing my swollen breasts.

"Tell Aunt Cookie you'll call her back." he whispered.

"I'll call you back Aunt Cookie." Taj took the phone outta my hand and hung it up before she could even say goodbye. He started kissing me on my neck as I removed his tie and unbuttoned his shirt. "I've been wantin' to hit this since I came home from the hospital." He moaned in a sexy voice.

"You are so nasty." I smiled, unbuckling his pants.

"You love me?" he said with his pants and boxers falling to the floor.

"I love you too much."

"Happy birthday baby." He turned me around and placed the palms of my hands against the wall. He slid his dick inside of me and started hittin' me off from behind with soft and long strokes. It took ten minutes for my legs to begin shake. As my juices slid down and ran between my legs I started thinking that maybe being 32 might not be so bad after all.

Aunt Cookie must've been timing my dick session, because as soon as Taj stopped shivering she was on my phone. "You comin' over here or what? I said we need to talk."

Taj patted me on the ass, "I'm going to take a shower." he whispered.

"Why can't you just tell me on the phone?" I said to Aunt Cookie, looking at my fur again.

"You gettin' smart?" she snapped.

"Aunt Cookie, please? Plus, Taj and I were just over there for Christmas."

"Oh hold up. I asked you to come and see me and you telling me about Christmas? I been reduced to only being seen on the holidays, like a lil' retarded cousin or something? Do you tell Taj's folks that? Especially since, you spent half of Christmas day in Newark. Smiling all in Betty Greene's big ass pie face. Just a ha-ha-ha all over the place, like South 14th Street is winter-fuckin'-wonderland."

"It wasn't even all that, Aunt Cookie."

"Yes, it was. You were happy as a drag queen in Boy's Town. All I know is that you better remember which side your bread is buttered on. When the shit go down, them is *his* folks."

I rolled my eyes, already I had a headache.

"Never mind. Fuck it." She said. "You ain't got to ride wit' me Shorty, I know its your birthday. It's all good. I almost forgot that your family don't mean nothing no more. Rowanda is a crackhead and I must be a two-dollar-hoe. You think ya Uncle Boy is a stick up kid, don't you? Taught DMX his tricks, jumpin' outta bushes and shit."

"Aunt Cookie please, don't you think that's going a bit far?"

"Naw, don't try and clean it up now. Its all good, na'mean? Humph, all of a sudden you're grown now, no more time for Aunt Cookie. But when you were a lil' girl and your birthday came I was the best thing since slice bread. Now, I ain't shit. You're gettin' dick on the regular and Aunt Cookie can't even get five minutes to say Happy Birthday."

81

"Aunt Cookie," I said trying to cut her off, before she started in on her, *Ungrateful-since-I-been-wearin'-Thongs* lecture.

"I'm talkin' Ms. Vera. Seems to me, that your G-string is glued too tight between yo' ass. Humph, truth be told, ever since you been wearin' thongs and shit, can't nobody say nothing to you. Don't worry it's all good. You got that, but I'ma tell you, if I had a mama—not sayin' that you don't because I ain't ya mama no how—but if I had a mama, I would come running when she called me. I would never put my lil' nappy-headed clients before her. But, I don't have a mama and I'm just yo aunt, so let me be quiet and let you go and take care of your business."

I took a deep breath, "I'll be over there in a few minutes." I hopped in the shower, came out, got dressed in my Gap maternity jeans, matching top, and blue Gucci loafers. I slipped on my full length Chinchilla, kissed my man goodbye, and headed to Aunt Cookie's.

Aunt Cookie really gets on my nerves! Never mind that I'm six months pregnant and feel like I'm about to pop the fuck open! I can hardly breathe, I piss every five minutes, and my legs and ankles are always swollen. *'You ain't got to ride wit' me Shorty'* is the smart ass shit she says, fuck all my pregnancy issues! I mumbled as I started driving. *None of that matters, all that matters is that she needs to see me right now.*

I pulled in front of Aunt Cookie's row house. My thoughts slowed down. Then suddenly they came to a complete halt. There was a cloud of black smoke floating from the porch and into the street. I pulled out my cell phone and hit 9-1-1. *Oh my God the house is on fire!* Just as I was about to press send, I could see Uncle Boy standing in front of a grill he had on the front porch, with a big ass bag of charcoal resting next to his feet.

I parked my truck and got out. "Uncle Boy!" I called from the sidewalk, "What are you doing?"

"Hey Baby Girl! Happy Birthday! I'm roasting some corn, pig feet, and steaks. You want some?"

I wanted to say *Hell no!* But instead I said, "No...No thank you." As I stepped onto the porch, the smell was making me wanna throw up. "Uncle Boy, do you know what you're doing? The house looks likes it's getting ready to explode. I almost called the fire department. You *know* the last time you started grilling, the neighbors complained."

"Be quiet," he said with an attitude. "All of a sudden you wanna act like Cookie Jr.? Go on in the house. Had you come earlier you would've seen your mama. She passed by here on her way to look for a job. We gave her a few dollars to hold her over for the week."

If Rowanda needed money, why didn't she ask me? That sorta hurt my feelings but I shrugged it off. The important thing was how far Rowanda had come in her recovery. She was entering the final stages of her program and soon would be able to come home for good. Finally, she was learning how to be independent; by looking for a job and solving her problems without getting high.

"Hopefully, she'll come by the shop today." I said.

Uncle Boy didn't respond. I think I hurt his feelings by turning down his bar-b-que. I went to apologize but smoke got all in my throat and I started to choke. "Uncle Boy," I coughed, "You need to cut that shit off! Somebody gon' file a complaint against you! I don't think you know what you're doing, Uncle Boy. You need to put that fire out. Not to mention it's almost January. Say it with me, Jan-u-ary."

Uncle Boy frowned up his face; he had a 40 oz. can of Colt 45 in his hand and slammed it down on the small card table next to the grill. "Vera, let me tell you something. When you was small I let Cookie discipline you, cause I felt that I needed to spoil you. Now, I'm thinkin' perhaps you need yo' ass tapped. Seems to me, that's you got it crooked. I'm grown and I don't need you in my business."

Is this Negro trying to tell me off? Wait a minute; did he just say that I had it *crooked?* "Uncle Boy, its no need for you to get an attitude."

"I don't have an attitude. I'm just puttin' my thang down, lil' girl."

Lil' Girl? This niggah talkin' to me?

"Cause you, Vera," he continued to say, "got it crooked. Fall back, Ma."

Oh hell no, I know this old ass niggah ain't tryna talk smack, is he? I cut my eyes at Uncle Boy. "First of all, what do you know about a' *fall back, Ma?'* And second of all, its got it's *twisted.* Not *crooked.*"

"Lil' girl, please." He said waving his hand.

"Lil' girl?" Seeing that he was obviously pissed off, I felt that making a point of how I was wasn't worth the argument. "Bump it."

"You cussin?" Uncle Boy looked at me as if he wanted to knock the taste outta my mouth. "You done turned 32 and you cussin' in my face? Cookie," he yelled, "You better tell this lil' girl somethin'!"

I can't believe that he's telling on me. "Whatever, Uncle Boy."

"Yeah, whatever. You and ya Aunt Cookie need to let me grill. I'ma grown ass man. If the *fuckin'* snow is fallin and *piss* is droppin' from the sky, and I feel like grillin', then dammit let me grill! If you don't wanna eat my shit, then don't eat it! I pay mortgage here, matter-fact the mortgage is paid off, which translates to mean that this is *my shit*! Understand *Lil' Girl*?"

"Uncle Boy, that's enough!" I turned away and walked toward the front door.

"Don't tell me! Humph, first Cookie, now you. Nawl, now

she might get a way with it. But you? Long as I raised you, you gon stay in a child's place. Hell, I been grillin' a lot longer than you been born. *Thank you*." He picked his beer back up and returned to his grilling. Judging by his actions he seems to think that he told my ass off.

He rolled his eyes as I walked passed him and into the house. After I let the screen door shut, I had to do a double take. I know damn well that my eyes must be playing tricks on me! I opened the screen door back up and...Oh my God! What the hell is this? This Negro is standing in front of the grill, turning over steaks with tight ass 1974 green basketball short shorts on; with two thick ass white stripes tracing the bottom of the legs and up the seams. He also had on a red du-rag, with a matching leather bomber, trimmed in red fox fur.

Just when I thought it couldn't get worse...I looked down and Uncle Boy had on black sheer dress socks pulled all the way up to his knees and one of them had the nerve to be slouching down! On his feet, he had burgundy, hard bottoms with the tassel hanging from the tongue.

"Aunt Cookie!" Now it was my turn to tell on his ass! "You need to get Uncle Boy. He standin' out here with a red du-rag on, with the string tied around the front and hanging on the side, lookin' like a old ass Blood!"

Uncle Boy looked at me, curled up his lips and growled. "Gon'! Get! Step ya lil' fast ass outta my sight! You in my space and all that belly you got is makin' it crowded."

Did he just call me fat? I thought. Oh hell no! This old ass wanna be Richard Roundtree ma'fucker! Ooh, if I could cuss his ass out and get away with it, I would! Looking at Uncle Boy, my eyes started hurting. I was convinced his ass was crazy. Suddenly, my stomach started boiling as I imagined what Disco Diva, Cookie Turner, was in sportin' in the house.

Uncle Boy looked back at me. "Be gone, Baby Girl!" Then he turned to his portable radio and raised the volume. Al Green was singing about how to stay together.

All I could do was shake my head, pat my belly and say, "Baby, Mommy sorry."

I walked back in the house and headed to the kitchen. Aunt Cookie was sitting at the table, taking a three-liter bottle of ginger ale to the head and a tray full of crackers were sitting in the middle of the table. Her eyes were droopy and even her big blonde wig seemed flat. I looked at her and knew she had to be sick.

"Aunt Cookie," I said placing the back of my hand to her forehead, "Are you feeling okay?"

"Na'll baby girl. Aunt Cookie ain't doing too well. That's why I'm glad to see you because we need to talk. I'ma give you your birthday gift tomorrow. It wasn't ready today. I had it specially designed."

Oh yes, it must be that Tiffany Heart toggle necklace I told her I wanted. "Can you tell me what it is?" I pleaded.

"Oh Baby Girl, it's bad. Got diamond chips in it and everything."

"Diamond chips?"

"Yeah. It's a three-finger ring with your name on it. I started to get you some bamboo doorknocker earrings, but they didn't sell 'em anymore. I remember how you use to like to step on 'em."

"Aunt Cookie nobody wears that shit anymore! Stepping on earrings went out with Salt and Pepa's "Push It". And a three-finger ring? Anyway, Aunt Cookie, I wanna know how long you haven't been feeling well. That's a little more important to me."

"About six to eight weeks." She said, taking a swig of ginger ale to the head.

"Six to eight weeks? And what have your symptoms been?"

"Baby Girl, I been throwing up everyday. Can't smell nothing, can't eat, can't hardly drink, sweatin' one minute, and cold the next. Not to mention that my breast are sore as hell."

When she said her breast, it sorta threw me off, but then I started thinking about how Taj's mother died from breast cancer. I started heaving, just thinking about my Aunt Cookie having to deal with that and maybe even dying. "Aunt Cookie, we have to take you to the doctor, right now. You have to get your breast checked!"

"I don't need that."

"Aunt Cookie, please don't be in denial. I couldn't live with myself if something happened to you."

"Baby Girl, you alright? Aunt Cookie done been through this twice before I got this."

"Twice? You got this? Got what?"

"All I need is for you to get me there by eight o'clock in the morning. Otherwise they won't take me."

"Take you? Eight o'clock? Who won't take you?"

"The clinic. I'm gon' get an abortion."

This bitch has lost it! "You're what! Oh hell no!" I started pacing the floor. "Oh hell no! What the hell you just say?" I turned to Aunt Cookie to make sure I heard right.

"Calm down Baby Girl, it's all good. I'ma get local, they ain't gon' put me all the way out. I got high blood pressure, that shit'll kill me."

"What?!"

"Yeah. It's alright." She said trying to get me to calm down. "Just take me in the morning and wait for me in the lobby."

"Aunt Cookie! What the hell is wrong with you? You think that I'ma take you to get an abortion? Are you fuckin' for real!"

"Hold up Baby Girl, you better watch ya mouth. You know how I do it. Sick and all I will break yo ass. Don't sleep."

"Don't sleep? Aunt Cookie, I am so embarrassed."

"Embarrassed for what? What, you think my man and me don't get busy? Where you think you get all your moves from? Shhiit..." she said with a sly smile running across her face, "You don't know me, I be droppin' it like its hot. If you don't know you better rent the video!"

"Yeah," I said sarcastically, "Which one? The bootleg R. Kelly tape?"

"Oh, hell no!" Aunt Cookie said, struggling to get out of her chair, "Have you lost your ever lovin' mind? Talking about R. Kelly? As long as he singin' "Happy People" he straight with me." She reached for me, but I jumped my pregnant ass back, I ain't crazy.

Suddenly, it clicked who Aunt Cookie's been creeping with. Oh, shit, Mr. Bennet! I looked at Aunt Cookie and said, "Whose baby is that? Is that Mr. Bennet's baby? Oh my God! That baby probably ain't even Uncle Boy's! Taj 'bout to have a lil' brotha. He gon' die! Oh my God, whose baby is that?" I started freakin' out, my voice getting louder. "You don't even know do you? Holy shit! Aunt Cookie doesn't know who the baby daddy is. Oh my God, *oh...my...God!*"

Aunt Cookie jumped back up from the table, knocking the ginger ale and crackers to the floor, "Take that shit down! Have you lost yo' goddamn mind?" she whispered through clinched teeth. "You tryin' to fuck up my shit, don't you see Boy on the front porch? Furthermore, fuck all that are you cussin' at me? I ain't ya lil' girlfriends. Don't play with me, cause I'll slap yo' ass slam in the mouth!"

"Well, whose is it?" I asked ducking.

"Get this straight, fo' I be forced to wreck shop on you. From one pregnant woman to the next, I will fuck you up over my man. Boy is the only one go up in this raw, yo' father-in-law, fine ass Taj Bennet Sr. straps the fuck up! Don't sleep!"

"Ms. Betty gon' kick yo' ass and so is Uncle Boy. You sittin' up in here pregnant by God knows who!" I grabbed a paper bag from off the kitchen counter. I felt like I was going to hyperventilate. "I need to leave Aunt Cookie." I said grabbing my purse. "I gotta go."

When I got to the shop DeAndre and Rosa, looked at me like I was crazy.

"Happy Birthday Diva! We gotta a cake for you!" DeAndre said, holding the door open for me and for his client that was leaving.

"Thank you." I said dryly.

"Problem?" DeAndre asked.

"Ya'll really wanna know?" I asked, taking off my fur coat and reaching for my black apron-like smock.

"Si, Mami tell us." Rosa said, sitting down in one of the shampoo chairs and crossing her legs. The shop was empty this morning. The rush wasn't due to come in for at least another hour. Lyfe's, "Hypothetically", was playing in the background.

I sat down in my station chair. "Aunt Cookie thinks she's in the family way." I confessed.

"Family Way?" DeAndre mumbled to himself. "Oh my God, Aunt Cookie thinks she's pregnant, oh shit. One of them change of life babies? Oh hell no, my mother had one of those."

"Papi," Rosa asked, "Would dat be de brother or de sista?"

"Dat would be de pain in de ass. Comprende amigo? All them ma'fuckahs that are born on the change are ADHD. Trust and believe something's wrong wit' 'em. They act like they can't sit still, bouncing off the walls and shit. What Martin Lawrence say, 'crazy and deranged? Yeah, that's it. Trust me when I tell you, you don't even wanna talk to none of them fools."

"Damn, that sounds rather personal." I said, feeling my baby kick.

"It is." DeAndre snapped, "I was the youngest child and here come this ma'fuckin criminal. Niggah been a thief since he was born."

"Who DeAndre?" I asked.

"My brother."

"DeAndre you shouldn't be like that." I frowned. "That's your brother."

"Yeah, well. I'm working on that. The psychologist said we'd discuss that when we meet again. I've had problems all my life. First, my oldest brother shoots Rudolph and then this change of life ma'fucker comes along. But Rudolph getting shot, now that was the worse. Do you know what that does to a kid?"

"It wasn't the real Rudolph." I said looking at DeAndre as if he had lost his mind. What the fuck was wrong with him? He was acting like he wanna cry and shit. Is this even for real? "DeAndre be quiet." I said. "You 'bout to scare the shit outta me. You actin' all crazy."

"De Papi is de loco." Rosa laughed, taking her finger and making the crazy sign.

DeAndre fell out laughing, "I'm just buggin' ya'll. For real, ya'll know I'm just buggin'."

For some reason I felt like his ass was quite serious, so I peeped at him with one eye closed. "Don't get to actin' like a ma'fuckin' fool up in here."

"Me? Act like a fool. Hell, the last fool that was up in here was Roger? Diva, you don't still talk to him do you? You did take out a restraining order, right?"

"No. I didn't. I didn't even tell Taj about that. I don't even wanna deal with that."

"Vera, you need to check that. All you need is for that fool to get outta hand again. Rejection is a ma'fuckah when you're insecure."

"DeAndre, paleeze."

"Ai'ight, all I know is that he better not come back up in here, *no more*." He turned to Rosa, "Rosa, turn the radio up."

The D.J. was pumpin' Junior Mafia's "Get Money" as Rosa raised the volume.

"Get money…" Rosa rapped, "Get Money…"

"Oh shit, this my part," I said, throwing my hands in the air, "Is Brooklyn in the house…"

"Without a doubt…" DeAndre rapped while noddin' his head, "I'ma swinger wit' clout er'body watch about!"

Instantly, Rosa and I stopped dead in our lyric spittin' tracks and looked at DeAndre, "What the fuck did you say?" I frowned.

"Oh no papi. Dat cokka is loca. Oh no, papisita."

I looked at DeAndre and rolled my eyes, "Rosa turn to CD. 101.9, the jazz station better yet, some country music. Hip-hop got DeAndre fucked up in the game. He done lost his damn mind!"

DeAndre hunched his shoulders, sat down in his station chair, grabbed his Starbucks latte, and started sipping. He looked at us and then he started laughing, "Aunt Cookie droppin' it on niggahs huh? What kinda men you think Aunt Cookie like?"

"De same like chou papi." Rosa laughed.

DeAndre snapped his fingers, stood up, turned from side to

side, "Excuse me, but I like *my* men, with their pants saggin, Tims draggin', straight thuggin' it! *Okay?*"

This man is crazy. I looked DeAndre up and down, with his tall, slim frame, medium brown flawless skin, and curly black hair. I had to shake my head at his pretty ass. Just plain pretty, didn't make no sense. His ass look just like a sweet Carl Thomas.

Taking a sip of his Starbucks latte DeAndre said, "Aunt Cookie is the original super freak. No disrespect and may Rick James rest in peace, but Aunt Cookie would put him to shame. She be snatchin' men left and right, *and* she *still* got a man at home. Now that's what I'm talkin' about. That's wassup."

"You a freak, just like she is." I said disgusted. "Aunt Cookie is doing some nasty and low down shit. I thought Angie was bad, but Aunt Cookie is the O.P.P. queen. Ms. Betty comes in here sometimes for me to do her hair and Aunt Cookie can't stop smiling in her face, all the while she fuckin' her man! Now she's pregnant, is that even for real? Somebody pinch me, shoot me, slap me, do something because I think I'm dreaming."

"Yeah, that's what I told my counselor last week, but he assured me that all this was real."

"Oh hell, DeAndre."

"Papi please," Rosa frowned, as she looked at me, "I agree Vera, Ti-Ti Cookie is too old to be pregnant, oh no."

"Hell yeah!" I said with my face frowned up and rubbing the side of my stomach, "She got ma'fuckers shootin' up in her and shit. Ill." Just as I said that, Taj and his father walked in. "Here comes the culprit now." I whispered to DeAndre and Rosa.

"Mr. Bennet?" They asked with their mouths dropped open.

"Mr. Bennet." I confirmed through my teeth, smiling at my beautiful man.

Taj glided in and I swear to God, every time I see my man,

he looks better and better. He walked over, gave me a kiss on the cheek, and whispered in my ear. "Damn you look good." I think the baby must've heard his voice because it started kicking and moving from side to side. I rubbed my stomach in an effort to try and soothe the baby.

"You want some head don't you?" I whispered in his ear.

He started smiling and instantly I knew that his dick was hard. Damn I still had it!

"You know you wrong for that." He smiled.

"You play your cards right and I got something to show you in my office."

"Keep talkin' smack and the nut that I'ma bust up in you, gon' have you pregnant for years." He said in my ear. I started blushing and cracking up laughing. I playfully pushed him, walked over, and kissed Mr. Bennet on the cheek. "Mr. Bennet, you know I heard something funny?"

"What, baby? Oh, and Happy Birthday."

"Thank you. The funny thing I heard is that your grand-child...well someone's grandchild, will have an aunt or uncle the same age." Then I watched his face and waited for a reaction. Taj looked at me like I had lost my mind. DeAndre and Rosa were rolling. Rosa was laughing so hard that not a sound was coming from her mouth. *Hell*, I thought, *that's what he gets for screwin' my Aunt Cookie. Nasty ass!*

Before I could follow up my comment with another food for thought, the phone rang. It was my cousin Dirty. "What up Ma?"

"Nothing. What's up with you? How's Nina and the baby?"

"They good. Me and Nina, not together right now. But we cool as far as the baby is concerned. You know, I love my lil' man. Cherise said she was coming by your shop today."

"Cherise? Biggie's ex-girlfriend?"

"Yeah. And yo' that ain't exactly his ex-girlfriend."

"Dirty please, she just told me that she ain't want nothing to do with him."

"Yeah, well, that's a long story. Look, you seen ya moms?"

"No, not yet why?"

"The program called."

When he said that my heart dropped. "And what?"

"They said she missed curfew, last night. Came in late and before the counselor could get to speak to her she'd already left this morning. You know I ain't feeling that shit right?" I looked around to see if anyone was looking at me. Of course Taj was, so I couldn't speak my mind, "Uhmm hmm."

"What? You can't talk?" Dirty asked.

"No, not really."

"Well, check this. If I find her on the street corner, I'ma drag her ass back to rehab. I mean that shit. Ain't nobody left, but us. You know Biggie upstate with the Feds. Now, he's on some football number type shit. When he was in the streets you couldn't tell that niggah nothin'. Trust and believe once I had my son, I wasn't feelin' bein' in the streets no more. My shit is legit. In a minute I'ma be up and outta these projects. You know I just started the police academy."

"Congratulations, Dirty. Oh, excuse me, Officer Wright."

"That's' wassup. Niggahs is buggin' and shit, calling me a sell out, but fuck'em I gotta do me. I wasn't never gettin' that much paper in the street any way. I was a broke ass hustler. But right now, I'ma have to put my street skills to the test and go find your mother. If she's high, God gon' have to help me."

"I gotta go, Dirty."

"Vee, you know I got love for you. Glad we ain't kids, no more. Rowanda and Towanda choices can't fuck us up. Na'mean?"

"Yeah, I feel you."

"Ai'ight cuz. Let me go, I gotta go find this lady. One."

Before I could hang up the phone, Rowanda was coming through the front door with Queen. Looking disoriented and out of place, her eyes were glassy and droopy.

"Hey Vee. I'm glad that I caught you," she said sniffing. That let me know right away she was high.

Paralyzed, I stood and watched Rowanda fade in front of my face. It seems like just yesterday I went to visit her in rehab. She was healthy, smiling, and reminding me of myself—so close to fulfilling the fantasy that I carried around in my heart as a child. But nevertheless, here we go again, back to the trash dump. Once I was able to get my legs to cooperate, I walked over to Rowanda, "Get the fuck out!"

"Vee, what's wrong?" When she didn't look me in the face, I knew for a fact she was high.

"Get out! And don't ever come back!" It's my fuckin' birthday and this is what I get from you? Damn Rowanda, wasn't dumping me in the trash enough? I'm telling you to get the fuck away from me!" I started to scream. Then I remembered that I wasn't in the shop alone. I had to be strong for appearance sake. I didn't want anyone to know how much faith and trust I had in Rowanda's being clean. For some reason I felt like her being clean would exonerate me, finally I'd be free of her demons and able to live my life. Now, I knew for sure that she could never save me.

"Vee, you can't be for real. You gon' have to listen to me." Rowanda looked at me and tears rolled from her eyes. She looked at Queen and then she looked back at me.

"Get out!" I was careful not to look anyone in the face. I can't stand here anymore. I just can't. I practically ran to my office and slammed the door. Once inside, I flopped down in my chair and placed my head on the desk. This was deja vue. I had been in this same spot, feeling this same way at least a hundred times, and just when I thought that things had changed, here I was again.

"Vera open the door." Taj said knocking on the door. I opened the door and wiped my eyes.

"What the hell is really wrong with you, that you think you can talk to your mother any kinda way?" he said obviously upset.

"Taj do you know-"

"Do I know what? How it is to be a dope fiend's kid? What it's like to starve? What, do I know that she placed you in a trash dump? I'm sick of that shit! Get over it! You're grown, you're getting ready to be a mother and you acting like a damn kid. I wouldn't care if your mother was high or not, the next time you disrespect her like that we got problems! You understand?"

"You're taking her side?"

"Taking her side? Vera please, I'm sick of you fuckin' complaining! I don't wanna hear it anymore. Now you need to just accept that you have a drug addicted mother and move on. So please stop it. I don't ever wanna hear you tell your mother to get the fuck out, again."

"Taj this is my shop!"

"I wouldn't care whose shop it is, don't you ever talk to your mother like that!"

"I'm pregnant," I cried. "I can't believe you're taking her side!"

"Pregnant?" he smirked, "Now being pregnant is a weakness? You were also pregnant when you treated your mother like shit. I'm not buying that one, Vera. I love your ass too much, that's part of your problem. But me loving you and you being pregnant has nothing to do with you embarrassing us. Rowanda is my child's grandmother and I won't have you disrespecting her again!"

"It just hurt so much to see her like that. I can't take it."

"Then baby, that's what you say." He said, calming his voice down and pulling me close. "Tell me how you feel and stop all this tough ass *get the fuck out* shit. Please stop it. I don't know what is hurting Rowanda so much that she feels she has to get high. But she's your mother, Vera, and that's not going to change. You gotta stop throwing fits. One day Rowanda may get clean, and refuse to fuck with you, 'cause when she was at her lowest you buried her. Understand?"

"Uhmm hmm."

"You need to apologize."

"Oh, I don't think so."

"You really need to. If my mother were still living, I would apologize all night long if I needed to. Think about that. I'll be by later," he said as he rubbed my stomach, "Let me use your truck. Pops and I caught the train over here. I'ma take him back to Jersey and I'll see you when I come back. Oh, I almost forgot. That slick shit that you said to my father earlier. Stop it. Whatever he and Aunt Cookie call themselves doing is none of our business."

Damn, this niggah don't miss a beat. "Uhmm hmm." I said, as we walked out of my office and into the shop. After Taj and his father left, DeAndre and Rosa didn't say a word, instead we pretended like the situation with Rowanda never happened and went on about our day.

At the end of the night, I came home and got right in the bed. How could Rowanda be getting high again? Didn't she think about me or my baby?

I started sweating and felt like rain was oozing through my skin and holding me captive to a river of tears. I wanted to rub my stomach for comfort. As I went to run my hands across my belly, it felt flat and hollow inside. I started screaming and fighting for dear life, "Where's my baby!" I screamed, "Where's my baby!" I couldn't stop feeling my stomach and I felt like I was drowning in the emptiness of my womb. "This can't be real." I said panting, desperately. Suddenly, I started running through the streets. I didn't have on any shoes and my bare feet were aching from the hard concrete. The pink nightgown that I wore flowed softly in the breeze, as I ran looking for my baby. I could hear her cry, as I got closer. I ran faster, losing my breath with every step. I ran, and I ran, and I ran, until I saw my baby, wrapped in a black plastic bag, lying in the trash dump. As I went to reach for her, Taj started calling my name, "Vera…wake up baby! What's wrong?!" he said rubbing my face.

"My baby…I reached down and started feeling my stomach. It was hard and round. I pressed on it softly and my baby started kicking. "Oh my God I was having a nightmare. I thought my baby was in the trash dump."

"Not again, Vera, damn I thought we were half-way through this…"

Blocked Shot

"You ain't gon' believe this baby girl." Once again, Aunt Cookie was ringing my phone, first thing in the goddam morning, as if all I have to do is wake up and talk to her. Jesus!

"What am I not going to believe? Uncle Boy took you to the abortion clinic?" I said sarcastically.

"Oh, you wanna be knocked the fuck out? You better take a break and recognize, you know how I do it. Anyway, I wanted you to know that I went to the doctor yesterday and he said that I'm going through a lil' change."

"What do you mean a lil' change?"

"A womanly situation."

"Like what? You have to speak plain English to me."

"All right. I ain't pregnant. I'm going through menopause."

"Menopause? Oh hell!" I sucked my teeth.

"Look," she said. "Check yo' attitude, cause it's extra nasty. Plus we got something else we need to discuss. Your mother called me yesterday, crying so bad that I could barely understand her. What I could make out was how you embarrassed her at the shop."

"Embarrassed her? She was standing in my shop high!"

"Look, Rowanda is sick with a lot of problems. Sometimes in life when you think things goin' straight is when everything turns upside down and it seems that all the steps you've taken were wrong."

"Like what, Aunt Cookie?"

"Like, your mama seeing Larry yesterday."

"What did you say Aunt Cookie?" I said, praying that I heard wrong, "Larry? Larry Turner? My father? He's still around here?"

"Yes, he was still around here."

"Why? And when did Rowanda see him? What did he want?"

"On Lincoln Street. She went to visit Queen and there he was. On the street watchin' her, he even started calling out her name. Rowanda said that everything rushed through her mind and she didn't know whether she was coming or going."

"So, she *was high*?"

"Vera!" Aunt Cookie screamed, "Did you hear what I just said! It ain't about you."

"Then, who is it about?"

"Rowanda, for once." Aunt Cookie snapped, "Don't nobody care about Larry, but Rowanda does."

"Please, Aunt Cookie, Rowanda should've told me that yesterday. She could've called me, came to me, something, and told me that. Instead, she was with Queen getting high and she called you to cry about it?"

"Did you give her a chance to speak? Or did you jump all on her like you jumpin' on me. I'm not making up no excuses for Rowanda bein' high yesterday."

"So, she was high?", I thought as I let Aunt Cookie continue.

"Rowanda is responsible for Rowanda," she said. "But you don't know the pain that that child is feelin', the pain that she carries around with her everyday. She cryin', Vera, she cryin'. Don't turn her away. Don't chase her to the point where she feels she doesn't have any one. Everybody need a lil' love, Vera, damn!"

"Yeah, well," I said bitting my bottom lip. "I don't want no parts of her being high. I can't deal with that. And Larry Turner, fuck Larry Turner. She still carrying around a thing for a man that pimped her, got her pregnant, and didn't even look back. Then she sees him and she can't stay sober long enough to cuss his black ass out! Let me see him and I'ma slice his ass! And you can put money on that."

"Well, you ain't gon' see him!"

"And why not, the niggah has disappeared again? Poof, he's gone. Well then, Aunt Cookie, you know what I think? I think," I said, answering my own question. "He could be cold in his grave with his ice on his bones and I wouldn't give a fuck. Fuck him! And if Rowanda wanna run around here and get high because she can't put a niggah in his place then, oh well."

"Vera, if I could reach through this phone I would slap the shit outta you! The man is dead. He dropped dead on the street. He was there lookin' at Rowanda, reminding her about how she use to be. He was beggin' her to come back and work the block. Be his bitch. That's when his girlfriend, the same one that sat at my dinning room table with the raised eyebrows, shot him to death. Killed him on the spot. Rowanda lost her mind! She started crying and screaming! She thought that woman was going to kill her. She cried so hard that she felt like her eyes shed blood, instead of tears. Here was the man that she loved and he was beggin' her to be a whore, begging her to come back and work the streets. Never seeing that she was a new woman, only seeing the old whore. How you think that made her feel? All of her life she's felt like less than nothing and just when she starts to feel good, here comes Larry with his shit. When he called here, I told him to leave her alone and he still bothered her."

"He called you and you didn't tell me?" I felt like Aunt Cookie had been lying to me. "You been lying to me Aunt Cookie?"

"Lying to you? I don't have to lie to you. Larry is not your problem. He's your mother's. I took care of you, I raised you. I'ma always protect you. Vera, you really don't know what it is to be in the street, fightin' every time you turn around, so let me inform you. I have fought 'em all, chile. My mama got her ass kicked by my step-daddy, her boyfriend, and a man she called my uncle. But in the end, she beat herself the worse. Because she didn't take time out and see what she'd been allowing to happen to herself all of those years. I had to protect me, so that I wouldn't be like my mother, which is why I protected you. My mother died because, along with men, life kicked her ass, and she could never stand on her own. Now, you and your mother have a chance to do better with your lives. I've had a lot of broken hearts and I'm trying to save you from one that doesn't heal. You have to make this right with your mother."

"I'm tired of always having to get things right with her, what about me and my life? I'm tired of the streets. Been there and done that."

"What you know about the streets, Vera, I mean, really? Let me let you in on something; Aunt Cookie has done it all to survive. Trust me, I've been in the niggah's house sleepin' with him, laying up with him, cause ain't no place else to go. Using him until I got myself on my feet. Humph, Aunt Cookie, know about life. No, I didn't get high; I did other shit to survive. I chose to go to school, be a home health aid and work. I met Boy and he loved me for me, despite all the shit that I took him through, there he was unmoved and untouched. Loving me all the way. Everybody needs that. And that includes your mama. Now, I don't know how you gon' do it, but I want it done. You *will* apologize. And I mean it. You're getting ready to be a mother, Vera, wouldn't you want your baby to love you no matter what?

Wouldn't you? Stop what you're doing and talk to your mother."

I couldn't say anything, because I was trying to digest what I was hearing.

"Your mother," she continued, "is back at the program. Everybody needs somebody. Go to your mother, all you got is one parent left. Don't waste your time with her and the next thing you know, you're really a motherless child."

I didn't know what to say. I didn't even know where to begin. My father was dead, my mother was in rehab because she couldn't stop getting high, and the woman that I love more than anything, my Aunt Cookie, the woman that I thought was stronger than steel, I just found out has a past filled with broken hearts.

"I'm sorry Aunt Cookie." I said, not knowing how to feel. "I'm sorry."

"Don't apologize to me, I'm straight. Cookie Jolene Turner, can take care of herself. You got other shit to attend to."

"What about the police? What about Larry's girlfriend?"

"The police arrested her this morning. Oh, and just so you know, Rowanda didn't get high until after she left your shop yesterday."

"How do you know?"

"Because that's what she told me."

"So, you're blaming me for Rowanda getting high?"

"Vera, please! Get your shit together. Please, do right by your mother. You only get one."

After I hung up with Aunt Cookie, I called Rowanda's rehab program. Bryce answered the phone.

"Hey Vee."

"Hey Bryce, how are you?"

"I'm makin' it."

"Bryce, is my mother available?"

"Well, Vera we don't usually let the patients here take phone calls, during the first stage of the program, but since you're family I'll do it this time."

"First stage of the program?' I said confused. "What do you mean? My mother should be coming home next month. Her six months are up."

"No, her six months started over again."

"I don't agree with that. Why would they start again?" I said with an attitude.

"Agree with what? Recovery is not up for discussion. I'ma be straight with you, because I care. But your moms relapsed. Therefore, she has to go back to the beginning. Recovery is forever, and every time you get high to solve a problem, you have to start over."

This ma'fucker was pissin' me off. He had a lot of nerve! As far as I was concerned, he needed to be worried about his own mother and not mine. "Whatever Bryce, can I speak to her?"

"Yeah, I'll let you speak to her this time."

This time? Fuck him. I took a deep breath and kept my thoughts to myself. Before he put Rowanda on the phone he said to me, "Think a brotha could come by and get his do hooked up."

He was sounding so corny all I could do was give him half of a laugh. "Perhaps, call me first."

I could tell he was smiling as he gave Rowanda the phone. "This is Rowanda." She said.

"Rowanda," I said, scared she might hang up on me, "It's me, Vera."

"I know who it is."

"Rowanda, I didn't know about Larry. I'm sorry…"

"Vera, just be quiet." She was pissed off, "I been waitin' for you to call, 'cause I have a few choice words for yo' ass."

"Excuse me?" I said, shocked.

"No, not this time. Vera Wright-Turner, I'm *so sick* of you being a lil' girl that I don't know what to do. I can't blame you for my actions because I'm responsible for me, but I'm sick and tired of trying to get you to love me. I thought that if I got out that hospital, stayed alive, and got clean that you would love me and your love would be all I needed. I should've known that all this shit was too good to be true.

When I saw Larry, I didn't know what to do. Do you know how many times I practiced in my mind what I would do when I saw that man…the man that my heart wouldn't let go of? How I would react? Do you know how many times I wondered how in the hell could I still love a man that turned me out and treated me like shit? Of course not, 'cause you weren't there, Vera! You weren't there!" I could tell she wanted to cry, but she seemed more determined to say what she needed to say, than to drop a tear. "You weren't there when this man, that I still loved, was beggin' me to be a whore for him. Beggin' and pleadin', telling me he would love me if I just turned a trick. That shit was sick and then for him to be killed in my face and die at my feet. Do you know that I had blood streaked down my face like tears? Do you know that? All you care about is nursing your own wounds and me setting you free from *my* addiction. Well, Vera, I got my own set of ma'fuckin problems! And I don't need you reekin' havoc on me because I'm not the mother you always dreamed of. Cuz guess what? You ain't the goddamn daughter that I always dreamed of! You're selfish, spoiled, and you keep throwing a fit about shit I can't fix! So, I tell you what, take your ass outta the trash dump and grow up! When you are a woman, that knows how to treat her mother, then we can deal. But, until then I will love you from afar because I have to get myself together and this time I'm gettin' clean for me!"

"What are you saying?"

"I love you Vera!" Rowanda said sternly, "But, you got to treat me better, if you need to learn how to do that then fine, but don't you ever lose your mind and treat me the way that you treated me the other day. You understand?"

"Rowanda—"

"You understand!" she screamed.

Rowanda had never spoken to me like this. For the most part, I wanted to cuss her ass out and tell her that I didn't give a fuck what she did, but I couldn't. I just couldn't. Instead Aunt Cookie's story rang in my head and all I could think about was Aunt Cookie saying, *'You'll be a motherless child'*. Instead of spitting out the first hurtful thing that came to mind, I quietly replied, "I understand. I do."

Rowanda told me she would talk to me later and that I could come see her when she was able to have visits.

"Here we go again." I thought, *"Starting all over from day one."* I laid my head down against the pillow, pulled the covers over my head, and cried myself to sleep.

Established Position

My father's funeral was empty, but full for a man who nobody knew. We each took turns standing over the casket, saying goodbye to someone we barely said hello to.

Taj and I paid for the service and the burial. Aunt Cookie and Uncle Boy paid for the broken wheel of carnation flowers that rested at the foot of the casket. The Army wouldn't give us anything, due to his dishonorable discharge. The money meant nothing to me, it meant more to me that Rowanda say goodbye to Larry and perhaps move on with her life. I felt like she needed to see him buried. Leaving him in the city morgue with a tag on his toe would never bring her any closure, but looking at him in a nicely carved, cherry wood box, would give her the strength she needed to say goodbye.

Taj and I sat on the bench, behind Rowanda, Aunt Cookie, and Uncle Boy. A borrowed church choir sang, "Amazing Grace." An unknown pastor shouted a sermon about a home going, and how it won't be long..."Don't weep for the deceased," the pastor said, "cry for yourself, for he has gone on, and we are still in the midst of the land, where the Devil is at hand. But glory be to Jesus!" The pastor shouted as the organist slammed on the intruding keys, "You can be born again! Hallelujah!"

Rowanda cried like I have never seen anyone cry before. Her constant jerks of emotions made me shudder.

The eight-year-old life that I had in Lincoln Street projects ran through my mind. I can remember looking in the cracked mirror that Rowanda and grandma use to argue over. "Hurry up Rowanda!" Grandma would say, "I need that goddamn mirror! Get ya own shit." I can remember holding that same mirror in my hand and turning it sideways so that I could see myself. "You ain't gon' be no fiend...no matter what they say." Then I would pretend that a dark reflection would sparkle in the mirror's background. It was Larry. My faceless daddy, looking for me. I imagined that he was tall and handsome, deep mocha in complexion, like Taj, with a small Afro, like Uncle Boy, and a soft touch like Aunt Cookie's. He would be extending his hand to me, motioning for me to come and go with him. He would promise to take care of me, forever and ever. But instead, it was Rowanda looking at me, with an empty face. She would grab my hand and together we walked out of the bathroom and into the bedroom. We'd sit on the bare mattress that had faded gray strips and towels for sheets and listen to the tranquility of the projects. The high pitch clapping of the steel doors to the medal frames, Ms. Johnson getting her ass kicked every night, and the how the two girls next door where more than just friends.

Later, when Rowanda thought I was sleeping I would wake to see her crying with tears dripping over her lips and sliding down the glass dick of the crack pipe.

I sat here determined not to drop one tear for a man who never loved or cared for me. Any of the tears that I cried today would be for my mother.

My baby constantly kicked and fluttered back and forth. The baby was moving so much that the movement could be seen through the black dress I had on. Taj kept rubbing his hands together, as if he were nervous. He kept pulling at his tie and when it seemed that he couldn't take it anymore he ran his hands across my belly, the baby kicked, and Taj closed his eyes, as if he were saying a silent prayer.

After a while, the preacher seemed to be at a lost for words. He'd probably never held a funeral for a man that only had five people in attendance.

When it came time for someone to speak, Rowanda dried her eyes as best she could and stood up. "I know that ya'll probably wondering why I'm standing." she said, looking around. "But, I want to say goodbye to a bridge that I never seemed able to cross. I have a heart filled with painful memories, but I'm standing here today to burry yesterday and welcome tomorrow." She cleared her throat, took the back of her right hand, and wiped her eyes. "All my life I wanted to find something to hate about this man. Be it the way he placed me on the street, or the way he seduced me into drugs and the fast life. I wanted something to hold onto so that I could spit on his grave, but I guess with him dying at my feet, was the universe's way of throwing karma around.

As I look at this dead man today, I see some smiles. Some good times, some of the love that he showed me. How can I hate everything about this man? He's a part of my child and my grandchild. If I hate him, then how am I suppose to love them, when he's a part of them? I'm moving on." Rowanda said to us "I suggest that everyone else here does the same. It's time for life to begin and the games to end. Pray for me and I'll pray for you."

When we arrived at the cemetery, I didn't know how to feel. I knew I couldn't cry, but a part of me felt sad that my father was dead. Not missing, not somewhere else, but dead. Gone. No possibility of ever returning.

Taj seemed to be affected by Larry's burial more than me. "Baby, I gotta get outta here. I feel like I'm about to choke." He snatched his tie from around his neck.

"When's the last time you've been to a funeral?" I asked him, while wiping the sweat from his brow with the back of my hand.

"When my mother died." Taj moved my hand. "I gotta go baby. I can't breathe in here."

After the 'ashes to ashes and dust to dust,' everyone started walking back to their cars. Rowanda kissed me on the cheek as she walked over to Taj's Escalade.

Still standing over Larry's grave, I looked down at the ground. "Well, well, Daddy I guess this is where we get off." I bit my bottom lip, I felt tears sneaking up. "You know I always thought about you, no matter what came out of my mouth. I didn't always love you, because you didn't always love me. But, nevertheless, I still dreamed of you being the perfect daddy. So, forgive me for not accepting you for the way you really were. And forgive me for not closing the door on the pain that you caused me and my mother a long time ago. Forgive me for not cutting you off the way that I really wanted to. And forgive me for still wondering how things would be, if you had given yourself a chance to get to know me."

I wiped my eyes and when I turned around Rowanda was standing there. "I thought you were in the truck with Taj?"

"I was but I'm here with you now?"

"I'm glad you are?" I said hugging her. I felt like I didn't want to let her go.

"Don't worry baby. It's over." she said, "and this is the day that we're going to start all over again."

Crossover Dribble

"I hope Lee's ass don't be acting funny 'cause I'ma punch her dead in her mouth if some slick shit comes out." I said to Shannon, stretching my legs across the couch.

"Vera please, you're always calling Lee out, but let's look at you."

"What about me?" I snapped.

"Excuse me diva, don't be catching no attitude with me, because I'm shoutin' *yo'* ass out. You know we have never held any punches, so I won't start now. What's up with your wedding? I see you rockin' the hell outta that big ass diamond, bling-bling all over the place, but I don't see you putting anything behind it to back it up."

"I'ma marry Taj." I said squinting my face up.

"When?"

"When the time is right. Right now, I need some room to breathe."

"I see you breathing rather well."

"Shannon—"

"Excuse you, Ms. Thing, I'm talking. Taj has been paying bills up in your house as if his name is on the mortgage. Anything you want, you get it. No worries, no nothing. He's fine as hell; from the stories, you tell his feet and his dick match. Yet and still, pregnant and all, you're looking me in the face with a blank stare like you're confused. Keep your shit up...keep it up and I won't be here to save you."

"Whatever." I reached for the bowl of grapes sitting on the coffee table and stuffed one in my mouth. *I'll be glad when Angie and Lee get here because I'm starving.* I picked up the remote control to the CD player and turned on the new Lyfe Jennings CD.

"That man knows he can sing!" Shannon said, crossing her legs and humming to track number one.

"Girl, you ain't never lied." I said, trying not to have on attitude with her about the comment she made to me about Taj.

"I'm tellin' you Vera, if I wasn't in love with Nile, Lyfe could get it. Fa'sho, fa'sho."

"In love with Nile? Are you for real? What about Quincy, who's not only in love with you, but lives with you?"

"I'ma break up with him." Shannon said casually, refilling her glass of Chardonnay.

"For good?" I asked.

"Yes. My heart is not in this anymore. I'm tired of his ass. He's never home and you know he hired as International pilot for American Airlines."

"And...the problem...would be?"

"I just ain't feelin' him." She shrugged.

"Oh hold up." Finally, I could call Shannon's ass on the carpet. "How the fuck you gon' call me out and you in the same damn position? What the hell is that? Then you sittin' here complaining about Quincy. A young black, thugged out pilot? Excuse me, Ms. Shannon, but I ain't the only one sitting up in here getting bills paid by a good man with a big dick. Only difference is I ain't cheating, you on the other hand..."

"Oh please. I won't even start on Mr. Bryce. If yo' ass wasn't pregnant, who knows what you would've done."

"I don't think so." I said shaking my head 'no.'

"Anywho," she said nixing me off, "When Quincy comes back from his international flight training in London we're a done deal."

"How long is he going to be gone?"

"Three months."

"Damn, that's a long time," I said. "I don't know how I would feel if Taj was gone for that long."

"Keep fuckin' up and not marry that man. As soon as that baby drops, you'll see what its like to be with out him."

"Don't be wishing that on me."

"Vera please," she said frowning. "I'm ya girl, I'm just being honest with you. Me, I'ma stop Quincy's shit at the door. Girl, let me tell you, the day that he got promoted, he came looking at me like he was getting ready to propose. I shot his ass a look, like don't even do it to yourself, baby boy."

As she said that, the doorbell rang. I got up to answer it. Finally, Angie and Lee were here.

"I know yo' pregnant ass is starving," Angie said, handing me the take out she brought from B.B.Q's. "Ya'll ain't gon' never guess who I just saw!"

"Who?" I said placing the food in the center of my marble dinning room table, so we could sit down and eat.

"Danielle Santiago! I told her we were discussing her book tonight. To bad for ya'll but I got my book signed. She gave me the inside scoop on her and Ashley Haynes too!"

"For real? She told you that?" I said taking a bite of my sticky wing.

"Uhmm hmm." Angie said with a mouth fulla food. "I told her all she had to do is say the word and I would slide his ass!"

"That's funny as hell!" Lee laughed, putting ketchup on her fries, "Now tell 'em 'bout Lil' Love and the tattoo with your name on it."

"Lil' Love?" I frowned, with a mouth fulla food, "Tattoo?" Shannon and I looked at Angie like she had lost her damn mind. I looked at Lee, "Come again?"

"The midget," Lee said breaking a piece of fish with her fork "has Angie's name tattooed on his chest."

"You got a big ass mouth!" Angie shouted at Lee, "It isn't exactly like that."

"Well," Shannon said, "What was it like?"

"I'm confused." Angie said, "And I keep wondering what did I do to wake up on the wrong side of the world that has me catching all these fuckin' losers!"

"What are you talking about Angie?" Shannon asked disgusted. "You mean to tell me there's more drama with Daddy-O-dot-fuckin'-com. Oh, excuse me, Lil' fuckin' Love?"

"I can't even believe that we are still having the conversation." I chuckled in disbelief. "A goddamn midget, with your name on his chest Angela? I mean really."

"Now that the tables have turned," Lee smirked, "don't go blaming me for the shit."

"Whatever." Angie said, "Whatever."

"Well tell us what happened." Shannon said, taking a sip of her lemonade.

"Ya'll ain't gon believe this shit." Angie said rolling her eyes at Lee and then mumbling 'dumb trick.' "Remember this chick," she pointed to Lee, "said she was going to introduce me to Jerell's friend, Keith. I knew was skeptical for a reason. But despite my gut feeling, I made up my mind to go. I should've caught the first hint when the niggah pulled up in front of my Brownstone an hour late, blowing his horn, yelling, *'Be about it Ma!'*

Angie laughed and continued. Ya'll know I rent out the downstairs apartment to a little elderly Jewish couple. They're nice and quiet people. Don't bother anybody, mind their own business, and they go to sleep at 9 o'clock. Well, this fool is blowing the horn, at 10:30 at night, yelling, *'Put some fire under ya ass Ma!'*

Now mind you, I'm standing upstairs dressed in my tailor made, three piece Vera Wang, baby blue silk suit, with three inch *'fuck me'* pumps to match. And this sucker is blowing the horn for me and calling me a goddamn 'ma.' That shit sent the lil' elderly couple crazy. The lil' woman's yelling, 'Ira, Ira! What's going on Ira!' Trust me, ole Boy was this close to gettin' cussed out, but, on the strength of him being a hook up from my girl, over here." Angie said pointing to Lee, "I didn't sock it to him. Instead, I ran downstairs and calmed the old people down. And assured them that they weren't getting jacked and that it was okay for them to go back to sleep.

Anyway, I got in the car with this ma'fucker and no matter what my mind said my coochie stood up and took control, that's when the clit said to the lips, *'This is the niggah that we been lookin' for.'* Divas," Angie said snapping her fingers, "Fine would be an insult to this man. There was no doubt that he was one of God's favorite children. Blue-black skin, baldhead, Gerald Levert thick. Make you wanna growl and shit. Now, as I went to click my seatbelt, he looked at me and said, 'Oh Big poppa can't get no hug?'

"Did you hug him?" Shannon asked, with her mouth hung open.

Angie took a sip of her drink and said "No."

"No?" we all frowned, "Why?"

"Please, that niggah was too fine. I looked at him and said, 'Boy, if I hug you I might fuck around and get pregnant."

"Oh my Lawd. Ya'll so ghetto'fied." Lee interrupted, "That's why ya'll are so messed up now, superficial shit. I haven't heard you say yet if he was a nice person or not."

"We need to get rid of you!" Angie said.

We looked at Lee like she was crazy, this bitch wanted to be slapped! "Anyway," Angie continued, "We went to dinner and a movie. I swear fo' goodness that I was feelin' this black man and every time I looked at him, my coochie would chirp. So, when he suggested that I come back to his place, I checked my bag for my stash of condoms and extra Motion Lotion. Once I spotted them, I was straight. Fuck it, we could all use a one night stand."

"A whore never changes her spots." Lee complained.

"And a dumb bitch never owns her coochie." Angie snapped.

"Trouble in paradise?" I asked, being sarcastic, "I know the traveling twins can't be getting pissed off at one another."

"All right all ready!" Shannon shouted, "Angie, will you tell us about your ghetto-fabulous date."

"All right." Angie sighed, "Well, let me tell ya'll this shit," she said pouring herself a glass of Hennessey and Alize. "When we pulled up in front of his house, I was trying my best not to get all worked up about home-boy's lil' section eight, townhouse hook up. This was a Jersey niggah mind you. No offense ya'll." She looked at me and Shannon. "But this ma'fucker lived in the heart of Newark, right off Rt. 78. Divas, I couldn't believe this shit. Here I was, use to a man with a penthouse suite, but somehow I ended up in Newark with Pooky and the Johnson Avenue crew.

So ai'ight. Still, ya girl gave ole boy a chance. When we got out the car, walked up the stairs, and he opens the front door, his family sittin' around lookin' like the Klumps live and in concert. Grandma at the kitchen table, with pink and green sponge rollers in her hair. Equipped with the tissue paper wrapped around 'em and er'thang." Angie said with a southern twang. "Now mind you the kitchen table was actually in the living room and the heifah was selling Chico sticks and lose cigarettes. Sitting next to her musta been the neighborhood wino, cause he had a bottle of Thunderbird and a squeegee in his hand. Then boyfriend's sister, Bon-Quesha, had three lil' dirty kids running around. And the backdrop to all of this was Mahalia Jackson singin' "Nearer Thy God to Thee."

'Yo, Ma.' Ole boy gon' say to me, 'You wanna come upstairs and get up on this pony?'

"What did he say? A pony? Oh hell no." I laughed.

"Guess what I did." Angie said, taking a sip from her glass.

"What?" we all said.

"I called Eugene to come and get me."

"The midget? Get the fuck outta here!" I screamed.

"Hell yeah and that lil' niggah was there in five minutes flat!"

"You lying!"

"I wish I was, but I'm not. I'm telling you, he pulled up in front of ole boy's house with the handicap van and all."

"Handicap van?" Lee frowned. " What did Keith do?"

"Nothing, I told him that my lil' afflicted cousin, needed me to drive him back to Brooklyn."

"And he believed that shit?" I asked.

"Hell yeah, especially after the kiss that I laid on him."

"You should'a copped a quick feel of the dick." Shannon laughed, fixing herself another glass of wine.

"I did," Angie chuckled, "I placed my hand on his dick and squeezed."

"Oh my God," Lee frowned, "where are your morals?"

"Morals?" I said, "Did I miss something or are morals and dick two different things?"

"True story." Shannon said, "I could've sworn that they were."

"Now that we've clarified that, ya'll want me to finish the story or not?" Angie asked.

"Yeah, finish." Shannon urged.

"Anyway, I squeezed his dick so that I could see what I was leaving behind. After that, I jumped in the van with Eugene. Oh my Lawd, that was a big, big, big mistake!"

"Why?" Shannon said, trying not to laugh.

"Because this lil' niggah invited his ass in my house. At first, I thought I left him in the car. But he was so short, that I didn't see him walking around, until I went to close the front door and there he was Grinnin' and shit. His mouth lookin' like Trick Daddy."

"Was he wearing that same tight ass Easter suit?" I asked.

"No, he was wearing baggy jeans and a long white t-shirt. Looking like the stinkin' ass baby from the Bey-Bey kids cartoon. Bragging about how he had on Sean John. I looked at his ass and said, 'You might have on Baby Phat, but I doubt it very seriously if you have on Sean John.'

'This *dick* ain't from Baby Phat.' he said, grabbing his shit and licking his lips. Then he lifted up his shirt and said, 'And this tattoo is my undying love to you. That's why its above my heart.'

"Did he really have a tattoo?" Shannon asked.

"The lil' niggah had a tattoo of my name across his chest and on his stomach he tried to have 'Thug Life.' But what made it so bad, is that his damn chest was so small that the fuckin' tattoo was wrapped around to his back. I was embarrassed! 'Pull your shirt down. Please.' I begged, 'I've seen enough.' A couple of times I said to myself, what the fuck are you doing, Angela? But I nixed my thoughts off. I can't even lie for a moment, Eugene looked kinda good and I was horny as hell. I figured, what the fuck, let's test the waters and see what's up. I practically laid on the floor so that I could be face to face with his ass and kiss him. He got off on that shit. I was disgusted, but I was determined to see what lil' man was workin' with.

This ma'fucker insisted on undressing me. So I figured, all right, lets get in the mood. I stood up in the middle of my living room with my eyes closed, waiting to feel the palms of his hands. Instead, I heard a chair dragging across my wooden floors! When I opened my eyes this ma'fucker had gone in my kitchen, grabbed one of the chairs, was now standing on it and trying to take off my clothes. By the time, he took off my bra. He had to get on his knees in the chair, just to suck my goddamn titties! And ya'll know I'ma A cup so you can imagine that the Lil' niggah was 'bout to fall.

When he tried to reach his short ass arms, toward my pussy, thinking he was playing with my clit; I had to tap him on the shoulder, with my tittie in his mouth and say, 'Excuse me, but that's my navel, not my pussy.'

'My bad.' He said, smiling. Then he unbuttoned my pants and I'm thinking okay he gonna come down off the chair now. Well Divas, all he did was pull the chair closer, sit down in it, with his feet swinging, and started nibbling on my pussy. I was so disgusted, but when he started licking that spot. His whole head was damn near swimming in my coochie. I started cum-min' all over the place.

So I figured fuck it, let's take this to the bed. Needless to say, he tripped while hopping out of the chair and I had to help him up. When we got in the bed, the dick was hard as a rock and it was an okay size. It was one of those that had a crook in it. I was in heaven. I got on top of him and tried to ride his dick. As soon as I went to buck, his ass started coughing. The next thing I know he was plastered against the headboard like the ma'fucker Pillsbury doughboy! Once he peeled himself off the headboard, he looked up at me and screamed, "You know I'm handicap! That I get S.S.I.! I'm tired of people taking advantage of me! I should've known better than to let you sit your big ass on me!' This lil' niggah tried to go off on me talking 'bout, 'I should've known that yo' old ass wouldn't be able to handle the dick!'

'What dick niggah?' I spat back at him, 'My pinky finger is bigger than that shit. It looks like a fuckin' hot dog from a Mighty Kid's meal!'

I grabbed his clothes, walked his ass to the door and threw him the fuck out! Retarded niggah! I wanted to go outside and gut punch his ass but I was scared that I might kill him!"

By the time Angie was done telling the story we were all holding our stomachs. I was laughing so hard that not a sound was coming from my mouth and I thought that I would piss on myself. After we finished laughing, we noticed that Angie didn't seem to be amused. I wiped the tears from my eyes and said, "What's wrong now Angie?"

"Vera," she said sucking her teeth, "I am 33 years old, with no children and no prospects. I'm tired."

"Angie," Shannon said, "Your time will come, you just have to be patient. And even when Prince Charming arrives you may find yourself changing your mind."

Angie frowned up her face and said, "What is that suppose to mean?"

"It means that although, I love Quincy—"

"So what's the problem?" Angie snapped.

"If you be quiet," Shannon said rolling her eyes, "I could finish. Anyway, I'm not *in love* with him. And yeah, he's fine, got a big dick, nice job, money in the bank, but I'm just not feeling him like that, anymore."

"Why not?" Lee asked.

"That's a good question." Shannon said refilling her glass of wine. "That's a damn good question."

Triple Crown Publications presents

Off the Dribble

I'm nine months pregnant and the closer I am to giving birth, the more I can't wait to be a mother. But I'm scared and desperately trying to figure out if I can be scared and be a mother at the same time. Is that possible? Right now, I feel like I need *my mother* to be here for me and my child.

I have to work myself up to being the child of the new and improved, clean and sober, Rowanda Wright. I've been Aunt Cookie and Uncle Boy's child, a dope fiend's kid, and my own woman all rolled into one. But never have I simply been Vera Wright-Turner, daughter of Rowanda Wright…and I'm not sure if I know how to be. You feel me?

Lately I've been thinking about how my father's death has affected me. It's been three months since he died and although I don't miss him, it's the fact that he was never a part of my life that bothers me. It's the not knowing that bothers me the most. Not knowing how he was, who he was, or what he was like. Was he a nice guy or a grouch? Did he like morning walks or late night talks? Did he like movies or music? When was his birthday? Did he ever think about me? Did he ever miss me? Or was out of sight truly out of mind? If only I could get a feel for how it would've been to be Daddy's little girl, I don't think him dying would be so bad, because then I would have more than his last name to remember him by.

And in the midst of all this confusion is Taj. The black knight in Kente cloth armor, here to save Vera from the gold diggin' streets. Can somebody tell me please; is it a crime to wanna be left alone sometimes? In the beginning, I loved the attention, the feeding me, foot rubs, constant I love you's, but now I'm losing it and all I see is Taj and this baby. Nothing else. I can't stand this fairy tale, ghetto ass shit. Give me a ma'fucker with some issues and some problems then I'll have the excuse I need to bail the fuck out. But right now, I have no choice but to stay. I've fallen' into the trap of loving Taj too goddamn much for my own good, and now I know for sure if he leaves that I'ma break.

I swear this niggah got me goin'. I love him more than any money, house, car, shoes, bag, or clothes that I've ever gold digged for. I can't even play my position of the chick that does- n't give a fuck anymore. This can't possibly be the flip side of the game, the way it's looking for me...the game is over.

I opened my double door stainless steel refrigerator, took out a bottle of spring water, and sat down in the breakfast nook. As I reached for the phone to call Aunt Cookie, it rang. "Hello." I sighed.

"Hey Boo."

"Hey Shannon. Quincy's party is still on, right?"

"Yeah," she said hesitating, "But why do you sound like that? What's the problem now, Vera? Ms. Betty and Samira calling you to watch the Baby Story again?"

"Nothing's wrong."

"Stop lying. I can hear it in your voice." she insisted.

"Well, since you really wanna know, it's this shit with Taj and everything else. I can't do anything without Taj being all in my ass."

"That's your fuckin' man, no excuse me, your fiancé. You're nine months pregnant with his child. He *should* be all in that ass."

"Yeah, but I need him to back up just a little."

"What? Vera, please. What do you want? A man that doesn't talk to you? Ignores you, could care less if you're having his baby or not? Or do you want an attentive and responsible brotha? I mean tell me because I'm dying to know."

"Ain't nobody said all of that." I snapped.

"Then, what are you saying?"

"I'm just saying."

"You're just saying a buncha shit." She sucked her teeth; "You better calm down and get your shit back in order. Fuck around and chase that niggah away and you gon' have more baby mama drama then you can handle. I don't know what you're waiting on, but you need to marry his ass. Snatch him up before he's gone."

"Yeah, like Quincy." I snapped.

"Vera please, I didn't want Quincy."

"You didn't, or you don't."

"I don't. He's going to London and that's what I need, him gone. Besides the man that I love is here."

"There you go snortin' that bullshit again." My other line clicked before I could finish what I was saying. I peeped at the Caller I.D. and saw that it was Ms. Betty. "Shannon, let me call you back."

"Bye baby mama!"

I clicked over and before I could even halfway say "hello," Ms. Betty was running her mouth.

When Taj and I first got engaged Ms. Betty, called here every-day, two and three times a day asking me how many people would I be inviting to the wedding. *My* wedding, mind you. This chick ain't offered to pay for shit, but she's all in my guest list.

"Hey Vera. Ms. Betty here." She's always fuckin' announcing herself like she's waiting on trumpets.

"Hi Ms. Betty." I said dryly. Don't think she noticed, she was so caught up in herself and whatever she needed to say, that she could care less about the way I was sounding.

"Taj has a big family." Fell out of her big ass mouth "I need to know how many of your mama's folks are coming? So, I'll know who to invite from my church. What about your Uncle Boy, is he going to be there?"

All I could think about was, how many ways to slam the phone down on this nosy bitch. "Ms. Betty, why are you asking me about my Uncle Boy? Is there a reason why he wouldn't come to my wedding?"

"No baby. I didn't mean it like that. What I meant to say was, your Aunt Cookie can be kinda lose—"

"Kinda lose!" I took the phone away from ear, looked at the receiver, and mumbled, *'Ms. Betty I fuck up old women, especially the ones who wanna step to my Aunt Cookie. Even if she is doin' ya man!'*

"Vera! Vera!" Ms. Betty was yelling when I put the phone back to my ear, "What did you just say to me? You fight who?"

I ignored her. "Ms. Betty what do you mean my Aunt Cookie can be kinda lose?"

"I didn't mean nothing by it baby I was just wondering if we were going to be coupled off. And Vera, who's giving you away, since yo daddy died? If you need somebody maybe we can ask Taj Sr."

I was this close to cussin' this old bitch the fuck out, "Ms. Betty, I don't need to borrow any relatives."

"Did I say that? I just wanted to know and one more thing is the baby going to be christened here in Jersey? You know this is where Taj's family is and his old girlfriend Taniesha, said she would love to come to the christening."

Oh, this bitch wants me to stomp a mud hole in her ass! "His what, wants to do what Ms. Betty?"

"Don't worry, she's married with her own husband and son, Kenya Amir. Isn't that a beautiful name? Besides, she told me that she'll let you have Taj. Plus her husband has his own business. O.T. productions. Ever hear of them?"

"What?"

"Plus, Philemon Missionary Baptist is our home church."

"Ms. Betty—"

"And another thing…" the bitch said, cutting me off, "What's the baby last name going to be? I hope you know that it has to be Bennet and please, Lawd Jesus, whatever you do, name the chile something that I can spell and pronounce. If it's a girl, I like Violet or Renee. Matter a fact it's a set of twins that live down the street name Taylor and Sydney. Whatcha think of them names? Hell, girl or boy just go ahead and name the baby Taj…and…"

"And nothing!" I snapped, "I have had just about enough. What I name my child is what I name my child. *My child* being the operative word here. Don't be concerned with that. And *don't ever* call yourself telling me what my child's last name should be. What's your last name Ms. Betty? Oh, I forgot it's Greene and not Bennet. And be sure that you tell Taniesha, I'm from New York and I gotta hundred gun, a hundred clips!"

"Vera! What in the world is wrong with your mouth? Taniesha is a nice Christian girl! She is a trustee in the church! Oh Lawd Jesus. I'm too saved for all of this. Wait till I tell Pastah Allen about this! I gotta go Vera. All I did was call myself being nice and you done cussed me and Taniesha out!"

I wanted to say bye bitch, but Instead I was respectful and said, "Bye Ms. B." and the bitch hung up.

After that, I walked in the living room and laid back on the chaise lounge. I stretched my legs and hit the remote control for the CD player and listened to Sade's *Is it a Crime*, and placed I on repeat. Then I picked up this month's issue of Shannon's magazine and started flipping through the articles. When I ran across the one that Shannon wrote about being *"in love"*, I started thinking about Taj.

For the past month, I've purposely made no time for him. No talking, no listening, no looking in his face to see whether my behavior is causing him pain. Nothing. The only speaking has been in the lovemaking, and the more silent I've become the more intense the lovemaking has been.

"We need to talk Vera." Taj scared the shit out of me, coming through the door. When I looked at him I noticed he hadn't given himself a chance to relax and take off his medical gear before he'd started shooting off at me, which could only mean that all the way home he'd rehearsed this conversation.

My heart was in the pit of my stomach and I could feel the baby's feet kicking it around. Taj flopped down on the couch, across from where I was laying, still trying to flip through the magazine.

"Put the magazine down, Vera." He said, sternly as if he were my daddy and not my man. I shot his ass a look, reminding him that I wasn't the one, nor was I in the mood. "Don't play me Vera." He said taking off his overcoat.

Reluctantly, I placed the magazine down and laid it on my stomach.

"Why have you been avoiding me?" he asked kneeling in front of me.

"I live with you. How the hell would I avoid you?" I couldn't look at him.

"Look at me." he turned my face toward his, "Vera. You're always at the shop. I'm surprised that you're home now. Since

I've been working the night shift, you come in the house after I leave. I call you on the phone and you toss me a fuckin' attitude like I'm a punk or something!"

"I do not!" I said feeling my baby kick.

"Get the fuck outta here! Yes, you do and you know it. Always mouthin' off with some garbage, over talking me and shit!"

"Taj—"

"I'm talking." he snapped. "Be quiet. We're talking about you running, avoiding shit, and what you're avoiding is me."

"What's your problem now, Taj?" I said sarcastically, rolling my eyes in my head.

"Vera, don't fuckin' play me!" he yelled, "You keep fuckin' with me, rollin' your eyes and shit, they're going to show up missin'!"

What did he just say? "What you say? Repeat that?" I looked at him like he was crazy.

"Fuck all that, I ain't feeling this. Did you forget that I asked you to marry me? I haven't heard anything about a wedding date, and we've been engaged for over six months. I stepped to you like a man, Vera. Even after I gave you that big ass ring that you rockin' the hell out of, I came back and gave you more. I gave you my mother's Bible, the keys to my Escalade, my bankbook, my doctor's tag, the deed to the two houses that I own in Jersey, and my co-op. I took everything I owned placed them on a silver platter and handed it to you. I took everything I had that was mine, with my name on it, and told you that I wanted it to be ours." He seemed to be holding back tears. I wanted to cry. I knew I was hurting him, but not this bad.

"Vera, I told you that everything *I* had now belonged to *us*. The same way my father put it down for my mother, I came and laid it down for you; and the only thing you seem to appreciate out of all of that, is that big ass rock that you sportin' around here with no fuckin' issue."

"You don't even know what you're talking about. Your mother's Bible is in the baby's nursery."

"The baby's nursery? I didn't ask the baby to marry me, I asked you. The baby's already mine. The baby doesn't have anything to do with the love that I have for you, it simply adds to it. Vera I love you because of you. The baby was created out of that love. Not the other way around. Now understand this—"

"Taj—"

"I already told you to stop *fuckin'* interrupting me! I'M TALKING! Understand! I will not be playing house with you. So, I suggest you let me know if you want me to be your husband, or if you want me to step. Set a date. Do more than let your mouth say yes. Be about it or I'm gone. It's all or nothing. Don't give me no shit about being the baby's father. That's my baby and not you, or anybody else, can take that away from me. As far as that's concerned I'ma be around for the rest of the baby's life. Now you, on the other hand, may be a different story."

"Oh, so now you're threatening me? All because I haven't set a date. Now should I marry a bully?"

Taj started laughing in disbelief. "Vera, how many times have I told you to stop running game." He got off his knees and started pacing the floor. Sitting back down on the floor, in front of me, he said, "You don't love me anymore?"

"Taj, I am so…in love with you…that I don't know what to do. I'm scared," I found myself admitting.

"Why baby?" I started biting my lip and looking at the floor. "Look at me." he said holding my head up.

"I'm scared because in the end I feel like I'll lose me."

"What do you mean?" I could tell by his face he was confused.

"I mean, what will happen to me if I marry you and then lose you?"

"Vera," he said motioning for me to sit on top of him, "I'm the pot of gold at the end of the rainbow. I'm your man and I'm with you for life."

"But you just said that you weren't going to play house with me. " I said now sitting on top of him, with my legs straddled across his thighs.

"And I mean it." He moved his hips and positing his dick under my ass. "I love the hell outta you," he said, caressing my breast, "but I have to stand for something. I love you and I want to marry you. I want you to have my last name. I want to grow old with you. I want you to have what no other woman will ever get from me, not just my baby. I wanna come home and call you Mrs. Bennet."

"Wright-Turner-Bennet." I said, enjoying his hard on.

"Three last names?" he said pulling my extra long pink *A Baby's In Here* t-shirt over my head and then unsnapping my bra, revealing my swollen 36 C's "Vera why don't you have on any underwear?"

"Because I knew you were coming home."

"Yeah right." He said feeling my ass, "Now back to the last names. I don't think I'm feeling three last names. How about, Vera Turner-Bennet?"

"No, I can't get rid of Rowanda's name."

"What about Vera Wright-Bennet?"

"No, I don't like that either. Then Aunt Cookie will have an attitude. Maybe I'll do, Vera W.T. Bennet. That sounds important."

"Yeah like an army sergeant."

I sucked my teeth, "Please."

"Please?" He smiled, "So tell me, Ms. Vera W. T. Will you marry me?"

I looked at him and fell deeper in love looking into his eyes and said, "I would marry you everyday if that's what you want."

"What do you want?" he asked, while I was taking off the top part of his scrubs and running my hands across his nipples and his nicely laid six pack

"You." I said, "And you only."

"You've got me. That's a done deal."

"Do you want a big wedding?" he asked.

"No, just you. On an island."

"What about your family? Rowanda, Dirty, Aunt Cookie, Uncle Boy, Shannon, Lee, and Angie?"

"We'll have a reception for them. The wedding will be for us. When do you want to get married?"

"I don't care what month it is, just make sure the date is the seventh."

"Why the seventh?"

"Seven is God's complete number and I want this to be right." By now, we were both naked. I was sitting on top of his hard dick, but he hadn't entered me just yet. He took my nipples and started kissing them again, going from one to the other.

"That sounds perfect." I managed to say in-between moans.

"I love you." He said laying down as I slid down on his dick. I looked him in his eyes as he moaned softly, and I said, "I love you more than you could ever imagine."

"I know you do." He said, "That's why I'ma make you my wife."

Out of Bounds

"I ain't gettin' into no mo' shit withcha girl, Lee," I said to Shannon, while helping to fix shrimp scampi and cheese puffs for the guests. "Damn if I'll be in church again." I ran my hands across my stomach as the baby started to move.

"I don't think it'll get that far," Shannon said, while placing parsley on the scampi, "We just have to figure out what's really going on with her, she hasn't been herself lately."

"Let me see," I cupped my hand behind my left ear, as if I were listening for something, "You hear that?" I asked.

"What? The chirping, it's the lil' birds outside the window over there."

"No, it's not. It's the dumb bitch alert."

"Be quiet," Shannon chuckled. "It's no secret that Jerell is playing her. Every time I turn around, they're arguing. They got the house together and just when Lee packed her things to move in with him, he told her that he didn't think them living together was such a good idea. 'Wasn't Christian-like,' he said. Especially, since he just left his wife."

"What a dumb hoe." I huffed, "Let's see, how do we spell...uhhh...stupid? Lee is all twisted up in the game. Uncle Boy said a mouth full when he said that some folks have it

133

'crooked.' Now me, if I was dumb enough to get that house in my name and then he tells me I can't live there, I would just burn the ma'fucker up! KA-BOOOOOM! BOO'YAH! Left Eye would-n't have shit on me!"

"You ain't never lied!" Shannon said shooting me a high-five, " But Vera, you know Lee is a lil' slow with men."

"Please, that's just a dumb hoe."

"Who's a stupid dumb hoe?" Angie said, walking into Shannon's kitchen. "Your guest are thirsty," Angie said, taking another bottle of Moet bottle out of Shannon's stainless steel refrigerator, "And I know ya'll was talking about Lee."

"First of all nobody said, *stupid* and *dumb*. Get it straight, I only said dumb. How do you know we were talking about Lee?" I said frowning at Angie's eavesdropping ass.

"Because she *is* dumb. Jerell treats her any way that he pleas-es and she takes it, like *oh well*. She must be thinking he's the last black man on Earth."

"Oh, he can't be the last black man on Earth," I laughed, "because then you would'a had him."

"You'se a dumb dumb." Angie laughed. "Straight stupid...but that's a good one. I'ma have to use that." Angie walked out the kitchen and immediately walked back in. "Just so ya'll know," she whispered, "The dumb bitch is here with her stupid niggah, so behave."

"Oh Lawd," I prayed, "Give me strength."

"Tell her," Shannon yelled, to Angie, "to come and help us with the cheese puffs and to bring the crab salad, that she made into the kitchen."

"No problemo!" Angie yelled back.

"Shannon, you're wearin' the hell outta that dress." I said, admiring her well fitted, Gucci dress. "I didn't know Gucci made plus sizes."

"Don't get it fucked up, cuz yo' ass lookin' a lil' chunky around the hips."

"For your information this is a size ten from Neiman's." I snapped. Humph, she just hurt my feelings with her slick fat comment.

"You're lying. That shit is from Lane Bryant, with yo overdue ass."

"Shut up." I said, "I'm sensitive about being overdue. And don't be calling me out about Lane Bryant. Actually, it's not my fault. Everyone always said that a baby takes nine months to have. They all lied. This baby been chillin' up in here for close to ten damn months."

"Vera, be quiet." Shannon chuckled.

"For real though, but don't get it confused; ten months or more, I look good." I started to break it down and hit Shannon off with some serious top model poses, so she could admire how good I looked. But instead I twirled around in my off the shoulders beaded maternity dress, with the split on the side. Twisting my lips I said, "Jealousy will get you no where."

"Whatever," Shannon laughed, "That Lane Bryant shit was funny, wasn't it?" I just her a look at her and before I could reply, Angie stomped back in the kitchen with an attitude, huffing and puffing, acting as if she wanted to explode.

"What's your problem?" Shannon asked.

"Do you know that...that *bitch*," Angie said pointing toward the door, "asked Jerell if she could come in the kitchen and he said *no*."

"What?" I smirked. "And what did she say?"

"You see she ain't in here right? Oh hell, no. I swear I'm 'bout to catch a case!" Angie said throwing punches in the air.

"Calm down." Shannon said, "Angie go sit and watch that fool. Ya'll know she a lil' slow."

"Slow or stupid?" Angie smirked.

"Bye Angie."

"I am not saving that hoe, *anymore*," I said to Shannon, as Angie left. "The dumb bitch is on her own. But I'ma tell you, if he's bossing her around while I'm standing there, I'ma kick his ass!"

"Vera be quiet. Taj'll lose his mind if you get out there fighting. Now listen, I'm thinking about breaking up with Quincy before he leaves for London."

"You must be stupid. That mofo got your bank account looking prettier than Denzell in Mo' Better Blues."

"Yeah Vera, but my heart doesn't belong to Quincy anymore."

"*My heart doesn't belong to Quincy anymore?* What kinda white-ass soap opera you been watchin'? That's some ole Erica Kane bullshit. Now hit me with the Oprahfied side, what's the real deal? Why are you in such a rush to break up with Quincy, why can't you wait for him to come back?"

"Chile for what? That crazy lookin' niggah gon' be alright."

"Crazy lookin'?" I frowned, picking the tray of shrimp scampi off the counter, "He lookin' pretty damn good to me, especially tonight. That Jack Spade suit he has on is tight. But fuck it. Give him away. The next trick is on the corner waiting."

"Wait a minute now—"

"No, no, keep messin' around and *Baby Girl*," I said sounding like Aunt Cookie, "you gon' have a new bitch slappin' her sloppy pussy on dem black balls."

"Your mouth is disgusting!" Shannon said, giving me the screw face. "Yes, Quincy is a good man. It's not him, it's me. I'm just not ready for what he's offering."

"Hey, hey now! Whatcha' workin' wit!" I heard Aunt Cookie yelling through the house. She must've just gotten here. Before I could resume my conversation with Shannon, Taj walked in.

"Aunt Cookie and Uncle Boy are here." He said.

"I'm coming…"I turned back to Shannon, once Taj left back out and said, "Be good to Quincy."

"Ms.Thing you got nerve! When is your wedding? My point exactly," she said answering her own question. *"Besides."* She stressed. "Let me break this down for you, Nile is *that niggah*. I can talk to him about anything. Quincy blows me off with a buncha, *'Uhmm hmm's'* and *'okay baby's.'* If I ask Nile for something, he'll say, 'What is it? Let me see it. No problem baby, you can have it.' If I ask Quincy for something, this niggah wanna show me a table fulla bills that he's paying for me. And to add insult to injury he'll bring me the Sunday paper and let me know when payless is having a buy one get one half off sale. I wanna say so badly, 'Do I look like Star Jones?' I don't shop at no fuckin' Payless!"

"Don't front, you know you bought them stiletto's from Payless."

"Vera please," Shannon frowned. "As I was saying, if I tell Nile, 'Nile let's fuck in the chair.' He's like, 'Okay baby, bend over.' Quincy, this missionary position-at-all-times-ma'fucker, looks at me and says, 'Shannon, the chair? That's a bit much. Let's try the floor.' Do you understand now? There's no competition."

"Damyumm…missionary position all the time?" I said, as Aunt Cookie walked into the kitchen.

"Missionary?" Aunt Cookie said with her lips tooted up, "Ya'll better get with it and start gettin' hit from the back."

Oh hell, here we go. "Okay, Aunt Cookie. We get it." I had to stop her before she went any further. I didn't wanna hear the rest of what she had to say.

"Yeah, I get it too, Baby Girl. You trying to shut me up?"

As we walked out of the kitchen, I noticed that for once Aunt Cookie looked really nice. Her blonde wig and sterling silver hoop earrings were still big as hell, but her gear was straight. She had on a nice, slightly fitted blue sleeveless dress, with a Chiffon jacket. To top it off she had on a double strand pearl necklace, with matching pearl earrings. Wow! I was impressed! So impressed, that I had to stand back and admire how beautiful she looked.

Then something caught my eye, Oh hell no...no. It can't be. Do her shoes have flashing lights in them? Are they fuckin' glittering? I must be mistaken. She had on clear Cinderella shoes, with two-inch heels and every time she took a step the entire shoe started bling-blinging like white and blue Christmas lights. Immediately, I had a headache.

"Hey, Uncle Boy!" Shannon said walking over and kissing him on the cheek. "How are you?"

"I can't call it." Uncle Boy said, "Uncle Boy just tryna keep his grind on." *Grind on?* What the hell is wrong with Uncle Boy? He looked up, saw Shannon's step-father, and made a Black Power fist as he started walking toward him. As Uncle Boy passed me, I noticed something from his shoulders seemed to be blowing in the wind. As he passed by me, I noticed he had a short velvet cape, hanging from the back of his sky blue tuxedo jacket. The white shirt he had on, had layers of ruffles going down the middle. But what killed it all, was his skintight matching tuxedo pants with the thick ass black stripes traveling down the seams on the side. The man thought he was sharp though. You couldn't tell him nothing as he did his pimp daddy strut across the floor; slapping Shannon's step father a high-five and walking toward Taj.

I could tell that Taj was speechless. He simply smiled and Uncle Boy said, "I'm sharp, niggah, what-what. Give a black man his props. Ma'fuckers been looking at me all day, admiring this shit. This is what me and Cookie wore to the Nelly concert."

"Word?" Taj smiled.

"Word up. See Taj see eye to eye. That's why you Uncle Boy niggah. Now see, had it been a little colder outside Uncle Boy would'a brought out the full length rabbit and blew all ya'll minds!"

"That's right baby," Aunt Cookie said, now standing next to Uncle Boy, "Tell 'em, don't sleep on you. Cause you always clean. Let me see you model for Chocolate Chip."

"You want me to break it down baby?"

"Do that shit Big Daddy!"

"Ahhh shit now." Uncle Boy said breaking down and bustin' out three different jailhouse poses.

I was so goddamn embarrassed I didn't know what to do. I tried to ignore them, so I turned to Shannon, who was standing next to me, "We still on for the wedding on Saturday?"

"Who's getting married again?" she asked.

"Monica. My client. Remember Lee's friend?"

"Oh yeah, that's right. I'll be there providing yo' ass is not in labor."

"Alright Shannon my feet hurt and I need to sit down." I went and sat next to Lee. Jerrell had just gone to the bathroom. I could tell in Lee's face that she was miserable, but she was too damn proud to say anything. So I asked, "You and Angie will be at the wedding on Saturday, right?"

"Monica's wedding? Yeah, we'll be there. I invited Jerrell but he didn't wanna go."

"Lee, I'ma just be straight. I wanna punch Jerell in the face."

"Vera please." Lee frowned.

Angie was sitting on the arm of the sofa, sipping on a Show Stopper. "I keep telling Lee, that just because I'm from the south, don't mean that I'm slow. I have sliced a plenty of ma'fuckers in my day."

"Angie please." Lee smirked. "Let's change the conversation...Vera, what the hell does Uncle Boy have on?"

While we were trying not to laugh at Uncle Boy flying, pass us in his cape. Jerell walked over to us, "What are ya'll talking about? You know, Lee, you always have some ole silly conversation going on. Stop being so stupid and childish."

"Oh hell no!" Angie said, looking around the room, "Somebody gon' have to hold my drink."

"Stupid?" I snapped at Jerell, "Childish? Who in na hell are you talking too?"

"Excuse me?" he rolled his eyes and turned to me. "You need to take yo' big overdue ass and waddle across the room. And you," he said pointing to Angie, "need to stay away from midgets, fuckin' with the handicap and shit."

"Big ass? Midgets?!" Angie and I said simultaneously.

"You been tellin' this asshole our business?" I stood up and got directly in Jerell's face, "Let me just set you straight, cause you got it fucked up. It doesn't matter if I'm overdue, but Angie, oh hell no, you don't need to be making fun of her. She can't help it if ole boy was a midget!"

"Whatever." Jerell snapped his fingers in a Z motion and practically rolled his eyes out his head.

I stood back, I was in shock. "Look at you, a grown ass man talking about a *whatever*! Snapping his fingers and shit! Do I smell D.L. on yo' breath? *How you doin'!*" I said with a limp wrist. "J.L. King in the house! Keep it up and see don't I call rainbow world immigration on yo' ass. Let me see ya green card, since you wanna talk trash. Fuck with me and I'll put a big ass hole in that canoe you floated in here on!"

"So now you're a bombclaude racist!" He said sucking his teeth, "You should be ashamed of yourself and her," he pointed to Angie, "needs to be embarrassed! Going on the Internet prowl and seeking out the disabled. Oh, Leola told me all about how you met Daddy-O.com. Oh, excuse me, Lil' Love on the computer and used him for some sex!"

I wanted to slap Lee in the fuckin' mouth! *"Leola Jones!"* I said, "I can't believe that you makin' fun of Angie's situation. She didn't know he was a midget at first! Angie s'pose to be your girl." Then I turned to Jerell and said, "Don't you worry about her dating a midget. She can date that roamin' eye ma'fucker if she wants to, don't you worry about it! Some people have trouble gettin' a man. You see what Lee ended up with. But you keep it up and see how I lower the boom on your ass!" I turned back to Lee, "Pastah James? Ching-Ching went the Tambourine. Ring any bells? How about the first lady and the entire congregation about to bust yo' ass! Don't you ever tell our business again!"

"Oh," Angie chuckled in disbelief, *"His ass really don't know me*...You bald headed, lil' dick, fag ass, ma'fucker! Don't be mad at me 'cause yo half-a-ball produces water! Wit' yo block head ass! Go suck your father, pussyclaude cunt! Didn't know I could cuss yo' ass out Jamaican style, did you? Ain't nobody scared of you!"

"That's right," I added, "You fuckin' mutt!"

"A mutt? Half-a-ball, produce water? Go suck my father? Excuse you?" he said to Angie.

"No, excuse you." Angie said, twisting her neck. "You heard me, pussy ass! You might talk that bull shit to Lee, but you ain't gon' get away with it over here!"

He pointed his finger and said, "Lee get yo' friends!"

"Go somewhere else and sit down." Lee said, stepping to us. "Why are ya'll always trying to ruin something for me? Mind ya business!"

Slowly, I looked this bitch up and down, I swear I was gon' tear this ma'fucker up! "Are you crazy? We s'pose to be your girls and you're acting stupid. Don't be trying to get gully with me, you better break bad with his ass."

"Get your lil' girlfriend," Lee snapped, pointing to Angie, "And step."

"Fuck ya'll!" I said walking over to Taj, who was talking to Quincy. Angie went to find Shannon.

"Excuse me Quincy," I said looking at him, he and Taj seemed to be engrossed in their conversation. I didn't wanna be rude, but I had to tell Taj. "Taj," I said rubbing my stomach, "Do you what *that negro* said to me?"

"Vera, call the man, a man. Now who are you talking about?"

"Jerell."

"Jerell? Who is that?"

"Lee's boyfriend."

"Why were you in his face to begin with?"

"I try to tell Shannon the same thing." Quincy interrupted.

I wanted to tell his ass to mind his business so bad, that I could taste it. *Trust me*, I thought to myself, *You got plenty' a shit of your own to worry about.* "Anyway," I said, slightly rolling my eyes at Quincy, "Jerell just came out the blue and told me off. I mean cussed me out! And poor Angie. He had her in tears. Lee, she's over there picking on us too. I never said nothing to either one of them."

Taj and Quincy started laughing like I was a comedian or something! "Do I look funny? Did you hear me?"

"Vera, baby. Stay out the man's face. Knowing you, you probably said something to him first. Did the man call you out of your name?"

"Almost, he had that look, like *Bitch please.*"

"Vera, please. Stay out of his face. I really don't wanna get involved. I'm having a nice conversation with my man here. Telling him about my lil' brotha's record company, Newark Illustrated. Plus I really didn't wear the right gear to be knockin' ole boy the fuck out." Taj looked over my head at Jerell. "Understand Baby?" He kissed me on my forehead.

"Uhmm hmm." I walked away and headed toward Shannon and Angie. "I'm done witcha girl." I said to Shannon.

"Lee?"

"I need some weed. I swear to God I need to get high." Angie said fixing herself a another drink.

"What?" Shannon and I said simultaneously.

"I'ma knock that niggah out." Angie was getting hyped up, throwing punches in the air. "I can almost taste it. Don't you know he's over there telling her ass off and she's standing there. I need some hydro to calm me the fuck down, 'cause I'ma box that niggah in the head and then I'ma slap her ass! I swear!"

"For what?" I asked. "She must like the shit, she's standing there taking it."

As Shannon was about to respond, Quincy started lightly banging his fork, against the Tiffany flute glass that he had in his hand. "Excuse me everyone. Excuse me…"

"Is he crazy Vera?" Shannon mumbled. "Does he know what that glass cost me?"

"Shannon, please come here." he said.

"What his ass want?" Shannon mumbled to Angie and me.

Angie and I had huge smiles on our faces. "Gon', get, Stella." Angie said.

"Yeah, he gotta grove waitin' for you." We laughed, not knowing just how funny the shit really was.

On her way over to Quincy, Shannon gave us one of those fuck you smiles, that only we could understand.

Quincy's mother, father, and two younger brothers were there. Before Quincy could continue, the doorbell rang. Uncle Boy flew pass us with his cape floating in the air, to open the door, "What up Uncle Boy?" a familiar male voice said.

"I can't call it." Uncle Boy responded, "Uncle Boy just tryna' keep his grind on." As Uncle Boy walked back into the living and dinning room area, I noticed that the man behind him was Bryce. Damn this niggah looked good. For a moment, I could hear my gold diggin' shovel calling me. Then I noticed Taj was staring dead at me. Bryce walked right over to me. "You look good as hell girl." He whispered. "Is that how your would'a looked had you kept our baby."

"What the fuck are you talking about that for?" I said to Bryce through clinched teeth but attempting to maintain a smile. "That was a long time ago. You see my man over there? You tryna get me killed or some shit?"

"Cousin!" Quincy yelled, across the room. My mouth dropped open. I had no idea that Bryce and Quincy were cousins. I walked over to Taj and held onto his arm.

"Did you know he was Quincy's cousin?" I whispered to Taj.

"Who?" Taj smirked, "You're new boyfriend? I haven't been introduced yet."

"Oh please Taj. You've never been introduced to Bryce? You don't know Bryce? That's Queen's son."

"Yeah, ai'ight. Queen's son is all he better be."

I didn't even acknowledge that. I just turned my attention back toward Quincy and Shannon.

"Ya'll know that I love this woman." Quincy said to the room filled with friends and family. He held Shannon by the waist and pulled her close. "I love you baby and I couldn't be happier in my life." As Quincy, talked Shannon made quick eye contact with me. I tooted up my lips; Shannon was on her own with that one.

Quincy continued, "You know that I'll be gone for three months but when I return I want you to be my wife." He got down on one knee, held Shannon's left hand, reach in his pocket and pulled out a two and a half carat pear shaped diamond ring.

Once Shannon got a good look at the ring, her mouth dropped open, she opened her arms wide and held hugged Quincy tight. "Yes, Baby! I'll marry you."

I looked at Angie, who gulped down the rest of her drink in one shot. That's when I noticed Lee grabbing her pocket book. She walked over to Taj and I, "I need to leave."

"What the fuck?" I mumbled.

"Vera, I just gotta go. Jerell is ready to leave. Tell Shannon I said congratulations."

"You tell her." I snapped, as she walked away.

Taj walked over to congratulate Quincy, and I found myself trying to ignore Shannon. I could tell she wanted to complain, but with the way Lee was acting, we had bigger problems to deal with. On our way out, I told Shannon that I'd see her for the wedding on Saturday.

Saturday came and Taj was preparing to leave for a weekend medical training.

"I don't want you to go." Taj said, calling a cab to take him to Penn Station. "I spoke to Rowanda and since she's able to get weekend passes, she's going to stay the weekend with you. I'll be back on Monday."

"Taj the wedding is today. Shannon's coming to get me. Plus, Lee and Angie are meeting us there." I said taking a sip of decaf.

"Vera," he said hanging up the phone, "I don't want you to go. You already know that the doctor said he may have to induce your labor. Therefore I want you close to home."

"If that's the case, then why are you leaving?"

"Because, I'm an emergency room physician and I have to take this training every year for my license. Unless you don't want me to work? I can be a scrub if you'd like."

"Ain't nobody say all that." I said talking another sip.

"Yes you did, you want me to be a scrub. Maybe I can be a sexy scrub." He squatted down with his arms folded across his chest.

"You look a hot ass mess!" I said, laughing. "Sure you ain't never had a mug shot taken?"

"You don't even wanna go there." He said grabbing a piece of bacon from the grill on the kitchen island. Then he started blowing his fingers as if the bacon was too hot to hold.

"Anyway, what am I suppose to do, if I go into labor and you're all the way in Philly?"

"The program already understands that if you call me, then I have to take the next thing outta there. In fact, the director told me that I could have the hospital helicopter come and get me, if that happens. I have it all taken care of."

"Yeah, I'm sure."

"Don't play with me Vera." He said grabbing another piece of bacon. "Stay put until I get back."

"Uhmm hmmm."

"Your mother will be here in an hour." He kissed me good-bye on his way out the door.

For it to only be, the second week in April is was hot as hell, at least 80 degrees. and since it was hot, I decided to wear my mint green sundress, with the Chiffon shawl, and rhinestone jewelry, to the forbidden wedding. I had a funny feeling that something strange was going to go down at this wedding and of course my hard headed ass was sho'nough gon be there. I slipped on a pair of mint green Marc Jacobs' open toe slides. My feet were too swollen for anything else. I called Shannon to remind her that the wedding was today. "I remember girl." Shannon said, "I was just telling Nile that we had to get out of the shower, because I had a wedding to go to. Girl, this niggah was fucking me like there's no tomorrow."

"Shannon, that's in the category of too much information."

"I know girl but listen. Last night Nile handcuffed me and ate whipped cream out my ass!"

"Oh my god, you're a hoe. What the fuck is your house the Red Light District? I can't believe he was eatin' yo' ass. What the fuck is wrong with him?"

"Well let me inform you when I started cumin' I was screaming like Kunta Kente gettin' his ass beat. I swear to God I let Nile call me Toby."

"Keep it up and Quincy gon show up out the blue and go postal."

"First of all," Quincy's in London and he lives here with *me*. Don't get it confused."

"Whatever Shannon, just get dressed so we can leave."

"I am. Anyway, Nile said that he had to get goin'. He has a business trip he has for the next two weeks."

"Shannon, I had a crazy thought, all these negroes are gone at the same time. You think maybe they're somewhere plottin' and plannin' to leave our ass?"

"Be quiet, Vera." Shannon said taking a deep breath, "Just get here within the hour. By the way, don't be slick and call yourself driving, take a cab please."

"You and Taj are getting on my nerves." I complained.

"Bye, Boo."

After I hung up, I called a cab. Walking out the door, my back started hurting a little, but I dismissed it."

I was careful about my time because I wanted to leave before Rowanda got here and started running shit for me. Its been at least a month since I've seen her and I prefer it that way.

When the cab pulled in front of Shannon's, Nile had just taken off like a bat outta hell. Shannon looked sharp in her Chanel lavender silk, and fitted dress, with a diamond shape cut in the middle of it, showing off her smooth mahogany skin. Shannon's low curly hair cut, that I'd dyed light auburn at the tips, was bangin'. On her feet, she had on lavender Chanel stiletto's that tied around her ankle with a chiffon strap. Under her arm, she carried a lavender Chanel bag, with the two embossed C's in the center. This bitch knew she was the shit!

"Damn girl," I said, getting out of the cab. "I'm scared of you."

"You're not the one that needs to worry," she said, as we got into her gold 745I and clicked our seatbelts, "It's the bride that better be on her game." She teased.

"All right *Angie*." I said sarcastically.

"Angie? I ain't Angie." Shannon laughed, "I'm working my way to becoming Aunt Cookie."

"Better cool it, Ms. O.P.P. You know that other people's property is eventually returned back to them."

When we arrived, at the hall, where the wedding was being held it was decorated black and white. The ushers, who were dressed in black tuxedos with black vest and old English ties, escorted us to our seats. Our table was located in the middle of the floor and from where we were sitting; we'd be able to get a good view of the wedding ceremony. I could only imagine that Monica must be extremely nervous. Then I started thinking about my own wedding, and imagining how nervous I would be. Angie and Lee were already seated at the table. Lee had worked my nerves so bad the other day that I really didn't wanna speak to her but Shannon kept nudging my elbow. So finally, I mumbled, "Hi Lee how are you?"

Lee rolled her eyes. "I'ma pretend that I didn't even hear that."

"Good," I snapped, "Then I don't have to speak no more." *Stank ass Be'atch!*

"Enough." Angie snapped. "Please."

I waved my hand, reached in my purse, and pulled out my checkbook. I made out the check, for Monica's wedding gift, and placed it in an envelope. Then I thought, and I hate to break ghetto, but I'ma have to call homegirl on the carpet if she walks down the aisle two hours later than what is on this invitation. Hell, I'ma have a problem with forty-five minutes, let alone a couple of hours. All I can say is, she can try it if she wants to, but every damn minute she's late, twenty dollars gets deducted from this check.

A few minutes later, the lights dimmed and the music went from Beyonce's *Dangerously In love*, to Gerald Albright's instrumental rendition of *So Amazing*. The music was absolutely beautiful.

I was so caught up in the moment, that I hadn't even noticed Shannon tapping me on the arm, "What?!" I said aggravated.

"Don't snap at me." she said seriously.

"What's wrong Shannon?" I said taking my tone down and then glancing at Lee and Angie, who had their mouths', hung open.

"The groom," she said. I could tell she was holding back tears. Immediately I started to look toward the front of the hall and peep out the groom. Oh hell no! My eyes must be playing tricks on me. "Ya'll is that who I think it is?"

"Yes." Shannon said falling back in her seat. "It's Nile."

For a moment, I'd never felt worse for a person. How could this be? I read Monica's invitation and the guy's name wasn't Nile. It was Anthony McNilen James. Oh, shit, I said to myself, *McNilen* that's when my heart sank for Shannon.

"Shannon, I'm sorry." She seemed to wanna break down and cry, that pissed me the fuck off. "Don't you drop not one tear!" I said to her.

"Not even a half a one." Angie added.

"See," Lee interjected, "This is the shit that happens when karma gets involved. Ya'll really need to learn the art of being faithful."

"I'ma stab you!" I grunted at Lee.

Lee patted Shannon on the hand. "Don't cry."

"I'm not, I got this." Shannon said clearing her throat, "I'm just trying to get my shit together."

"Yeah you do that, because revenge is sweet." I snapped.

"And a divafied scorn is a bitch." Angie countered.

All during the ceremony, Shannon collected herself. By the time the pastor got to the part, "...Does anyone see fit as to why this couple shouldn't be married..." I had already downloaded my cell phone to sing, *Congratulations*, by Vesta Williams.

The Divas and I, including Lee, who eventually started to get pissed off at the fact that Nile had straight played our girl, had already practiced the Ms. America smiles and waves that we were going to lay on his ass when the phone rang. And suddenly like a thief in the night, BOOM! Wouldn't you know it, as soon as the preacher said, "Speak now or forever hold your peace..." the cell phone alarm went off. Hot damn and who turned around staring dead in our face, you got it, ole boy. Oh hell yeah, it was on!

Nile looked as if he wanted to pass the fuck out. During the rest of the ceremony, he kept looking at Shannon; and every time he would look, she would shoot him a Miss America smile and wave. Monica was so stupid that she didn't know any better. I was pissed that I had DeAndre hook the bitch's hair up. But then I started to feel sorry for her dumb ass.

Shannon wiped her eyes a couple of times, as Nile said his vows and then kissed his bride. "Quincy lookin' better and better, ain't he?" I whispered to Shannon.

"When you get Nile alone, " Lee mumbled, "Tell that niggah off. That sick bitch!"

After the ceremony was over and the bridal party had taken their pictures, the reception began. The coordinator introduced the wedding party and then came the part where people could make a toast. This is the part that I've been waiting on.

"Ching-Ching-Ching" went the glass that I was tappin' on. "We have something to say," I announced. Nile just about lost control. I looked at Shannon and said, "You want me to set the cell phone for background music.

"Don't worry, "Shannon said, winking at Nile, "I got this."

"You better work that shit too, girl!" Angie said.

"First of all," Shannon said, standing up, looking the bride up and down and then the groom, "You all will never know what it means to be here today. God works in mysterious ways..."

Don't ask me how, but some kinda-way the cell phone started singing Congratulations by Vesta, as Shannon started talking. I grabbed the phone off the table but it just so happen that the phone was stuck on repeating the tune. I looked at one of the guest sitting at the table with us and said, "Some phones just have a mind of their own."

"I have known Nile," Shannon continued, "for some years now and he has been er'thang to me." she said, sounding Ebonically correct. "To the bride I wish you the best of luck. May your husband never cheat and always be there when you call him. I'll try and be sure to kept my phone on the hook, to be sure that you get through. Be Blessed." As Shannon sat down, she slammed me a high-five. Others made toast, but who knows what they were saying. I was too busy taking my damn check outta the envelope. As we went to leave, the bride and groom were coming around to greet their guest. When they got to our table, Nile was looking directly at us. "Oh dear," Shannon said to Monica, "You are so beautiful."

Then she said to Nile, as she grabbed his hand, "Boy you know you look good. But this isn't what you had on this morning? Or was it? By the way, what's that red spot on your neck?" Monica looked around on Nile's neck. Damnyumm, Stevie Wonder would've been able to see that pink ass passion mark on his neck, just slightly covered by the collar. By the time Shannon moved the collar back, the passion mark was fully exposed.

"Oh boy," Shannon said, placing Monica's hand on Nile's shoulder, "You better cover that up."

Nile played it cool, though, because he didn't even flinch as Monica straightened up his collar. Then he seemed to get agitated and pushed Monica's hand down, "Stop it." He said.

"Trouble in Paradise?" I said, as we rose to leave.

"Listen," Shannon said, as we stood up, "Monica I'm going to give you some advice." Shannon bent over and whispered in Monica's ear, loud enough so that we could hear it, "Be sure to have Nile go to the doctor and get that mole in the middle of his left ass cheek, looked at. It's changing shapes, and you know skin cancer is on the rise." Shannon took a step back smiled, "Smooches."

As we turned to leave I started thinking, that I need to have a talk with this crazy broad, saying that shit to bride. Doesn't she see all these big ass bridesmaids? As soon as I thought that, I felt a swift wind. When I turned, it seemed as if four fists started flying outta nowhere! Holy Shit. All I could see was Monica's head boppin' and Shannon knockin' the shit out of her, "I will whip yo' ass bitch!" Shannon yelled, "You gon' try and sneak me on the way out the door! I ain't the one you need to be fighting! You need to kick his ass!"

Ain't that just like a stupid ass bitch! Almost immediately, Monica's family rushed toward the fight. Angie started jumping up and down, pushing the bell sleeves of her dress back and screaming, "Oh hell no! Lets be 'bout 'bout it!"

Nile jumped in the middle of Shannon and Monica, breaking them apart. But not even his 6'3", 240 pound frame could contain them. Before he could get a good hold of Monica, Shannon had snatched her ass and placed her in a headlock. Then it seemed that about fifty people rushed toward us.

Lee was standing there saying, "I can't believe they're fighting! I can't get in that, my face gonna be all messed up!"

"Punk ass bitch!" I mushed Lee in the head.

Angie jumped dead on whoever called themselves jumping Shannon from the back. Surprisingly, Lee ran over toward the fight, got a good look, at the bride's face, punch the shit out of her and said, "Oh God, who did that?"

Nile jumped back in the middle of Monica and Shannon, "You were fuckin' that bitch!" Monica yelled! "I can't believe this!"

"Yeah bitch," Shannon said, "he was and ask him how the crack of my ass taste! You might've thought he had a milk mustache, but think again, cuz that's me all over his lips bitch! Just know my ass hole is sweet! And everyday he's not with you, just know whose ass he's licking!" Monica reached for Shannon again.

The entire hall was in an uproar! The next thing I know Angie was fuckin' up Monica and Shannon was slapping Nile in the face! That's when Lee ran back toward the fight, got another good look, and snuck Monica's ass again. Nile looked as if he wanted to hit Shannon back, and I know I was wrong, but I had to get a lil' somethin' in there. Ain't nobody gonna hit a pregnant woman, so I took my fist and pounded this niggah in the head. Teach him to fuck with my girl!

"Everybody put their hands up!" yelled the police and the reception hall security. "What the hell is going on here?" The police yelled, "This is supposed to be a wedding, not summer slam!" That's when Monica reached for Shannon again, and ended up punching the officer in the face. She punched him so hard, that he started stuttering. But what he did manage to say was, "Everybody's under arrest!"

The next thing I know, me, Lee, Angie, Shannon, Nile, Monica, the bridesmaids and two of the groomsmen, that were trying to break it up, were all handcuffed and shackled together like common criminals.

I couldn't believe that this was happening to me. Here I was overdue and on my way to jail. I looked at Shannon, "You didn't see all those bridesmaids, bitch? You couldn't just make the toast and be out. Naw, you had to break bad and show yo' ass."

"Shut up! Vera," she said. "Just be quiet."

It took two officers to help me into the paddy wagon. All I

could think about was how Taj is gon' kick my ass when he finds out.

When I got to the station, I wanted to bang my head against the wall; it was the same precinct that Roger worked in. Before I could even complete my thought, there was Roger, staring at me. My heart jumped in my throat as I thought about how he placed a gun to my head. "To what do I owe this special occasion?" Roger asked, running his hands across my cheeks.

"Get off of me." I jerked my head away from his sweaty hand.

"Get off of you? You weren't signing that tune when you were playin' me."

"Roger, do I look like I wanna argue with you?"

"No." he said looking me up and down, "You look like you wanna go into labor any moment. How about I push you to the point where you go in labor and then I have social services take your baby and place it in the garbage."

At that moment, I felt like I could spit on him. I felt myself losing control as I started cursing Roger out. That's when Shannon stepped to Roger, who was now walking us to the holding cell. "You stank ass ma'fucker! I can't wait to report your ass!"

Lee, was already sitting next to Angie, and crying so bad that her nose started bleeding. Meanwhile, Angie kept saying to us, "Did ya'll see how I cold copped that bitch!"

"Captain," one of the officers yelled at Roger, "You wanna release them on their own recognance?" he said pointing to us.

"Uhmmm, let me see." Roger said slamming the cell shut.

"You ain't got to see shit for me." I said to Roger, "You think you got away with putting a gun to my head, but I'ma fix yo' ass!"

The other officer looked at me like I was crazy, "Vera, do you think you're in the position of threatening me?" Roger said tightlipped.

"Fuck you!" I said.

"I gave you that opportunity, but you didn't rise to the occasion."

"That's because you just *couldn't* rise to the occasion."

Lee looked at me and mouthed, "Shut the fuck up!"

"Vera, you still talk a lot of shit." Roger asked. "I got a good mind to send you off so you can see what they think of a pregnant woman on Riker's Island." Roger turned to the officer, "Get their paper work together for their release. But only on one condition, they have to be released into someone's custody." Roger cut his eyes at me. "Let's go call ya man."

This Negro was crazy ass hell. When he walked me to the phone, I dialed Aunt Cookie's number. Damn she would have a block on the phone. Oh yeah, Rowanda...but shit, she doesn't have any keys to my house, so how will I call her? Dammitt! I started rubbing my forehead. My back was starting to ache. I broke down and called Taj's cell phone.

"Vera," Taj said, "Why am I pressing two and accepting a collect call from you."

"Cuz...what had happened was...uhhh..."

"Vera," Taj said nice and slow, "Baby, don't tell me you're in jail. When I left you earlier you were so cute, all pregnant, feet all big, nose all wide, providing me with everything that I needed to keep me sane. So please...I'm beggin' you, Vera Wright-Turner, don't make me black out."

"Well...I won't tell you I'm in jail, I'll just say that by the time you get down here we may have a bail."

"What the fuck did you say?!" Taj screamed in my ear.

"I was arrested, " I mumbled.

"Oh hell no! What? Where are you?"

"In the precinct downtown."

"I swear to God Vera, if this is behind some stupid shit, I'ma mush yo' ass in the head! I'll get the hospital's helicopter to come and get me."

"How long is that suppose to take?" I snapped, "What, you think we should sit here for fuckin' ever?!"

"We? I should'a known!"

"Yeah." I said quietly,

"Don't get quiet now." Taj snapped, "You so fuckin' bad! Gettin' arrested and shit and then we? Tell me, Vera, who's we?"

"Me...Shannon..." I mumbled.

"Speak up Vera!"

"Lee...and Angie..."

"I'll be damn Vera. The game ya'll playin' needs to be over."

"What is that suppose to mean?"

"All of ya'll get arrested and at the same time? Then who's going to get who outta jail. Somebody gotta always walk with the bail money."

"Whatever, Taj. How long before you get here?"

"I'll get there when I get there! You should'a thought about that before you and your friends got arrested. Sit in the goddamn bullpen and think about this shit. Vera, I'm telling you now, if you fuck around and have my baby in jail, you and I are fin-ished!" He hung up.

When Roger brought me back to the bullpen, I looked at Shannon and said, "Don't even speak to me."

Within the hour Roger got up from behind his desks, watching me, and said, "I just got a call from the front desk, ole boy is here."

Roger brought Taj to the back. The back of the precinct was an open space where the bullpen was surrounded by various hard wooden desk and a mini counter with a computer.

I just shook my head. Fuckin' jail, I really couldn't believe this! I was so embarrassed that I didn't know what to even think, let alone do. I was just praying that Roger released us and then left me the fuck alone. I was too afraid to say anything, especially knowing what he was capable of. I could see the hurt on his face when he looked at me and saw that I was pregnant. Please God just let me get out of this.

Taj came rushing toward the cell. Once he spotted me, I turned my head. I had to bring myself to look at him. As Taj went to say something Roger pulled him by the arm and escorted him further into the back. A nearby officer gave Roger a strange look.

"He's on that shit again." The officer looked at his partner who walked up.

"That's one crazy mother fucker." The second officer said.

"For real though."

"Why you got me back here man?" Taj asked Roger. "Let me just pay the bail and release them. What's the point of having them in the cell like that and shit. They're harmless." The way Taj was talking to Roger I knew he had no idea who Roger was. A part of me was relieved.

"Harmless? Yeah, well, tell that to the bride, the bridal party, and the groom that they fucked up."

"Bride? Groom?" Taj shot my ass such a look that I knew

instantly that our conversation from earlier was playing in his mind. Taj let out a deep breath and took out a wad of cash from his pocket. "You got that man, what's the bail?"

"I'm releasing them," Roger smirked, "but I'm telling you if you keep trying to front on me? This shit is over."

Taj looked at Roger like he was crazy, "Excuse me? Front you? On what? You got something for me to front you on? I just said I'm bailing all of 'em out. Problem with that?"

"I don't give a damn who you bail out, but you need to be worried about me."

"All right man. What about you?"

"I'm Captain Roger Simms. I know you know my name, bruh."

Taj's left jaw started thumpin'. I could tell that he had to swallow some of what he wanted to say and how he really felt. Not one to cause a scene Taj looked at Roger and nonchalantly said, "Your point?"

You could tell in Roger's face that Taj's response took him for a loop. "What you say?"

"Listen man, what's up?" Taj said pointing and elevating his voice, getting some of the other officer's attention. "This is some retarded shit. For real. I'm tired, I'm aggravated, and now I gotta get four grown ass women outta jail, for some shit that should've never happened in the first place. So please, I'ma say this as nice as I can, stop fuckin' with me."

"Oh I ain't started yet." Roger got a solemn look on his face. "I'm Roger Simms. I took that bitch in and loved her and she left me for you!"

"I don't know any bitch, so fall back. Now, what's the bail?"

Two police officers stepped over to the escalating argument, "Problem?" one of them asked.

"I'm straight Officer." Taj turned to Roger, "You good, Bruh?"

"I'm not your ma'fuckin' bruh! So shut the fuck up, unless you want yo' ass beat?"

"The ass beatin' you plan for me, make sure it doesn't turn out to be the one planned for you." Taj said.

"Hold the fuck up—"

"No, you hold the fuck up, cause right about now, you takin' it there. Now *look*, if you're releasing them on their own recognance then do it, otherwise call the judge."

"You threatening me?"

"This niggah is crazy, when did I threaten you?" Taj said looking at the other officers.

"Oh you threatening me? Roger walked over to the counter to where the computer was, "This punk ass is testin' me." Roger took out his gun, laid it on the counter, and pointed it toward Taj. My heart was jumping in my chest. The other officers were looking at Roger like he was crazy.

"Captain Simms," one of the officers, said with his hand on his own gun as if he felt unsafe himself. "What are you doing?"

"This niggah testin' me." Roger said. "Don't be mad, *Taj*, because I had a taste of that fat pussy long before you."

Taj chuckled in disbelief, "You're just an old and disrespectful motherfucker. But I tell you what, the way I see it, you couldn't taste no pussy if it came in a jar."

Roger picked up his gun and pointed it toward Taj.

"What the fuck are you doing?!" One of the officers yelled at Roger.

For a moment, that station seemed paralyzed. I started screaming, "Taj! Taj!" Lee was bent over holding her stomach in pain.

Angie, who was sitting next to her, was in shock. "This can not be happening," she mumbled. Shannon couldn't believe it either.

"Vera," she said, "just calm down please.

"Fuck calm down!" I yelled. I was holding onto the bars of the cell, desperate for Roger to stop.

While Roger was pointing the gun and telling Taj how much he hated me for ruining his life, another officer was sneaking up behind Roger, with his gun pointed. Then there was another officer stooped down on the floor with his gun drawn. As Roger went to get a grip on his aim, the officer behind him put the gun to the side of his thigh, so that Roger couldn't see it. He placed his hand on Roger's shoulder and quietly said, "Captain Simms…Don't do it. Please, don't ruin your life. Come on man. We can get you some help."

Tears started to stream down Roger's face, as he looked at Taj. He broke down. "You don't understand. I love that girl. I sit outside her house late at night. I sleep in my car across the street from her shop and still she doesn't notice me. Do you know how many nights I prayed that she would have a baby by me? And nothing." Roger started to cry and looked down. That's when the officer tried to reach his hand over Roger's shoulder.

"What are you doing?" Roger asked.

"Please give me the gun, Captain."

Roger kept blinking his eyes. Looking at me and then at Taj. The officer that was ducked down on the ground with his gun pointed, jumped up, and tried to grab Roger's gun.

As he did that, Roger's gun went off! "Taj!" I screamed, "Oh my God!"

Roger started shaking, threw his gun down, and screamed, "What did I do?!"

Suddenly Taj and the officer standing next to him both fell to the ground. My heart stopped!

"Damn this shit stings!" The officer laying on top of Taj yelled. He stood up as best he could and revealed a bulletproof vest. At the same time, an army of officers swarmed down on Roger.

Taj was pushed to the ground by the officer who was shot and from what I could see Taj wasn't hurt. Roger started kicking and screaming. It took three officers, in riot gear, to take him out.

An hour later the girls and I were released, the officer that let us pulled me aside. "You're not the first woman he's done this to, but I'll see to it that you're the last."

Before we left precinct, Taj and I got a restraining order against Rodger in the hopes that we would never have to see him again.

Time Out

I kept trying to tell Taj how much pain I was in, but he wouldn't hear anything that I had to say. He was still upset by all that had just happened with Roger. We had already dropped Angie and Lee off at home. Shannon, who was sitting in the backseat, was catching an attitude with Taj, because she could see the pain on my face.

"Taj—" I said.

"Be quiet! Vera!" Taj said, "I don't wanna hear it!"

"Taj!" Shannon yelled. "Would you listen, damn! She's having your fuckin' baby."

I started crying and screaming, "My back is killing me and my water just broke. You're sitting here telling me to shut up!"

Taj got an apologetic look on his face. He looked at me, and then he looked down at the floor of his truck where my water had just broken. "Oh shit, I'm so sorry baby, it's time."

First, Taj called my doctor and then Aunt Cookie and Uncle Boy, so that they could meet us at the hospital.

When we arrived, I was taken straight to the delivery room. My OBGYN came in, checked me, and saw that I was already fully dilated. The doctor couldn't believe that I had labored for so long, without being in the hospital. I was too far-gone for any medication. Once the doctor told me that, I felt like the pain became more intense.

"The baby seems a little stressed." The doctor said, "I want to prepare you for delivery, but I have to be honest with you, if at any time I feel that the delivery is too stressful for the baby then I'm going to have to do an emergency C-section." I started to cry. I felt like the baby was literally falling out. I wanted to push so badly, but couldn't.

"Don't push," the doctor, said, "When you feel a contraction, I want you to hold you head to your chest, push while counting to ten, and then stop."

Taj held my hand and coached me the whole time. On the fifth push, I heard a cry. Taj gave me a huge smile, "It's a girl, Vera!"

"Would you like to cut the cord Dr.-, excuse me, I mean Daddy?" The doctor asked handing Taj the scissors.

"I would love to." Taj cut the cord and the nurse held the baby up so that I could see the her. She was covered in a little blood but she was still beautiful. The nurse weighed her, cleaned her, wrapped her in a blanket and handed her to me. Instantly all of this started to feel surreal. It was a feeling that I've never felt before, it was as if all of the anxiety that I had inside of me was now gone. Now I'm overwhelmed with love, a love that I have never felt before. Now on April 17th at 2:11 a.m. I was now someone's mother. I felt like I had finally been given the chance to exhale and let go of the aggression that was living in me for 32 years.

I looked in my baby's face and saw Rowanda. I couldn't believe that she looked so much like my mother. Coal black hair, melted caramel skin, with a darker shade of chocolate around the edge of her ears. I think she's going to be the same color as her daddy. She had Rowanda's eyes, nose, and tooted up lips. Taj stroked her hair. "Look at my baby."

The doctor and the nurse that were in the room, told us that they would be back in an hour to take the baby to the nursery for some newborn tests. I panicked, "Is there something wrong?"

"No, baby." Taj said, "newborn test are standard procedure."

When they left, Taj was still amazed by his daughter. "I can't believe I'ma daddy. Vera, look at my baby."

"Yes, you're a daddy…You know we never settled on the name." I said to him, while looking at the baby. For a moment, everything that we had been through was gone.

"How about Skyy Imani?" Taj suggested,

"Let me see," I said holding her 7 pound, 8 ounce body. Do you look like a Skyy?" The baby's eyes were wide open and she was looking at me, like she was wondering who I was. "I'm your mommy." I said to the baby, then I started to smile, "Skyy Imani Bennet, I love you so much." I could tell that Taj wanted to hold her, so I said, "Lil' Miss Bennet, go to your daddy."

Taj started laughing, "Vera," he said taking Skyy into his arms. "I think, I must be the happiest man in the world, right now. And I would do it all over again, if I knew that this very moment is where I would end up." Taj sat on the edge of the hospital bed, "She's beautiful Vera. Thank you." I laid my head against the side of his arm and looked at our daughter, "Yes, Taj, she is beautiful."

Four Point Play

Skyy and I stayed in the hospital for three days before we were discharged. Taj picked us up and when we got home, there was a banner hanging over the front door that read: "Welcome Home Skyy!" When Taj opened the door, everybody jumped out and yelled, "Surprise!" In the background, McFaden and Whitehead's "Ain't No Stopping us Now" was playing.

Ms. Betty, walked over to me first, "Let me see what we have here." She took the baby out of my arms, while kissing me on the cheek. I still could barely stand her ass, but for the baby's sake, I would tolerate her.

There were pink balloons and streamers floating throughout the room. Aunt Cookie, Uncle Boy, Rowanda, Dirty, Dirty's son, Jamal, Lee, Angie, Shannon, DeAndre, Rosa, Mr. Bennet, Taj's brother, Sharief, sister Samira, and his niece Tay-Tay, were all laughing and having a good time as I walked in slowly, still sore from labor.

"Show me whatcha' workin' wit', Baby Girl." Aunt Cookie said walking over and squeezing me on my shoulders. She mumbled, "Don't forget we need to talk. I wanna know when you gettin' married." *Damn, I'm just getting home from the hospital and she's starting all ready.*

"Cookie," Uncle Boy said, "Leave the girl alone. She just had a baby. Damn."

"Oh, hold it." She said to Uncle Boy holding her index finger up, "This is an A and B conversation and you need to C your way out of it."

"Whatever," he said nixing her off, "I got food on the stove, any how." Uncle Boy started walking away. "Taj, my man, what you call yourself doin?" he yelled.

Taj was standing and looking at the stereo. "Uncle Boy," he said, "How is the music coming from the speakers but the CD player isn't hooked up?"

"CD player?" Uncle Boy smirked, "Taj, that ain't no CD player, that's an eight track."

I was so embarrassed, but of course, Uncle Boy was proud. He walked toward the kitchen with his long bell-bottom jeans on and his black polyester shirt, half way open. The hairs on his chest were sticking out just a little and hanging from his neck was a sterling silver chain with a cross on it. He was snapping his fingers, and humming a tune. Uncle Boy slid toward the kitchen, with a 1977 pimp daddy strut. The strut where one leg is dipped and one arm is thrown back as if he's fighting off a cool breeze. Just as he got to the kitchen door, the hook of the song started to play. Uncle Boy threw his arms in the air, and sang, *"No stoppin'…no stoppin'…there'll be no stoppin'….Heyyy!"*

All I could do was shake my head, walk away, and sit down, placing my feet on the couch. Shannon was now holding Skyy and walking toward me. She bent down and kissed me on the cheek. "Girl," she said, "This baby lookin' every bit like Rowanda."

"Uhmm hmm," Angie said walking over, "Girlfriend, we might need to give Rowanda a blood test and make sure that she didn't have this baby."

"I know." I said to them, "That's all everyone's been saying for the past three days."

"Don't worry," Lee, said, flopping down on the couch next to me, and knocking my feet to the floor, "Rowanda is beautiful."

"Yeah she is," I said, looking at the side of Lee's face; she had a bruise on her left cheek. "Lee what the hell happened to your face?"

"Nothing," she said looking away.

"What do you mean nothing?"

Shannon and Angie were standing there with a dumb look on their face. "Oh ya'll niggahs can't talk now? For some ole bullshit, ya'll mouths are flappin' but now I don't hear a word."

"All right," Lee said, taking a deep breath. "Jerell and I got into a fight."

"A fight?" I frowned.

"Actually, I started it."

"Now, I know you're lying because you're a punk. You won't even fight a female, let alone box a man. I'ma tell you what, although I just had my daughter and if I have to get on my grind and do some time for fuckin' up your boyfriend you better be prepared for that niggah to die."

"Vera, please. You and Skyy just came home from the hospital don't start."

Shannon, who obviously didn't wanna talk about Lee, sat on the arm of the couch, "So, Divas, does this mean that we're grown? Since we're having babies and shit."

"Well," Lee said, looking at us with her face twisted up, "Technically, you three could have been grown a couple of times, but we won't talk about that."

I just looked at Lee and shook my head. Some things never change.

"Whatever Lee," Shannon snapped, "Vera, DeAndre, and Rosa are dying for you to open their gifts, so you may as well open them."

I started with an envelope that contained a note. The note read: *Thank you for allowing me to be a part of Skyy's life. Please let her wear this with pride.* When I looked up Rowanda was standing there with a light spring jacket on. She must've just come in, because Uncle Boy was shutting the front door.

"It was your dress, when you were a baby. I hope you don't mind." Rowanda said. I couldn't help but cry. Rowanda walked over and hugged me tight, squeezing the box between us. "Don't cry baby. Don't cry." she said. I wiped my eyes and squeezed her hand.

Aunt Cookie was so busy being slick and smiling in Mr. Bennet's face, that she didn't hear me announce to everyone that she and Uncle Boy had bought all the furniture in the baby's nursery.

The girls gave me saving bonds, money, and three tall Bloomy Baby boxes filled with clothes. Skyy seemed to have enough clothes to last her for years.

Taj's family gave Skyy a stroller, walker, high chair, rocking chair, clothes, and crib bedding. Ms. Betty was so busy bragging about the gifts they had given; she didn't even notice how she was being swindled out of her man.

After we were done with the gifts, the girls made me wear that silly Baby Shower hat as they took pictures. Finally, it was time to eat. Taj told me that Uncle Boy and Rowanda had been here earlier and cooked the food. They both set the table and fixed everyone a plate of fried fish, baked chicken, potato salad, crab salad, collar greens, candied yams, cornbread, and Red Velvet cake for dessert. Once they were through fixing the plates of food, and everyone was getting their eat on and laughing, Rowanda came to me and asked if she could hold Skyy. "Of course." I said. She walked over to Taj, who was holding the baby. Taj placed a bottle of breast milk, that I'd pumped at the hospital, in Skyy's mouth and then took it out. Causing her to cry. He handed her to Rowanda. Rowanda placed Skyy on her shoulder and patted her back. She took the bottle from Taj's hand

and went to sit in a remote corner of the living room and placed Skyy in the crook of her arms and started feeding her.

Uncle Boy grabbed his plate and eased over to where Aunt Cookie and I were sitting on the couch eating. I was listening to Aunt Cookie's, *"Don't have more than one baby and ain't married"* speech. Uncle Boy had a serious look on his face. He tried to nudge Aunt Cookie on the arm without me seeing him. Every time I peeped up at him, he just smiled. He nudged Aunt Cookie again. "What do you want?" she asked him, obviously, annoyed.

"Cookie," he tried to whisper, "You see Rowanda holding the baby?"

"Yeah, Boy," Aunt Cookie said agitated.

"You see her right?" He said again, while looking around.

"Yeah, goddamit, I see her, why?"

"Good," he said, looking over his shoulder, "You keep an eye on her, while I go hide the Hefty Cinch sacks and the garbage cans."

"Boydon Brown!" Aunt Cookie said, "Get the fuck away from me!"

For the entire time that Rowanda held Skyy, Uncle Boy wouldn't take his eyes off of her. He managed to step away for a minute and go into the kitchen. Then he came back out and seemed to be enjoying himself.

A few hours after every one had been at the house and the baby shower started to wind down, Taj started cleaning up, in the kitchen. "Anybody seen the garbage can?" he yelled.

Aunt Cookie shot Uncle Boy a look, "No you didn't, niggah!"

"Taj, my man." Uncle Boy said, "Let Uncle Boy hollah at you for a minute."

As everyone started to leave and kiss us goodbye, Rowanda continued to sit in the corner holding Skyy. She had changed her pamper, burped her, brushed her hair, and played with her hands and feet. This was the first time since Rowanda came out of her in-patient rehab program that she seemed to be in so much peace. Dirty and his son, who had given me $200 for the baby, walked over to where Rowanda was and they both kissed her on the forehead. "See you when you get home." Dirty said. Then he walked over to me, "You should'a had a baby a long time ago, if this is what it took to make us a family again." I gave Dirty a tight hug and then he left.

Angie, Shannon, and Lee all left together. "I'll be over here tomorrow." Shannon said on her way out the door, "Don't tell ya other two girlfriends." I had to laugh, because little did she know, but Lee and Angie had already told me the same thing. "Trust me. I won't say a word." I looked at Shannon and smiled. Aunt Cookie, Uncle Boy, and Taj's family left next.

Once everyone was gone, Taj came over to me, "Baby, I need to run to the hospital and get some of my things that I left in my locker. Especially since I'll be on paternity leave for a couple of weeks." He smiled.

"No problem," I said, trying to stand up, after sitting in the same spot all day. "We'll be here."

"You better be." He said chuckling on his way out.

When he left, I saw that it was just me, Rowanda, and Skyy. Rowanda walked over to where I was. She placed Skyy in my arms, "I couldn't have asked for anything more than this."

"Really?"

"Yes, Vera. Girl, you just don't know," she said. "Sometimes I look around and I can't believe that I walked around high for so long. Especially, when I think about all that, I've missed out on. I know that it'll take some time for us to be close, but I wanna be close to you and I wanna watch Skyy as she grows."

"As long as you do the right thing, we won't have a problem."

"Vera, I plan on doing the right thing. I've been clean for months now and it ain't been easy. But I've been doing it, one day at a time. I wanna ask you something."

"What's that?"

"Let me keep the baby for you, when you go back to work."

"Rowanda, my baby will never step foot in Lincoln Street projects."

"Vera, Dirty moved last week to a small apartment in Spanish Harlem. Just a train ride away. I could stay with you during the week and go home on the weekends. I just stared at her. When she saw that I didn't have an answer right away, she changed the subject.

Rowanda and I spent so much time together, laughing and joking. She helped me with the baby and for once in my life, I felt like I had the mother that I've always wanted. When the night was over, we both agreed on her keeping the baby for me.

Boxing Out

I'd stayed home with Skyy until she was three months old. It was now the middle of July and this was my first day back at the shop. And I'm not quite sure how I feel about that. I'm sad because I feel like I'm going to be missing something special that Skyy may do. But on the other hand I feel like if I stayed in the house any longer I was gon' die. Finally, I can talk to adults instead of walking around, placing milk on the back of my hand, testing the temperature, whipping out my tittie every five minutes, waiting for Skyy to go to sleep and then checking to make sure she's breathing. Jumping every time she sneezes and shit like that.

In all honesty, I'm happy to be back at my shop although, part of me is uncertain about leaving my baby with my mother. How can I trust her when she got high all of my life? I know I'm dead wrong, but yesterday, I had Bryce come and hook up two small cameras for me. One in the baby's nursery and one in the living room. I didn't tell Taj, because I know he can't stand Bryce. Also, I didn't wanna hear his mouth; not about the video cameras, but about Bryce. The shop's computer controlled the cameras, so I could watch Rowanda and the baby while I worked.

At home, I checked the cameras to make sure they were working. I had already called DeAndre to tell him to call me when he saw me on the computer screen. As I went to stand up in the chair, he called. "Hey Diva!"

"Hey Dre!"

"I see you Vera."

"Good then it works. I'll be there as soon as Rowanda gets here." I hung up. Skyy started crying and as soon as I picked her up, the doorbell rang. It was Rowanda. Holding Skyy in my arms, I walked Rowanda around the house. In the kitchen, I opened the fridge. "Here's her bottles and the two in the corner are her cereal bottles. Her pampers are in the living room in the wicker basket, the little cartoon character goes in the front. When you give her the bottle, you have to stick it between her lips and wait for her to pull on the nipple. That how you know she's eating. Another thing all of Taj's and my numbers are on the refrigerator, see, this is how you dial on the phone..."

"Vera," Rowanda said, reaching for Skyy. "Stop, while you're ahead. Goodbye."

I bit the corner of my lip and took a deep breath, "Okay, I'm leaving but I'll call you in an hour."

When I walked in the shop, there was DeAndre, dressed in beige linen pants, a beige fitted tee and dancing to a serious club mix on the CD player. Rosa was washing Cherise's hair. Cherise, Biggie's ex-girlfriend, was still very close with my family.

I was so happy to see them that I didn't know what to do.

"Damn ya'll," I yelled "Can a Diva get a group hug!"

"My niggah ya'll!" DeAndre yelled, "Niggahhhh!" he said sounding like the foster mother in *Antwan Fisher*, "You come home niggah!"

"You so stupid," I said playfully mushing him on the side of his head.

"Ma'mi," Rosa screamed, "Look at cho, ma'misita. You look'a good. Almost like de Rosa. Heyyy!" Cherise sat up in the chair and Rosa came over and gave me a hug.

"Vera!" Cherise said, amped as hell, "A bitch is too glad to see you, these mofo's been losing their minds since you been gone! One time I walked up in here and there was a fish fry goin' on."

"What?" I said looking at DeAndre and turning the computer on. When the picture came up, Rowanda was kissing Skyy on the forehead and telling her how much she loved her. "Nana's boom, boom, boom!" Rowanda was saying. At this point, Skyy was starting to get fat and she had a double chin when she smiled. "You're mother don't think so," Rowanda said, "But you look just like she did, when she was a baby." Skyy started crying and Rowanda started pacing the floor with her.

"Vera!" Cherise yelled, "You need to be shot, you got a goddamn low jack on yo' baby and shit. See, a bitch like you don't ever need to leave your kid. Rowanda gon' cuss your ass out, if she find out that you're recording her. Oh, that's fucked up."

I shot Cherise a look. "You want your hair done up in here?"

"Vera, now you know you're wrong."

"Be quiet." I said motioning her to sit down in my chair. I started combing through Cherise's hair to see what style I wanted to put it in. Skyy was screaming at the top of her lungs. "Oh hold up." I walked over to the screen. "Rowanda," I knocked on the screen, "Skyy is crying…See," I said to DeAndre, "Oh hell no, I gotta go and get my baby."

"Calm down Diva." As he said that, Rowanda walked back into the room where Skyy was, "You were raising all that sand. Nana, had to go to the bathroom, Boom-Boom." She cooed, now holding Skyy.

"Oh," I laughed, relieved. "She had to go to the bathroom ya'll."

"Uhmm hmm," They all said, looking at me out of the corner of their eyes.

"Anyway," Cherise said, changing the subject, "I see ya girl's man got a lil' spot over on Avenue D. with his *new* girl."

"What are you talking about, Cherise?" Deciding that I would corn twist her hair, with zigzag parts, going straight back.

"Ole girl." Cherise said. "Lee."

"What do you mean his new girl? He's with Lee."

"Please Vera," Cherise said, twisting her lips. Her face got serious. "Damn, Vera, Rowanda 'bout to drop the baby." I whipped my head around so fast I almost got whiplash. When I looked, Rowanda was in the living room changing Skyy's pamper. "Made you look!" Cherise said, falling out laughing. "Siked yo' mind!"

I took my comb out and slapped the shit outta of her, in the back of her head. "Stop fucking with me! Now tell me about Lee."

Just as I said that Lee came through the door. She walked over and gave me a kiss on the cheek. She spoke to everyone else by name and when she got to Cherise she just said a dry ass, "Hi."

"Vera," Lee said, "I just came by to drop off these outfits for my goddaughter."

"Thank you, Lee." I smiled holding up a cute little sundress.

"You're welcome." She said while leaving out the door. "Talk to you later." Not until she left did I realize that she had on sunglasses the entire time that she was here.

"Dumb bitch can't beat my ass, that's all I know." Cherise mumbled.

"Would you finish telling me the story," I said to Cherise, "and don't talk so loud."

"Well, ole boy lives with a girl that I use to go to elementary school with."

"Elementary school?" I frowned.

"Wait a minute." She continued, "Tamela, Jerrel's new girl, Saboo, and the baby, on Flatbush."

"Sa who?"

"Saboo from Flatbush. He hooked Tamela up with ole boy, because that's his Uncle. They met last year at the West Indian Day parade."

"Oh, that's his baby?"

"That ain't Saboo's baby. Just listen. She got a baby by Devine's aunt's lil' sister on her father side, mother, baby father's play cousin. That's her baby daddy. And he said that Tamela was living there, but the baby don't live there, the baby live down south with the grandmother. So anyway, Tamela baby's father cousin, told me that Jamillah from down the hill, called Tammy from over on Church Ave. and told her that Tamela was living with an old ass man, and that she's bout to marry him. When I was walking on my way to the train station, I saw the happy couple, coming out of the house together and she was locking the door. Which has to mean, she got keys. Now tell me, am I on my C.S.I. shit or what? You know ole girl livin' up in the spot."

"Wait a minute, now, oh hell no!" I said to Cherise, "So, what you're saying is Jerell is living with Tamela? He thinks he can play my girl?"

"No, yo' girl playin' herself."

"True, true." I had to agree.

"Can you find out some more information for me?"

"For you Vera, but as far as your girl, you know I can't stand her ass."

"Just do it for me then."

"Ai'ight. I'll let you know." she said, "Vera, can I bring my friend around here so you can do her hair?"

"When? Now?"

"Yeah in a few."

"Okay, no problem."

I finished Cherise's hair and then she left. While I waited for her to return, I called Shannon at her office to tell her the scoop.

"Hey Boo." I said to Shannon, "Your girl, Lee, was in here today with shades on. You think ole boy beatin' her ass?" I asked.

"I don't know, but I *will* be asking her," Shannon said sucking her teeth. "Ole boy gon' fuck around and I'ma have him beat the fuck up."

"Or shot."

Shannon snickered a little. "You always about to shoot somebody, better stop that shit."

I laughed. "Girl, you know I ain't shootin' nobody, I'm a mother now."

"That's right…Vera," Shannon's voice got weak, "I saw Nile today."

"Where at? Shannon, I know you ain't still fuckin' with his ass!"

"Hell no, girl, please. He came by my office today and was trying to talk some ole garbage about he needs me to understand that he married her because they had been together so long, but that he loves me…and wants me back…and so forth and so on."

"What you tell his ass?"

"I picked up the phone and told that niggah to call his wife and tell her that shit."

"What he do?"

"He just looked at me. Then I said, 'That's what I thought.' Then I told him to get the fuck out and not to ever come back." I could tell that she wanted to cry.

"Are you crying?"

"Girl," Shannon said, taking a deep breath, "this shit got me goin' crazy. The niggah that's perfect for me, I don't want him. The one that ain't no good and married a bitch, literally in my face, I'm sitting here in tears over. One thing's for sure and two things for certain, I got too much pride to be fuckin' with Nile's ass ever again. I wouldn't care if I gotta cry every goddamn day. That niggah will never get the satisfaction of being with me again."

"What about Quincy?"

She sucked her teeth, "I ain't feeling his naggin' ass either. He fulla fuckin' complaints. I think when he comes back from London, which will be soon, instead of finding a wedding planned, he gon' find his bags packed."

"Are you serious?"

"Watch me."

"All right, well let me go." Since she said 'watch', I need to go and watch Rowanda with my baby for a little while. After I hung up, I went back to the front of the shop and watched Rowanda on the computer. Skyy was sleep, but there was another voice in the house. As the person came closer to the camera, it was Queen. I knocked on the screen, "Get that bitch outta my house!"

"Queen," Rowanda said, "This gon' hurt me to say this. But you can't stay here! You gotta go."

"Rowanda, you putting me out?" Queen asked surprised. "You s'pose to be my bestfriend."

"I am and I love you like a sista but you need help. Queen

look at you." Rowanda said looking her up and down. Queen looked as if she hadn't taken a bath in days. She constantly sniffing and scratching the same side of her neck repeatedly, "I feel sorry for you," Rowanda continued.

"Feel sorry for me?" Queen snorted, "All of a sudden you think you better than somebody, cause you clean? And how long you gon' be clean? For a day, a month, until shit hit the fan and you can't deal? You was the only somebody that I had, ain't nobody else ever gave a fuck about me. And now you telling me that I gotta go?"

"Queen, I love you like a sista and sometimes the best love is the toughest. It hurts me more than you can imagine having to say this to you, but I got a life here that I'm trying to live. I got a daughter and a granddaughter, that's depending on me. This baby is my opportunity to get it right. God has blessed me with a second chance and I can't have nobody mess that up for me. Now please, if Vera or Taj come here and find you here, all high, then they gon' think the same thing about me. I may never get to see my granddaughter again."

"Rowanda," Queen said clearing her throat, "do you remember who you talkin' to? I was the one who pulled *yo'* baby out the trash! I was the one that told you not to toss her away, but you did. Now you look at me like I'm nothing…like I ain't shit, but a used up fiend. We been clean together, relapsed together, shot up together, done time together, lived on the streets together; everythang that you can think of, we been there together.

Who was there for you when Larry came back looking for you? Wanting you to be his whore? Who was there when Larry died and Vera cussed you out like a dog shit on the street? Me, Queen. I gave you my last. I was the one on my grind, workin' that block, beatin' down that money, feedin' both our monkeys when you was too sick from dope to go and get some. I made sure you had it. Now you're so high and mighty, cause finally your crack baby done grew up and need a damn baby sitter of her own!"

"Don't talk about my child."

"Rowanda," she cried, "If I leave out that door, then I ain't gon have nobody."

"If you get your life together, not only will you have me, but you'll also have Bryce. He needs a mother, Queen."

"I ain't no mother. I'ma junkie. Ain't that why you putting me out, cause I'ma junkie, who ain't good enough to be a part of your lil' family here?! Ain't that the reason?"

"Naw," Rowanda said, opening the front door, "That ain't the reason, the reason is I love you, but I love me more. I'ma pray for you, Queen, because I can't live like that no more. I just can't."

After Queen left, Rowanda flopped down on the couch and cried into the folds of her arms. That's when I peeped Bryce standing in front of me. Caught off guard, I clicked the computer off.

"Hey girl, is it safe?"

I smiled. "What do you mean is it safe, what's suppose to happen?"

"You know ya man can't stand me, I don't want his ass jumpin' out on me."

"What, are you a punk, scared of Taj?"

"Scared of Taj," Bryce smirked, "Taj better be scared of me."

"Negro, don't be threatening my man. Ma'fuckers have died for less than that. Needless to say, we don't play those games."

"Yeah, well, what games do you play?"

"Why?" I playfully frowned up my face and said.

"Because," he said reaching over the counter and stroking my hair, "I play to win."

I took his hand down. "You've already lost."

"You got that. I just came by to see if I could make an hair appointment. I got a date."

"Whaaaat? You better act right."

"There you go. Can you do my hair?"

"When? Tomorrow?"

"Yeah, tomorrow about 4:30."

"See ya then."

After he left, Cherise came in with her friend. When I looked, I couldn't figure out whether the friend was a man or a woman. I mean, he or she, or she or he, looked like a woman, sorta, but not really. Then I looked at the person's throat, saw an Adam's apple, and knew then he was a man...but being that he looked like a she, I decided to call him Shim, a combination of she and him. Shim was dressed in fringed bottom jeans with a purple tee shirt, and a floral print silk scarf tied around shim's waist like a belt. As soon as I opened my mouth to speak, Shim cut me off by screaming, "Peaches!"

"Peaches" I thought, *"Who the hell is Peaches?"* I looked at Cherise.

"Peaches!" Shim screamed.

"Tasty." Cherise said, "Who the hell are you talking to? You are suppose to be getting your hair done."

"I can't get my hair done now, I gotta take care of my heart."

"Your heart," Cherise smirked. Hell, she seemed just as confused as I was.

"Wait a minute," I said, pointing to the guy, "Your name is Tasty?"

I looked around the shop to see who the fuck Peaches was. Everybody but DeAndre was looking at this fool like he had lost his mind.

"Peaches! Peaches! Peaches!" Tasty stomped his feet. "I know you hear a bitch calling your name. I know you feel my pain of seeing you in here and I ain't heard from you! I know you do, Peaches."

I looked at DeAndre, "Mofo, are you Peaches?" At this point nobody could contain it anymore and we all fell the fuck out laughing. I was laughing so hard that I thought I would pee on myself. Goddamn Peaches. "Peaches!" I said, "Go see what Tasty want…What's wrong Tasty?" I turned my back to DeAndre. "You can tell me." I walked over and placed my arm around Tasty.

Tasty wiped his brow like he was about to faint. "I'm in so much pain, Miss Thing, that I don't know what to do."

Before Tasty could continue, DeAndre walked over and grabbed shim by the arm, dragging him out of the shop. Once the door slammed behind them, we cut the radio off so that we could hear every word.

"Tasty," DeAndre said, "What the hell is your problem? Coming up in here showing your ass!"

"Oh you wanna see my ass?" Tasty said, "All this time I've been trying to get with you and now you talking about my ass. It's always sex with you, Peaches."

"Look go home and we'll talk later."

"No Peaches, I can't, I'm in pain. I'm in pain. Every time you say, 'Bend over Tasty', Tasty bends over, but afterwards Tasty can't find Peaches nowhere. Wassup Peaches?"

"Go home Tasty. I will call you later," DeAndre said.

"You Promise?"

"Yes." We all knew he was lying.

"Okay, now Peaches don't lie to me. I'll be waiting."

When DeAndre walked back in the shop we all said in unison, "Wassup Peaches!"

DeAndre looked at us, "Fuck ya'll!"

After a few hours, I closed the shop and went home to my baby. When I got there, Taj was on the couch with Skyy lying across his chest. They both seemed to be sleep, but as I went to pass by the sofa, Taj reached out and touched me on the arm. "Hey, daddy." I said.

"Is that Daddy-Daddy, Big Daddy, or Daddy-like, you better have my money, Daddy."

"That depends on, who's on top tonight." I said playfully.

"On top? I planned on bangin' it from the back."

"You are so nasty." I smiled.

"Isn't that what you like?"

I bent down and kissed him. His tongue tasted like fresh peppermint.

"How was the shop today?" he asked.

"It was cool. Where's Rowanda?"

"Upstairs with Aunt Cookie."

"Oh, Aunt Cookie's here? Let me go upstairs." I walked upstairs to the second floor and went into my dressing room.

Aunt Cookie was in there puffin' on a cigarette, wearing tight leggings, the ones that have the strap underneath the foot, a white blouse, and red high heels. She was talking to Rowanda. "You're too young to be looking at these walls all day. Go on out there and get it p-poppin'. Plus, my girlfriend, Carol, the one that throws the card parties, say that he's a nice man."

"Who's a nice man?" I said interrupting their conversation.

"Whatcha workin' wit baby girl! I'm trying to hook your mama up with a man."

"She don't need no man." I frowned. "She ai'ight."

"Excuse you," Rowanda said, squinting her eyes at me. "I beg to differ."

"Oh hell, why would you wanna man? Why?"

"Slow it down, Baby Girl," Aunt Cookie said, smacking on a piece of gum and tapping her heels. "Stay in a chile's place."

"I am not a child, and who is a nice man?"

"Jimmy Charles, from Utica."

"Jimmy Charles? She doesn't need to date anybody named Jimmy Charles, sounds like he's old as Moses."

"Vera, cut it out." Rowanda laughed.

"I'm sorry, you're right" I said, "but *Jimmy Charles*, come on now you can do better than that. He sounds like he's 77 years old."

"For your information, he's 39." Rowanda snapped.

"Thirty-nine? *Oh, hell no.* I'ma just leave ya'll sittin' right here, because this shit is makin' my stomach burn. I feel like I'm about to pass out."

Rowanda and Aunt Cookie continued talking. I don't even remember when Aunt Cookie left. I went downstairs and breast fed Skyy, came back upstairs and dropped some hot hoochie moves on her daddy.

The next morning, I went to the shop extra early, around seven, and Bryce was waiting out front for me.

"Hey Bryce, what are you doing here so early?"

"Hey Vera, I wanted to come and holler at you for a minute." His eyes looked glassy.

"What's wrong?" I opened the door and motioned for him to come inside. I looked at the computer, but decided that I would cut it on a little later.

"I got a call last night from the police." Bryce said.

Immediately, my heart started pounding, ever since the crazy ass incident with Roger, I can't tolerate much of anything that has to do with police. The girls and I hired an attorney for the simple assault charges that Nile's wife pressed against us. The attorney, just about promised us that the charges would be thrown out, because her husband wouldn't testify against us. We're just waiting on a court date.

"What did they say?" I asked Bryce, biting my bottom lip. Not knowing what to expect.

"Vera," his words were getting caught up in his throat, "They found my mother dead in an alley off of 132nd street. My business card was in her pocket...she overdosed."

"Oh my God..." my heart started pounding.

"I figured I would come and tell you. Especially since she and Rowanda were so close."

"I'm so sorry to hear that, Bryce."

"I don't know if I can face Rowanda and tell her."

"Don't worry, I'll tell her." I placed my hand on his shoulder.

"Thanks, baby. I can't do that." he said, clearing his throat, "Vera, I never thought that I would be in so much pain behind losing a woman that I never knew."

"Bryce, it's not easy being born to a drug addict. It's like you're always in the midst of some shit. But they're in pain, that's why they act the way they do. They can't help it."

"She could've helped it. I was here. Hell, I work at a rehab. She could've come to me. But no, she turned to the streets! Damn!" He pounded his fist against the counter.

"Bryce," I grabbed some tissue from behind the counter and started wiping his tears away. "Baby, all she knew was the street. That's it. It was everything to her, for whatever reason, but she was your mother." As I continued to wipe his tears I thought about him crying once before over his mother, when we were a couple. She came to his high school graduation high as a kite. That turned out to be the first night that we ever made love.

Bryce kissed my hand as I continued to wipe his tears away. "Vera, you were the only one I could ever talk to about my mother."

"I know, sweetie, I use to feel the same way."

He grabbed me by my waist, "I still love you, Vera, I never stopped."

"Don't say that." I stepped back. "I can't love you like that. I'm in love with Taj. I have a child with him. I'm marrying him. Your mother just died and you need someone. But, I can't give you what your looking for; and I can't say that I'm sorry about that."

"I don't expect you to be sorry about loving someone…I'm the one who should apologize, I'm way outta line." He hugged me and placed his face in the curve of my neck. "Thanks, Vera." He said, seemingly struggling to keep his throat clear of tears.

As I squeezed him tight and prepared to let him go from my embrace, I could hear the front door swinging open.

"What the hell is this?" It was Taj. Bryce and I jumped back and let each other go.

"Taj, hey baby. I was just comforting Bryce, his mother, Queen, died," I spat out, so that he would know right away I was comforting Bryce and that's it. Taj shot me such a look that I felt I needed to back the fuck up.

"I'm sorry to hear that." Taj said to Bryce, but still looking me up and down. I started to feel self conscious in my tight black capris, black Old Navy top, and throw back pumas. When I looked down at my hand, I remembered that I took my shower this morning and left my engagement ring soaking in the diamond cleaner. Damn! When I looked back up at Taj, his eyes were glued to my hand.

I started to give Bryce another hug before he left, but then I figured that wouldn't be the best move. "Bryce, do you plan to make any funeral arrangements today?"

"Yes, my father told me that he would help me. Also, since Quincy'll be back later on this afternoon, he'll be able to help me out."

"I'm going to go home and tell Rowanda," I said.

"Thanks." And he was still crying as he turned to leave.

I knew that Bryce was hurting when he walked out the door. "Nothing against my man," Taj said, once Bryce walked out, "but is there some shit going on? Did you use to mess with him or something? Now's the time to tell me, because after today I don't know how I may take it."

"What are you talking about Taj?" I said shutting the lights off.

"You got feelings for him?"

"Hell no!" I snapped, "What do I look like to you? Remember *we're* suppose to be getting married?"

"Yeah, I remember. Do you?"

"Taj, please his mother just died."

"I understand that. Hell, I knew Queen, but Bryce, I ain't feeling him. Whatever ya'll got goin'on, end it, or I swear to God, I'ma catch a case."

I just rolled my eyes and locked the shop's door. Taj, walked out before me and we each jumped in our cars and headed home. When we got home, Rowanda was laying Skyy down in her cradle in the living room. Right away, Rowanda looked at us and could tell that something was wrong.

"Why ya'll lookin' like that? Ya'll havin' problems?"

"No, Rowanda." I said trying my best not to feel the same way she just described. "Taj and I are fine."

"Then where's your ring at?"

"Good question," Taj smirked.

"It's soaking in the diamond cleaner." *Damn, how did she notice that?*

"Well you need to put it on." Rowanda insisted.

"Rowanda," I said cutting her off, "That's not what I came here for. I need to tell you something."

"What?"

I sat down beside her and grabbed her hands; "Bryce came by the shop this morning."

"Yeah," Rowanda said sounding scared.

"Queen passed away last night."

Rowanda started crying and screaming! "She did what? Oh Jesus, why?" she screamed, "Why?! She didn't have nobody! Nobody should have to die alone."

For the rest of the day Rowanda stayed in her bedroom and cried. She told me how she told Queen to leave the night before she died. Already knowing the conversation, I sat there feeling guilty. Snot dripped from Rowanda's nose and tears poured from her eyes, for the only friend that she ever had in the world. Queen, was gone.

Queen was buried three days later. It rained all day. At the funeral, Rowanda was quiet the entire time. Aunt Cookie and Uncle Boy didn't even say much. Not even, a 'whatcha workin' wit' or a 'I can't call it.'

Bryce was visibly upset at his mother's funeral. Besides Taj and I, Shannon and Quincy, and Bryce's father were there for support.

Queen looked to be at peace laying in her casket. She didn't seem to have the traveling lines of pain covering her face. As I looked down at her, I almost felt a relief that she was gone. I remembered the look on her face, when Rowanda asked her to leave and to never come back.

"Queen was walkin' around dead." Rowanda told me after the funeral. "And now that she's dead, she almost seems alive."

Personal Foul

When Taj and I woke up the radio alarm clock, was tuned to KISS FM's, morning show. It was the Wake-Up-Club's *'Confessions Hour.'* At first I wasn't paying any attention, I was focusing more on the big black dick that I wanted for breakfast.

For the past month, since Queen's death, I've been trying my best to get Taj and me back on the right track. Thinking that if I woke him up with me riding his dick, that that would be enough to get us going.

As I started to caress Taj's dick with the palm of my hand I heard a voice sounding just like Uncle Boy coming across the radio, except I could tell that the person, was trying to disguise his voice. The caller said his name was Boydon James, and since Uncle Boy's name was *Boydon Brown*, I nixed the caller and attempted to get back to handling my business. As soon as I got Taj to whispering my name and what he wanted me to do, I heard the caller say to the D.J., "Hey, I can't call it."

That's when Taj and I both looked at the radio. I though to myself, *"What the hell is Uncle Boy doing?"*

"Boydon James, what's your confession?"

"Hey, my confession is that I been livin' with my woman, let's just call her Cookie Wright, for over twenty-five years. We raised one child together, let's call her Vera Hairstylist, and my grandbaby lets call her Crack-a-Dawn."

"Mr. James, get to the point. Air time is limited."

"Well, me and my woman have been together for twenty-five years. All this time she's been thinking that I'm divorced, but I'm not."

Let me say this nice and slow, my...mouth...dropped...the fuck open.

"So, let's get this straight," the D.J. interrupted, "You live with your lady, Cookie Wright, and she thinks you're divorced?"

"That is correct."

"Tell us what's goin' on Mr. James?" The D.J. asked, while dropping Usher's "Confessions" in the background.

"See, when I met my woman, I planned on gettin' divorced but, I just never made it happen. After we'd been together for three years, that's when she told me I had to get divorced or leave."

"And you didn't wanna leave?" the D.J. asked.

"Hell no. I love that woman. That woman be puttin' it on Uncle Boy...I mean *Boydon James*."

"She be droppin' it like it's hot?"

"Sizzle-sizzle." Uncle Boy laughed.

I'm about to be sick. Taj was so embarrassed, "What the hell is wrong with Uncle Boy?" he asked, shaking his head.

Uncle Boy continued. "Let me explain. I had the money to get the divorce and back then it was only two-fifty for a quick one. But see, let me explain, what had happened was, uhhh...See, there was this lil' candy store round here, actually it was a number runners' place. One Friday night, I was playin' the numbers in there and the placed got raided."

"Whaaatt," the D.J. yelled, "You're an old gangstah, huh?"

"Old G., that's me." I could practically hear Uncle Boy's lips crack a smile through the airwaves, "Anyhow, when they raided the place, I needed to use the divorce money to get me outta jail. So that's about it."

"Okay...you're callin' today because you want us to call yo' woman and tell her the truth?"

"Yeah man, I need some help with this. Lately, I've been feeling like I wanna marry my woman and I can't with this cloud over my head."

"Well, that's it's called a confession, it cleanses the soul. So, how you feel about doing this so far?"

"I can't call it."

"Hold on Mr. James, we're about to make the call."

When we heard that shit we had to sit up.

"Wait a minute," Uncle Boy said; "Before you put me on hold I just wanna make a shout out to my man, Taj. I see you boy."

Taj had a look on his face like, '*Oh hell no!*' Uncle Boy continued, "And I wanna make a shout out to Big Dawg, Young Blood, Melly-Mel, June Bug, Sip Jr., and Goody, down at the barber shop on Lenox. This is *Boydon*, reppin' for the whole of Uptown. Not to mention is Brooklyn in the house?"

"Mr. James," the D.J. interrupted, "Can we call your lady?"

"Yeah, go 'head."

When the D.J. placed Uncle Boy on hold, my phone rang. It was Shannon.

"Vera, is Uncle Boy on the radio?"

"Yeah, girl."

"Aunt Cookie gon' kill 'em."

Before I could tell Shannon bye my other line clicked, "Let me call you back." I said to Shannon. Angie was on the other line.

"Vera! Turn the radio on, Uncle Boy is on the air." She hung up. That's when Rowanda yelled through my bedroom door, "Vee, turn to KISS. Boy is on the radio…" It was as if everybody in Brooklyn knew this niggah was on the radio showing his ass.

When I focused back on the radio, a telephone was ringing, "Nursing Aid service," Aunt Cookie answered.

"Cookie Wright, please." The D.J. said.

"No Cookie Wright here, but this is Cookie *Turner*."

"Okay…Ms. Turner do you know a Boydon James?"

"No. I know a Boydon *Brown*. Who are you?"

"This is Jeff Foxx, from KISS FM's morning show and I'm calling because—"

"Hold up!" Aunt Cookie screamed, "Barbara, Faye, Sharon, Carol, Mae, Phyllis, Gerri, Renee, Phine, and Deborah, come on in here, I think we won that office party thing with Lloyd Banks."

"Lloyd Banks?!" One of the women said in the background. All of the others were screaming, then they started singing in unison, *"Its on fire…up in here…its burning hot…we on fire, Tear the roof of dis ma'fucker, set the roof on fire…what you say…"*

"Ms. Turner," the D.J. said, interrupting their tune.

"Whatcha workin' wit baby boy, Lloyd comin' down now?" Aunt Cookie asked.

"Ms. Turner this is 'Confessions Hour' on the radio."

"Hush ya'll…" Aunt Cookie said to her co-workers in the background, "Confessions?" she said to the D.J., "Who set this up? Betty Greene from Newark?"

"No, Ms. Wright."

"Well, I know that Taj Sr. didn't do it, right?"

"No, Cookie, damn." Uncle Boy said interrupting, "Its me, Boy."

"Boy!" Aunt Cookie screeched, "What are you doing calling me on the radio?"

"I got a confession."

"A what? You couldn't wait till we got home to confess?"

"No, I gotta do it now?"

"Boydon Brown, if you take this time and tell me that you're gay and comin' outta the closet, I'ma beat yo ass!"

"Oh hell no, Cookie. I ain't no homo thug!"

"Then why you got me on the radio?"

"Remember Mare-Helen?"

"Your ex-wife?"

"Well, yes and no."

"What about her?"

"Well…she's not exactly my ex-wife. We're still married and I'm gon' get divorced; don't get it crooked, though. You know I loves you Chocolate Chip, which is why I'm confessin'."

"Oh, wow." Aunt Cookie, said surprisingly calm, "Thanks for telling me, now you can get yo' shit and get the fuck out…" the radio was beeping after every other word, "You sorry," Aunt Cookie continued, "no good…son-of-a…beep-Jack-beep,

Monkey…beep-don't even leave your stankin 'mother…beep-drawls behind…you gon' call me on the…beep-radio. Here I am thinkin' I won lunch with Lloyd Banks and you clowin'! I done called all my homegirls around me thinkin' we 'bout to get a honey up in here and this no good…beep-playin' me! Oh sucker you gots to go!"

After that, the line went dead, "We'll be right back." The D.J. said.

Simultaneously, Taj and I threw the covers off of us, "Go get dressed!" Taj yelled, "I'll throw on something. Meet me outside, so that we can go and help this old man. If Aunt Cookie get to him first, she gon' slam his ass!"

I ran in the bathroom, threw something on and told Rowanda to watch Skyy. I ran out the door and jumped in Taj's Escalade. We took off. Anxiously I kept tapping my foot. Flatbush had more goddamn traffic than a little bit. It was worse when Taj cut over by Prospect Park. Being that it was early August, the kids had the caps off the fire hydrants and were jumping in the water. By the time we got to Uncle Boy, Aunt Cookie was dropping every got damn thing that Uncle Boy owned out the window!

"Aunt Cookie!" I yelled, opening the truck's door and practically falling out, "Stop it! Cut it out!"

"Catch this!" she screamed. Poor Uncle Boy was moving like a damn centipede, trying his best to catch his eight tracks and his clothes as they fell. I couldn't believe this shit. Taj was helping Uncle Boy, collect his things.

I looked up at the second story window, of their row house, that Aunt Cookie was hanging out of and said, "Aunt Cookie! I can't believe you're handling your business like this in the street."

"You can't believe it? This Negro was on the radio this morning. Embarrassin' me. Hurt me. Here I've been livin' with him all this years and he been playin' me? Get yo' shit and get to steppin' Old G.! Ya jack ass monkey!"

"Cookie," Uncle Boy said, with a lil' base in his throat, pointing his finger and sticking his chest out, "I told you the truth! Now I pay bills here and you gon' stop it right now! Right goddamit now! You understand me!"

"Understand you? Understand this, kiss my ass!" She threw one of his white leather platform shoes and hit him in the head.

"All that ass!" Uncle Boy, ducked, covering his head, "That's a bit much." Slowly he stood back up, "Furthermo' what you need to be tellin' me is why you would think, Taj Bennet Sr. or Betty Greene would be callin' you on confessions? You got somethin' you wanna share? Don't make me light Taj Bennet Sr. the fuck up! He might see in the streets but the niggah don't know me. Understand? Now stop what you doin' and don't throw out no mo' of my stuff!"

"No problem." Aunt Cookie said, "I won't throw out no more of your stuff, cause all yo' shit is already outside. Oh, wait a minute, I almost forgot ." She left the window, came back, and threw a suitcase, slam on his head.

Uncle Boy had fucked up royally; and I wasn't the one to be going upstairs and fucking with Cookie Turner this morning. She wasn't going to beat me to a pulp. I turned toward Uncle Boy, "Where you s'pose to go?"

"Cut it out Vera," Taj mumbled.

"Come on Uncle Boy," Taj helped Uncle Boy pack the suitcase and then he said, "Let's Go."

At first, Uncle Boy staying with us was okay until this nasty niggah started fartin' in my baby's room and saying shit like, 'Better out than in...or better to lose a friend than bust a gut.' He'd walk around with stinkin' ass Magic Shave on, funk up the whole house, and act like he'd just sprayed perfume.

The Escorts, Ray Goodman and Brown, Blue Magic, and repeats of Jimmy Swaggart were non-fuckin'-stop on a Sunday morning. Uncle Boy left newspapers all over the house and he had an opinion about every goddamn thing under the sun! He drank Pepsi colas with peanuts, ate banana sandwiches with mayonnaise, potted meat mixed with sardines, and every evening his nightcap would be a Colt 45.

He's been here for two weeks and truth be told, I don't how long he can keep staying here. Let me tell you what happened last week. I came home early and Uncle Boy was scratching his balls, listening to Sam Cook, and frying bologna. Standing at my stove with mixed matched long johns on. The shirt was beige and tight as hell, squeezed his arms and shit, and the waist stopped right above his hairy ass navel. The pants were gray and sagged in the ass. They made him looked like he was carrying a sack fulla shit. "Uncle Boy!" I screamed, "What in 'na world?" I closed my eyes real tight and placed my hands over them, "Please put some clothes on!"

Tonight I came home and this man had his feet soaking in Epson salt and alcohol in my baby's tub. When I asked him what he called himself doing, he told me that he was 'wetting his calluses'. After he wet his calluses, he took a razor blade and peeled off the dead skin.

Then, as if that wasn't bad enough, when he finished soaking them, he dried them on my baby's *Proud Family* throw cover and commenced to cutting his gritty ass toenails. In addition, for an extra-added bonus, he took the original Ben-gay, not the new and improved scent, but the original that makes your eyes water, and started massaging his bunion. That's when I picked up the phone and called Aunt Cookie. She had Betty Wright's, "No Pain-No Gain," playing in the background and I could hear her girlfriend, Ms. Carol say, "I got the deck of cards for tonight."

"Aunt Cookie!" I was pissed off that she was acting like Uncle Boy being gone was no big deal.

"Whatcha workin' wit Baby Girl?" I could hear her taking a pull off her cigarette.

"I can't call it," Fell outta my mouth. What the hell was

wrong with me, I don't even talk like this. "Aunt Cookie, please can this man come home?"

"No."

"Why not?" I asked, practically begging.

"Let me tell you somethin', Ms. Vera. See ya Uncle Boy, who all these years you been thinkin' is hot shit, been playin' Cookie Turner."

Her girlfriend Ms. Carol was in the background saying, "Cookie, don't believe the hype. That niggah ain't no good! Don't even do it to yourself girlfriend. Let's not forget how he was on the radio in front of millions of people. Had you runnin' round the office like a damn clown, lookin' like a straight fool, niggahs laughin' and shit! Show'd his natural ass!"

"Ya hear Carol, Baby Girl?"

"Tell Carol she need to mind her fat ass business and stay outta yours!"

"Have you lost your mind?!" Aunt Cookie snapped. "You wanna be slapped for being disrespectful! Yo' Uncle Boy thought he was smart. Thought he got that off, cause he been walking around me sayin' slick shit about keepin' his grind goin' on. How he ain't the one to be messed over. Shit like that. What was all that suppose to mean huh? Well, I'll tell you," she said answering her own question. "That meant, you a fool like a ma'-fucker, Cookie Turner, causes I'ma slick niggah."

"Aunt Cookie, that's a bit much."

"Let me tell you somethin' Baby Girl, I'm bout it bout it. And I don't play them games. Fuck over me and you gots to go! Now he wanna come home? Cause he missin' me. Tell him I said to call that porch-monkey-bitch, Mare-Helen and cry in her ear, cause I ain't for it. Hell, ever since Nelly's Sweat came out, Cookie Turner been gettin' her eagle on! Remember Earl Gatling?"

"Yeah."

"Well he a souljah! Now hollah atcha gurl!"

Tears started running from my eyes. "Aunt Cookie, you don't understand, I can't take it. Please Aunt Cookie, Mare-Helen don't want him and neither do I. I can't keep living like this. Aunt Cookie, you're the only one that can love him the way he needs to be loved, everybody else is tired. For Christ's sake, you've been with this man for over 25 years! Don't you miss him?"

"Miss him? Yeah he use to lay it down, but your fine ass father-in-law ain't too bad. Therefore I will roll over in hell before that mother-sucker, jackass monkey come up in here again. Damn, if he gon' play me for 25 more years. And make sure you tell him that he can't come back through this door until he is divorced and the papers are in his hand. Otherwise, you can keep his sweat-socks-to-the knee-wearin'-ass, in the summer time, right there with you! And until then, like I said, I'm gon' get my eagle on. Now, tell Rowanda I said get ready."

Oh God, I'ma die. Just take me now. "So just forget about Uncle Boy?"

"Pretty much. Just tell ya mama what I said."

"What is she getting ready for?"

"Vera, don't play with me. Matter-a fact, why don't you and your girls come on over and play some cards with us. We having a lil' get together."

"Who's we?"

"Me, Janet, Carol, and ya mama."

"Maybe Shannon and I'll run through. Angie's on a date and Lee…well…don't even get me to lying."

"Come on and bring ya mama with you. I'll tell Jimmy Charles to pick her up after the party is over…Oh Baby Girl, don't come up in here empty handed. This is a B.Y.O.S. party."

"What?"

"Bring ya own shit."

"If that ain't bout ghetto. How the hell are you inviting me to your party and then you want me to bring my own shit. Like what?"

"Well, I got the food here. So bring your own drinks, cause you know Janet and Carol'll be sipping on a case of Golden Champale."

"Golden Champale, they still make that?"

"See, I'm hanging up cause I feel a cussin' coming on and I don't wanna take it there. You better take a break and recognize. Humph, you know how I do it."

"But Aunt Cookie—"

"Baby Girl!" Uncle Boy yelled sternly, interrupting my conversation.

"He talkin' to you?" Aunt Cookie asked. "Now he know I ain't nevah allowed him to discipline you, that's my job."

I cocked my neck to the side, "Hell yeah. What could be his problem calling me like that?" Suddenly, I felt the need to either cry or cuss...or both. Before I could decide which one, I smelled Uncle Boy coming this way. He spent all day eating pork-n-beans, so I knew it was only a matter of time before he lit the house up! I rolled my eyes as he stood in front of me, with his brown corduroy housecoat on and the belt tied super tight around his beer belly. On his feet he had on matching corduroy house shoes, white sweat socks pulled to the knee, a cigarette tucked behind his left ear, and on his head was a floral print shower cap. *Wait a minute! Wait one damn minute; is that my damn shower cap?* "Uncle Boy is that my *damn* shower cap?"

He reared back on his legs and started looking around, "Hold up Baby Girl, I can't take a shower 'round here? First you don't cook," he said as he rubbed his belly, "and now you wanna monitor how I wash my body? Oh hell naw! Now get off the phone!" He was looking at me with a serious attitude, holding a bag of bar-b-que skins in one hand and a Colt 45 in the other, "Every time I turn around you on the phone! You need to get off that phone and cook some dinner or something around here. The damn baby 'bout to starve, all she do is eat milk..."

"She's four months old."

"Stop making up excuses! When I was four months old, I was eating grits and eggs! Now, she can do more than eat milk."

"You can't eat milk."

"Oh you bein' smart? Girl, don't make me have to put my skins down and come at you! You worse than yo' Aunt Cookie!"

"Tell that niggah to keep my name out his mouth!" Aunt Cookie snapped.

I was in complete shock. Did I miss something or did his crazy ass start paying bills up in here? Oh my God, if he keeps fucking with me he gon' catch a major beat down!

"You hear me?" he said with his eyes bulging out. "That goddamn receiver gon' explode in yo' ear! You gon' mess around and that phone bill gon' be through the roof. You just taking advance of Taj. Humph, I ain't seen you cook yet! And that's what you need to be doing! Now hang up! Hang...it...up! And I mean now!" He took a sip of the Colt 45 he had in his hand, let out a small belch and said, "Right now, Baby Girl."

"Oh hell no, Baby Girl put his ass on the phone!" Aunt Cookie demanded.

"Aunt Cookie wanna talk to you." was all I could manage to say.

He practically snatched the phone outta my hand, "Hey Chocolate Chip. You missin' ya Boy?" I could hear Aunt Cookie cussin' him out. "A monkey?" Uncle Boy was in disbelief, "Cookie you called me a monkey? A signifying-jack-ass-porch monkey? I look like Dolomite...sit down...with my viagra needin' ass...Do you Cookie, cause Boydon Bruce-Lee Brown ain't nevah scared! What-What?...Bring it then...Harlem World represent! Look Cookie, I done apologized fifty-eleven times. But it's all good, it's always a ram in the bush...You gon' do what? Well, bust a move then Cookie. Bust a motherfuckin' move! Hello...hello...oh she done hung up on me!" He gave me back the phone, popped a skin in his mouth, chased it down with his Colt 45, and looked at me. "Now hang up the phone and stay off of it for the rest of the night!"

I rolled my eyes so hard at Uncle Boy that it's a wonder they didn't get stuck. I picked the phone back up, right in his face, and called Aunt Cookie. I told her that I would see her in an hour. Now, I see why she doesn't want his ass back home!

I got off the couch and walked up the stairs where Taj and Skyy were in our bedroom. "Taj, I'ma go out for a while. I need some air. If you need me, me and Shannon'll be at Aunt Cookie's for her card party."

Before I left, I changed into a mid-calf jean skirt, a matching Christian Dior top, and slipped on my black-wedged Christian Dior sandals. Rowanda had already left, she caught the train. She told me that she wanted to stop by her 'friend's' house before she went to Aunt Cookie's. I looked at her because from the smile on her face, she must've been going to see a man. I called Shannon and told her that I wanted her to go with me to Aunt Cookie's.

"Well, Vera," Ms. Janet, spoke into a stream of cigarette smoke, as she collected her book of spades, "Ya'll might have to hold a 'Comin' to Jesus meetin' on Lee's ass."

"That's what I told them," Aunt Cookie slapped her deuce of spade down on the table, "They gotta get with that ass and make her listen. Hell, if Lee is suppose to be your homegirl then you don't hold no punches...don't cheat now, Carol." Aunt Cookie said turning her attention toward, Ms. Carol, "You know I get the damn kitty if I have the deuce of spades...Don't play."

Ms. Carol, who wore what she called baby hair slicked down around the front of her hairline, mashed her cigarette in the clear ashtray, "I'm gettin' a lil' sick of ya'll. Just 'cause I did a lil' time for credit card fraud, don't mean I'ma cheat. I'm saved now. So I suggest," she said pointing at Aunt Cookie and Ms. Janet, "that ya'll stop fuckin' wit' me."

"Be quiet Carol and drop a card." Aunt Cookie said. "You did time for more then fraud, you got locked up messin' wit' that no good niggah."

"That was my niggah wasn't he? I'ma ride or die to the mother fuckin' end."

"Ya'll needs to stop talkin' like that." Ms. Janet, whose hairstyle consisted of a single sponge roller in the front of her hair for a bang and the rest combed straight to the back, took a sip of her Golden Champale; "Take time out for the Lawd. If it wasn't for Him ya wouldn't wake up in the mornin'. Get it straight." Shannon and I sat off to the side like too little girls, listening to a *'grown folks'* conversation.

"Wait a minute Janet." Ms. Carol said, "I always got time for the Lawd. You better fall the fuck back and stop gettin' it confused." Before she could go on, her cell phone rang, "Praise the Lawd, chile of Gawd speakin'."

Shannon nudged me on the arm and mumbled, "That's how she answers her phone."

"Uhmm hmm," I said sitting at the makeshift bar in Aunt Cookie's kitchen, fixing myself a drink.

"Ai'ight dawg," Ms. Carol said hanging up, "I'm out...Hey ya'll, Barbara from down at the job, wanna know what we cookin' for the repass tomorrow? You know he had thirteen kids and we damn near will be cookin' for an army. Remember when Jam Master Jay passed, they ate all yo' Red Velvet Cake, Janet."

"Jam Master Jay?" Rowanda frowned, looking over her hand of cards, "Ya'll cooked for his funeral? Were you invited?"

"Invited?" Ms. Carol screeched. "Who ever heard of being invited to a funeral? It ain't a birthday party Rowanda. All you got to do for a funeral is show up."

"Sho'nough," Aunt Cookie said, "and Janet's cake was a big hit. I'ma tell you that cake was so good it'll make you slap yo' mama!"

"Yeah I know." Ms. Janet bragged, "I put my foot up in that cake."

"I'd shoulda known that grit I was tastin' was from that big ass hammer toe you got." Ms. Carol said, cracking up laughing.

"Hold it now, don't talk about my hammer toe. Shit, I can't help it if I had to have the bones takin' outta my feet."

"Carol," Aunt Cookie blew out an O of smoke, "You need to be quiet, you know Janet sensitive about them feet she got. Just like you sensitive 'bout that nappy ass baby hair plastered across your forehead."

"Don't talk about my baby hair, now, Cookie. 'Cause ain't nobody said nothing to you 'bout yo' man showin' his ass on the radio. *Mr. I got a confession.*"

"Carol don't make me roll out on yo' ass, okay? So let's just skip all that you talkin'and tell me what you cookin' for the repass?"

"Aunt Cookie," I asked, with a confused look on my face, "Who died?"

"Old D.B. from the Wu-Tang Klan."

"Oh, hell no." *Why'd I even ask...*

"Well, the only way I'm cookin' for the repass," Ms. Carol said collecting her book, "is if I can get up on M-e-t-h-o-d man!"

"Ya'll a mess," Rowanda chuckled. "But can we get back to the girls? Vee and Shannon trying to get some real advice on what to do about Lee. Now let's talk to 'em and tell 'em some things. Now me, I have been through it all." She said looking at her hand of cards. "And that ain't no secret. But what I've learned is that there are times when a person can get so lonely that not even they can comfort themselves. Ya'll need to talk to Lee and find out what's really going on. Tell her that love doesn't hurt and if it does then it's not love anymore."

"Rowanda, you sho telling the truth." Aunt Cookie agreed," snatching up her book that Ms. Carol was trying to steal. "I use to date a man before I met Boy and he thought that he was suppose to treat me anyway that he wanted to, just because he felt like it he was the man. The king of the castle. It took me a while to get outta being 'in stupid.' But once I realized that I was the prize, I understood that if he couldn't treat me like I wanted to be treated then he needed to leave or better yet, I needed to go."

"Ain't that the truth, Cookie," Rowanda said, "There's no compromise when you're being treated bad. Ya'll really need to talk to Lee."

"And once you've talked to her," Ms. Janet said, throwing out a card, "And she gets over being in love with his ass, then you sock it to him!"

Aunt Cookie slapped her a high-five, "Teach that Negro a lesson that he'll never forget!"

"Shit, yeah!" Ms. Carol laughed, "Send him a dildo's in the mail, fuck with him and make him think twice the next time he wanna dog somebody!"

"I'm telling ya'll don't sleep on this. If Lee is your homegirl then you gotta look out for her." Aunt Cookie laughed.

"Please," Rowanda added, "Don't let her suffer. I'm a witness that sometimes suffering isn't always that easy to get away from."

After I dropped Shannon off and was driving back home, I

started to think about Lee. I know that we don't always get along, but she is my girl. One of my daughter's godmothers and I can't see her go out like this. If that niggah is really beatin' her ass, then I'ma personally roll out on that ma'fucker!

I parked my X5 in front of the house and dragged my self to the stoop. I was so tired from the long night that I couldn't wait to get in the bed. I have some brand new Laura Ashley sheets on my bed and I know I'ma sleep real good. I turned my key in the door and flicked on the light in the living room. "Ahhhhh!!!! Mother fucker!" I practically jumped outta my fuckin' skin! "Uncle Boy! What are you doing here sitting in the dark?"

"Do you know what time it is?" he sneared, "It's two o'clock in the damn morning and you been out running the streets! You are somebody's mama and don't no mama have any business being in the street this time of the night! You couldn't, call Vera?"

"Call?" I clutched my chest, my heart was still beating fast.

"What? All of a sudden, the word calling is Greek to you? Any other time we can't get you off the phone, but now you don't know how to use it."

"Now wait a minute Uncle Boy, you getting a little carried away! I am grown, I don't have to call. Now, what you need to do is loosen up that tight ass belt you got on and go upstairs."

"All I got to say is don't let it happen again!"

I didn't even address him. I simply walked past him and headed up the stairs toward my bedroom.

Triple Crown Publications presents

Defense

"Pregnant! Lee is pregnant!" I couldn't believe what Shannon was calling to tell me. Taj, who was lying next to me in bed, mouthed, *"There you go in somebody else's business."* I pressed my index finger against his lips, and mouthed back, *"Be quiet"*

"Be quiet. Oh, I got your be quiet." He said, licking my earlobe and caressing my breast. I tapped him on the shoulder for him to stop as Shannon continued to tell me about Lee. "Yes, girl, she's pregnant *and* she's keeping it."

"How far along?"

"A few weeks. She still has to go to the doctor. She's only taken a home pregnancy test."

"That's about one stupid broad. I guess the morning after pill doesn't work for her ass?" By now, Taj had his hands underneath my nightgown circling his fingers in my wetness. I was doing my best not to moan in Shannon's ear. When I looked down to tell him, *'Not now'*, he was kissing my thighs, pulling my panties off, and working his head beneath my nightgown.

"One minute Shannon," I covered the mouthpiece with my hand. "What are you doing?" I whispered to Taj.

"I'ma lick that fat clit." He whispered back.

"Taj, I'm on the phone."

"Keep talking, just be real quiet when you cum."

"You are so nasty."

I placed the phone back to my ear, "Shannon, I hope Lee doesn't think that Taj licking…" *Damn, I almost told Shannon all my business, either Taj is gon' have to stop or I'ma have to get off the phone.*

"Vera, what the hell are you doing?" Shannon asked sucking her teeth.

"Nu-nu-nuthing."

"You mean nu-nu-nuttin'. Bitch, you fuckin'?"

I started laughing; I couldn't hold it in any longer. "Oh, you such a nasty trick!" she chuckled, "Hurry up and call me when you're done, so we can go see Lee."

"Are you crazy?" I tapped Taj on the shoulder for him to stop for a minute. He didn't stop, he just started kissing my thighs again, turned around, and positioned himself for a 69. "One minute Shannon," I took my hand and covered the mouthpiece again, "Taj," I whispered, "One minute, baby. Let me finish talking to Shannon."

I picked the phone back up while massaging his dick, "I'm not going over there for ole girl to show her ass. You remember what she did the last time? Homegirl broke fly and was like, *You can't give me no advice…Tell it to the hand…Ya Oprah and Gail King wanna be's.* Nah fuck that! This time I'm going to the movies with my baby's daddy, all else will have to wait. I know what Aunt Cookie and Rowanda said, but I'll have to check Lee when I come back."

"You are such a bitch."

"Did I say I wasn't going? I'm just saying that if she shows her ass, I'ma molly whop it!"

"Be quiet Vera and get your nut. Call me when you and Taj get done. I mean get through, damn, you know what I mean. Get back from the movies. Or just have him drop you off here when the movie's over."

"Bye Shannon." I hung up the phone, turned over to Taj and was preparing to bust out the nastiest 69 in the world. "Where were we?" As we got ready to get our groove on, Uncle Boy starts yelling our names and pounding on the bedroom door, *What…the fuck…does he want?* I looked down at Taj and said, "Ask that bamma what he wants because if I ask him, ain't no telling what may come outta my mouth!"

"What's up Uncle Boy?"

"Taj, I thought we were going to the movies to see Ray?"

To the movies? This niggah wanna go to the movies with me and my man? Oh hell no.

"*Taj and I* are going to the movies Uncle Boy!" I yelled.

Taj looked at me and said, "Don't talk to him like that." he whispered.

"Don't talk to him like that? Do you know how he's been talking to me? Treating me like I'ma kid and shit."

"Be quiet," Taj said, waving his hand for me to hush up.

"Uncle Boy, Vera and I were going to go the movies to get away for a lil' while. We haven't really been out alone since the baby was born, so we wanted to spend a lil' time…if you know what I mean."

"Oh I get it. Cause I been thinkin' that ya'll need some time together, too. So, if you could just *drop me off* at the movies I would appreciate it. I don't need nobody to talk to. Ever since Cookie put me out, I'm use to being alone. Ya'll go ahead and be a happy couple. I know I'm on my own. So I'll be waitin' for you to simply give me a *ride* to the movies."

"No problem, Uncle Boy." Taj said.

After Uncle Boy walked away from the door, I looked at Taj and said, "I don't even wanna fuck with you no more. Punk ass." I went to get up from the bed and Taj pulled me on top of him, "Ai'ight now lil' girl, don't let me have to put these skins down and get up in ya."

I couldn't help but laugh, "Why I gotta be on top? What about the 69?"

"Because I changed my mind," he said cupping my breast, "I want you on top now."

"You know what I want?" I said as I slid down on his dick and started gyrating my hips.

Taj closed his eyes, "What?"

I took my index fingers and arched his eyes open. "I'ma get on my knees and beg Aunt Cookie to please take Uncle Boy back home."

"Uhmm, baby. I really don't wanna hear about Uncle Boy right now. I gotta hellava visual goin' on and he ain't in it."

When we got to the movies, Uncle Boy sat his ass in the same aisle...three seats down from us.

"Uncle Boy, you want some popcorn?" Taj asked him when we first sat down, before the movie started and the aisle got full.

"No, thank you. Uncle Boy just gon' sit right over here and leave ya'll alone." Fifteen minutes into the movie and the aisle is now full, guess who's moaning, loudly, about how he wish he had some popcorn, but his knees hurt too bad to go and get some?

"Uncle Boy, you want me to go and get you some popcorn?" Taj whispered.

"Oh, would you son? I would appreciate that."

Taj left and returned with the popcorn. Ten minutes later, guess who's fuckin' gagging off of a popcorn kernel?

"Uncle Boy?" Taj said, "What's up? You ai'ight?"

"I guess." Uncle Boy coughed out with his left hand wrapped around his throat, like he was about to die or something. People were looking at him and some of them were even sighing and complaining about the noise. "I'll be alright, Taj." Uncle Boy said with in a scratchy throat. "Just sitting here about to choke off this dry ass popcorn you brought me back. You couldn't get me no butter?"

"Uncle Boy, you have high cholesterol. So, no, I couldn't get you any butter."

I was fuming. I hadn't said a word because I didn't wanna cuss Uncle Boy the fuck out and have to apologize later, so I sat there quietly.

"I'll get you something to drink, Uncle boy." Taj said.

"Here you go." Uncle Boy smiled, pullin out a super-sized plastic Burger King cup. "I gotta lil' Seagram's Seven in the bottom. Just put a lil' ice and Sprite remix in here and mix it up real good."

I swear I could've kicked his ass.

"Here's your drink, Uncle Boy." Taj said returning to the theater. Forty-five good minutes into the movie, Uncle Boy hadn't said a word. We almost forgot that he was there. Then we started hearing, "Excuse me, let me pass. Excuse me, let me pass." When we looked, it was Uncle Boy, crossing over every single person in the aisle, to go to the bathroom! When he came back, he had to cross over the same people again! I was fuming. I looked at Taj, "If he gets up again, I'ma cuss his ass out!"

Twenty minutes later, Jamie Foxx, who was playing Ray Charles, starts singing and so does Uncle Boy. *"Hit the road Jack and don't you come back, no more-no more-no more-no more..."*

"Uncle Boy!" I couldn't hold it in any longer, "Be quiet. This doesn't make any damn sense. Now hush before I have to spaz out!" *I really wanted to say shut the fuck up! This was one time I wished Uncle Boy could read my mind.*

As I settled back in my seat to finish watching the movie, the shit was going off. I was pissed! I told Taj that he and Uncle Boy could leave, but that I was staying here to catch the next show. Taj kissed me on the way out. Uncle Boy rolled his eyes. I didn't give a fuck.

I paid for another ticket, sat in the theater, and watched the movie by myself. Afterwards I caught a cab to Shannon's.

Once Angie got off work, she met Shannon and me in front of Lee's co-op. Shannon opened Lee's door with a pair of spare keys. "Oh, she gives you an extra set of keys, like you just Queen Bee and shit." I snapped.

"Vera," Shannon said turning the knob, "This is not the time."

Lee was asleep on the couch, when we walked in and saw that both of her eyes were swollen and black.

"Leola Jones!" Angie screamed, "What the fuck is goin' on!"

Scared shitless, Lee jumped out of her sleep, "How the hell did ya'll get in here? You ever heard of knocking?"

I looked at Shannon and mouthed, "She startin'." Then I plopped my ass down on the love seat, placed my feet on the ottoman, and waited for the bitch to jump bad.

"I asked ya'll a question. Why are you here?"

"Look at you." I said in disbelief. "You lettin' some no good niggah beat on you? And wait a minute aren't you pregnant?"

"Shannon!" Lee said, "I told you not to say anything."

"I didn't. I only told Vera and Angie." Shannon said sitting down next to Lee.

"Anyway," I snapped, "That ain't the point."

"Vera, don't start!" Lee screamed, "You don't even know what you're talking about, so please."

"Please, what?"

"Lee," Shannon said, as calmly as possible, walking over to her and grabbing her hand, "Please tell us what's going on."

"I'll tell you what's going on," Angie spat, while sitting on the arm of the love seat. "Lee's getting her ass kicked!"

"I second that motion." I twisted my lips and rolled my eyes.

"First of all, nobody asked any one of you to be in my business first of all!" Lee said while snapping her fingers.

"See all that energy you got to be nasty," I said, "That's how you need to be treatin' that niggah."

"Every time I get a man ya'll asses find a fuckin' flaw." Lee snapped. "Did you all ever look at your own men? Crooked ass thugs, hustlin' their way to be legit. Mr. Doctor and Mr. Pilot! Any way you put it, they are *still* street niggahs and Angie, don't even do it to yourself girlfriend. 'Cause you don't even want me starting in on Lil' Love!"

"Scallywag!" I screamed, "You talking about my man? My baby daddy? Oh I will bust your mouth wide the fuck open," I stood up and started walking toward Lee.

Shannon stood in front of me and said, "Sit down Vera!"

I kicked my foot, pounded my fist in my hand, and looked Lee directly in the face, "Don't let me catch you outside, ya stank ass, skeezin' ass, broke the fuck up pregnant punk! Bummy ass hoe!"

"Takes one to know one," she replied.

I reached for her and Shannon pushed me back. "You know

what Lee," I said, sitting back down, "You always got a lot of mouth when it comes to taking up for a no good ass hole! But who's always there when the shit doesn't go right with the mofo? We are. I swear, an orgasm was the worse thing that could've happened for you, because you lose your fuckin' brain cells. Now you need to stay the fuck off Taj and Quincy. 'Cause I don't know about Shannon, but I don't play that shit."

"Whatever!" Lee sucked her teeth.

"See, Shannon, see. Just one time let me mugg her ass! I ain't gon' kill her, I'ma just knock the shit out of her!"

"Calm down, Vera."

"Oh I'ma calm down, it's all good. At least I ain't gettin' my ass kicked! I betchu my man stay on the grind for me. Cause I get whatever I want. And he damn sure doesn't have a ma'fuckin crib that he shares with another bitch. My man is at home. Where's yours?"

"You tell me." She spoke with tears falling from her eyes, "It seems like you know. You know what? You, you, and you," she said pointing around "Can get the fuck out!"

"Wait a minute now, slow ya roll homes." Angie said twisting her neck, "Cause I ain't for the shit. Now I've been quiet this whole time, but you need to calm the fuck down. Get it together, and take a deep breath. Don't take the shit out on me. I'm not Shannon, so I will not be treating you like a baby, and I'm not Vera so I'm trying not to completely cuss *you* the fuck out. All I have to say is that I hope and pray that you have more sense than to stay with a man who's beatin' your ass. Regardless of whether you're pregnant or not."

"Lee," Shannon said, "Why didn't you use something? Right now is not the time to be having a baby by this man."

"Don't tell me about my man and my baby."

"That might be your baby." I said, mean muggin' Lee's ass,

"But ole boy damn sure ain't your man. I'm certain Tamela would argue that point."

"Tamela?" Lee cried in disbelief, "Nobody told you that but that fuckin' Cherise. That's why I can't stand her!"

"So you know about this chick?"

"She is nothing to him. It was only one time and she came on to him. Men will be men."

I'm about to pass the fuck out! All I could hear were sirens and shit. Bells and whistles goin' off and screaming, *Dumb bitch alert!*

"Do you know how hard it is for him to be out of work?" Lee cried. "Do you know how hard it is for a black man period?" Lee said.

"Do you know how hard it is for you to be a baby mama," I said to Lee, " and the niggah don't want you, he wanna be with the next bitch? What? You think that shit is a joke? You're 32 years old, *you* should know better!"

"Lee, he's out of work?" Shannon asked in disbelief.

"Yes and…"

"And? And that was the day you should've left his ass." Angie said pointing her finger, "Unemployed niggahs need to be looking for a job not fuckin'."

"Fah sho'!" I snapped, "He's unemployed and he's kicking your ass? What he got a platinum dick?"

"All you think about is dick!" Lee screamed, "I love Jerell, Jerell loves me. Every couple goes through shit! Don't you know Ms. Vera? Or should I remind you about Bryce's resurrection?"

"Let me explain something to you, Bryce is not my man, therefore I am going through anything with him. Taj is my man and one thing he never does is put his hands on me!"

"There it is." Angie said. "Let me tell you something Lee. I know what it is to be going through something with a man. I was so in love with my husband that I couldn't tell his ass from his lips because I was in it so much. Honey, I was so in love with this man that I forgot about me and what I liked to do. Where I liked to go and the things that I liked to see. I forgot that shit because I was so busy chasing this no good niggah, thinking that if I could somehow show him that I was the bomb bitch, he would act right. So, I withstood his cheating, his dogging, his degrading, him having no money. If I could stand by that, then I was superwoman. Right? And he would see that he had the whole package in me? Right? Wrong!" Tears were streaming down Angie's cheeks as her voice started to crack, "It hurts me to see you like this, because looking at you reminds me of how I felt living with a niggah I had to convince to love me. But how could he love me when I wasn't even loving me."

"Jerell is under a lot of stress!"

"Fuck his stress! What the hell is he doing for you?" I snapped, "Are you stupid? You think we like coming here and having to convince yo' ass that you deserve better than what you're getting? You think I like looking at you, all beat the fuck up? Instead of you saying I need help, you're screaming some bullshit; defending this bum niggah! Fuck all that. You have to want more for yourself and your baby!"

"They're right, Lee." Shannon agreed.

"Do any of you know what it's like to always be the one to finish last?" Lee cried.

"Finish last in what Lee?" Shannon smirked.

"At everything. I was always the tallest in class,"

"Bitch yo' ass is 5'5", you're far from tall!" I said.

"Yeah, but I've been 5'5" since the fourth grade and I was always fat."

"You ain't fat. You just big boned." Shannon chimed in.

"Please, I was the one who always teased."

"You were always startin' shit." I snapped, with my face twisted.

"Be quiet Vera!" Shannon snapped.

"I'm just sayin'."

"Hush!"

I sucked my teeth and let Lee continue, "I always had to be the funny one…"

"I don't remember you being funny." I know I wasn't helping any, but this bitch was sounding ridiculous.

"If you say another word!" Shannon snapped at me, "I'ma stuff my fist in your throat!"

I shot that heifer a look like, *try it please.*

"Don't think I won't." Shannon said, as if she could read my mind.

"Go on Lee, please." Shannon said, stroking Lee's hair away from her face.

"Being the fat kid; I had to put up with a lot of things because people think that a fat kid doesn't have any problems, besides over eating. You should just be jolly and fat. Well, guess what…I wasn't! I was miserable and unhappy. Out of all the goddamn problems in the world, I had to have a dead daddy and a weight problem! And when it came to boys; paleeze, young boys don't like fat ass girls. You know who they like? They like your friends. The skinny ones. They come to the fat girl for advice on what they should do to get with your skinny friend…and all the while, you're saying, *But I'm the one who likes you. What about me?*"

"But Lee," Shannon said, taking a tissue and wiping Lee's tears, "You had boyfriends."

"But it's so much more than that, Shannon. Don't you see? All the guys that I dated wanted fat ass girls. I wanted someone that wanted me. And Jerell is the first one who just wants me, Leola. Don't you understand, even though I'm grown I still feel like that same fat ass kid."

"Oh please, I'm dying in here. What the fuck," I said interrupting them, "is it me or do you hear violins? This ain't no *'feel sorry for me cause I'm fat'* session, this is about that niggah beatin' yo' ass. You sitting up here trying to convince me of shit that I just don't see. You're 5'5" and a size sixteen, so what? You look good to me. You be wearin' the hell outta that tight ass shit you be puttin' on."

"It's not about you, it's about me!" Lee took a tissue and blew her nose.

"And him kicking your ass is about *him* and not *you*. Now look, I understand that you may have issues with yourself but then you deal with you, you don't let a niggah discipline you because you got issues. Don't you ever, ever; let a man mistreat you because you're carrying issues about what you use to be or what you are. You have to be important to you and that's how you become important to someone else. So you let him beat your ass and what?"

"What do you mean, *and what?*" Lee cried.

"This is what, look at yourself Lee, all you do is date somebody's husband and believe his lies. Why? He's married; the bitch with the legal ties is numero uno. Unless you want a crazy ma'fucker like Roger to damn near kill you and anybody else in his path." I couldn't help it but I started to get emotional, "Don't you know that we love you? But the love you have for yourself means the most. I use to think that beatin' a niggah out of his money was the bomb ma'fuckin thing to do. It paid my bills; it got me what I wanted. Nuccas were always sweatin' me. But in the end what, happened? Nothing. They used my body just as much as I used their money. Trust and believe, ain't no bitch out here gold diggin' and ain't giving up the pussy, it doesn't work like that. Don't do it to yourself. Believe me in the end, all that is left is you and your issues."

"But what am I suppose to do…"

"You need to get it together." Shannon said.

"Please," I chuckled, "he lives with somebody, anyway."

"Vera!" Lee screamed, getting off the couch, "I'm so sick of you always trying to degrade my man. Bitch!"

"Bitch? Let me explain something to you, you damn real I'ma bitch, and a bad ass one at that. But you? You a hoe, and a dumb hoe at that. See the difference is, bitches get rich and hoes get dicked. Stupid ass!"

"That's enough Vera!" Shannon yelled.

"No, fuck that! This hoe think's she is so smart! Come on Lee, let me show you where the niggah lives with the bitch, oh excuse me, the hoe."

"Oh no!" she said snatching her house keys off her coffee table, "You are so fuckin' wrong! Cause you don't even know where he lives."

We all stormed out of her house and jumped in Shannon's 745I. I gave her the address on Avenue D that Cherise had given me. Once we pulled up I grabbed Lee by the arm, "Don't punk out, come on. Let's go knock on the door."

"No!" Lee started screaming, pulling her arm back.

"Why not?"

"Because he's getting out the car with her, right there. He's right there…and she's pregnant!"

Jerell was standing in front of us, holding the door open for who I assumed to be Tamela, she appeared to be at least six months pregnant. He grabbed her by her waist and kissed her.

"Please take me home." Lee cried, "Please. I've had enough."

"Oh you're just gon' let this niggah punk you in the street, with his bitch and shit?" I asked in disbelief, "You're sitting here all beat the fuck up, pregnant, and this mofo living swell? Oh I don't think so, you better get yo' ass out the car and confront his ass!" I opened my car door and said, "Let's go."

"Jerell!" I yelled, stepping outta the car, "I know you hear me niggah!" The girl looked and said, "Who the fuck are they?"

" My name is Vera and you are…"

"Tamela."

"Well Tamela, this is Lee and we're here to see Jerell."

"Jerell?" the girl frowned, "Oh sweetie you must be mistaken, this is Rasheed. Rasheed Hill."

I looked at Lee in disbelief, "This mofo tryin' to play us the fuck out. His name is Jerrell, just as sure as I'm standin' here."

"It damn sure is." Lee said. I motioned for Angie and Shannon to come over where we were. I knew they would never believe this one.

"Sweetie," Tamela said, "his name is Rasheed Hill. Period."

"Well," I said placing my hands on my hip, "Why don't you let him speak for himself.

He looked at me and rolled his eyes. He looked at Lee and said, "This is why I didn't tell you my real name, because I knew you would stalk me. Why don't you accept the fact that I love my wife? Please if you continue to follow me around I will have to press charges on you." He grabbed Tamela by the arm and they walk toward their house.

"Lee!" I said, "You better drop kick that niggah in the fuckin' back!"

"No, I'm, not." She cried, "Please, I just gotta get outta here. I already told you that I've had enough!"

"Dumb ass niggah!" I yelled at Jerell, "I don't know why she would end up pregnant by your ass anyway!"

They walked in the house and slammed the door. Lee cried all the way home. We were going to spend the night with her, but she insisted on being alone.

I was in a deep sleep when the phone rang, "Hell-lo..."

"Hey Baby." Taj said.

"What time is it sweetie?" I said wiping my eyes.

"It's three o'clock in the morning."

"What's wrong?"

"Lee's here in the hospital."

"What?!" I screamed, reaching across the bed and cutting the light on. "Why? What happened? Is she okay?"

"She had a miscarriage. She won't press charges but Jerell beat her up pretty bad."

"I'm on my way!"

I called Shannon and Angie. We met at the hospital. When we arrived, Lee had just been admitted for overnight observation. She had a broken arm and her face was bruised. She wouldn't look at us. "Lee, please." Shannon said, "Please leave him alone. Please."

"Lee." A female voice said from the doorway, "May I come in?" when we looked it was Tamela.

"What are you doing here and what do you want?" I asked. I was giving this bitch five minutes, pregnant or not I was gon' beat her ass if she came up in here to start some shit.

"I didn't come for any trouble." She said, "I lied and told them that I was your sister so they would let me in. I know Rasheed did this to you and I'm so sorry." Tears were flowing from her eyes, "I followed him to your apartment and I heard everything outside the door. He didn't see me when he left out. I was the one who called the ambulance. I'ma go now, okay?"

"One minute," Lee said, "thank you. I just wanna say, thank you."

I walked her to the door and slipped her my card, "If you ever need to talk. Please call me."

***

"Well, Shannon," I said, while I was touching the color up in her hair, "I didn't expect the bitch to call. I was just being nice, but I picked up my cell phone last night, and there she was telling me her whole life story. But I'll say this, we need to get with her and fuck Mr. Jerell...Rasheed...whatever the fuck his name is up! He need his ass stomped anyway. Dirty told me all I had to do was say the word and he would stomp the shit out of him. Even Taj told me that he would call his brother, Sharief, if we needed him to and pull a drive by on that monkey ma'fuck-er and break his shit up!"

"That's the same shit Quincy suggested. Let's just talk to Tamela and see what she wants to do. Then we plot, while the bitch is still willing."

"True," DeAndre said, while sitting in his station chair, sipping on his coffee. "You better catch her ass now. You know how bitches do. One day she'll want revenge and the next day she'll want him back."

"There it is DeAndre." Angie said, while Rosa was washing her hair. "The best thing to do, is use the hoe's info to get some leverage on Jerell's ass. Tell her shit like he was using both of ya'll."

"Yeah, Angie," I said, "Then I'll hit her with this shit. 'You're a pretty girl, you seem to have something going for yourself, why get stuck with him? You see what he's capable of doing. Just take your baby and leave him. If you leave now, who knows maybe he'll get himself together for you and the baby."

"Great minds think alike," DeAndre laughed, "And once ya'll hit homegirl with that, you know she'll believe it and tell you everything that you need to know.

"Alright, I'ma call her now, ya'll be quiet. DeAndre, finish basing Shannon's scalp for me."

I spoke to Tamela for about an hour and repeated to her everything we'd just discussed in the shop. Just as we expected, she told me everything I needed to know. About how Jerell left his first wife to be with her. That his wife claimed Jerell use to beat her, but she didn't believe it, until she saw what he did to Lee. Anything I wanted to know she told me. When I got off the phone, I turned to them and said, "Let's skip the crazy shit and go straight to having his ass kicked! Stomp a mud hole in him!"

"No, Vera." Shannon said, "We have to save the best for last. Now let's put a plan into action."

"Whatever you say, but it starts tomorrow."

Day one: Angie bought a dildo to the shop. It was the prettiest black penis I have ever seen—balls and pubic hair included. Angie had a slight, she didn't wanna give away a good dildo, but hell, this was for our girl. So we sliced it up and poured fake blood in the cracks. For a nice touch, I put drops of mayonnaise in the cracks so it would turn yellow and look like puss. Then we sent it in the mail to Jerell, with a note that read, "Make sure yours never looks like this." Tamela called me right away after Jerell opened it.

"Vera!" she said, "He got it. He's in the kitchen right now holding his crouch and pacing the floor." He didn't bother Lee, because he was scared she would press charges on him. Especially after we sent Dirty and his friend over there acting as detectives; with an active warrant. As we suspected Jerell, was a bitch and told him that nobody by the name of Jerell or Rasheed lived there. Every since then, Tamela says that he jumps when the doorbell rings.

Day two: Come to find out Jerell was never unemployed. He just told Lee that, so she would never ask him for anything. So, I had Bryce hack into computer system at work. Luckily we were able to get the needed information from Tamela. Jerell worked for an advertising firm, which allowed him to work from home at times. Bryce took the information we had and ran with it. Hooked the shit up where we could send a nice lil' email, from none other than ole boy himself (Rasheed Hill must've been his real name, because that's the name he was using at work). Tamela told me everything I needed to know to lower the boom. The email went something like this, *"Hey ya'll. A niggah sittin' here scratchin' his nuts trying to figure out where my viagara is...and then I remembered that I gave my last pill to my supervisor, Dave. Did you all know that Dave was gay and he's taking it in the ass? Oh by the way, speaking of fags, Francis from accounting use to be a man. And Sally and Amy, from clerical, well let's just say that Amy likes to play with Sally's Kitty Kat. Two fine women, bumpin' pussy. But shit, I know I would like to watch! By the way Calvin, the senior Vice president, his baby is the mailroom guy's baby, he just doesn't know it yet.*

Oh well, all ya'll be blessed. Much Love

Rasheed Hill."

Tamela called the next evening and said that all the other fucked up gifts that we send would have to come straight to the house. Because ole boy's been suspended without pay until his upcoming trial for disorderly conduct. When he arrived at work the next morning after I sent the email, his co-workers jumped him in the bathroom. But he was the one, who the head of the department, suspended.

Day three: I pulled some shit outta my hat from when Shannon and I use to run game on a slick ma'fucker that thought he was the shit...Jerell had a bangin' ass custom designed Jag, with chrome wheels and the whole nine. This ma'fucker prided himself on this car. Tamela said that when he first got it, he wore olive green clothes for a week, so that he and the car would match.

Well, late one night Shannon and I took the tags off the car, called the cops, and reported that a vehicle with no tags was sitting on the street, The cops towed the car away and Jerell's been looking for it ever since.

Day four: The day I've been waiting on. The girls and I, this time including Lee and Cherise, went over to ole boy's spot to do some damage. We told Tamela to stay out of it, since she was pregnant, but she insisted that we bring her the same hoody and sweat pants that we would be wearing.

We covered our mouths with matching black bandanas and over our eyes we had on black Jackie O shades. Cherise was playing DMX's *Where The Hood At* to get us hyped up on our way to the spot. Cherise had already packed six wooden bats, wrapped in duck tape; or as Aunt Cookie calls them, *'Niggah Be Cool Sticks'*. Needless to say, we were strapped.

As we each stepped out we grabbed our weapons and creeped up to the stoop. Tamela let us in, as she ran around the back and got dressed in the gear we brought for her. We waited for her to come back before we made our move. When she came back, it was on.

This bum niggah was laying in the bed sleep. "WAKE THE FUCK UP!" Cherise screamed.

"What are ya'll doing?" Jerell asked, waking up sleep drunk. When he saw six thugettes standing over him with hoodies, sweats, and niggah be cool sticks, he started screaming.

"Shut the fuck up!" I said, "Screaming like a lil' bitch!"

"We gon' give you a chance, niggah," Shannon said, "to get the fuck out and if you don't make a move in two minutes, we gon' fuck your ass up!"

"Wait a minute. Wait a minute." Jerell said as started laughing, nervously, "You can't be serious?"

Shannon threw a crazy laugh in the air, "Hey y'all," she said, quoting the rapper, T.I., "It's a lot of niggahs that gotta lotta shit to say,"

"But when you confront 'im." Cherise growled, "They can't stand up for what they fuckin' said."

"Yeah," Shannon continued, "They be like, 'Naw, I ain't said that, he said that. Niggah," she pointed at Jerrell, "Stand up!"

He seemed to scared to move. BAMMMMMMMM!!!!!!! Shannon's stick hit the nightstand

"I-I-I…" Jerrell studdered, "Ain't goin' no where!"

"Ya, gotta alligator's mouth," I said, "And a humming bird's ass."

"Your mouth writin' checks," Angie followed up, "that ya ass can't cash!"

She moved closer to him, slamming her bat into her hand.

"We ain't no joke." Cherise said, "We use to let the mic smoke!"

We all looked at Cherise, like she was crazy, *that is not what we rehearsed.*

"He ain't moved yet!" Angie screamed.

I figured that it was my turn to flex a lil' bit so I took my stick and broke the ma'fuckin flat screen TV on the wall, *"Oh hell no!"* Tamela yelled, *"That was my shit!"*

"Tamela?" Jerell said in a thick West Indian accent, "I tought dat twas you! Whatcha doin' mun? Why?"

"Cause niggah, you play too much!" Tamela said, starting to cry.

See, what I mean about a bitch with feelings. Now look, Lee's punk ass ain't said a word yet, and Tamela is falling apart.

"Get up and get yo' shit!" I said demanding, trying to stop whatever was going on between these two.

"I'ma drop kick yo' ass! Niggah!" Cherise yelled.

Lee was still standing there like a bump on a log, so I nudged her slightly with my elbow. "Speak bitch."

Lee looked at Jerell, walked over to him and slapped the shit out of him. "That's wassup!" We all cheered.

Then she lost control and started beating his ass like a damn gangsta. She took her bat and banged him in the knees. Then she took it and started swinging it wildly. Hitting Jerell wherever the stick landed.

"Lee!" Shannon yelled, "Chill!" Lee still didn't stop. Since when did this chick get balls like this?

"Lee, you gon' fuck around and kill him. Just wait." I screamed.

Jerell seemed too scared to hit her back, so he kept covering his face.

"Stop it!" Angie screamed and then she snatched Lee off of Jerrell. "That's enough!"

"Why ya'll doing this? What I ever do to ya'll?" Jerell cried.

"Jerell," Lee said, "Why did you beat on me? I lost my baby because of you!"

"I told you to get an abortion! Stupid ass!" Jerell was still talking shit but we could tell that he was scared. Limping in pain, he started taking some of his things and packing them in a gym bag.

"Hurry up, punk, before I burn this ma'fuckah down!" I yelled.

After I said that, I peeped out the window and saw Dirty and his boys waiting for Jerrel outside.

After Jerell packed what he could, in-between shaking he said, "Where am I supposed to go?"

The answer was BAMMMMMMMMM!!!! Angie stick slammed against the floor, "Oh baby boy you 'bout to have three hots and a cot!" Angie sneered.

"West Side!" Cherise said in a high-pitched voice.

Tamela started mushing Jerell in the head. "Dumb niggah. Punk niggah. What niggah. Say somethin'. I dare you."

"Get off me, Tamela!"

"Do somethin'!" She said, "I dare you."

"Let me just go, before I hurt you!"

Jerell asked permission to walk pass us. We followed closely behind, tapping him on the shoulder with the stick, every step of the way. When he got to the living room, he turned to Tamela and Lee, "Ya'll was some lil' bomeclaude hoes." Then he opened the front door and tried to run out. Only to be greeted by Dirty's fist. Dirty slammed him to the ground and said, "You like to beat women huh? You a punk? Huh? Beat me then ma'fucker!" Dirty took Jerell and beat his ass so bad that we had to beg him to stop. "And now," Dirty's friends who were standing around watching spoke, "Rasheed Hill, we have a warrant for your arrest." What nobody, except Shannon and Angie knew, was that, my cousin Dirty had just finished the police academy and was now a NYPD police officer. I had already given Dirty all the information on Jerell that he needed, so that the state would have a domestic violence case without Lee having to give up any information. Now the State of New York could pick up the charges.

I looked at Lee as they placed Jerell in the back of the police car, "No matter what we go through, I will never let anybody fuck with you."

"I love you too, Vera." She said hugging me, "I love you too."

Flagrant Foul

"Why do you have to go?" I asked Taj, as he packed his bags, "Didn't you just leave and go to a seminar?"

"Vera, I'm teaching the seminar this time, baby."

I was sitting on the edge of the bed in my green and white silk nightgown, pissed off. Every time I turned around Taj had something to do out of town. I sucked my teeth and crossed my legs, "Do what you gotta do, but am I gon' get some dick before you go?"

Instantly, I could tell that he had a hard on. He slipped out of his CK boxers and walked over to me, "This dick is all you care about ain't it? We've been engaged forever, you ain't mentioned a date yet."

I threw both of my legs over his shoulders. "Yes I did, December 7th."

"And when was I going to be informed of this date?" Taj said, moaning his way in.

"I wanted to surprise you."

"Get the fuck outta here, Vera." He started grinding and his dick felt like it was reaching for the pit of my stomach.

"You told me to pick a date and run with it, so I did." *Lawd I hope this man, can't tell that I'm lying. December 7th is the first date I could think of...Damn why is he fucking me so hard?*

"I know you're lying. What's up with that?" The more he spoke the harder he was grinding, the sound his balls slapping against my ass was like a wet towel hitting my skin.

"Nothing baby," I said jerking from the roughness, he was throwing my way. "The seventh of December, is there a problem? You don't like that date?"

"It's not the date, it's you."

"What about me?" My head bouncing slightly off the bed from his hard ass strokes.

"You're playing me."

"No, I'm not. Taj," I was trying to take my legs down because his grinding was starting to hurt.

"Don't take your legs down." He placed his arms around them, holding them tightly.

"Well you gotta slow down. You're knockin' the hell outta me."

Instead of stopping he started grinding harder with each word. "When...I...come back...there better be....some wedding plans in motion or...we gotta...problem...Understand?"

"Yes baby." I said, surrendering.

An hour later Taj was on his way to the airport. The cab was outside waiting for him. As he got in the car, the mailman walked up the stoop and handed me the mail. The letter sitting on top was from the court saying that the charges filed against me and the girls for wreckin' shop at Nile's and Monica's wedding had been dropped. Before I could look up to tell Taj the good news, the cab had already taken off. By the time I walked back in the house to see if Angie, Shannon, and Lee, had received their letters, the phone rang. It was Shannon.

"Hey Boo! Did you get the letter from the court?" I said.

"Yes and no. The letter came, but Quincy received it."

Holy shit, what did she just say? "What did you say?" I asked, not believing what I just heard.

"*I said* that Quincy received it."

"What happened?"

"He saw a letter for me addressed from court and he opened it, being fuckin' nosy and he got his welcome home present."

"What did you tell him?" I asked, still in shock.

"I told him that I was sorry but that I needed a break from our relationship. I didn't want him to find out like this...you know...receiving a letter in the mail, but everything happens for a reason."

"Get the fuck outta here. Just like that? And at what part did Quincy lose it?"

"Girl," Shannon exhaled, "This ma'fucker went crazy."

"Did he hit you?"

"Hell no! But he threw some shit around. Said how he couldn't believe me. That here he was a black man puttin' his thing down and I was fuckin' playin' him. I just sat there, what was I going to say, 'No, I didn't play you.' Hell, he had it in black and white. So, I just told him as much as I knew he could handle. My heart ain't here no more."

"Damn, Shannon, where's he at now?"

"He left. He told me he would be by to collect the rest of his shit at another time."

"Damn, Shannon, I'm not so sure if you should've done that."

"Well time'll tell, but all of these games have to end. I'm done with it. If Quincy wants to step, then he probably should. I've given him no reason to stay. I just need a break." She got choked up, "Let me call you later, Boo."

I made up my mind, by the time Taj came back I would have some locations for the wedding in mind. I made a couple of phone calls to some wedding consultants. Afterwards, I played with Skyy until it was her naptime and we both fell asleep. When I woke up, Rowanda was knocking on my bedroom door telling me that she was going out for a little while.

"Excuse me?" I frowned. "How come all of a sudden," I said looking her up at her black halter dress, three-inch heels, with her short, blonde frosted, and spiked hair cut, "You're going out every weekend?"

"Because," she smiled.

"Because what?"

"You want me to really tell you, really?" she blushed.

"Yes."

"I have a boyfriend."

"Oh please, that's ridiculous." That was the last thing I wanted to hear.

"See, that's why I didn't tell you." She walked in and sat next to me on the bed.

"Well, who is he? " I sat up, Skyy started cooing. "That 39 year old man?"

"No, this guy happens to be 42. I'ma few years older than him, but so what?"

"Oh, hell no! How are you going to have a boyfriend and we've never met him?"

"You wanna meet him?"

"Yeah." I said expecting her to make up an excuse.

"Good, he's downstairs, come on."

Rowanda practically raced down the stairs like a schoolgirl with a crush on the captain of the football team. I had an attitude when I stepped into my living room and saw how fine this man was, instantly I became pissed. Because I knew that there was no way that she wasn't screwing his fine ass. He stood at least six feet tall, with a milk chocolate complexion and hazel brown eyes. He had a salt and pepper beard with a low haircut to match. It didn't make any sense for my mother to have a boyfriend that was this fine.

"Craig, this is my daughter and my granddaughter." Rowanda said pointing at me and Skyy, who was in my arms.

"Hello," he said, sounding like Barry White, "I've heard so much about you. How are you?"

"I'm fine and yourself?" It was killing me to be nice.

"I'm well. I'm glad I got a chance to meet you." He looked at Rowanda and said, "Baby, we need to get going."

Baby? I frowned, is this mofo retarded, calling my mother 'baby' right in front of me? Rowanda smiled, "No problem." She grabbed her chiffon shawl and after ole boy was standing outside on the stoop, she looked at me, winked her eye, and said low enough so that only I could hear, "Don't wait up for me."

After Rowanda left Uncle Boy walked out of the kitchen and said, "Baby Girl, you seen my toe nail clippers?"

I wanted to cry all over again.

"Hey Diva," DeAndre said coming into the shop. "How do I

get this I spy shit off of the computer. You never watch it any way. I'm trying to get on the Internet."

"Damn!" I said, "I've been meaning to take that shit outta my house. When I go home I'll do it. Just remind me, please."

"I'll remind you, but don't forget, because if Rowanda finds out that you've been watching her, she's gon' lose her mind."

"I know DeAndre, it'll be off tomorrow." Sitting at the desk I played with the computer trying to get the camera off. Uncle Boy was on the camera with Skyy sitting in her carrier looking at him. I could hear Rowanda yelling from the other room, that she was coming.

Uncle Boy had his feet propped up on my couch with his gigantic ass toenail clippers out preparing to clip his toenails. I started knocking on the screen, "Take that shit somewhere else!" Well, the next thing I know Uncle Boy clips his big toe's thick ass nail and it musta been too hard to crack., 'cause the toenail clipper broke and popped my baby in the forehead! Skyy started screaming. The last thing I saw before grabbing my purse and rushing out was Rowanda racing into the living room to see what happened to the baby.

I flew through the streets of Manhattan and into Brooklyn like a bat outta hell! When I arrived at my brownstone, I ran inside. "Uncle Boy," I was breathing heavy and was out of breath, "you hit my baby in the head wit your nasty ass toe nail clipper?!" Rowanda was feeding Skyy and she looked at me like I was crazy, "How do you know that?"

"Because..." I stalled, realizing that I was caught out there and had no choice but to drop the bomb.

"Vee," Rowanda said, laying Skyy down in her cradle, "How do you know that Uncle Boy made a mistake and hit Skyy?"

I didn't know what to say, so I took a chance on trying to explain. "Well, see...these cameras they go in the baby's nursery and the living room and they allow me to see the baby, from the shop and uhhh..."

"So you've been watching me?" Rowanda said. "Here I've been taking care of Skyy and you've been video taping me?"

"It wasn't everyday. I haven't watched you in a long time...and..."

"Oh Baby Girl," Uncle Boy said, "Now you dead wrong! Apologize to your mother!"

"No!" Rowanda said, "She ain't got to apologize to me. I can show her better than I can tell her!" She stormed upstairs to her room and started packing her things.

"Rowanda, what are you doing?" I said following behind her.

"I'm getting away from your selfish ass! Here I've been giving up my life during the week, to be a good mother and a good grandmother and you've been spying on me all this time? Oh hell no!"

"But you gotta understand, this is my baby. I didn't know-"

"Didn't know what, whether I would put her in the trash?"

I couldn't believe that she said that.

"Well, I'll admit I was a little reluctant myself." Uncle Boy said, standing in the doorway, "That's part of the reason I moved in here." *I wish I had a gun to shoot this lyin' ass niggah.*

"Well to hell with both of ya'll!" Rowanda shouted, "Vera you take your cameras and shove 'em. I'm outta here!"

"Rowanda, wait!"

"Rowanda...wait...hell!" She stormed out, ran down the stairs, and slammed the door behind her.

I couldn't believe this shit! I looked at Uncle Boy, "You need to go home. Right now!"

"Don't take it out on me, Baby Girl!"

I called Aunt Cookie on the phone. I was crying so hard that she couldn't understand one word I said. "Baby Girl," she said, "Don't say nothin', just wait there for Aunt Cookie, I'm comin'. I was comin' anyway to tell ya Uncle Boy about his ex-wife or whatever the hell she was."

I cried the entire time until Aunt Cookie came. When she finally arrived, I told her everything that happened from beginning to end.

"Baby Girl," she said, once I was finished, "You know you were wrong." She hadn't even acknowledged Uncle Boy, who kept clearing his throat and walking past the bedroom door.

"I know but—"

"You know, but what? Now get it together, go find your mother, and apologize. I'll take Skyy home with me." Finally she spoke to Uncle Boy, "Not that you need to know, but June Bug down at the barber shop, told Carol's man, that you ain't have no reason to confess. Mare-Helen has been dead for over a year now. Her third cousin on her daddy's side and June Bug are related."

"Thank you, Jesus!" Uncle Boy said, hugging Aunt Cookie, "Well, I didn't exactly mean it like that. Look, Chocolate Chip, I miss ya, and I need to be with you. Please let me come home."

"Come on Boy, Chocolate Chip been missin' you too."

Uncle Boy looked at me and said, "Baby Girl, I know you don't want Uncle Boy to leave, but you know that I gotta go home. Maybe I'll come over and visit more often." He smiled.

I didn't respond.

After they left I jumped in my X5 to find Rowanda. She was still upset but, thankfully, safe at Dirty's new apartment.

"Can I speak to you...please?" I begged her.

"Speak." She said with an attitude sitting on the couch.

"I'm sorry. I really am. Rowanda this is my first child and I was taking a hellava chance with you. I didn't really know you, but I still left my baby with you. I love you Rowanda, more than you will ever know, and I'm so sorry that you'll never know how much." The tears started flowing, "All I can ask is that you forgive me and know that it'll never happen again." I kneeled down in front of her and placed my head in her lap.

"I'm your mother, Vera. I can understand how you feel or felt, but I won't tolerate it." She said wiping my tears.

"I'm taking it off tonight." I looked up at her with pleading eyes.

"Not tonight, right now!"

"Yes, I promise. Please forgive me?"

"I don't know what I'ma do with you. You gotta learn that trust goes both ways. If you ever do something like this to me again, I will never stay in your house, again Understand?"

"I understand."

She gave me a hug. At that moment, nothing else mattered in the world, because I had my mother.

That night Rowanda came back home with me. I unhooked the cameras and threw them in the garbage. We put the baby to bed, ordered Chinese food, and exchanged boyfriend stories; both only sharing what we knew the other could handle. I knew she didn't wanna hear about my sex life and I damn sure didn't wanna hear about her's. Afterwards we ate some chocolate cheesecake and drank wine. Relaxing on the couch in my bedroom, we watched Disappearing Acts on DVD, cussin' Franklin's ass out the entire time.

The next thing I remember is Skyy waking up for her six a.m. bottle.

Technical Foul

Since yesterday, my X5 has been giving me trouble and today it won't start. I told Taj, last month, that I wanted to get a new one, but he insisted that we have priorities now and buying a new truck isn't one of them. But shit, the councilman I was fuckin' with a few years back gave BMW too much paper for this ma'-fucker to be acting up.

Uncle Boy and Aunt Cookie came by and picked up Skyy and Rowanda. Rowanda's, what's-his-name, was hanging out over Aunt Cookie's house and wanted to see her and the baby.

When ole boy called this morning and Rowanda told him to meet her at Aunt Cookie's, I was relived because then I could get a break for a little while. Now that they were gone and I have a little freedom, my goddamn truck won't start. To make matters worse, I have an appointment this morning with an afro-centric wedding consultant that I really need to see, before Taj gets back this evening.

In the midst of trying to figure out what to do my cell phone rang. Fuck! I just knew it was Taj telling me that his flight was coming in early. I didn't even peep at the caller I.D. when I flipped open the phone.

"Hello?"

"Wassup Ma!" I couldn't make out the voice, but I knew this wasn't Taj.

"Hi." I said distantly, to give the person a hint that I didn't know who they were.

"Vera, this is Bryce."

"Oh, hey Bryce, what you got poppin'?"

"Oh, what, you're a rough neck now?"

"Please," I said, "My freakin' truck is acting up and I just don't know what to do. Taj'll be coming in soon. I'm suppose to go and see a wedding coordinator. Can't drive Taj's Escalade because it's being detailed! Hell, I'm just screwed."

"Vera, please." Bryce chuckled, "Is the horn blowing?"

I pressed on the horn. "No."

"Is the truck turning over at all?"

"No."

"The battery is probably dead then."

My other line clicked. "Hold on Bryce...Hello?"

"Hey, baby!" Now this was Taj.

"Hey, baby." Don't ask me why but with Bryce on the other line I felt like I was playin' Taj. This has to stop.

"What's wrong?" Taj asked. "Is my daughter okay?"

"Yeah baby, she's fine. She's with her grandmother or grandmothers I should say, and Uncle Boy. I swear I've never seen one little baby have so many adults wrapped around her finger."

He chuckled, "Baby, my plane has been delayed, the weather is horrible down here. I may be here a few hours. When I get to JFK I'll call you."

"Okay Taj, be safe. Call me as soon as you get here. I love you."

After I hung up with Taj, I clicked back over to Bryce. "Damn you had me on hold a long time."

I'm sorry that was Taj, but look I gotta go, I have to call a mechanic."

"I can take a look at it if you want me to. The only thing is, I got a lil' date and I'll need to change at your house, after I'm done looking at your truck, that is."

"Date with who?

"With a young lady, I met. Now, do you want me to come take a peep at your ride?"

"Bryce, I thought you were a drug counselor, not an auto mechanic."

"I'm a jack of all trades. Remember?"

"Uhmm hmm, well, hurry your ass up because I have to be on time to get Taj from the airport."

It took Bryce about fifteen minutes to get to my house, when he got here he had a change of clothes in his garment bag. So, he was serious? He really had a date. Still, I played stupid. "What are those clothes for?"

"Girl stop playing," he said opening the hood of my truck. "I told you I had a date. I gotta look for somebody, especially since you don't want me."

Is this niggah for real? "Are you for real?"

"Very." He said, propping the hood up and then stepping into my personal space. "Look Vera, I know you gotta man, but I'm feeling the hell outta you. You know what we had was special. Let's stop playing this game and lay the shit out on the table."

"Special? Boy, I was practically a kid. I'm grown now and there's nothing to lay out on the table. I'm marrying Taj. I love

245

him. I'm in love with him. That's my niggah and I ain't giving him up for nobody. So stop it, please, and if you don't, I'm gon' stop fuckin' with you all together."

"So, essentially you're telling me to step off?"

"Not essentially. That's exactly what I'm saying."

"So, you don't want me?" he pressed.

"Is there a certain dialect of retarded that you want me to translate rejection into?"

He started laughing. "It's all good Ma, maybe the next life-time."

"I'll be looking for Taj in that lifetime, too."

"You got that." Bryce chuckled, returning his attention back to my truck. "It's the battery, let me turn my car around so I can give you a jump."

Bryce turned his car around and gave my X5 a jump, "Ai'ight you should be good now...You know what, since you're a woman, and probably never think of it, let's check your fluids."

"What the hell you mean, since I'm a woman, *let you check my fluids?*"

"Just that...no pun intended." He winked his eye and while twisting the cap off the oil gasket he sighed, "Just as I thought, you need to be oiled. What you want? You want me to hit it? Or you wanna wait for your man to do it?"

"You use to ride the slow bus to school didn't you? Stop play-ing with me. I'll get the oil outta the back of my truck so that you can put it in my gasket...I mean the oil gasket."

"I'm sure you did." He smiled revealing his perfect teeth.

This niggah gotta get the fuck outta here. He got me sweatin' and shit, trying not to blush. I can't take it. "Look, here you go,"

I twisted the top off the oil bottle, handing it to him, and…"Bryce! What the fuck?! I can't believe that you! Shit! You dropped oil all over my Gucci sneakers? Do you know how much these cost me?"

"Nobody told you to open it. Shit look at me, this shit is all over my pants, my hands, and my arms, and you got the nerve to be complaining about some damn knock off sneakers! I got a goddamn date!"

"Knock off? That's some ole bullshit and you can kick rocks wit' it. The only thing knocked off will be that fake ass hoochie you wish were me."

"Her, not being you, was your call, not mine."

"Bryce, let me explain something to you. I got a man. I don't need you. So, stop with the bullshit. You gon' fuck around here and get us both knocked the fuck out!"

"By who? Doctor boy?"

"Doctor boy? Niggah, don't make me spit my switch blade at your punk ass!"

"Punk ass?" he started laughing, "Yeah I got your punk…but whatever Vera, let me stop playing with you. Shit, I gotta go home and shower. I'll never meet up with this lil' chick on time!"

"Boy just come on in my house and use the downstairs bathroom. And make sure you hurry your ass up because I gotta be ready to pick up *my man* when he calls."

"Yeah ai'ight!" Bryce said playfully, "Just show me to the bathroom."

I mushed him on the side of his head and he laughed.

"Vera, remember when we use to live on Lincoln Street and…"

"Yo' ass use to jump Double Dutch with the lil girls." I said unlocking the front door.

"Oh you tryin' to play me?" he said nudging me with his shoulder causing me to trip through the front entrance. "Don't make me fall." I chuckled.

"I would catch you."

I shot his ass a look and said, "There you go with that bull-shit."

"Yeah ai'ight."

"Bryce, just go take your shower. There's a linen closet inside the bathroom."

I ran upstairs, took off my clothes, and jumped in the shower. My ankles and a parts of my legs were splashed with oil. As I was stood in the shower, the steamy drops of water slid down my skin and I started thinking about laying on the edge of the tub and fucking Taj like no tomorrow.

I jumped out the shower, dried off, and tried to throw the towel on the chaise, but it landed on the corner of the bed. That's when I realized that I hadn't made up the bed this morning. Fuck it; I'll do it after I get dressed.

After I dried off, I slid on Taj's favorite green apple Victoria Secret's bra and panty set. Then I slipped on a pair of super tight blue Juicy jeans. No sooner, than I snapped my jeans closed, did I hear Taj yelling my name at the top of his lungs, "VERA!!!!" My heart stopped. Shit!

"What the fuck are these?" He asked, holding a pair of men's boxers in his hand. Immediately our eyes locked. He looked me up and down. Staring slowly at my tight jeans and his favorite bra. He peeked behind me and glanced at the unmade bed and the red terry cloth towel laying on the edge. There were two wine glasses lying on the floor. The same wine glasses that Rowanda and I had from last night.

"You heard what the fuck I said! Whose are these?" Taj demanded.

"Are those yours?" I said biting my lip.

"Stop that biting your lip, shit! What are you so nervous for?"

"How did you get here?"

"You fuckin' with me? Did you forget that I live here? The plane turned out to be on time, so I caught a cab home. Plus you didn't answer your cell phone. Now I'ma try and be calm because I'm waiting for you to tell me somethin' so I don't lose my fuckin' mind."

Taj started walking closer to me. "Taj, please don't be upset. I can explain…"

He stopped dead in his tracks. "Start explaining." As he said that Bryce ran up the stairs, without a shirt on and fumbling with the belt in his pants. "Vee, you ai'ight?" As he said that Taj turned around and left hooked the shit outta him!

"Stop it!" I ran around Taj and jumped in front of Bryce. Taj drew his fist back and I cringed. "It's not what you think, let me explain!" I said and ducked down.

"Stand the fuck up!" Taj screamed. "And look at me!"

I stood up slowly and turned toward him, he had tears in his eyes. "Taj—"

"Vera, how could you do this to me? This is why you weren't answering your cell phone? You left me at the airport cause you were fuckin' this niggah?!"

"I wasn't fuckin' him! Why would you even think some dumb shit like that?! Please, don't hit him anymore, let me explain…"

"Now you taking up for this niggah? What is he suppose to be? Your ma'fuckin man! This is why you been actin' funny?! This niggah has been your problem!"

"What the fuck are you talking about?!" I screamed. I turned around toward Bryce who was holding the side of his face. "Ma'fucker you better say somethin'! Why the hell you just standing here?"

"I don't have to explain shit to his ass!"

I couldn't believe this was happening to me. I turned back around toward Taj, "Taj, baby please..." Before I could finish what I was saying, Taj reached over me and punched Bryce so hard in the face, that it forced Bryce to do a spin just to catch his balance.

I tripped and barely fell outta the way as Taj started giving Bryce some work for his ass. This shit has got to be a dream!

"Taj stop it!" I yelled getting up off the floor.

"Stop it? You got this niggah in my ma'fuckin house where my daughter sleeps! Are you fuckin' crazy!" That's when Taj seemed to completely black out! Taj started hooking the shit outta Bryce and I was screaming for him to stop. With every blow that he landed to Bryce's body I kept feeling like Taj was going to kill him. *Oh, God please, make him stop!*

I started pulling Taj at the waist to get him off of Bryce, "What the fuck are you doing? What the fuck, you gon' kill him! Please stop! Please stop! Don't kill him! Oh God!" For a moment Taj seemed to catch himself, that's when he backed up and told Bryce, "You got two seconds to get the fuck out!" Bryce looked at Taj and charged toward him, knocking him on the bed, Taj flipped over, kicking Bryce in the stomach, Taj chuckled, "What the fuck are you, stupid!"

I grabbed Taj, by his waist and yelled, "Stop It!"

Taj got up from the bed charging at Bryce. Real quick, Bryce pushed him back and I was able to get in between them. Taj grabbed me by the arms and spun me around. "You got one more time to pull me off his ass, and I'm knock yo' ass the fuck out!"

"I don't believe this shit, Vera!" Bryce screamed with blood all over his chin and chest. I help yo' fuckin' ass out and this niggah fuckin' attacks me! What the fuck! I should'a just fucked you, again, if I knew it was gon' be all of this."

Again? What did he say? "What did you say?" I said to him, "You must be goddamnit crazy to say some shit like that?" Before I could continue, Taj reached over my shoulder and pimped slapped the shit out of him. "Now you wanna die!" Taj yelled.

Bryce looked at Taj and said, "I'ma shoot you ma'fucker!"

"Do it niggah, what?"

"Punk ass fuckin' doctor! You think you runnin' some shit!"

"Ma'fucker, that's where your game is all confused, I'm from the ma'fuckin Bricks, I'ma street niggah first and foremost and the quickest way to get fucked up is to play with my life. It's either me or you niggah and the way I see it, it's like you comin' for my throat! But I tell you what, just remember that the same ma'fucker that pops the bullet gotta be able to wear that ma'-fucker! And when you shoot, shoot to kill, cause if you don't it, its gon' be on, forever!"

"Fuck you, niggah!" Bryce yelled. "Bring it!"

"Bryce!" I said, "You like gettin' yo ass kicked or somethin'? You don't have no work up in here, please stop talkin' shit and go. I'm begging you please. You gon' fuck around and Taj's crazy ass gon' kill you! Please, I'm begging you, to leave!"

Finally, Bryce started backing out of the room.

Taj was standing there looking crazy. I was scared as hell, so I started walking behind Bryce. As soon as my foot touched the other side of the door way Taj yanked me back into the room and said, "Where the fuck are you going?"

I pulled myself away and said, "I need to make sure Bryce gets the fuck out!"

I practically ran down the stairs. When I caught up to Bryce I had some choice words for his ass, "I can't fuckin' believe you would do this!"

"You can't believe *I* would do this?" He was standing in the doorway with the rest of his clothes in his arms. "Vera I had your heart before that niggah was even thought of! I was your first lover and you wanted me back, don't even act like you didn't!"

Taj appeared out of nowhere, reached over my shoulder and slammed the door in Bryce's face. "Your first lover! I knew it was something extra with you and that ma'fuckah. I knew it!" Taj yelled, the warmth of his breath floating over my shoulders. "You lied to me and you've been lying to me all along?! I can't fuckin' believe this!"

I turned around. "What are you talking about? That was fifteen years ago!"

"I wouldn't give a damn if it were four days ago. I asked you to tell me the truth and you lied!"

"I didn't do anything, just let me explain!"

"I can't believe this shit! Your first love? You were still fuckin' him?" He completely blacked again. "I can't believe this shit! I just can't fuckin' believe it!" He picked up the marble coffee table and slammed it against the wall. It made a thumping sound as it hit the floor. Then with one swoop Taj knocked over all of my retired Annie-Lee figurines and Aroma candles off the mantle. He picked up a picture of us and threw it against the wall, the glass from the picture frame sent pricks of glass into the air. "All for a niggah, Vera? What, my dick wasn't big enough?" Tears were streaming down his face. I was scared as hell. Taj looked at me and said, "I gotta get the fuck away from you!"

"Taj, what the hell is wrong with you, nothing happened, let me explain! Are you listening to me? Are you? Ma'fucker you better listen to me! Ma'fucker you hear me!"

"No! Get the hell outta my way. Because if you keep standing in my face I'ma knock you the fuck out!"

"Taj please let me explain!" I couldn't believe that this was happening. I started following him around the house and up the stairs as he started packing his things. "Why won't you listen to me, I WASN'T FUCKIN' HIM...JUST LISTEN!!"

At first, he seemed unfazed and then he snapped, "Do you know what the fuck it takes for a niggah to stay with you? How much I put up with? How much I tolerated and then you get a punk ass, stick up kid and you fuck him? You couldn't get no ma'fucker that had some work for me? You, Ms. Ma'fuckin-Gold Digger. Ms. Goddamn Gamer, and all you did was play yourself! I swear on my mother's grave that I'll never fuck with you again. Ever!"

WHAPPPPP!!!!!!!!!!! I hauled off and slapped the shit out of him. "Who the fuck you talking to? Me? You stupid ma'fucker! You ain't the grandest niggah in the world! I ain't have to fuck with you. But I love you. I ain't never loved no man, but I love you. But you ain't shit! You wanna leave? You wanna leave? Get the fuck out and don't come back!" I started pulling his shit out of the closets and throwing it on the floor. "Fuck you! Fuck all this shit! Fuck this crying! Fuck loving you! Fuck marrying you! FUCK YOU! Get the fuck out and don't ever look back!" I started kicking his clothes all over the floor. Then I looked at him and ran toward him. He grabbed me by both arms before I could punch the shit out of him. "You want me to beat the shit out you? Let me get my shit and go!" I slapped him upside the head. "Vera, if you hit me again. I'ma stretch you the fuck out!" When he let me free from his embrace, I hauled off and right hooked the shit out of him. He grabbed the side of his face and I ran in the bathroom and locked the door. I was waiting for him to call my name or bang on the door, but he didn't. I sat and waited for almost a half-hour and nothing. When I opened the door to peek out slightly, he kicked it open with his foot, grabbed me around the neck, and yanked me out. "I dare you to punch me in my goddamn face, again! Crazy ass!" He pushed me on the bed and then he ran down the stairs.

Regaining, my balance, I ran behind him. As he went to walk out the front door, I mushed him with all my might in the back of his head! He turned around and said, "You really want me to beat your ass don't you?"

"You think I'm scared of you. Fuck you!" I stood on my tip toes and tried my best to look him in the eyes.

"Fuck me? Just get the fuck out of my face. Fuck me? Good, I'm out! And don't *you* look the fuck back!"

"So that's it? This is it?" I cried, trying to block his path. "You gon' just leave! Fuck me, fuck us, fuck everything. All for something that you *think* happened? We just had a baby, niggah! Are you for real? I changed my life to be with you and this is what you do to me."

"Vera, you ain't shit! I don't even know why I was fuckin' with you in the first place! We're finished. Stay the fuck away from me! And when I come and get my daughter don't even fuckin' breath in my face!" He went to slam the door and then he turned back around and said, "Do you realize that that cop ma'fuckah had a gun in my face? That I could've died, fuckin' with you, and this is what you do?" I took my entire hand and mushed him in the face! Then I pushed the door closed, locked it, grabbed a chair and placed it under the doorknob.

I looked out the living room window, watched him toss his things in the backseat of his Escalade, and take off.

Last Quarter, five seconds left...

Black space, with silver stars and white lines shooting through.
The music from the traffic outside echoed in my ears and
reminded me of how people were leaving one another all the
time...and some of them never coming back.

My heart ache had split in to so many pieces that I couldn't
tell whether the pain started at the top of my head or at the bottom of my feet. I thought that the first time Taj left me, I would
die...but that was my fault. I was actually fucking around. This
time I stopped, took a breath. "This is the flip side of the game,
Vera. Catch ya'self."

I know I was fuckin' up, I know I was. But I never stopped
loving Taj. I was just feeling some ole, extra shit. I never loved
Bryce. Never. But I loved Taj, I still love Taj, but now I'm sitting
here in the midst of moonlit darkness, trying to figure out what
the fuck is going on.

Convinced that Taj would be back later and that we'd be
able to talk about what happened, I picked myself off the floor.
Then I moved the chair from underneath the doorknob and
unlocked the door. Most of my figurines were broken, so I threw
them in the trash. The candles were broken into pieces so I
swept them up. The glass from the picture frame I picked up one

by one. In the midst of cleaning up, I felt a knocking in my chest and suddenly my mouth started trembling and without any warning, the tears flooded back, sweeping me into a wave of hard pounding and crashing jolts of pain. I picked up the phone and called Shannon. I was crying so hard that all I could do was gasp for air.

"Vera?" Shannon said, "Is that you?"

"Yes." I managed to spit out before the involuntary jerking started again.

"Stop crying, please."

I couldn't stop crying and the more I tried not to cry the more the tears came.

"Is Skyy okay?"

"Yes."

"Rowanda?"

"Uhmm hmm." I said biting my bottom lip.

"Vera, sweetie, tell me please, what's wrong?"

"Taj...he left...Bryce...but I didn't do anything...I swear I didn't..."

"Calm down and speak slowly."

I tried to keep my bottom lip from trembling so that I could keep the words that fell outta my mouth steady. "Taj came here and he thought that Bryce and I slept together."

"What?! Did you? Please tell me you didn't."

"No, I didn't fuck him! I tried to explain that but he wouldn't listen."

"Vera, where is Taj now?"

"He left me. He's gone…" that's when I knew that I would die if I didn't get off the floor and walk around. "Shannon, I gotta go. My head feels like its gonna explode." I started walking around and then I had to sit back down again. I took the chair from under the doorknob, and then I started pacing the floor again; repeating to myself from the beginning what exactly had gone wrong.

The words weren't coming fast enough, "Think Vera. Think! Oh my God! I started screaming, "Oh my God!" I couldn't stop screaming. I kept trying but I couldn't. "Please God. Please God. Help me." I sat back down and cried into my knees.

I didn't hear Shannon when she came in. She stood over me and looked down. I was crouched with my knees softly pressed to my chest and my arms clasped together around my legs.

Shannon slid down the wall next to me. "Damn," she said pulling my head against her bosom, "What the hell are you doing here, like this again?"

I sucked the snot back into the bridge of my nose and said, "It's all my fault. I was being so stupid."

"No, you were being Vera. Fucking up, but not meaning to fuck up."

"But, I didn't do anything."

"That was *yo' niggah*, Vera. That was *your man*. When he first told you he wasn't feeling Bryce then you should have given him that, and cut Bryce off, completely. But you didn't and now here we are. You kept playing…damn, Vera."

"Oh, so you're blaming me?"

"I'm not blaming you, I'm just letting you know that this could've been prevented."

"You don't even know what happened! Fuck his ass! He wanted to leave, then good, he's gone…he's gone…Shannon, he

257

should've trusted me. I kept trying to tell him. I kept trying!" I started crying again.

"It's not always the here and now that hurts us the most. Sometimes, it's what we've been going through all along."

"Please, Shannon."

"Come on Vera, let's be for real. How long has Taj been on you about setting a date, making some wedding plans? And you did nothing. How many times did he catch you with Bryce and still the niggah didn't go away, even after he told you that he did-n't want you fuckin' with him. Sometimes, Vera, it's the shit that happens over and over again that does the most damage and then when something happens...even if it's really nothing...it still blows everything the fuck up. That's just like when Quincy came by the other day. He stood at the door and he said, 'All I wanna know, is, how long? How long were you going to lead me around, blind'?"

"What did you say?" I asked, raising my head from her bosom and wiping my eyes.

"Nothing. What was I going to say? I fucked up."

"What did he do?"

"He looked at me and said, 'If I could get over loving you, then shit would be much easier for me. Then he left...Vera, I don't want you to make some of the fucked up decisions that I've made. I got my shit all fucked up. I been walking around here thinking that if I could somehow find the right man, then I could somehow find the right me. Then I discovered that that's some dumb shit. I can't change me, because I change men. I need to change me because I need to change me."

"Do you wanna change you?"

"I don't know, girl. But I gotta do something with myself because I'm fuckin' up. You know what, or better yet, you know who I've been thinking about lately?"

"Who?"

"Bilal."

"Why are you thinking him?"

"Because I can't get him back."

"But he died Shannon."

"I know, and that's so hard to deal with. I have felt guilty about his death for years and just recently with Quincy leaving me, I am starting to accept Bilal's death. Remember when he died Vera?" She said wiping tears from her eyes.

"Shannon, but you can't go blaming yourself for his death. How were you to know that he was going to die?"

"Come on Vera I knew what he did. I knew the type of man that I was playing with, or better yet fell in love with. Bilal was a hustler, plain and simple. And I was right there every time the shit went down, sending bail money, getting cars and shit in my name. Knowing that at any moment, it could all flip and then where would I be? That's why I had that abortion. I couldn't take the chance of having a baby in that life..."

"Remember, I called you at your dorm room when you were in NYU and said, *'Thanks for the money. I got the abortion yesterday. It was no way I could keep Bilal's baby. He's a typical street niggah, a scallywag, hustlin' his way through life. I need more than a man's whose future involves hittin' bricks and doin' stints. Bilal on some ole bullshit, that's why he'll never get a baby outta my ass. Fuck that...'"

Shannon looked at me, wiping her eyes, "When I hung up with you, Bilal was standing in the doorway of my dorm room. He looked at me with the worse look in the world, as if I had just spit on him and said, *'I'm glad that you feel like I'm just a street niggah...a scallywag. That I ain't shit...cause I'm damn sure stupid to be standing here and coming all the way from Brooklyn every other fuckin' weekend, to Tennessee, to be with you. You*

damn sure don't need no baby by a typical street niggah, a hustler. But the funny thing is, maybe we need to tell the Gucci store, Prada, Coach, Louie V. and Chanel about me being a street niggah and maybe they'll give me my paperback. Or better yet, let's go to the accounting office and see if they'll give this typical niggah back his money for the tuition he paid. Then we'll take this goddamn ring that I brought your ass back to the store and get my typical money back...since I ain't shit. Shannon I thought we were so much better then this. You were my ma'fuckin heart. I loved you. You were my lover...my fuckin' friend! I was trying to wife you and you couldn't even have a baby by me? You kill my baby and you don't even tell me.' He reached in his pocket and threw five hundred dollars at me and said, *'Pay your girl back. Sorry for the inconvenience. I don't need nobody paying for my problems. The next time, we fuck, if there is a next time, I'll be sure to leave the abortion money on the nightstand!'*

The next time I saw him I was kissing his cold forehead in his casket. I felt like I killed him."

"Shannon, you didn't kill him. He died in a drug bust."

"I know, but I killed us." She was crying so hard that her chest was heaving in and out, "Vera, I don't even have my baby to remember him by. And I don't want that for you. Get yourself together, and work things out with Taj. You don't wanna be wishing how things could've been different."

"Well, Shannon," I said wiping her tears with the back of my hand, "I fucked up and all I can do is pray that he comes home...but you have to stop blaming yourself...and if your looking for Bilal in Quincy, Nile, or any other man then you'll be looking forever..."

We sat there for the rest of the night, until the wee hours in the morning and then somehow we ended up falling asleep at one another's feet.

When I woke up the sun was blinding me, Rowanda was touching my shoulder and she said, "What happened? I came in here last night and if weren't for you, both, being here I would've thought that someone had broken into the house."

I didn't respond. Because in a weird sorta way it was true, someone had broken into my house. "Where is my baby?" I said.

"Upstairs." She responded.

"Where is Taj?"

"He's gone." I got off the floor, careful not to wake Shannon who was lying beside me and I went upstairs to see my baby.

Skyy was laying in her crib, smiling at a sweet dream, and all I could do was think about her father and wonder if he were thinking about me.

I sat up for two nights straight, praying that Taj would come home. In between the praying and never ending spells of crying, something told me that I had managed to take a bath or at least a shower. Having lost all track of time, I couldn't place the exact moment when the soap and water graced my skin, but I knew I had on fresh underwear.

Skyy was crying from the other room. I peeked out my bedroom's window and the sun was out. It was show time. Time to get up and pretend to be ever so happy that I was a new mother, despite the fact that I had a broken heart. I moved as if I were remote controlled, reciting all the right things, singing all the right lullabies; all the while looking at my precious daughter, but saying to myself I just want five minutes to cry.

At some point during the day when I was playing the doting mother, I remember being slightly amused at the hardy laugh Skyy had this afternoon. As the day went on and nightfall came, Skyy fell asleep around eight o'clock. I knew she was out until she woke up for her midnight feeding. Relieved, I could stop holding my stomach in, breathe, and stop the pretend. I could sit in the dark again wondering when the phone was going to ring. I didn't eat because my stomach was already upset and food would've made it worse.

The next day was a repeat of the day before.

I got up this morning, held my tears long enough to take care of Skyy, pretending all was well with the world. Despite my appearance, despite me dragging around, and despite me never turning a light on as I moved, I managed to smile and laugh with her, regardless of how I really felt.

After I took care of Skyy, I carried her to Rowanda's room, went back to my bedroom, crawled in the bed, laid down, and fell asleep at three o'clock in the afternoon. When I woke up it was three o'clock in the morning.

I couldn't take it anymore; I picked up the phone and dialed Taj's cell phone number. There was no answer and I didn't leave a message. Two minutes later, I called again. No answer. I almost left a message but then my mind said, "No, you gon' look stupid." So, I hung up. Five minutes later I picked up the phone and called again, this time I left a message, *"Taj, this is Vera, please call me back."* I waited one hour; he didn't call me back so I pressed redial. *"Taj,"* the next message said, *"Please call me. I really wanna talk to you."* I waited a half an hour. The next message was, *"Taj, why are you doing this? I didn't do anything. Please, I'm damn near beggin' you to come home."* Five minutes went by and it felt like fifty-five minutes, *"Taj,"* my message said, *"I just wanna talk."* Two minutes later, two more of the same messages.

Forty minutes later the messages changed, *"I can't believe you, as much as we've been through, you start buggin' over some shit that didn't even happen. Fine, if this is how you want it, fuck it!"* The next one, *"I'm sorry I didn't mean that."* The next one, *"I ain't gon' be sitting up here begging you at five o'clock in the morning to come home and talk to me..."* The next one, *"It must be some other bitch that you got in the street. That's why you're acting like this. Fuck you and that bitch! I tell you what, don't ever come home!"* Then came the one that always commands attention, *"...And since you wanna leave you can forget about seeing your daughter."* I hung up, turned over, and buried my face underneath the cover.

Ten minutes later, the phone rang. It was Taj. I let it ring. Two minutes later, the phone rang again. It was Taj. I picked it up. "What?!" I snapped, "What is it?"

"Let me tell you one THING," Taj said with some major bass in his voice, "Don't fuck with me and my daughter, that's the quickest way to get hurt! There will be no baby-mama-baby daddy-from the block type shit, so save the drama! If you ever call my phone with that young girl bullshit again, I'ma show you what I can do!" And he hung up. I cried for three hours straight, thinking about how he was listening to my messages the whole time and straight out ignoring me, this ma'fucker really didn't care.

The next thing I knew Rowanda was coming into the room, flicking on the lights, "This don't make no kind of damn sense! Get up!" She threw the covers back.

"Rowanda, please." I rolled over.

"Please, hell. Now get up. I have watched you mope around here for three days like you were going to die. The next thing I know I'm on the phone with Cookie and Taj calls here like a bat outta hell, screaming in my ear about his daughter and what you said from what you didn't say and so forth. If you ask me, both of ya'll some selfish asses, this chile needs two parents and though I love Taj, you're my child. I will not sit by and watch you wither away. You have a child, a business, and a household to run. If you look at the caller ID, you'll see that Mr. Taj has been calling from work. Translation, he's going to work. Some place you haven't been. Guess what, I got another thing, in order for Mr. Taj to be healthy enough to go to work, he's been eating, something you need to do. And one more thing he's been doing, is getting dressed everyday, at least dressed enough to leave out his house. Unlike you, who's been sitting here like a dead ass bump on a log, acting ridiculous. Get yo ass up and out of that bed!" This time she pulled the pillow away, "You're just gon' be pissed off with me, but I want you up."

Reluctantly, I got up, took a hot shower, went to the shop for four or five hours, and came back home. Something about my house seemed different than when I left.

"He was here," Rowanda, said, "He came by to see Skyy and fell asleep with her on his chest. He left an hour before you got here." Rowanda pointed to the mantle and said, "Taj left you a check for five thousand dollars for the shit he broke." My heart felt like it was going through electric shocks, I sat down on the couch, picked up the silk pillow that contained his smell and cried into it. Rowanda didn't say a word; she took Skyy and went upstairs.

An hour into crying and the situation remaining the same, I called Shannon, Lee, and Angie and I didn't get an answer, immediately I got pissed. Where they fuck could they be? Did they go on another trip? I decided to call again. This time I tried Shannon's cell phone.

"Hello." She said.

"Where yo' ass at?" I asked.

"Home," she said.

"Doing what?"

"Talking to Quincy."

"He's speaking to you?" I asked surprised.

"Oops, do I detect haterraid?"

"Be quiet. I just didn't know that ya'll spoke."

"Something like that."

"Well tell him," I said, "When I catch his cousin, Bryce, he'll need to say his prayers."

"The message has already been delivered." She said.

"By who?"

"Taj."

"He told Quincy that?"

"Pretty much, but I can't talk now. Call me in the morning." She hung up.

I was pissed. How in the hell does she expect me to wait until the morning for a phone call, doesn't she know that my nights are long? As I got off the couch to go upstairs and see Skyy, the phone rang again.

It was Ms. Betty. "Hello"

"Vera, this is Ms. Betty, Taj home?"

"No."

"Where is he?"

"Try his cell." I hung up. She called right back, but I didn't answer, I let it go to my voice mail.

Then I went upstairs, kissed my baby on the forehead, and apologized for ruining our family. After my apology, I broke down and started crying again. That's when Rowanda walked in, "Vee, tell me what happened."

"I fucked up."

"How?"

"Because, Taj thinks that Bryce and I slept together, but we didn't. The truth is that, yeah, Bryce and I kicked it for about three months back in the day, and at that time, I really like him. But I was seventeen. I never loved him. Taj is the only man I've ever loved."

"Is that what Taj is upset about? You and Bryce?"

"He feels like I lied to him, because I didn't tell him about me and Bryce. The way he found out was fucked up. Bryce told him."

"Oh Lawd, when it comes to men, baby, you have to pick and chose what you take to your grave." I could tell she was trying to get to me crack a smile. "Finish telling me the story." I cried the whole time that I talked. When I finished she looked at me and said, "Stop crying. Right now!"

"But I—"

"But nothing! I can understand why Taj would get upset, however, as much shit as ya'll been through he should've listened to you. Right now Skyy is the most important person and she needs you to get it together."

"Rowanda I won't lie, I love my baby and I wouldn't trade my child for nothing in the world, but I'm in so much pain, that sometimes I just wanna disappear. How could he not believe me?"

"I don't know baby."

For the next three days, I walked around like a zombie, taking care of Skyy and forgetting about me. The same shit that I was afraid of happening when I was pregnant is happening now.

When I woke up this morning, I decided to take a long, hot bath. I turned on the radio and Toni Braxton's *'Another Sad Love Song'*, was playing. Fuckin' figures. I turned from Kiss FM and went straight to the Hip Hop station, 105.1 and they were having a slow jam moment, Mary J's *"Can't Live Without You"* was playing, I laid back in the water, closed my eyes, and tried my damnest not to cry.

Floor Violation

"So'oooo pissed off, looking at life through the glass that you shattered,

Little shit like love doesn't matter anymore

Baby wassup...

Niggah, you...so ticked off...

Can't let up long enough to get over it

Brotha can I live...can a sista live...goddamn!"

I was naked and sitting on the edge of my bed, massaging Victoria's Secret's Apple Butter into my thighs. Angie Stone's *'Pissed Off"* was playing on the radio and I was singing at the top of my lungs and bobbing my head. Without thinking twice I started flipping through my CD collection. Yes, here it is! Angie Stone's *Mahogany Soul*. I slid the CD into the CD player, turned the volume all the way up, hit track number three, and whoop there it is...my theme song—Pissed Off, *"Baby what's wrong wit' you...can't get along with you...but now you pissin' me off...and I don't wanna be'eee stressed out...cuz I gotta live my life-gotta, live my life..."*

I took the towel that was laid across the bed and wrapped it around my body, walked over to Taj's dresser, and started taking all of his shit, that he left behind, out. Once I got all of it on the floor, I walked over to the closet and started taking his coats, suits, and thugged out gear, the fuck out. I looked under the bed, where he left a pair of Tims, pulled those out, and wrote *'Bitch ass Niggah'* across the toe in permanent marker.

I gathered all his shit and threw what I could into a suitcase, the rest of the shit I called the Salvation Army to come and pick it up. As far as I was concerned, Taj could kiss my ass. I was sick and tired of being sick and fuckin' tired! I've been stressed out long enough. But not anymore. Skyy's 6 month's old and I'm only 32. I gotta live a Lil' better then this. I can't keep crying everyday. Oh hell no, somebody dial 911 cause a silly bitch done kidnapped me! But oh, this sista is about to be back on track!

I got dressed in my Ralph Lauren denim skirt with the slanted hem line, my long sleeve, sky blue, Michael Stars tee with the V-neck, and my signature Gucci stilettos with the satin tie that criss crosses up the leg.

Rowanda and Skyy were at Aunt Cookie's, so I was free to go without anybody questioning me. I grabbed Taj's shit, my Angie Stone CD and headed out the door.

The brisk October wind cut against my face as I hoped in my truck and started to pray, *"Dear Lord please don't let me find a bitch over here at this niggahs co-op because I've forgotten how to tuck my razor blade under my tongue, which will force me to bust her ass with my bare hands. And I ain't in the mood"*

I walked in the building and opened the apartment door with the spare key that I had. No one was here. I checked the bathroom, only one toothbrush. I checked the bedroom no unusual clothing, then I went into the kitchen and saw two plates sitting on the table. That pissed me off! I could hear Angie Stone singing in my head. As each lyric went through my mind, tears started flooding my eyes and before I knew it, I was wailing and talking to myself at the same time. *"Fuck his ass Vera! He wants to leave you and treat you like ya'll ain't never had shit? Who the fuck*

does he think he is? Oh hell no!" I started in the living room first and kicked the wicker truck over. The trunk opened and all of his shit flew out. Then I took the curtains and the blinds and yanked 'em from the window. I took one hand and swept all the pictures he had of his family along with the two he had of us, onto the floor causing the frames to break apart. The only ones I didn't break up was a picture of his mother and another of Skyy. *"Oh you just gon leave me niggah? Just fuck me? Come over here and set up shop like I ain't mean shit to you! Oh hell no. Do you know how much I love you?"* I walked into the bathroom and tore down his shower curtain, threw the towels on the floor. Cut the hot water in the tub on, clogged it up, and let the shit run! *"Fuck you Taj! Let this be the last time I fall in love with your ass and you leave me over some shit I didn't even do!"* I went in the kitchen, grabbed the sugar, went into the bedroom, pulled the covers back on his bed and sprinkled a five-pound bag of sugar all over his white sheets. Then I made the ma'fucker up like nothing had ever happened.

I went in the linen closet, and took all his towels. Walked in the living room, went over to his CD collection and stole his Lyfe, DMX, Biggie Smalls, Tupac, Ludacris, John Coletrane, and James Brown CDs. Then I took my Angie Stone's CD slid it in the CD player, kicked it to track number three, *"Pissed Off,"* turned the volume all the way up, and placed it on repeat! I wanted to be sure he was greeted by some theme music when he floated in here.

His shit that I dragged here from my house, I dumped in the middle of the floor and threw the shit I stole in the suitcase. Then I placed the Tims with *'Bitch ass Niggah'* written across the toe on top of the CD player. *'Now, Dr. Taj Bennet you may kiss my entire ass! Courtesy of Baby Mama Drama!'* and then I walked out as smoothly as I came in.

By the time I got back home, I noticed Taj's Escalade and the Salvation Army's truck parked in front of my Brownstone. As I walked up the stoop, the two people from the Salvation Army were standing there looking at Taj, who was holding the front door open, with the veins in his neck popping out. "Who's shit are you giving away?"

I ignored him, walked into the house and up the stairs. "I know you aren't giving my shit away?!" he said following me to my bedroom.

I nicely took his pile of clothes that I had in the floor and placed it in garbage bags to take down stairs. "Vera! You hear me talking to you?"

I still ignored him. Fuck him!

"Forget it, talking to you is useless!" He stormed out and I could hear him tell the Salvation Army people that they would no longer be needed. I could hear his feet pounding as he ran back up the stairs. "I pay the mortgage up in here, don't be giving away my shit!"

"Let me explain something to you." I said taking his cologne and aftershave off my dresser and throwing it into an open garbage bag. "I don't need yo' ass. You got it fucked up. I can pay my own mortgage, I have my own money. So you can take a slow boat to hell with all that!"

"Whatever, kid."

"Whatever, kid? Whatever, kid? Fuck you Taj! I don't know why the hell I fell for your crazy lookin' ass anyway!"

"Oh now you wanna play me?"

"No, you playin' you!" I gathered the garbage bags that I packed. "Give me my ma'fuckin keys that you used to get in here, take your shit, and then skip yo' happy-dread-lock-havin' ass the fuck outta here!"

"There you go with that bullshit! Anyway, I just came by to let you know that I wanted to come and get Skyy for the weekend." Before I could answer, he treated me as if I'd said yes. "I'll be by Friday evening and I'll bring her back on Sunday. I hope you can keep your ass home long enough to perhaps have her dressed. But it's all good if you don't, because I bought her some things. So, it's not like we need clothes or anything. So if you plan on performing like yo' ass is crazy let me know, so I won't expect you to pack up shit!"

"You finished?"

"Why?"

"Because you're taking up too much of my time. Get the fuck out!"

"You know what? You are such a kid. I wouldn't give you the time of day even if I wanted to. Here's a check for Skyy and the mortgage. If you don't wanna pay the mortgage, don't pay it! I don't give a fuck what you do, as long as you take care of my daughter, then its all good, kid!"

Oh hell no! "Let me tell you something ma'fucker, I have had just about enough of you. Fuck you! Take your money," I said handing him back his check. "And get the fuck out! You seem to think that somebody needs you around here for something. See all this shit here I had before you skipped yo' ass up in here. Now if you wanna see Skyy, then you see Skyy! But don't you ever try and play me!"

He rolled his eyes, smirked, and said, "Whatever."

He stormed down the stairs and slammed the door. I tried my best not to cry, but I couldn't seem to help it.

An hour later the phone rang, "What the fuck did you do!" Taj yelled. " My shit is all fucked up! There's water everywhere! Hot ass water! Why would you come over here and fuck up my shit! I can't believe this! Vera, you hear me?! Answer me!"

"Whatever, kid." I said yarning. Finally, he was feeling some of what the fuck I was feeling.

"Vera!" Taj yelled, "...oh no, my goddamn shower curtain and my towels, where are my towels Vera?" A few seconds later, "Vera I ain't playin' with you. Where my goddamn CDs? Oh I'ma, fuck you up! You know that? Oh I'ma hurt you!"

"I don't think you wanna catch that charge. You put your hands on me, I'll make sure you go to jail!"

"All this fuckin' water! I can't believe this! My wooden floors, my carpet. My fuckin' big screen TV! Vera, my goddam Lyfe CD? You know I wake up to *Stick Up Kid* in the morning! Where my damn CDs? Oh, I'ma kick yo ass!"

I could no longer hold it in, so I fell out laughing. Taj hung up on me.

An hour later, he called back and said, "Just wanted you to know, I got sugar up my ass!"

I laughed so hard, that I cried myself to sleep. This time they were tears of joy.

Bank Shot

It's Friday and I'ma make sure Skyy and I aren't home. Fuck Taj. Its not that I don't want him to see Skyy, I'm just not going to make it easy for him to do it.

Rowanda kept calling my cell phone, to remind me about Taj picking up Skyy. But I figured, fuck Taj. As far as I was concerned, Taj could lick the crack of my ass, which is exactly why Skyy and I are spending the night with Shannon.

"Bitch, you know you're wrong." Shannon said with a slight chuckle as she played with Skyy. "Look at these legs." Shannon said, "Where did you get my godchild's outfit from? It's too cute." Skyy had on a Baby Gap light pink jumper with a long sleeve, beige, turtleneck underneath. On her feet, she had on baby throw back pink and white Pumas. In her ears, she had diamonds and dangling from her arm were two gold bangles. Now, that she was 6 months old, she started teething and sucking on her wrist. Slob was all over Shannon and Skyy.

"I'm telling you, Vera," Shannon said, "Don't fuck around with that crazy ass Taj and have him doing a drive by over here."

"Please, he won't even know that I'm here. Plus, he doesn't wanna talk to me and he treats me like shit when he sees me, so fuck him."

"Girl, Taj is so in love with your ass that he's fuckin' stir crazy. By the way, I heard, *again* about how you fucked up his co-op. Quincy told me and I pretended like I didn't know a damn thing."

"What's up with you and Quincy?"

"I don't know, but I do know that I'm not trying to be on no living together type shit, no more. I need some space."

"He still workin' that dick?"

"Damn, you know me too well." Shannon smiled.

Skyy started crying and reaching for me. I picked Skyy up and gave her a bottle. "I can't believe that Quincy's ass is even fuckin' with you again." I said amazed, "Here you really fucked another niggah, but yet and still your man is speaking to you, not to mention every thing else ya'll doin'. Me, I ain't even suck the dick, let alone put some pussy on it, and I can't even get a niggah to look at me straight."

"Oh wait a minute now, you ain't fucked him *recently* but I do remember a time when Bryce was tearin' some ass up."

"Tearin' some ass up? Please that niggah dick game was ai'ight," I said waiving my hand from side to side, "But Taj'll bury that ma'fucker."

"Well then, make up."

"Make up? Please Shannon we're not you and Quincy."

"Don't get the shit confused, Quincy and I didn't start talking outta the blue. I got my share of being cussed out. One night Quincy told me off so bad that I told him he had one more time to say how much I was acting like a bitch before and I was gon' go straight Lorraina Bobbit on his ass."

"That shut him up?"

"No, but it damn sure got him put the fuck out."

274

We both laughed, that's when Shannon's doorbell and my cell phone rang at the same time. When I peeped my cell phone, I noticed the number was blocked, I started not to answer but then I figured fuck it, so I answered. Big Mistake, it was Taj.

"You need to grow the fuck up!" I hung right up on his ass. When I looked up Shannon, was walking back in the kitchen with Quincy. Quincy shot me a sly smile, "You pretty much on the most wanted list."

"Quincy," Shannon said, "I thought I told you that you could use your keys again."

"Oh, I'm using them." Quincy said, walking right behind her.

Shannon was too caught up in the sly feel that Quincy just copped on her ass, to even notice his slick ass comment. Instead, she kissed Skyy on the forehead and picked her up again. They sat down on the barstool, next to me.

"Somebody in here belongs to you?" Quincy said seemingly outta the blue. Shannon and I looked at Quincy, who was standing in the kitchen doorway. In walks Taj.

"How did you get in here?" I asked.

"He used my key." Quincy smiled.

"I can't believe ya'll two." Shannon said, shaking her head.

"Yo'," Quincy laughed, pointing to Taj, "This is my boy right here. We go back like biscuits and gravy, yo."

"Oh, please." Shannon chuckled, "You are way too cute to be so corny."

"Vera," Taj said, walking toward me, "You live here now?"

"No, do you?" I replied.

"I probably need to, after you fucked up my spot."

"Your point?" I smirked.

"This lil' show you got going on here is done. I need to speak to you alone. Get your stuff and let's go."

"Oh, hell no," I said looking around the room, "Did my father just resurrect from the grave?"

"Whatever." Taj said, "Let's go."

I had to laugh because this ma'fucker had lost it. "I wish I would."

"Look," Quincy said, taking Skyy from Shannon, "Shannon and I will take the baby with us to eat and ya'll stay here and talk."

"Pssst, please. I'm all talked out." I said looking at Taj. I felt a need to get up. I started gathering Skyy's things so that we could leave. I couldn't stand to look at Taj anymore. I knew it was only a matter of time before I started crying.

"Vera," Shannon said, "let me speak to you for a minute."

Reluctantly, I got up. We walked into the living room, and as I passed Taj, I bumped his arm like a niggah pissed off on the street. "Look it's apparent that we slept on their game and we got got. Talk to Taj." Shannon whispered.

"I don't wanna talk to him." I rolled my eyes and twisted my lips, "Fuck him!" I said the last part loud enough for Taj to hear.

"Well, Vera," Shannon said through clinched teeth," Who would you like to talk to him? One of those lil' nurses from the hospital that's dying for some well-paid delicious doctor dick?"

"Shannon, please." I smirked.

"Look, do what you wanna do, but don't come to me crying."

"Shannon please."

"Vera, just see what the man wants."

I let out a deep breath and hunched my shoulders, "Whatever, but I'm only giving his ass five fuckin' minutes and then I'm out."

Shannon called Quincy into where we were. When he walked in he was holding Skyy in his arms, "You look kinda cute." Shannon said, "Holding a baby like that."

After they left I stood in the middle of Shannon's afro-centric living room, bouncing my eyes from one piece of eclectic art work to the next. Taj came and stood in front of me, "We need to talk." He said, reaching for my hand.

I snatched my hand back, "You said *talk*."

"You wanna sit down?" he asked.

"No. I want you to get to the point and quick."

"I know that you were telling me the truth about you and Bryce."

I felt like my whole body shut down. I looked at him and tears flooded my eyes. "What did you say?"

"Look, I'm not always right and this time I was wrong. I got my shit fucked up."

"Who told you that?"

"Quincy."

"Who told him?"

"Bryce."

"And Quincy told you, what Bryce said?"

"Yeah, he did."

"And you believed him?"

"Yes." Taj said slightly agitated.

"So in essence you believed Bryce over me?"

Taj stood there a moment, "Why you twisting up my words?"

"I ain't twisting shit! I'm calling a spade a spade. I have a question for you, why would you do that?" I said trying to hold tears back. "The man you damn near killed, you took his word over mine, even after I begged you to listen to me? I'm the one who loved you. Me, and you didn't even believe me?"

"Vera, I'm sorry you feel that way, but…"

"Are you fuckin' for real?" I said with my neck cocked to the side and peering at Taj with my eyes squinted tight. "You can't be serious? You're sorry? Are you as sorry as I have been for over a month? The fuckin' pain that I've been in. The cryin', the don't know whether I've taken a bath today, or yesterday, shit. The *what did I do that was so wrong*, shit. After all of that, you come along and you're sorry? Suppose he said that I fucked him, then you would believe that too?"

"Vera, come on."

"*Vera, come on* my ass! I changed my life to be with you. I broke down walls. I challenged myself to do the right thing. I let you into my life. I wanted to marry you. Hell, I even had a baby by you and then you fuckin' left me!" I started poking him in his chest, "You left me! You fuckin' left me. Night after night, I cried…I cried, and I fuckin' cried! I begged you to come home; to please listen and you gave me your ass to kiss, so you know what?" I said pushing him in the chest, "Fuck you!" I let loose punches into his chest, that got progressively weaker as Taj grabbed and held me tightly. I was so devastated by him treating me the way he has, that I couldn't stand the fact that I loved being in his arms. "Just let me go." Tears started to roll down my cheeks.

"Wait a minute, wait a minute." He said kissing my tears and holding me tighter. "What do you think I'm made of, steel? You don't think I cried? You think I didn't sit up at night wondering, why? Why, did I leave? Why, didn't I listen to her? Maybe, she was telling the truth. Maybe I would still have the five G's I paid you for the shit I broke." He chuckled.

"Nothing's funny." I started biting my inner cheek to keep from cracking a smile.

"You know you wanna laugh." He said, "You know you fucked up my shit? I had to get my floors done again and my T.V. was ruined. I'm glad my Escalade wasn't there, I might've met all my damn windows on the ground."

"True." I smirked, resting my arms over his.

"Yeah ai'ight." He started kissing me on the neck." I love with you, Vera. I'm in-love with you. I need you."

"Did you cry?" I asked.

"Yes."

"Did you stay up all night thinking about me?"

"Yes."

"Good, keep it up." I removed his hands from my waist, "Now I gotta go."

"No," he said pulling me back in between his arms, " Don't leave me. I know I fucked up. I should'a listened to you, but right now I need...we need...to work this out. I miss you man," he said kissing me on the neck again, "I miss us. Please, I'm in-love with you, I don't wanna stay away. I love you too much."

"You can love me all you want," I said stepping out of his embrace, Oh, and by the way, the locks on the brownstone are changed." I said lying. "So, stop calling it home. You have a co-op remember?"

"Hold up," Taj chuckled in disbelief. "How are you going to change the locks on a house where I pay the mortgage?"

I didn't even acknowledge that. "Are you keeping Skyy tonight?"

"I wanted to."

"Good. Vera needs to go now. She's got shit to do..." and then I put on my best bill collector's voice, sounding politically correct, and enunciating every syllable, as I said, "Ciao bella muth'er fu'cker..." I looked at Taj and rolled my eyes, "I'm out." And for the first time in weeks, my strut was starting to come back. I could feel him watching my ass on the way out, so I threw a little more motion in the ocean. When I stepped outside I flipped open my cell phone and called Shannon. "Hey girl," I said, "When you come back, give Taj Skyy's baby bag, he's going to keep her tonight. "Love ya, speak soon."

At exactly seven o'clock the next morning, Taj was on my phone. I could hear Skyy cooing in the background.

"May I help you? *Stop*," I said into my background before Taj could speak.

"Stop, what?" Taj asked.

"Oh no, not you baby." I said smiling, picking up the remote control and turning on BET. Videos were playing so I turned the volume all the way up.

"*Turn that down*," I said in a slight whisper, talking to no one in particular. This was the type of shit that drove a beggin' man crazy.

"Vera! Who are you talking to?"

"No-body. Damn, Taj. Say what you gotta say." Then I paused, "Hold on." I didn't even put the phone down, I just held it to my ear, and said, as if I were talking to someone, "*I don't know why he's calling this time of the morning*." Then I turned back to the phone and said to Taj, "Why are you calling so early?"

"You fuckin' with me right?" Taj snapped.

"Fuckin' with you, how?"

"Oh, now you wanna play games? Let me come over there and find a niggah and I swear to God I'ma crack his shit open!"

"Please, I do not have time for that. Plus, I'm not going to argue with you. I gotta go." I was doing everything in my power to keep from laughing.

"What you say?" he snapped.

"I said goodbye." And I hung up.

I give him exactly thirty minutes and his ass will be ringing my doorbell. I jumped up and went in the shower. After I came out, I told Rowanda that I needed to go to the shop and do some billing and would be back in a couple of hours. Also, to please look out for Skyy and Taj.

As I pulled off, Taj was pulling up. I knew I was going to take my time now, because if I played my cards correctly ole boy would be at the house when I got back. After I did my billing at the shop I took a ride down to The Mall at Short Hills and bought Skyy some clothes from Talbot's kids. Then I went to theLil' nasty diva's shop and purchased me a fun fur nightie from Fredrick's'. Afterwards, I ran into a lil' boutique and purchased myself a tight ass platinum number that was sure to look like it was poured on.

Last, but not least, I went to the floral shop and bought myself a bouquet of red roses. Afterwards, I drove home and just as I thought, ole boy was still here. When I walked in, Skyy was sitting in her high chair. When she saw me, she started kicking and laughing. Taj was feeding her and her face was full of food. I walked over and kissed her, getting some of the food on my chin. It was now six o'clock in the evening and being that it was early fall it was starting to get a little dark outside.

Taj was staring at me like I had lost my ma'fuckin' mind! I

ignored his ass. Believe me it was hard, 'cause he was looking so good, with his tight wife beater on and baggy jeans. He had his hoody hanging on the back of the kitchen chair. His wife beater was caressing the hell outta his pecks and his biceps made me wanna scream. We need to break up more often if this niggah gon' come back with a body like this. His cocky ass caught me peepin' him out. *'Ole boy you think you got shit with you, well check me out, cause you ain't seen nothin' yet.'*

After Taj finished feeding Skyy, I took her upstairs with me and gave her a nice bath and before I could snap her sleeper together, she had fallen asleep. I placed her in her crib and headed for the shower. When I came out, I was wrapped in a plush Charter Club yellow towel, and smelling like Victoria Secret's Green Apple. I stepped in my bedroom to change into my brand new platinum number that I purchased this afternoon; Taj was sitting on the edge of my bed complaining about a headache. I ignored him. Rowanda knocked at the door and said, "Vee, Craig is downstairs, I'll be back in a little while. You want me to take Skyy with me?"

"No, Taj is here, he'll watch her."

"Okay." Although I wasn't crazy about what's-his-name, I was glad to see my mother happy.

Taj started coughing, "Taj'll watch her? Who said I was babysitting?"

"Oh, is that what keeping your own child is called?"

"You know what I mean."

"Yeah, I sure do."

He started coughing again. "Just spray Lysol on whatever you touch," I said. "I definitely don't want my baby sick." Then I went back to ignoring him. I was standing in front of my full length oval, cherry wood, mirror, applying my Mac press powder and I could see Taj staring at me from behind with a look that said, *'this bitch.'*

"Excuse me," I looked at him in the mirror. "but I need to get dressed. Can you, go in the other room?"

Immediately he started coughing and moaning about how he didn't feel well, "You just want me to leave like that? As sick as I am?"

"Excuse you, *Dr.* Taj Bennet. Can't you take something? Please. Are you going to leave, so that I can get dressed?"

"Just fuck, me huh?"

I sighed. Seeing that he wasn't going to leave, I stood in front of him, dropped my towel to the floor, stood butt naked and commenced to putting my clothes on. I slipped on a strapless bra and thongs. Then I slid on my platinum number, that fitted just like a glove, my four-inch, *'hit it with one leg over the shoulder,'* pumps, let my hair down, shook it out, and headed toward the door. Then as if I had forgotten something I stepped back into the room and slowly rubbed body glitter all over my cleavage. I looked at Taj and smiled. "The baby's bottles are in the fridge. I'm leaving."

"Vera," he coughed, "I'm sick."

"You'll live."

Then I left, went over Angie's, and forced myself to sit there for three hours. Seeing that all this bitch did was eat bon-bons and drink coffee at night, I left her sitting there and came back home. When I got there and went upstairs, Taj was laying at the foot of my bed, asleep. He looked so pretty just lying there. To be honest, I wanted to fuck the shit out of him, but I knew I couldn't take it there. I threw on a cotton tee, one that smelled like his cologne, and got in the bed next to him. When I woke up Taj looked at me, "This ain't right. I won't be laying in bed with you, unless I can make love to you." I didn't comment, I just turned over and internally agreed.

Taj was in and out of my house for the next three days. Every time I looked at him, I felt my resistance getting weaker. I woke

up in the middle of the night to Skyy screaming at the top of her lungs. It scared the shit outta me! I jumped and ran into her room. Rowanda and I damn near knocked each other over, coming to check on Skyy. When Skyy saw me, she reached for me and I could feel her skin was burning up. Instantly, I started to panic.

"Get my phone, Rowanda!" I said frightened. Skyy had never been this sick. When Rowanda handed me the phone, I called Skyy's doctor and by now, I was in tears. Instead of getting the doctor herself, I got her answering service. When I looked at the clock, it was 3:30 in the morning. I left a message with the answering service and they told me that the doctor would be calling me back any minute.

I paced the floor with my screaming baby in my arms. I didn't know what to do. Rowanda stood there looking at me. I looked at her and said, "What do I do?"

"I don't know." She said, with a look of concern on her face.

"What do you mean you don't know?! You had a baby didn't you?"

"Yes, I had you."

"Well, then, what did you do when I was sick!"

"I don't remember."

"Why don't you remember?!" I was screaming and crying by now.

Rowanda wasn't screaming but she was crying, "I was high Vera, when you were a baby, I was high. I'm learning how to be a mother just like you." I couldn't believe this shit! I just couldn't. I held my baby tight to my chest and I slid down the wall. I couldn't believe this was happening to me. Every fuckin' body else could ask their mother what to do when their baby was sick, but leave it to my mother to announce to me that she doesn't remember, because she was high. I felt like shit. Somehow, I

managed to talk myself into calming down, until the doctor called back.

"You may want to take her temperature, Vera." All of a sudden Rowanda was, thinking of bright fuckin' ideas. I got off the floor and took Skyy with me in the bathroom so that I could take her temperature. It was 101 degrees. My heart started racing. Then the phone rang, it was the doctor.

"Hi, Doctor Johnson, Skyy has diarrhea and a temperature of 101 degrees."

"How long has she had diarrhea and a fever?"

"Just this morning, she woke up screaming."

"Sounds like she has a virus, which needs to run its course. Give her Tylenol every four hours until the fever goes down and only give her Pedialite for today."

Before I opened my mouth and cussed the doctor out, because she was diagnosing my baby over the phone, I said to her, "I think she needs to go to the emergency room."

"Mrs. Bennet, I'm sure that your husband, Dr. Bennet will agree…"

"My last name is not Bennet," I said to the doctor, "and *I'm* calling you, not Dr. Bennet."

"Okay," she said taking a deep breath, "If her fever gets any higher, after you've given her the Tylenol every four hours, if the diarrhea gets worse, or the baby seems lethargic then call me and I'll have you bring her in. Please don't go running to the emergency room, Mrs. Bennet."

I looked at Rowanda and mumbled, "Why does he keep calling me Mrs. Bennet?" "Okay." I said, gritting my teeth as I hung up. Afterwards I ran to the twenty-four hour CVS and purchased Pedialite and Tylenol.

When I came back home I gave Skyy a warm bath and a bottle of Pedialite. "Your daddy must've really been sick when he was here, the other day. I'ma kill him for making you sick." I started to call Taj but then I changed my mind.

"Dada..." Skyy said, with her bottle in her mouth, as if she were the saddest little baby in the world. Then with the nipple in her mouth, she started crying again. Her crying spells went on for four to five hours straight. After a while she fell asleep. I placed her in her crib and sat on the floor to try and gather the tee shirts and sleepers that she threw up on. Before I knew anything, I laid my head back and fell asleep.

When I woke up, Skyy was screaming all over again. I took her temperature, which had gone down, and changed her pamper. Although the diarrhea seemed to be easing up, she still seemed aggravated. I fed her some more Pedialite and then I massaged her little stomach. She smiled a half smile, but I could tell she was still sick. When I sat her up on the bed, she just looked at me. Usually she'll crawl around so much that I'll have to catch her, so she won't fall off the bed. However, now she was looking at me. I gave her a bottle and she laid down. Then I thought, *let me call her daddy before he finds out that she's sick and be pissed off that I didn't call*. I called and got his voice mail. I hung up.

Later that evening Skyy started to feel better. I told Rowanda not to worry and if she wanted to go out, then to go ahead. She said that she would call and check on Skyy periodically. By now, it was seven o'clock in the evening and I was exhausted. I gave Skyy a warm sponge bath and laid her back down. The doorbell rang as soon as I went to walk out her room; Skyy woke up and started screaming all over again. I felt like I was going to pass out if I didn't get any sleep. I picked her back up and we walked to the door. I didn't even look out the peephole I swung the front door open. It was Taj.

"Why didn't you use your key?" I said turning around and walking into the living room.

"You changed the locks remember?"

"Please, I just said that. I didn't change no damn locks."

"You play too much." He laughed, walking behind me. "What's wrong, why is Skyy crying like this?"

"She's been crying all day. She has a virus, that you gave her and she had a fever, but it's going away."

"Let me see her."

Gladly I handed him his screaming child, walked into the kitchen, fixed her another bottle, and walked back into the living room handing it to him. After I handed him the bottle he stared at me. "I look a mess don't I?" I laughed.

"Naw, you look beautiful to me." he said, holding Skyy in one arm and using the other to take off his overcoat. Taj had on Versace dress pants and a matching olive green button up, "You did rounds today?" I asked.

"Yes and then I came over here, after I saw you called me."

"I'm exhausted."

"Go upstairs and take a bath. I'll take care of Skyy."

I kissed him on the forehead as I walked pass him. He grabbed me by my forearm. "I miss you." I just looked at him and then went upstairs. I decided to soak in my octagon shaped Jacuzzi, play a little Jill Scott, and straight chill. I felt like I hadn't been to sleep in what felt like days. I lit some aroma candles that were on the edge of the Jacuzzi and turned down the dimmer, closed my eyes and laid back.

I must've fallen asleep, because I heard Taj knock on the door. I smiled and for a moment I felt like things were okay. "Hey Baby," I said.

He peeked his head in, "Ahh, hearing that is like a breath of fresh air," he smiled.

I smiled. He walked over to the Jacuzzi and I noticed that his clothes had changed. "I hope you don't mind," he said, sitting on the floor, pulling his knees up to his chest, "I had some extra clothes in my gym bag. Skyy seems to be out for the night. I put her in her crib."

"I'm glad she's sleep and no, I don't mind if you changed your clothes." I said looking at his long velour shorts and extra crisp wife beater. I was getting horny just looking at him. "You don't think nothing of being naked around me, do you?" he smiled.

"Don't you like to see me naked?"

"No." he said, "I like to be up in you naked."

I laughed, "Filthy mouth."

He cracked up, "I miss you man. You know you use to be my niggah."

"Use to be?"

"Well you still are, but you're acting more like my ex-girl then my best friend."

"Things are different." I said, feeling myself getting emotional. I bit my bottom lip because I was determined not to cry.

"They don't have to be." he said dipping his hand in the water.

"I don't even know where we would begin."

"Right where we left off." By now, he was on his knees facing me with both of his hands in the water.

Not knowing what else to do I eased closer to him. "You still love me?"

"I love the hell outta you." He smiled, with his hands exploring my body underneath the water. I looked at him and as if we had both been waiting for this moment. We kissed passionately.

Suddenly, I broke the kiss. "Do you know how many nights I cried over you? Do you know that you hurt me? I mean, really? Taj I ain't nevah, nevah, evah cried over a man. No man, not even my daddy and here I was on my knees crying over you. You broke every piece of my heart and now you want it back? How can I do that?"

"You don't have a choice."

"What do you mean I don't have a choice?"

"You love me too much and I love you too much. You think I'm walking away? Humph, you don't know me. I camp out in this ma'fucker and never leave."

"I'm serious." I laughed.

"Me too…Look Baby, we all make mistakes, but I'm sorry. I love you. I wanna make love to you. I need you in my life. I swear I don't want nobody else, ever. This is it. Please, baby. You gotta forgive; cause there's nobody else for me but you. Nobody else that I wanna love and become a part of." Gently pulling me close to him and kissing me softly on the neck he whispered, "I love you…I love you…I love you…"

I got out of the Jacuzzi and slipped on one of Taj's long white tee's that came to the middle of my thigh. Underneath I had on no bra and a pair of silk panties.

I met Taj downstairs in the kitchen so that I could do his hair. As I was washing his hair I felt the same way I felt the first time I laid eyes on him. After I finished, he sat down in the kitchen chair, drinking a Heineken, and I started twisting his dreads from the roots. He laid his head back against my full bosom and I kissed him on his forehead. Neither one of us were talking and the only music that filtered in the background besides the sexiness of the late night New York City traffic, were the sounds of Boney James' *Seduction* CD.

After I finished twisting the sides, I carefully pushed his head forward and twisted the back. When it came time to twist the front, I stood in front of him and began twisting his hair. As I twisted his locks one by one, Taj began to run his hands up and down my thighs and back up again. Smoothly, he slipped his hands in my panties, moving the seat to the side and parted my vaginal lips with his fingertips, lightly stroking my clit.

Still to the best of my ability, I twisted his hair. After he finished caressing my inner lips and clit with his fingertips, he pulled his hands out. Then he licked his fingers and said, "I've been waiting to taste this for a while." My heart was thumping and my pussy was soaked. Still determined to keep my composure, I continued what I was doing as he slowly began to suck my nipples through my white tee shirt. He was starting to break me down, but I kept doing what I was doing, despite how much he was moving his head. While I was trying to keep up with his tongue sucking my breast, he took his hands and raised my tee shirt above my waist. He took my hands down, wiped them clean of the Lock-It-Up gel with the towel that was around his neck.

"Come here," he said seductively, but almost demanding that I comply.

He pulled me gently as he stood up. I pulled his velour shorts and boxing shorts down in one sweep. They fell to the floor and he stepped out of them. I lifted his shirt above his head and pulled it off, revealing his nicely chiseled six-pack. When I looked down his dick was looking like a delicious piece of chocolate. He sat back down in the chair and he said, "I need you to come here." I straddled my legs across his lap as he gently entered me. I rested my head on his shoulder, feeling like I just found a part of me that was missing.

"Damn baby," Taj whispered. "this pussy is tight."

"I know," I moaned, "it's because I've been saving it for you…"

Field Goal

"SURPRISE!!!!!" We yelled as Rowanda walked into the living room trailing behind Craig. Immediately she started crying once she realized that this was a surprise birthday party for her.

"Oh, my God!" she said, looking around the living room at all of us. "You did all of this for me?" Tears were falling from her eyes as she held her hand over her mouth.

"This is all Vera's doing, Rowanda." Aunt Cookie smiled.

"Oh, my baby," Rowanda cried.

"I wouldn't miss celebrating my first birthday with you for nothing in this world." I fought hard to hold my tears back, "I love you and I wanna celebrate just being able to be with you and you being my mother."

"I love you too, Vee. I really-really do!"

"Enough of that!" Dirty said, walking over and giving us a group hug "Let's get this party started right!"

As soon as he said that, Uncle Boy, who seemed to be itchin' to showcase his D.J. skills, took it upon himself to introduce the song, "This is Kells…happy people baby!"

I laughed as Rowanda tried to step with Craig.

"Rowanda." I said, holding a brandy glass filled with Amaretto and Orange Juice, "That's not how you do it. It's step-step-side-to-side. Craig has it down packed but you looking a hot mess!"

"Hold up," Aunt Cookie's girlfriend, Ms. Janet said, "Give me a minute and I'll break down the Pop and Lock for you. Let me just hit this Boston real quick."

Aunt Cookie and her girlfriends, Ms. Janet and Ms. Carol, were gathered around playing Bidwiss, slamming down cards, and arguing over who was running a Boston and who was bull-shittin'.

"Don't cheat, Carol!" Aunt Cookie yelled, "You gon' get put the hell outta the game."

"The next person that says Carol-Ann is a cheat can get it. And that's on my word!"

"Hush Carol and throw out a card!"

"Hold my drink Angie…" I said. "Look Ma, it's like this." And I started stepping from side to side.

Rowanda looked at me and said, "Oh, it's Ma, now?"

"Yes," I said, while dancing.

"Vera, sweetheart, let me show you how we do in Chicago." Craig said.

"Chicago?"

"Yeah baby, that's where I'm from…Now let me show you."

Craig grabbed my hand, Uncle Boy started the track over and Craig and I began to dance. *Step-Step-Side-Side-Round-and-Round-Getting' down…step in the name of Love…*

"That's it baby!" Craig said, excitedly, as we dipped. "Damn girl, you got it!"

"Oh, wait a minute now, Craig." Mr. Bennet said, who was standing by Taj and watching Craig and me, "That's my daughter-in-law, and from what I see, I may need to cut in."

"No offense. Mr. Bennet, but we got this." I said.

"All right." He said, smiling. "Who wanna step with Mr. Bennet?"

"I got this." Aunt Cookie said, throwing her cards down on the table and excusing herself from the game. "Let me show ya'll what I'm workin' with."

"Oh you got a little work." Craig smiled as Aunt Cookie and Mr. Bennet danced. "But check this out, Let's do something new, let's all do it as a group."

That's when Taj stepped up, "Well then, we gotta do this with the right women. You got mine, Bruh." Craig, stood back and smiled. "By all means." Then he grabbed Rowanda and said, "Come on ya'll."

Shannon and Quincy were behind Taj and me. And we were behind Aunt Cookie and Mr. Bennet. Rowanda and Craig were leading.

Ms. Betty was looking and seemed to have a slight attitude, but she tried to be pre-occupied with the baby.

We started to dance as R. Kelly sang, *"Somebody touch somebody and tell somebody you love somebody…"*

After we finished dancing we sat down to eat. We laughed and joked with one another. Rowanda laughed so hard that she cried.

Toward the end of the night, as everyone started to leave, Rowanda was helping me clean up, "Thank you so much, Vera."

"You're welcome! We've come a long way, wouldn't you say." I said passing her a dish.

"Sho'nough "

"Well...I have to say Craig doesn't seem so bad. But he better be good to you."

"He will be. I promise..."

"He better be, because I love you Rowanda."

She hugged me and said, "That's ma to you!"

Game Over

"Guess what bitch got hooked up with a doctor!" Shannon screamed, coming into the shop. The shop had been busy all day. It was getting late, but some of the clients, who already had their hair done, were still hanging out.

It was December 5th and the last day that I would be in the shop before becoming Mrs. Taj Bennet. I couldn't believe my wedding was two days away.

Jay-Z's Black album was bumpin' through the shop's surround sound.

DeAndre looked at Shannon, "How you know I'm fuckin' with a doctor, which one of ya'll been listening to my voice mail again?"

"Oh no, Papi." Rosa said, "De Rosa don't play dem games. I've had enough of chu voice mail. Ahh ya'i-ya'i."

DeAndre rolled his eyes.

"He is crazy," Shannon laughed, "Angie. Angie met a doctor. A damn gynecologist. You know that bitch is in heaven."

"Well," DeAndre said, "I know that wasn't me, because I would prefer a urologist, Hollah!"

Shannon slapped DeAndre a high-five and he said, "Work that shit, Shannon, show'em what I taught you." DeAndre laughed, then Shannon started throwing her ass in the air and placing her hands on the floor, *"Face down, ass up, and this is the way he likes to fuck!"*

"And you know this man!" DeAndre laughed snapping his fingers.

Everybody in the shop was practically on the floor laughing.

A few minutes later, Cherise walked into the shop singing, Floetry's *"Say Yes."* Cherise said "hello" and walked over to me, "Vera, I can't believe that you gon' let a hoe up in your wedding."

"There ya'll go." DeAndre said, "Talking about me again."

"Si papi," Rosa said, "Dis time Vera say chu gon' be de flower girl!" When she said that everybody burst out laughin' again.

"Keep it up" DeAndre said. "Keep it up. And ain't nobody gettin' on that plane to Trinidad, let alone being in a wedding."

"What ya'll talking about?" Angie said, walking into the shop with Lee walking behind her.

"Where have you two been?" I said, looking at them like they were crazy. They were supposed to be here over an hour ago. "Ya'll gotta stop thinking you can come up in here anytime you feel like it and get your hair done. That's what appointments are for."

"Uhmm, with an attitude like that," Angie said, "somebody ain't been gettin' dicked on the regular."

"Oh, hell no!" DeAndre said, "Rosa, somebody, please hold me back, this trick is all up in my business!"

"Stop acting silly!" I said falling out laughing and pointing for Cherise to come and sit down in my chair.

"Ya'll seen Dirty lately?" Lee asked out of the clear blue. Everybody looked at Lee as if she had lost her damn mind. This bitch has never in her life asked about my cousin Dirty, as a matter of fact she refuses to even call him Dirty, she'll only call him by his government name Diwan.

"You mean Diwan Wright?" I said, "My cousin Diwan?"

Lee rolled her eyes, "Yes. Problem with that?"

"Why are you looking for him?"

"Because I saw him the other day and he helped me out by taking boxes into my classroom for my children. I wanted to say thank you."

"Didn't you say thank you, when he finished helping you?" Angie asked.

"Yes." Lee smiled, "but still and all."

"Oh, hell no," I said to Lee, "See, this is where I draw the line, if you think you gon' be turning toward thugs and start fuckin' with my cousin then you got another thing coming." Lee rolled her eyes. That's when her cell phone rang. Her face lit up and she stepped outside. "That bitch knows she's confused." I said to Shannon and Lee.

"She always been confused." Cherise said, "I don't know how ya'll put up with her anyway."

"Cause that's my girl," I said to Cherise, "Don't *you* get it confused."

"You got that Vera," Cherise chuckled.

Lee walked back and whispered something to Shannon and Angie. Angie looked at Cherise and winked her eye.

"What the hell wrong with your eye, Angie?" I said, wondering why in the hell would she be winking at Cherise.

"Hey-Hey, now! Whatcha workin' wit!" Aunt Cookie said, before Angie could respond. I placed a black cape over Cherise and started basing her scalp.

Uncle Boy waved at everybody in the shop "What it be like ya'll? I can't call it." Rowanda came in behind Uncle Boy. "Where's Skyy?" I asked her.

"With her daddy. Hell, daddy back home now and Nana needs to do her thing, just a lil' sumthin' sumthin'."

"Hey-Hey now!" Aunt Cookie said, "I don't see nothin' wrong with a lil' bump and grind."

"Ya'll crazy," DeAndre said, "Uncle Boy you ready for your hair cut?"

Uncle Boy smiled with his front gold tooth shining and said, "Ain't nuthin' but a word Dre, but Uncle Boy 'bout to be outta here."

Ain't nuthin' but a word? What the hell? I looked at Aunt Cookie and Uncle Boy and almost passed out from being embarrassed. What the fuck did they have on?

Aunt Cookie flopped down in the chair across from my station. I kept blinking "Please, God tell me I'm wrong!"

Aunt Cookie had on a skin tight, silver and gold cat suit. Her lipstick was ruby red with a black lip liner, and the platinum clip weave that she made me do for her last week needed to be redone. The spikes that were once standing up and were now bending over. This bitch looked ridiculous.

"How much longer, Baby Girl?" Aunt Cookie asked, "Before you get to me?"

I wanted to say, "Not fast enough, call 911 and see if they have a hair stylist on board, cause you look like a damn cardiac arrest just waiting to happen!" But what killed the game was Uncle Boy. He was rockin' a brown corduroy jumpsuit with a long black leather trench coat on looking like a cross between Shaft and Kool Moe Dee in the Wild-Wild West video. The elbows on the trenched coat were patched. But what had me about to keel over was the three finger ring that his ass had on, looking like an old and out of place Big Daddy Kane walking around here.

Oh, hell no! If I look down again and this ma'fucker has on starched white, patent leather Stacy Adams, I'ma die. Oh, shit! Somebody call the morgue, *cause I'm comin' Elizabeth!*

I just blinked my eyes and stared at Aunt Cookie and Uncle Boy, in disbelief. I could tell that Cherise was a bit taken aback by these two herself. But if she knew like I knew she won't open her mouth. Because Aunt Cookie and Uncle Boy might look ridiculous, but they're my goddamn ridiculous surrogate parents, and Vera don't play no slick talkin' shit, when it comes to these two. I glanced at Cherise, and shot her ass a look like, don't even go there. She seemed to catch the drift, because she started telling me about her date tonight.

"He's an older man." Cherise smiled. "A lot older than these du-rag wearin' ma'fuckers I been around here dealing with…Let me tell you, Vera," She said before I could digest her first statement, "You know this niggah Abdul got a bitch pregnant and he's still calling me."

"Abdul? That's the older guy you're dating?"

"No, that's my man that was locked down for a minute. He came home yesterday."

"I thought he was in there for life?"

"I ain't never told you that. That was Fa'roo."

This bitch must be crazy, "Fa, who?"

"Fa'roo? But I ain't with him no more. I cheated on my ex-boyfriend, Abdul, with him."

"What?" This bitch was confusing me. Quite frankly, I ain't wanna hear no more, but she kept going. I noticed as she was talking, one of DeAndre's clients was dead in our mouths, especially when Cherise said something about Abdul just getting out of jail.

"...I'ma give this niggah another chance, but this gon' be it. I can't take no more babies. Plus he knows that the baby I'm carrying is his. I'm just gon' blame it on the old man."

"Yo' ass must be crazy." Before I could continue what I was saying, DeAndre's client that had been staring in our mouths, interjected.

"Excuse me, I'm sorry to be in your conversation, but do you know someone by the name of Abdul Jackson?"

"You talking to me?" Cherise asked, sounding a little indignant. "Yeah, I know him. The question is do you know him?"

DeAndre's client, an older lady, who seemed to have a lot more sense than Cherise said, "I know him quite well and yourself."

"Oh hold up, Vera" Cherise said, "How you know Abdul?"

"Cherise, would you let me put this perm in your hair. You said that you ain't wanna be bothered with him anymore, so it doesn't matter how she knows him."

"Nawl, fuck that." Cherise insisted.

"How do you know Abdul?"

DeAndre's client looked Cherise up and down, "That's my husband."

"Bitches need to stop lying! That shit you talkin' is what I call too much playin'."Cherise turned all the way around toward her.

At that moment, it seemed like everybody in the shop shut up. "Seems like it's 'bout to be some shit up in here." Aunt

Cookie said, "Ya'll can get started it if you want to, but Aunt Cookie don't play, so I think ya'll need to take it down."

I looked at Aunt Cookie and she was carefully taking off her shoes and removing her clip weave. That's when a big, fine ass, honey glazed, big brown eyed man, with fresh sweat on his upper lip, walked in wearing a pair of baggy cut up denim shorts, with construction boots, a cut up white tee, and a tool belt. Fuck the argument this mofo had our attention.

"Abdul!" Cherise and DeAndre's client started screaming, and then suddenly the lights went out and out of no-where smoke started rising up from the floor. Then disco lights started sparkling around the room. That's when Donna Summer's hot stuff started playing and I realized that I was in the midst of my own bachelorette party! Oh my God!

The stripper also known as Abdul walked over to me and started grinding on me. Uncle Boy started yelling, "What the hell! Uncle Boy s'pose to been gone. Cookie get yo' shit and come on outta here!"

"Boy," Aunt Cookie said, "leave me alone and get *yo'* ass outta here!...Abdul!" Aunt Cookie yelled, "Show ole Chocolate Chip whatcha workin' wit!"

Uncle Boy stormed out the door and DeAndre started screaming, "That's wassup! That's what I'm talkin' about!"

"Cherise," I mouthed, over the stripper's shoulder "Is this *your* Abdul?"

"Nope," she laughed, "Siked your mind! We made all that shit up! Hollah!"

By the time the stripper was undressed down to his jock strap, he already had about three hundred-dollar bills at his feet. I'm sorry but I had to peek, so I placed a dollar bill right in the middle of his jock strap, and wouldn't you know this niggah had a python tucked away in that G-string!

"Come over here and let me try!" DeAndre yelled.

The stripper looked, winked his eye at DeAndre and DeAndre started going, "Woo-Woo-Wooooo..." that's when we knew what was up.

Time flew by and by the end of the night; we were too excited to be going home to sleep for our flight to Trinidad the next morning.

Me, Shannon, Lee, Angie, Rowanda, Cherise, Aunt Cookie, Rosa, and DeAndre sat around and finished off the rest of the Moet.

"Damn girl." Shannon said, "I guess the game is over. We about to married and having babies and shit."

"We," I said to Shannon, "You getting married?"

"No," Rowanda said, "But I am."

I looked at her and she couldn't stop blushing. I couldn't believe this, here my mother, a woman that had been a dope fiend all my life had turned her life around and, was now getting married. I didn't say anything, I just looked at her. "What, Vera?" she said, "He ain't gon' come in between us. You're my child."

"No, it's not that, it's just that I would've never thought..."

"Rowanda be droppin' it like it's hot!" Aunt Cookie yelled.

"Now go ahead, Shannon," Rowanda said, "tell us your good news."

Shannon looked at me and said, "I'm having a baby."

"What?" Don't ask me why but tears where coming to my eyes. "A baby? Quincy's?"

"Heifer!" Shannon laughed, "Yes. We didn't expect it. It just sorta happened."

"Yeah that's what happened between me and Dirty." Lee admitted.

I almost fell outta my chair. This bitch had lost her mind. "What sorta happened between you and Dirty?"

"We just sorta clicked and we been going out for a minute."

"Oh, hell, no!" I said, "What the hell Lee gon' do with a thug."

I turned to Angie, "What, what you got going on?"

"I'm straight." She said, "I got me a coochie doctor and I'm good."

"Times up." Shannon said, "Game's over. We got a plane to catch."

The Winner Is...

December 6th at 3 p.m., Taj and I took separate flights to Trinidad. We were to meet up again at the stroke of midnight, December 7th, on Maracus Beach by the shore.

The moon glistened in ripples across the Caribbean Sea as I stood on the balcony of my hotel suite reflecting on a time when I thought that none of this would be possible. I've come a long way since the piss pew hallways of the Lincoln Street projects and the haunting of a dead grandmother's ghost. I could feel tears of joy dancing in my throat and slipping out my eyes.

My mother wiped my cheeks with her bare hands, "I have waited all of your life for this moment."

"Me too." I said, nervously biting my lip. "It's a moment of peace, of being safe, and suddenly I'm not afraid anymore."

"Afraid of what?"

"Of loving him. I just pray for it to ever end."

"Then it won't," she said grabbing my hand, "As long as you work for love, love'll work for you...I think you need to be getting dressed, Ms. Vera." She smiled.

I untied my robe and slipped into my undergarments. My stomach was turning three different ways.

The girls came into my room, filled with excitement. They all looked so beautiful! Shannon, Lee, Angie, Cherise, Rosa, and Taj's sister, Samira, were dressed in silk strapless peach dresses with pearls trimmed at the bust line. There was a slight V-dipped in the front of their dresses going into the cleavage. Their jewelry were white pearls and rhinestones. For flowers they each had a single Calla Lilly. Aunt Cookie, Rowanda, and Ms. Betty had on similar beige Afro-centric dresses, but with different mud-cloth trim.

"The men are outside," Shannon said, "And they look wonderful!" The men: Taj, Taj Sr., Taj's brother, Sharief, Quincy, DeAndre, and Dirty were dressed in black Versace tuxedoes, with silk ties and matching vests. Taj insisted on picking out Uncle Boy's clothes. Uncle Boy wore a black tuxedo, with a bow tie and matching cummerbund. Since we were getting married on the beach, no one wore any shoes.

I was so nervous that I went to the bathroom to throw up at least three times. DeAndre was the only man allowed in the room with me, he wanted to be sure that not one strand of my hair moved out of place. My hair was braided into three goddess braids like a crown and with spiral curls hanging loosely around my hairline. My MAC was flawless and my three carat diamond earrings sparkled as bright as the moon shining into the ocean.

I couldn't stop crying. Rowanda started helping me slip on my gown. "When you were a little girl, I use to pray that you would have the life that I always dreamed of. I prayed that you would have a black knight come and save you from the dungeon of the streets. With you being the princess of his dreams. That's what I always wanted." I could tell she was trying not to cry. "Never in my life have I been happier. I've been through it all, men, friends, dope, all kind of shit, but right here at this moment makes it all worth it." By now, I had slipped on my eggshell Cinderella wedding gown. My gown was detailed with hand-sewn rhinestones sprinkled all over and every time I moved it gave the appearance as if I were wearing diamonds. As a finishing touch Rowanda placed on my rhinestone tiara and when she was done, I felt like a princess waiting to meet my knight.

As I stepped out of a glass buggy pulled by two white horses, two men dressed in Kente cloth attire, sounded their trumpets to announce me. All of the guests stood up, while the band began their rendition of Natalie Cole's, "*Inseparable*."

The runner was covered in white rose petals and lined with bamboo torches and sparkling flames. The bridesmaids were standing on the left side of the runner and the groomsmen stood on the right. Aunt Cookie and Skyy were sitting and had already walked down the sand laced aisle, with Aunt Cookie carrying Skyy, who was now seven and a half months, on her hip. Ms. Betty and Taj's father were sitting on the opposite side of Aunt Cookie.

As I pressed my feet onto the runner, sprinkles of sand blown by the wind covered my feet and some of the rose petal floated in the night air. I looked up and my eyes locked with Taj's. He smiled, "You look beautiful." he mouthed, as tears started to run from his eyes.

Uncle Boy and I locked arms and began to walk down the aisle, "This is the day that I've been waiting for," Uncle Boy whispered as he walked me to the middle of the aisle, where Rowanda was waiting to take me the rest of the way. I tried my best to keep it together but it was hard.

Taj looked at me as I stood on the side of him, "I love you so much." He mouthed as the ceremony began. After two spiritual passages and a solo, the pastor asked, "Who givith this woman to this man?"

"We do." Aunt Cookie, Uncle Boy, and Rowanda stood up to say. They sat back down. Taj and I were now facing each other. It was time to recite our vows. Taj reached for both of my hands. "Vera, I have never loved the way that I love you. I want to be in love with you beyond the end of the time. Infiniti could never understand the depths or the ends of which my heart would travel to love you. You are the mother of my child, the lover of my heart, and I thank God that from this moment on, we will be joined as one."

Speechless, I stared at Taj because I didn't have any vows planned, I figured that I would say what came to me...So I began, "I have come from the bottom of the Earth to meet you, to be with you, and to love you. There are no more games to be played. It can't flip anymore; there are no more steps to take, and no more moves to make, but this one. This is the highest level that I could reach and that is marrying you. If this were a game the winner would be my heart, because now it would know the pleasure of being in love with you, forever."

After our "I do's." we jumped the broom. As we kissed, I felt as if we were soul tapping and with each stroke of the other's tongues our hearts made love. For the first time in my life, I felt as if time had been gracious enough to stand still.

ORDER FORM

Triple Crown Publications
2959 Stelzer Rd.
Columbus, Oh 43219

Name: _____

Address: _____

City/State: _____

Zip: _____

		TITLES	PRICES
		Dime Piece	$15.00
		Gangsta	$15.00
		Let That Be The Reason	$15.00
		A Hustler's Wife	$15.00
		The Game	$15.00
		Black	$15.00
		Dollar Bill	$15.00
		A Project Chick	$15.00
		Road Dawgz	$15.00
		Blinded	$15.00
		Diva	$15.00
		Sheisty	$15.00
		Grimey	$15.00
		Me & My Boyfriend	$15.00
		Larceny	$15.00
		Rage Times Fury	$15.00
		A Hood Legend	$15.00
		Flipside of The Game	$15.00
		Menage's Way	$15.00

SHIPPING/HANDLING (Via U.S. Media Mail)   **$3.95**

TOTAL $_____

FORMS OF ACCEPTED PAYMENTS:

Postage Stamps, Institutional Checks & Money Orders, all mail in orders take 5-7 Business days to be delivered.

ORDER FORM

Triple Crown Publications
2959 Stelzer Rd.
Columbus, Oh 43219

Name: _____

Address: _____

City/State: _____

Zip: _____

		TITLES	PRICES
		Still Sheisty	$15.00
		Chyna Black	$15.00
		Game Over	$15.00
		Cash Money	$15.00
		Crack Head	$15.00

SHIPPING/HANDLING (Via U.S. Media Mail)   **$3.95**

TOTAL $_____

FORMS OF ACCEPTED PAYMENTS:

Postage Stamps, Institutional Checks & Money Orders, all mail in orders take 5-7
Business days to be delivered.

"MENAGE A' TROIS Sexy Flicks"
The Ultimate in Visual Entertainment

Experience visual entertainment at its best! Our photos of sexy ladies will take you far and beyond your imagination.

Order a Sampler Set today for only $9.99* + Shipping & handling $2.00
(Assortment of (10) Hot photos)
Send $2.00 for a preview Color Catalog+$2.00 shipping & handling
Send $6.00 for a multi-page Color Catalog-Includes Free shipping

Quantity	Item	Price
	"Sampler Set" (Assortment of (10) Hot photos)	$9.99
	Preview Catalog	$2.00
	Full Catalog **(INCLUDES FREE SHIPPING)**	$6.00
	Merchandise Total	
	Shipping & Handling	$2.00
	Total	

Send All Payments To:
MENAGE A' TROIS
2959 Stelzer Road Suite C
Columbus, OH 43219

*The Sampler Set is pre-selected
This is a limited time offer.

(As of January 2005)
*Free shipping & handling applies to full catalog orders only.